New York Times and USA Today Bestselling Author

LORA LEIGH

SARAH'S Seduction

ELLORA'S CAVE
ROMANTICA PUBLISHING

What the critics are saying...

ॐ

"She excels at creating a sexually charged atmosphere without the underlying story being lost among the love scenes." ~ *Timeless Tales Reviews*

"Ms. Leigh writes compelling characters... She has a knack for exploring sexual awakenings and complicated human relationships." ~ *Simegen*

"Sarah's Seduction once again displays Lora Leigh's talents as a writer." ~ *The Romance Studio*

"Sarah's Seduction is a tale that takes you on a journey filled with suspense and intense, sizzling love scenes that will hold you enthralled until the very end." ~ *In The Library Reviews*

"SARAH'S SEDUCTION delivers outstanding characters, tension and chemistry" ~ *Romantic Times*

An Ellora's Cave Romantica Publication

www.ellorascave.com

Sarah's Seduction

ISBN 1419950304, 9781419950308
ALL RIGHTS RESERVED.
Sarah's Seduction Copyright © 2003 Lora Leigh
Edited by Sue-Ellen Gower
Cover art by Syneca

This book printed in the U.S.A. by Jasmine-Jade Enterprises,
LLC.

Trade paperback Publication May 2007

Excerpt from *Heather's Gift* Copyright © 2003 Lora Leigh

Content Advisory:

S – ENSUOUS
E – ROTIC
X – TREME

Ellora's Cave Publishing offers three levels of Romantica™ reading entertainment: S (S-ensuous), E (E-rotic), and X (X-treme).

The following material contains graphic sexual content meant for mature readers. This story has been rated E–rotic.

S-*ensuous* love scenes are explicit and leave nothing to the imagination.

E-*rotic* love scenes are explicit, leave nothing to the imagination, and are high in volume per the overall word count. E-rated titles might contain material that some readers find objectionable—in other words, almost anything goes, sexually. E-rated titles are the most graphic titles we carry in terms of both sexual language and descriptiveness in these works of literature.

X-*treme* titles differ from E-rated titles only in plot premise and storyline execution. Stories designated with the letter X tend to contain difficult or controversial subject matter not for the faint of heart.

Also by Lora Leigh

ᔟ

About the Author

ᔥ

Lora Leigh is a wife and mother living in Kentucky. She dreams in bright, vivid images of the characters intent on taking over her writing life, and fights a constant battle to put them on the hard drive of her computer before they can disappear as fast as they appeared. Lora's family, and her writing life co-exist, if not in harmony, in relative peace with each other. An understanding husband is the key to late nights with difficult scenes, and stubborn characters. His insights into human nature, and the workings of the male psyche provide her hours of laughter, and innumerable romantic ideas that she works tirelessly to put into effect

Lora welcomes comments from readers. You can find her websites and email addresses on their author bio page at www.ellorascave.com.

Tell Us What You Think

We appreciate hearing reader opinions about our books. You can email us at Comments@EllorasCave.com.

SARAH'S SEDUCTION

જી

Dedication

ຄ

For Karen, Chari, Chris, Nikki, Nicole
And Terri, Marty, Robin, Ruth and Lue Anne.
For all of you, because you read it over and over, and never got too aggravated to read it again. Thank you for your time, your comments and your friendship

Prologue

ೞ

Sarah was everything he wanted, everything he had dreamed of for over a year now. He had waited, put aside any thought of her until she turned eighteen, ignored his rising lust each time she smiled at him. Just as he now ignored the little voice in his head that said she was still too young. Much too young for what he needed from her.

But how could he resist her any longer? His body ached for her, his cock throbbed with a constant erection, his hands itched to stroke her silken skin. He was starving for the touch, the taste of her, and could no longer deny himself the pleasure he knew he would find in her.

So, he watched and he waited, planning just the right time, just the right way to draw her to him. She wanted him; he could see it in the soft golden-brown eyes, the flush that mounted her cheeks when she looked at him. The way her hands trembled and her breasts rose and fell with her quickened breathing.

And he knew when she left the party after receiving his note to search the shadows of the house for him, that she needed him, too.

"Sarah?" He moved from where he hid as she stepped hesitantly toward him. "Where's your shadow?"

Mark Tate had been damned near impossible for him to get rid of.

"Mark?" She bit her lip nervously, glancing back at the corner of the house as though afraid the other man would suddenly appear. "He went off to the barn with some of his friends." She turned back to him, watching him intently in the dim light of the full moon. "He's just a friend, Brock."

Mark wanted to be more. Brock was determined he wouldn't be.

"I was afraid you wouldn't come." He moved closer to her, feeling the warmth of her body that seeped into that cold, dark place in his heart.

He watched as she swallowed tightly, her big brown eyes following him, looking up at him as he stopped within an inch of pressing against her heaving breasts.

"You asked me to come," she whispered on a sigh. "You knew I would be here."

Her admission was like a fist of desire to his loins. Brutally sharp, agonizing in its intensity.

"Will you come for me every time I ask?" He was more than aware of his play on words.

Sarah frowned, her face turned up to him, her lips tempting him. "If I can."

God, she was too innocent for him. Too soft, too vulnerable.

"You have no idea how much I want you, Sarah," he told her, fighting to keep his voice soft, tender. "How desperately I want to touch you."

She took a deep breath. Her breasts brushed against his shirt, the light material of her sundress doing nothing to hide the hard little nipples beneath it. She licked her lips nervously, and Brock was lost.

"Come upstairs with me." He lifted his hand, touching the fall of dark blonde hair that brushed her bare shoulders. "I promise not to hurt you, Sarah. Whatever you want. Just come with me."

Her hand, small and graceful, the fingers slender with delicate pink nails touched his chest. He felt that touch clear to his soul. She looked up at him, her eyes wide, hungry.

"I'm nervous," she whispered. "What if I can't—"

He would explode, but he would accept it.

"Then I won't," he promised her. "Whatever you want, Sarah."

She was scared. He could see it in her eyes. Scared, but she wanted him, wanted him just as much as he needed her.

"Just us?" She asked the question almost fearfully. "Just me and you, Brock?"

Gossip was the spice of life. Had she heard the gossip, the truth of what he was?

"Just us, Sarah." He lowered his head until his lips could brush her temple as his hand smoothed up her bare arm.

He heard her breath catch, felt her body melt against him. He clasped her other hand in his as he moved back. He drew her into the house, then up the stairs to his room. The barbeque was in full swing outside. Laughter and music drifted into the house, though it seemed distant, unreal. The only reality for Brock was Sarah as she followed him up the stairs, down the hall and into the room he had prepared for her.

Tall, thick candles graced the walnut dresser and bedside tables. Their soft light spilled over her, creating a soft glow on her creamy skin. She trembled, a blush stealing over her cheeks as she glimpsed the bed, turned down and inviting.

"Sarah," he whispered her name as she halted in the middle of the floor. "I promise. Only what you want."

She followed him, her steps careful as he moved her to the bed.

"I've never—" Her voice shook.

"And you don't have to now." His cock was raging at him; his heart was breaking for her. "I just want to hold you, kiss you."

He needed her like sunlight. God help him, she brought light to his soul when nothing else had in years. He would do anything for her; kill to have her. But he didn't think he could survive another night without holding her.

13

He stopped by the bed, pulling her against his body, unable to wait another minute before he touched her. His lips covered hers, catching the breathy little moan that escaped as one hand clenched in her soft hair.

Her hands were on his shoulders, her soft belly pressing against his cock, and Brock knew he was on the edge of his control. He pressed his tongue to her lips, sinking into the dark velvet of her mouth as she shuddered against him. Her nails bit into his shoulders, her tongue tangled timidly with his, drawing him deeper in the maelstrom of pleasure that touching her evoked.

Moving slowly, his lips still covering hers, Brock lowered her to the bed. He wanted her until he couldn't breathe. Her skin was soft, her moans heady as he pulled his shirt from his shoulders, tossing it to the floor. Her cry was mingled with shock and pleasure as he lowered the bodice of her dress, pressing the hard points of her nipples into the muscles of his chest.

His lips were at her neck, nibbling, licking the fragrant skin as she trembled and gasped in his arms.

"I could eat you up," he growled, kissing a soft line to the rising mounds that tempted him. "Like candy, Sarah. Like a man starved for the taste of you. Just you."

A fever of need burned inside him. Lust had never been like this. It had never stolen his control, had never wiped the pain of his memories from his mind. It had never sent his heart beating so fast it shuddered through his body. It had never made him tremble from his hunger.

His lips reached her nipples and for a moment, he could do nothing but stare at the perfection he was ready to devour. The tips were hard, dark pink, the perfect mounds swollen and flushed as they rose and fell sharply from her agitated breathing. Watching the hard little points carefully, his tongue distended and swiped over the delicate bud experimentally.

He felt the muscles of her stomach clench beneath his hand, her hips bucking sharply.

"Brock?" There was fear and desire in her voice. A husky little moan of pleasure that frayed the last threads of his determination to go slow.

His head lowered, his mouth covering her nipple as his hands worked her dress from her hips. She arched to him, her hands locking in his hair as he began to suckle the engorged nipple. She was chanting his name and he was drowning in it. God help him, she was so hot, so soft and sweet he could barely breathe for it.

He let his tongue rasp her nipple as he sucked at it. He pushed the dress from her hips, down her legs, surprise flaring in him as she kicked the material free with an impatient move of her legs.

His hand smoothed up her thigh and she stilled. Opening his eyes, he moved with greedy hunger to her other breast, his gaze locking with hers. Her golden-brown eyes were wide, dazed as she watched him. His hand neared the humid heat emanating from her cloth-covered cunt as his tongue licked her unattended nipple in slow strokes, his eyes never leaving hers.

Her head jerked, her eyes darkened. His hand covered the hot mound of her cunt and she cried out brokenly. The sound went straight to his cock. Lifting his hand from between her legs, Brock quickly worked his pants open. Careful to keep her pleasure building, he nibbled at the hardened tip of her breast as he worked his pants and underwear from his body.

He was so hard he wanted to scream from the agony. When he was finally free, finally naked, his hand went back to her thighs, his fingers running over the damp silk of her panties. She jerked in his arms, twisting against him now as her own hunger began to reach a fever pitch. Her eyes closed, and Brock couldn't help but watch her. Watch her cheeks flushing, her lips opening in a strangled gasp of pleasure as he

15

moved the crotch of her panties aside, his fingers sliding into slick, damp honey.

"Sarah." Brock panted her name as he lifted his head from her breast.

He couldn't control his desire. His need to touch her. He had to have her. He had to taste the sweet honey of her or go crazy from it. He planted soft, sweeping kisses across her chest, her neck, back to her lips. She was hungry for him, her lips opened, her hands tightened in his hair as her hips arched to his fingers.

"So sweet," he growled against her lips, then stroked them as his fingers slid into the wet velvet crease between her thighs.

She stilled, her eyes opening again, staring up at him as she whispered his name beseechingly. His fingers moved slowly through the slick crease to circle her swollen clit slowly.

"Oh God, Brock." Her thighs opened wider, her hips pushing against his hand.

"You feel so good, Sarah," he whispered, desperate, his need to ease her, to draw her to him with his tenderness rather than the wild hunger driving him insane.

He clenched his teeth as her hands left his hair, moving to his shoulders. She was watching her hands now, smoothing them over his chest. Curiosity lit her expression, amazement washed over him in waves that she would draw such joy from touching him.

"Yes, Sarah," he groaned, hearing the fierceness of his voice. "Touch me. Please God, touch me."

His fingers moved through slick honey to the tender opening of her vagina. Her hands stroked his clenched stomach as he slid his finger shallowly into the tight, hot entrance.

Sarah cried out his name, her muscles clenching on his finger as her hand encountered the thick stalk of his cock rising to meet her fingers.

"Sarah, I have to have you." He was dying for her. The need was a white-hot agony radiating through his body. "Dear God, Sarah, please—"

His hand moved from between her thighs. He wanted to draw the panties from her hips, show her caution and tenderness. The sound of fabric tearing shocked his dazed senses but did little to cool the fever raging through his blood. The widening of her eyes, the glitter of excitement in them shocked him further. His sweet, shy Sarah liked having her panties ripped from her? What else, he wondered, would she like as well?

* * * * *

Sarah cringed inwardly from the excitement that flared through her body like a burst of heat as Brock ripped the panties from her hips. His face was a portrait in sensuality, his gray-blue eyes dark and hungry, intent. She could see the need in his expression, the rapid loss of control working through his body, and it thrilled her.

Her hand clenched at his shoulder, sun bronzed and hard from the tense muscles beneath as he stared down at her. His gaze locked with hers, watching her, intent on her. Thick, black lashes were lowered over his eyes; his black hair was mussed about his face from her fingers.

"I want you, Sarah," he whispered desperately. "If we're going to stop this, now is the time to do it, baby. I may not be able to later."

His voice was incredibly gentle, at odds with the hard sensuality in his expression. His hand smoothed over her shoulder, her breast. Sarah arched in his arms, hearing the involuntary whimper that issued from her throat. His hands were so warm; they felt so good.

"Brock." She arched against him, feeling the heated length of his cock against her thigh, his hand as it smoothed over her body, setting up an electrical firestorm of need that she had no defenses against.

"Sarah, I need you so bad." His face buried in her neck, his lips tasting her skin like a man more than starved. "Let me have you, Sarah. Please, let me have you."

His voice was tormented, his body tense.

Sarah moved against him, unable to halt her body's response to his plea. As his lips moved over her cheek, then took hers in a kiss that destroyed any objections she may have had, she could do no more than give into him.

Her lips opened to him, her tongue twining with his as he moved against her, pressing the hard length of his shaft against her thigh as he groaned into her lips. Her hands clenched at his shoulders as his chest rasped the tender tips of her breasts her neck arching as desperate kisses ran across her jaw, her neck. He licked his way to her breasts, but didn't stop there.

His hands roamed over her body as she tossed beneath alternate stinging nips and fiercely hot licks to her flesh. Each touch sent her spiraling higher, her fears of his possession overshadowed by the electric currents of arousal pulsing through her body.

His lips moved to her abdomen, tongue stroking, then teeth nipping as she tossed against him. His touch moved lower then, his hands spreading her thighs as he went between them.

His head was moving below her hips, his breathing a hard, rumbling groan as he moved lower, then lower.

"Brock?" Sarah stilled, forcing her eyes open, her breath catching at the hungry look on his face.

"I'm going to eat you like candy, Sarah," he whispered, his voice deep, dark. "Just liked I've dreamed of for months now."

His head moved, lowered, his hands arching her closer as his tongue swiped through the curl-shrouded, slick folds of

18

her cunt. Sarah cried out, her fingers clenching in the blankets as he did just as he promised her. He ate her. Every inch was stroked, licked, sucked. His tongue pushed inside her pussy with a slow, even stroke, drawing yet more of the thick liquid from her pulsing center.

Sarah was insane with arousal now. She bucked against him, pleading for more, desperate to still the raging fires burning through her body. Each second she could feel her body tightening further, reaching higher. She shuddered, gasping, begging. Then his lips enclosed her swollen clit, suckling lightly as his finger sank shallowly inside the humid depths of her throbbing pussy.

Sarah felt herself exploding, coming apart. Her eyes flew open, her first sight that of the doorway at the far side of the room and Brock's twin, Sam, as he turned from them. In an instant she saw his arousal, his assurance, and Sarah knew the rumors about the August men were true.

She stiffened, fear washing over her, the hot slide of depraved excitement flaring inside her. She knew the rumors that were whispered of about the August men. Their sexual conduct, the perversions that tied the three men together and in that instant, she knew it was the truth. And she knew, to the depths of her soul, that she would never find the strength to deny Brock whatever he wanted, if he took her now.

"No," she cried out desperately as Brock rose over her, pushing between her thighs, his cock stroking over her moist cunt lips as he positioned himself.

His gaze was shocked, so desperate she wanted to retract the denial, wanted to sooth the pain from his face and give him whatever it took to wipe the shadows from his mind. Whatever it took, even if it meant taking his brothers as well.

"I can't." She pushed against him, horrified by the knowledge that swept through her in that second.

"Sarah?" He was breathing hard, fighting for control when her hands went to his shoulders.

She was desperate to escape. She had to leave, get out of there before he possessed her forever. Because, God help her, she would never find the strength to deny him anything he wanted otherwise.

"No," she cried out again, mortifying tears brimming from her eyes, fear shaking her body as the thick, bulging head lodged at the entrance of her cunt.

"God, baby. Sarah." His voice was a cry of pain, a desperate dark plea that shook her to soul. "Please, Sarah. Don't do this."

"Let me go." She couldn't control her cries, the soul-shocking pain and fear that assaulted her now. "I can't. I won't, Brock. I won't do it. Please don't make me. Promise me you won't."

All he would have to do was ask her. She knew it. The flare of added arousal she had felt at the sight of Sam had shown her that.

"No, Sarah." He dropped his head, his expression tortured, tormented. "Don't do this."

She pressed at his shoulders, fighting to escape not just Brock, but also the dark needs rising inside herself. She was sobbing now, unable to stop the fear that overshadowed her arousal.

"God damn." His curse was fierce, angry as the head of his cock parted her, throbbed at her entrance. "Son of a bitch."

He jerked away from her. His curses sizzled the room, his fury was a like a beast—wild, untamed.

"Go, damn you! Get the fuck out of here!" he yelled at her, his expression so angry, so dark and so filled with pain that Sarah couldn't bear the sight of it.

She jerked her dress from the floor as she jumped from the bed, stumbling in her haste, barely catching herself from falling. She struggled into it, crying, shaking as she rushed for the door.

"You'll be back, Sarah," he bit out as she rushed from the room. "I swear to God, I won't let you go."

Chapter One
Six years later

&

The bar was crowded, the music pulsing. The crush of bodies on the dance floor moved in a strange synchronization that amazed Sarah. After nearly a full hour hiding in the shadows, she was still in awe of the limber bodies on the floor. When she wasn't watching the man she had come to find, that is. She sat in the corner, nursing a warm bottle of beer, her gaze flickering from the dancers to the object of her lust who stood a good twenty feet away from her.

Tall and well muscled, he exuded testosterone. A perfect male in his prime, his muscular body shown off to perfection in the snug jeans he wore, and the gray striped, cotton dress shirt. A wide leather belt circled his slim hips and hard stomach. Propped against one of the wide, wooden posts that separated the dance floor and the table area, his casual position shouted confidence. The position he assumed was mouth-wateringly sexy. All that hard muscle lounging comfortably, arms crossed over a wide muscular chest, long, masculine legs crossed at the ankle, leading to muscled thighs that framed a more than impressive male bulge. She swallowed tightly. She knew exactly how impressive that bulge actually was.

Turning her gaze from him, Sarah remembered years ago, a stolen night, hard, hot kisses in the silence of his room, and the thick, hard erection beneath those well-worn jeans. It made her body heat alarmingly, remembering his touch. His hands, work-roughened on her sensitive young breasts, between her thighs. His fingers sliding through thick moisture, his voice humming with approval as his fingers penetrated, then stopped at the evidence of her innocence.

Then his mouth. Her eyes closed as she remembered that hot, seductive mouth and the fear that washed over her as he threw her into her first and only orgasm. He had lapped at the rush of moisture, holding her hips still as his tongue dipped into her vagina, penetrating her, eating her decadently. His mouth had been hot, his tongue voracious, the sounds of his pleasure vibrating against her clit in a manner that had her crying out in bliss over and over again.

She had opened her eyes then and behind him she had seen the identical version of the man whose tongue had lapped so desperately at her flesh. Brock's twin, Sam. He had been turning away, but Sarah had seen a look, an assurance in his eyes that terrified her.

You'll be back, Sarah. I won't let you go! The memory of his last words to her six years before whispered through her mind.

She shook her head, fighting the betraying weakness that had assailed her then as well. She took a long drink of the beer, grimacing at the warm taste. What the hell was she doing here? What made her think she was any braver now than she had been then? That she was any more accepting. What made her think he would even want to touch her now, an older version of that scared little girl, helpless in the face of her own passions and the fears that made her run? She had been eighteen; Brock had just celebrated his twenty-fifth birthday. Six years. She sighed. He was more handsome at thirty-one than he had been when he was younger. More handsome and decidedly more dangerous.

The rumors concerning his and his brother's sexual practices had only grown in that time. Enough so, that Sarah knew they were based in fact. She had known it before though. Known it to an extent that she had never forgotten her own dark desires as she saw his brother turning away from the sight of Brock lapping at her pussy.

"Hello, Sarah." She froze at the sound of that dark, male voice. There was no mistaking the rough timber of it, the dark intoxication of hearing it roughen with lust.

23

The breath stilled in her chest, birds wings, not butterflies, beat at her stomach. She felt the wet evidence of her desire for this man pulse from between her thighs. Sarah swallowed past her nerves and allowed her eyes to rove over his masculine form. Up. Up. Past the thickened bulge, noticeably larger now, over the flat abdomen and wide chest, up to the dark, blue-gray eyes that watched her with arousal.

The muscles in her stomach bunched, tightened. Fingers of arousal danced over her breasts, teased her inner thighs. She felt her breathing deepen as lust lanced through her body. It was like a mild electrical shock being sent through her entire system.

It had been years since she had allowed herself to be anywhere near him. She had avoided any place he could be, went the other way if she saw him coming. She had avoided him for so long that it became a habit. A need. She knew if she was in his company for longer than a second, then she would be begging him to fuck her. It amazed her that he had approached her now. Amazed and terrified her.

"Hi, Brock. It's been a while." She tilted her beer in a small, courageous gesture before tipping it to her lips and taking a long drink. False courage. She needed it badly.

She wasn't normally a bold person, or a forward one. She had always been the one hugging the corners at parties, reluctant to step out. How she managed to get up enough nerve to come to the bar in the first place, she wasn't certain. It had been an impulsive move to take this one night for herself. Just one night. A night to remember, to hug close to her during the long, lonely nights to come.

"Have a cold one." He set a chilled bottle in front her, then swinging a leg over the back of the chair, sat down across from her.

The graceful male movement had her breath catching in her throat. The loose limbed straddle, the shrug of his shoulder, the wry tilt of his lips. Not quite a smile, but the hint that it could be if he could get past the shadows that lurked in his eyes.

Sarah slid the empty bottle over and picked up the cold one. She lifted it to her lips and sipped. The bitter bite wasn't pleasant, but she knew the much-needed salve to her nerves would be welcome when it hit. When breaking out of one's shell, one needed to do it right.

"Thanks." Her eyes flickered to his, then back to the bottle. He had only grown more handsome in the past six years. Where she had just grown older. His face, strong-boned and cut into firm, determined lines, showed a man who knew a little too much and had seen more than his share of pain. His dark hair was overly long, brushing the collar of his white shirt. It was black, glistening like midnight silk and tempted her hands to run through it.

"I haven't seen you in a while." *Six years.* The thought strained at her nerves.

The secluded corner gained them a measure of quiet from the band at the front of the room, keeping him from having to yell at her. His voice was still raised, though, the husky timber stroking over her.

She looked into his eyes; saw the measuring, considering look there. He would push her. But he still wanted her. God, so much had changed in six years. Why hadn't the desire that pulsed between them dissipated as well? It was like hot, velvet bonds, impossible to break as it sizzled in the air, making it impossible for her to forget his touch, or to ignore the needs that had tormented her over the years.

She shook her head, glancing quickly at him, then back to the bottle as she shrugged, biting her lower lip enough to make it smart.

"I've been busy." Stupid was more like it.

She squelched the flare of anger. Mark, her ex-husband, had kept her home, convincing her that was where a good wife stayed. The truth was, his cheating was so extensive he had been terrified someone would finally tell her. No one had to tell her what a fool she was. She knew the first week they were married. A completely blind, misguided, stupid fool. Strangely enough, she wasn't hurt in the least, just embarrassed. Embarrassed, humiliated and totally ashamed. Three progressions that left a taste more bitter than the beer in her mouth.

"So, you aren't busy anymore?" There was a thread of amusement in his voice, a question that went beyond the words.

Her gaze met his. She read the speculation, the sexual intent they contained. She held the look for long seconds before her gaze lowered. Her fingers picked at the paper on the front of the bottle for a minute before she shook her head.

"No." She tipped the beer up for another drink, swiped at the fringe of long bangs that drifted over her forehead. "I'm not busy anymore, Brock."

What was she doing? Was she insane? The cautious, frightened part of her screamed the question. Jump up. Run away. She wasn't about to. She had deliberately come to this bar, sat here for nearly an hour, waiting. For six years the memory of one night had tormented her, the incompleteness of the act driving her mad with the need to finish it.

She licked her lips, fighting her nervousness, then tipped the beer up for another long drink. At the same moment, her eyes met his once again. She swallowed the beer hard then took another for added courage. His eyes were hot, heavy-lidded, his firm, finely molded lips just a bit full, the expression on his face intense as he concentrated on her lips. He looked sensual, hungry. She knew his sexual appetite was said to be voracious. She shivered in yearning.

She ran her tongue over her lips and wanted to whimper as she set the bottle down. His eyes followed each movement she made. When it disappeared into her mouth once again, his eyes rose slowly to meet hers. She was caught. Trapped like a deer by a bright light, helpless, bound by the sheer sexuality he exuded. It vibrated through her system, soaking into the pores of her skin until she felt sensitive, overheated.

She wanted him and he knew it. Sarah could see that knowledge in the dark look he gave her. He could feel it, just as she could. Like a physical wave of energy coming off them both.

"Still scared, Sarah?" He mouthed the words more than he spoke them.

He had no idea just how scared. She trembled beneath his look, remembered the lava-hot sensations that poured through her body so many years ago. The loss of control, the desire, the need to give this man whatever he wanted, any way he wanted it.

"Terrified," she answered in the same manner.

His gaze held hers. She watched shadows shift in his eyes; emotions so fleeting she couldn't decipher them flashed through his gaze. Then resignation, acceptance settled into his expression. As though he too knew that the memories of that hot summer would never just go away. Sarah was afraid giving in would only make it worse as well.

"Dance with me." He rose to his feet, holding his hand out to her.

Sarah looked at it, so hard and broad, then into his eyes as she reached out slowly. He pulled her from her chair as a haunting ballad filled the air. The words of Gary Allen, whispering how he would prove he was the one, began. Her breath caught in her throat as Brock took her into his arms at the edge of the dance floor, pulling her tight against him.

Heat and the scent of masculine arousal enfolded her. His arms were strong, protective, causing her heart to clench painfully with the realization that one of her greatest needs over the years was being fulfilled. She was in his arms again. The remembered feeling of security, of peace and longing rushed over her in a fiery wave of sensation so intense she wanted to cry. His chest was broad, hard, but he cushioned her against it with tender hands. The remembered feel of his bare flesh caressing her breasts made her nipples harden. He had danced with her in his room that night, slowly removing her clothes as his lips possessed hers, his body weaving in hypnotic circles to the slow, sultry beat of the music outside.

His erection was like a brand on her lower stomach. His arms wrapped around her waist, leaving her to place hers at his shoulders. One big hand lifted to hold her head to his chest. His heartbeat was hard and imperative beneath her ear, his chest rising and falling with swift motions as his hands rubbed over her back, slow and easy. If he kept this up, she would be a boneless pleading idiot in minutes.

"Are you playing with me, Brock?" she whispered as he gripped her hips, moving to the music in a way that pressed his hips more firmly against her, making her breath catch in her throat, her vagina to clench, weep in urgent demand. Please God, she prayed, don't let him be playing with her, she didn't think she could stand the tormenting demand of her body much longer.

"Maybe I should be asking you that question." They turned around the dance floor, ignoring the other couples, drifting in a haze of warmth and arousal.

He bent his head, nuzzling her neck, his lips smoothing over the skin beneath her ear. She shivered, her nails biting into his shoulders as fiery sensations wracked her body. She breathed in harshly, a strangled whimper startling her when it came from her throat.

His lips were warm and rough; the moist rasp of his tongue nearly sent her into climax then and there. He licked seductively with each movement of his lips against her skin, driving her insane with the heat that spread through her veins. Her womb contracted, her heart beat hard and loud.

"Are you finished running from me, Sarah?" He nipped the lobe of her ear as though in retaliation for the lost time.

"Was I running?" she gasped. "I thought I was married."

He tensed. The corded muscles in his body tightened instantly.

"Don't remind me of that, Sarah," he warned her cautiously. "I'm trying real hard to forget it."

His fingers clenched at her hips, not painful, but forceful, grinding her body against his as the song came to its last, pulsating note. Sarah lifted her head as Brock paused, staring down at her. She was breathing hard and she knew her expression was filled with the pleading desperation raging through her body. So long. It had been so long since he had touched her, held her. She needed him, and God help her, she needed him now.

"Let's finish that beer." His hand settled on her back as he led her back to the table.

Chapter Two

Sarah was surprised. She had expected him to want to leave. She didn't expect him to walk her back to the table and help her back into her chair. Then he sat in his and surprised her once again.

Brock moved, chair and all until he was crowding her into the corner. One arm went behind her back, the other to the table as he leaned forward, blocking her from view of the other bar patrons. She felt enclosed, sheltered and warm as he surrounded her. At the same time she could feel excitement gathering, pooling, making her cunt slick and hot.

"How terrified are you, Sarah?" He whispered the words at her cheek now, staring into her eyes as an involuntary whimper issued from her throat.

Her nipples hardened beneath her new dress, her breasts swelling, straining the fragile buttons that held the bodice together. His gaze dropped to the rapid rise and fall, then returned slowly to her eyes. That single, hungry look electrified her. She wanted to beg him to kiss her, stroke her, fuck her until she couldn't move.

"You should be outlawed," she told him desperately as the hand that rested on the table moved to encase hers.

His long fingers caressed the sensitive skin of her wrist as the hand at her back began to rub several inches of her spine slowly. She wanted to arch against him, like a cat begging to be rubbed.

"How scared are you, Sarah?" He repeated his question, his expression intent as he watched her. "And be very certain that you tell the truth this time."

Her chest tightened at his warning. He still wanted her. She could see it in his darkening eyes, feel it in the heat radiating off his body. Just like before. He enclosed them in his sexual need, his determination to have her. His hunger for her.

Just one night, she reminded herself. What harm could come from just one night?

"Not scared enough," she admitted desperately. "But scared, Brock. Real scared."

She wouldn't lie to him this time. Not now, not while she needed him like this. Like a hunger, an obsession that stole her breath. His hand rose to her neck, beneath the soft fall of her hair, cupping the back of her head as he urged her to look into his eyes once again.

"I won't stop this time, Sarah," he told her gently, but the expression on his face was savage. "Do you understand me? If I get your panties off again, I'll fuck you, no matter how hard you cry. I won't have the control to let you go."

She had cried before. As he rose over her, his erection nudging the slick heat between her thighs, she had begged him to let her go as she pushed against his chest, fighting to be free. She remembered how hard he fought for control. The head of his cock had buried inside her before he jerked away, cursing her, raging at her as she scrambled to her feet, jerked her dress on and stumbled from his room.

"I won't beg you to stop." That was all she could promise.

His jaw clenched, satisfaction flaring in his eyes. His hand went from the table to her thigh. She jerked in startled awareness as it moved slowly beneath her dress. A test? She swallowed hard, her chest suddenly tight, her breathing harsh as his fingers inched up her thigh. She looked into the crowd nervously, wondering who could see.

"No one can see what I'm doing, Sarah," he promised her, his voice husky, throbbing with passion.

A test? A passionate form of torture to see how serious she actually was? With Brock, anything was possible. She

31

knew his sexual excesses were whispered of, much as the demons of old once were. Hushed whispers, as though speaking them clearly would bring them to life. He, like his two brothers, was Madison's favorite topic of gossip.

"Would you care if they did?" She blinked, her lips parting to fight for breath as those diabolical fingers inched forward.

They were hot on her skin, the slight friction making her muscles clench with the need for more. She would never get enough of his touch and she knew it.

"I would only care if another man actually saw what is mine now, Sarah," he told her ruthlessly. "Make no mistake. You run into the arms of another man to escape me again, even that ineffectual husband of yours, and blood will be shed."

She shivered. She swallowed tightly. Blinking up at him she tried to make sense of the possessive light filling his suddenly darkened gaze. This wasn't right, she thought. One night. That was all she wanted. She needed closure to the memory that haunted her day and night. She couldn't handle more. She wouldn't allow it to become more. She would have protested his statement, but as her mouth opened and she felt his fingers moving closer to the throbbing center of her body, her eyes widened.

They were a bit calloused, warm. They drew intriguing designs above her knee, then upward to her thigh. His thumb rubbed in silky circles, causing her breath to catch on a low moan as his fingers reached the edge of her panties. Her blood thundered with excitement, with the forbidden.

"Easy now." He gripped her thigh, tugging at it as he urged her to scoot down on the seat marginally.

"Brock." Her small protest was one of feminine fear.

She was riding an edge, close to the barrier of common sense and insanity where her lust for this man was concerned. It terrified her to think of the lengths she would go to, this one night, to fulfill the fantasy of him possessing her body.

"I just want to touch you, Sarah," he whispered at her ear. "That's all, just touch. I promise not to embarrass you."

She moved forward, his hand stopping her as her buttocks neared the edge. Satisfaction glittered in his gaze as the hand behind her urged her to settle against the back of the chair. Sarah looked up at him wanting to beg him not to do this. Not here, where everyone could see.

"No one can see, Sarah," he promised her. "Just sit here a minute, that's all."

His fingers moved again to the edge of her panties, burrowing under them, touching the soft curls that shielded the hot, wet folds of her feminine flesh. Sarah's eyes fluttered.

"Watch me, Sarah," the order was rough, growling in intensity. "Don't close your eyes. Watch me."

Her eyes met his. A gasping moan escaped her throat. His dark face was set in lines of concentrated desire, the edge of his control reflected in the dark depths of his pupils.

She felt his fingers, coated now with the creamy essence of her need. Her moisture lay thick and hot along the lips of her cunt as it flowed from the hot depths of her vagina.

"Damn, you're wet," he growled. "How much wetter can you get, darlin'?"

Sarah knew she could get much wetter. She did often, thinking about his touch, his kisses. When her fingers stole to her hot flesh, she dreamed of Brock, his touch, his possession, and she got much wetter.

"Brock, please—" she pleaded, snared by his eyes, by the fingers entering the narrow cleft he caressed.

Was he punishing her? Would he tease her here, then leave her as she had left him, begging for more?

"I'm going to fuck you, Sarah," he told her as his fingers moved slowly over the drenched lips of her quivering cunt. "But I won't be left begging again, do you understand me?"

She wasn't able to answer. Her eyes widened, she gasped, moaned. Where she had been empty, she was suddenly filled, stretched, long broad fingers were testing her, plunging deep as the hand at the back of her neck kept it from falling back in ecstasy.

"I wish you could see how pretty you are, trying to hide what I'm doing, all flushed and shy and aroused." His fingers moved deeper, spreading her, testing the tight, inner recess of her body.

"Brock," she gasped his name, unable to say more as her flesh clenched over his fingers, drenching them further.

"So wet and ready for me." A smile tipped his hard lips.

She whimpered in need as his fingers retreated, pulling away from her, leaving her gasping, nearly begging him for more. Then slowly, his movements teasing, taunting, he filled her once again. Her nails bit into his arm, her heart raced out of control, making breathing more than difficult. Small whimpering moans escaped her throat, helpless desire flooded her system, washing over his fingers to drench the silk of her panties. Each time he retreated she felt empty, where she had been filled before. Achingly aware of the brief moments where the edge of release taunted her, made her reach, yearn for more. Then she was filled again, pushed ever closer to the mind consuming moment where she knew her body would explode into a pleasure so intense, so violent it would shatter her sanity for those brief moments.

"Will you leave with me, Sarah?" he asked her softly. "Right now. We'll leave. Go wherever you want. But when we get there, I'm going to rip those panties off you and thrust so hard inside that tight, wet pussy that you'll scream out your orgasm."

Her vagina spasmed. Sarah felt the betraying muscles clench in hunger at the vivid images that hit her brain. Brock, rising over her, the thick expanse of his erection pounding into her. She fought for breath. She was so close to orgasm right now that she could feel her cunt grasping in an anguished plea for it. Her juices trickled over his fingers, making her inner body slick, accessible to whatever he desired to do to her.

"Yes." The betraying sigh was so filled with longing that Sarah knew she would writhe in shame later.

His eyes narrowed, his own breathing rough now as he watched her.

"Where?" he asked her, his voice hard as his fingers slowly pulled completely from her, then plunged home forcibly.

Sarah bit her lip, fighting a scream of pure, electrified sensation. Her hands gripped the edge of the table in desperation, her thighs quivered with the hot flash of impending release. She gasped, whimpered. Tears came to her eyes as the pulsating demand for more had her almost begging. She wanted to beg. She wanted to plead with him, here, now.

"My house." She saw the surprise flare in his eyes. "My bed."

He smiled slow and sure, approval reflecting in his expression. His fingers pulled free of her body with a slow, regretful motion. He carefully tucked the silk of her panties back over her protesting cunt, watching her intently as he did so. He stood to his feet; a slow, graceful movement that made her breath catch in her throat. Then he was holding his hand out to her, watching her carefully. She placed her hand in his, allowing him to draw her to her feet, then lead her slowly from the bar and into the starry night.

His hand rode low on her back, never breaking contact with her. His broad chest brushed against her as they walked, she had never been so aware of another man's body next to her. Even years ago, he had done this to her. Made her frighteningly aware of her femininity, her weakness and his strength.

"Did you bring your car?" he asked her as he led her into the dark parking lot. He kept his hand at her back, moving her to the Jeep with the trademark August Ranch logo on the side.

"No. Cab." She could barely speak, the need pulsed so heavy in her body.

When they moved to the side of the Jeep, she gasped harshly as he suddenly turned her, pressing her into the side of the vehicle.

"Six years," he snarled, lifting her against him as his head lowered. "Six fucking years, Sarah."

His voice was tormented; his lips were hot, hard as they covered hers, his tongue sinking into her mouth as he wedged his erection hard against the soft pad of her cunt.

Sarah's self-control was never at its best with Brock. She cried into his kiss, her hands locking desperately into his hair as she fed on his passion. Their tongues twined together, licking at each other, groaning in their need. He ground his pelvis against her, his cock a hard, throbbing heat beneath the jeans that separated them.

"I could take you here," he growled. "I should."

His lips and teeth were nipping at her jaw, then her neck.

"I should rip those panties from you and fuck you now before you have a chance to beg me not to." His voice was rough, hungry. Sarah had never heard such a sensual sound in her life.

She moved against him, her head falling back as his lips went to the neckline of her dress, caressing the swollen mounds of her breasts. She didn't care. He could take her anywhere he wanted to, it didn't matter as long as she got his cock inside her, deep, hard, sating the hunger that had tormented her for so long.

"So soft, Sarah." His raspy voice was a low, agonized groan. "So soft and sweet. God baby, if you're not serious about this, tell me now. Tell me, Sarah, because I don't know if I can stop later."

He raised his head to stare down at her, his face shadowed, his breathing rough.

Sarah raised her hand to touch his lips, feeling the exciting warmth, the swollen curves that tempted her as nothing else could.

"Take me home, Brock," she whispered. "Take me home to my bed. I want you there with me, all night."

The silence of the night was filled with nothing now but their harsh breaths, their needs.

"I won't let you go tonight," he growled. "All night, Sarah. I'll keep my cock buried in you all night long."

She took a deep, hard breath. "The night is moving fast, Brock. If we waste any more time, that won't be for long."

He moved fast. He jerked the door to the Jeep open and helped her quickly inside before closing her door carefully and moving quickly to his own. The Jeep started and within seconds he was pulling quickly from the driveway.

Heavy intent lined his expression, tautened his powerful body. They rode in silence, and as each minute drew them closer to her house, Sarah realized the ache in her body only grew. Grew until it was a hunger, a need, something she was terrified she would never be free of.

Chapter Three

ஐ

Maybe it was the beer. Maybe it was the fact that today she had signed away the last six years of her life. She had finally convinced Mark to sign the divorce papers. Waiting until he was furious, outraged at the fact he believed he had finally gone through the last penny of her inheritance. He wasn't aware he had only gone through the portion bequeathed to her by her mother. Or maybe it was the fact that Brock was so dangerous, so sexual, so intensely male that she just couldn't forget, nor resist his touch any longer. She had spent her adult life so far fighting the attraction, the need, until she was weak, starved for his kiss and his touch as she had never starved for anything.

Whatever the reason, Sarah found herself letting them both into her home late that night, and trying to stem the attack of nerves that left her hands shaking. Could she satisfy him? Of course, she knew it wasn't possible. But she knew she would try. She knew she had to.

"You're trembling." Brock took the keys from her fingers and laid them on the small antique desk just inside the door.

Sarah shrugged. Why was she shaking? It wasn't like she was a virgin with her first man. Or was she? Brock August was definitely not in her league, so wouldn't that qualify as a cherry of sorts? She stifled her runaway laughter at that thought.

"I'm not used to bringing men home with me," she finally sighed as she turned and faced him. Damn, he was gorgeous.

Sensual knowledge glittered in his eyes, sexual intent lit the banked fires that were said to burn hot and bright. Rumors of his sexual prowess, his carnal desires had been running rampant through Madison for years. Sarah was under no illusions that she could hold this man's attention longer than it would take for him to climax and walk back out of her life. But the illusion he gave her satisfied her need to believe, just for a little while.

"Women perhaps?" He angled his head as he asked the question, watching her curiously.

Sarah felt the heat that seared her face at his question.

"No," she shot back. "Not women. Why would you ask me something like that?"

He sighed, a small smile quirking his lips.

"You are a very beautiful woman, Sarah. There are no rumors of you taking lovers, or wild weekends, despite your husband's infidelities. I was merely curious if you had a female 'friend' instead." He stressed the friend part. The look in his eyes said the thought would do little to dampen his desire. Sarah had a feeling it would only heighten it.

She shook her head. "No lovers, male or female." She nearly choked on the words as he began to crowd her slowly against the wall. He was big and broad, hot and hard. Her hands flattened on the tight muscles of his stomach as he pressed against her, feeling them clench, tauten in anticipation.

"You have one now," he whispered, his hands going to her hips, his fingers testing the flesh there. "Or at least, you will have if you don't shake yourself to death first."

He was almost smiling at her. His full lips were tilted in a sort of half grin, his expression was patient, if a bit amused. He was so handsome he took her breath.

"I didn't expect you to still be interested," she said a bit desperately, staring up at him, wondering at the sudden flare of intensity in his eyes. "You're very much out of my league, Brock. Then and now."

"There's a class system, then?" he asked her gently as his head lowered, his lips smoothing over her jaw line as her breath caught in her throat.

"Just for you and your brothers," she gasped weakly.

His lips were warm, his breath moist and caressing as a hand framed her face, tilting it so he could stroke his lips under her jaw. His soft laughter raced through her blood stream, pooling between her thighs as the muscles clenched in arousal. She couldn't believe Brock was touching her. That his mouth was sipping at her skin as though he found the taste of her pleasant.

Quiet, unassuming Sarah Tate had drawn the interest of this man, for this night, once again. She could barely comprehend it. But he was definitely here, holding her, one hand caressing her hip above the light cotton of her sun dress, the other holding her neck lightly as he tilted her head so he could experiment with the soft skin beneath her jaw.

She was shivering with the pleasure, fighting to contain her gasps, the little whimpers of delight as his tongue reached out and stroked her skin. Her hips lifted against him when he pressed his jean-covered erection against the softness of her lower belly, a strangled cry escaping her lips as heat surrounded her

He took her mouth as though he needed her taste to survive. His lips moved over hers, his tongue stroking past them, tangling with hers as he groaned against them. Sarah's hands rose to his shoulders, her nails biting into the soft shirt he wore as she pressed her breasts desperately against his chest. His kiss was addictive, the taste of his lips, his tongue like a dark, seductive liquor.

His body, hard and carefully controlled, moved against hers. The muscles were tense, his hands moving her. His kiss overpowered, washed over her with darting shafts of electric sizzles throughout her body. She couldn't believe this was happening. She wanted to relish each moment of it. Every touch, every kiss. Oh God, was he groaning like that because her touch pleased him?

She stroked her fingers over the side of his neck again, gasping as he bent his knees and drove his hips against the vee of her thighs, his moan dark. Dangerous. Like an animal anticipating the coming meal. The sound exhilarated her, made her bolder, more confident. She had spent too many years in a sexual void. Mark's infidelities had ruled out sex with him. His claim that she was frigid, that her body did nothing to excite him, had left her too unsure to seek another lover. Until now. Until the dreams and the need and the sexual cravings had pushed her further than her fragile control could bear.

Brock's lips moved from hers and swept over her jaw again. He asked for nothing. He took, he stroked over her, claiming her, stealing any resistance she may have possessed. She angled her head, desperate to taste the tanned flesh of his neck as his mouth ate at her skin. Her tongue stroked and he stilled, a shudder wracking his body.

"I'm sorry." She drew back, suddenly frightened. Why had he stopped? What had she done wrong?

"Sorry?" He was breathing roughly as stared at her. "Why are you sorry? Damn, Sarah-love, why did you stop?"

"You liked that?" She couldn't stop her incredulous whisper. Mark had hated to be touched on his neck.

Brock's face was sexually flushed, his eyes glittering behind heavily lashed lids.

"I don't know," he growled. "Do it again, for a long time, so I can decide."

She saw the gentle teasing in his eyes and moaned in longing. He bent close again, rubbing his neck against her chin, and it was all the encouragement she needed. Her lips rubbed over the heated flesh of his neck, her tongue licking delicately as she savored the taste of his skin, her teeth nipping at his flesh, hearing him groan deep and low as his hands roved over her back, her hips, then began to draw the material of her dress to her thighs.

His taste intoxicated her. She couldn't get enough. Those strong fingers seared her flesh as he stroked the skin of her

41

outer legs, and the way his thigh tucked between the bared flesh of hers sent a feminine thrill of sexual heat pulsing through her body. She felt fevered, each taste of him making her crazier by the second as her mouth moved along his neck, her fingers pulling at his shirt frantically as she fought to taste more of him. His chest. She needed to stroke her tongue over the hard muscles of his chest, test and taste the resiliency of his skin.

"Sarah-love," he growled as her fingers fought with the buttons of his shirt. She trembled, shaking so hard she couldn't manage to release the slippery little devils from their mooring. "Easy, baby. We have all night. It's okay."

"I can't wait," she cried out, mortally ashamed of the clawing need that had her writhing against his thigh with tight, desperate movements.

It had been so long since she had known a man's touch. Had she known a man's touch after Brock's, all those years ago? Her husband had never made her feel this way. The touch of his hands on her body had been moist, not firm and dry and work calloused. She was burning alive, crying out as she fought desperately to release the burning tightness in her lower body. The harsh, driving ache that made her aware of her own emptiness, the ache in her clit, and the desperate rush of moisture soaking through her panties.

She felt the perspiration that dotted her skin, the sudden fullness of her breasts as his hands whispered over them. Oh God, he was releasing the small buttons, his movements deft and sure as the edges fell apart and her full breasts were revealed. She closed her eyes, terrified of seeing the same disappointment she had seen in Mark's eyes. Her body bucked. She cried out, her fingers clenching at his shoulders as she felt the heated moisture of his mouth on her nipples.

It was too much. She fought for air as the little buds hardened to the point of pain. She fought to still the racing of her heart, but the scrape of his teeth wouldn't allow it. She was desperate for him. Dying, aching inside unlike anything she had known in her life. If he didn't take her soon she knew she would die.

"Bedroom," he growled as he moved to the next breast, covering it, nipping at the sensitive bud as she arched in his arms, her hands holding him tight to her.

Who needed a bedroom? Her head fell back against the wall as his thigh ground against the moist center between her thighs.

"Now, Sarah. The fucking bedroom." He jerked the dress to her waist as his lips went to her neck, drawing the flesh between his lips, licking erotically, biting at her skin with hot, desperate nips.

She couldn't think. Where was the bedroom? She felt her panties tear. She heard the rend of the material as his lips covered hers harshly, his tongue sweeping in possessively as his fingers pushed between her thighs.

Sarah stilled. Breath suspended, eyes opened wide in disbelief, she stared at him as his fingers plunged inside her. She cried out harshly, wondering at the lack of shame that she was so wet, so desperate that the sticky fluid seemed to gush over his fingers.

"Son of a bitch," he groaned, his eyes dark, his face flushed. "Too fucking late for the bedroom now, Sarah."

He dropped to his knees as she stared at him in surprise. His hands pushed her thighs apart, then as one hand held the dress to her waist, the other slid out of her hot entrance and his mouth consumed her.

Sarah shuddered, crying out desperately as she felt his tongue swipe through the slick folds of skin. He was licking her. Oh God, like a cat licking at cream, he was licking her, groaning in pleasure at her taste. He was making hot, desperate sounds of hunger as he drew the wetness into his mouth, savoring it. She felt her womb tighten, spasm and more of the hot cream seeped from her vagina.

She couldn't stand it. Sarah felt her knees weakening as the pleasure rose inside her. It gripped her stomach, tightening it almost painfully as the waves of near ecstasy washed over her again and again. Her hands were clenched on his shoulders, her thighs spread wide, his lips and tongue playing with her clit as his fingers thrust repeatedly into the hot channel that wept with the attention. She knew she was spiraling out of control. The fires searing her body were making her buck against his mouth, thrust into his fingers, tightening her body, drawing her into a vortex of such mind numbing pleasure that she exploded.

Sarah heard her own keening cry as she felt her body come apart. She tightened, thrust against his immoveable mouth and lost her breath as extreme pleasure flooded her entire being, bursting over her flesh and leaving her shaking, gasping in completion as she slowly wilted.

Brock was there to catch her. His arms went around her as he stood to his feet, his eyes staring down at her in stark lust.

"Where is the fucking bedroom, Sarah, before I take you here in the middle of the hallway." His voice was dark and rough, rasping with the force of his own need.

"Upstairs," she gasped as he swung her into his arms.

He took the stairs quickly, his big body sheltering her smaller one. He glanced around the hall, then turned to the first door. He pushed it open, then stopped abruptly.

"Who the fuck is that?" His tone was only mildly curious, but the pulsing fury underneath it concerned her.

Sarah glanced in confusion at the bed, then her eyes widened in horror. He hadn't. He wouldn't. But he had.

Mark was entwined, in her bed, with his young lover. The room reeked of alcohol and sex. Her bedroom was in complete disarray. Clothes were thrown everywhere, the lamp had toppled to the floor and a chair lay on its side. She shook her head, unable to believe it.

"God, this could only happen to me." She shook her head as Brock set her slowly on her feet.

Her knees were weak, so it took her a moment to steady herself, and all she could do was stare in shock at Mark and what was her name? Sarah could never remember. But there they were, nude, enfolded in each other's arms, snoring softly.

Tears filled her eyes. Not from pain at seeing her husband, or ex-husband in her bed with his lover. But the deeply humiliating pain of knowing the man behind her was slowly, furiously aware of the situation.

Sarah fought to draw the bodice of her dress back over her body. She struggled with the small sleeves, dragging them up her arms, all the while more than aware of Brock's tense anger.

"Where're your clothes?" He surprised her when he went to the closet and began rummaging through it. The dresser drawers were lying on the floor, her underwear, bras and T-shirts scattered along the carpet. It would be hard to find anything salvageable in that mess.

Brock jerked several dresses from the small closet, laid them over his arms and came back to her. He took her arm and pulled her quickly from the room. Sarah followed him in a daze, nearly stumbling as he strode from the room and back downstairs.

"Your purse." He picked the small handbag up and pushed it into her hands. "Anything else you have to take?"

She shook her head quickly, blinking up at the harsh features of his face.

"Where are you taking me?" she asked numbly as he dragged her out the front door and slammed it behind them furiously.

Brock didn't stop, he didn't ask permission to drag her out of her house, away from yet another of Mark's humiliations of her. Not that it mattered as much now. They weren't married anymore and she was more than thankful for that. Still, she couldn't believe the lengths he had gone to this time to shame her.

"To the ranch," he growled. "I'll take care of that bastard in the morning. But I'm telling you, Sarah, I'm so damned hard and hurting tonight that you may be days getting back in that house."

He threw her dresses into the back seat of the Jeep, then pushed her into the interior with hard hands.

"Buckle up, or would you prefer to stay here with hubby and company?" His eyes bore into her in the dim light of the Jeep. Anger pulsed; lust arced like white-hot, invisible strands of electricity between them.

She shook her head desperately, fumbled for the seat belt and snapped it in.

Her dress was still unbuttoned. As Brock started the engine, she fought to re-fasten the tiny pearl buttons that held the front of the cream-colored sundress together.

"Shit." His expletive had her flinching as he turned in his seat and quickly fixed it for her.

Tears gathered in her eyes. Her body still hummed with desire and she was terribly afraid he was going to be disappointed in her now. No mature, sophisticated woman would have such trouble buttoning her own dress at this point.

She felt as immature, as sexually inept as she had been at eighteen, and the shame of it had her cringing inside.

Then Brock was tilting her face, his lips taking hers in a kiss so hot, so furious, she reeled under the invasion. Her arms went around his shoulders again, her lips opening, her tongue twining desperately with his.

Hunger assailed her with such blinding intensity that there was no other thought, no other need, but for that of Brock's touch. His kiss. Her hands tangled in his hair, fingers clenching in the thick strands as she arched closer to him, demanding more.

"Enough," he growled, jerking away from her. "Dammit, we'll both be lucky if I make it out of town before I bury myself inside you."

The Jeep pulled out of the driveway with a squeal of tires. Sarah sat silently, still in shock, still pulsing with lust. He was taking her to the ranch? Dear God, was she insane? What had happened to her night of passion? Why had it suddenly gone to hell? She sighed deeply. Mark. He had ruined this night just as he had ruined every night of her life since she married him. Someone needed to shoot him and put the world out of the misery he brought to it.

Chapter Four

Brock couldn't believe the ending to this night. He was hard, hurting, achingly aware of the quiet young woman sitting in the seat beside him, twisting her hands nervously as she sneaked long looks in his direction. He knew she was worried, confused. She didn't understand why he was taking her back to the ranch and in the heat of the moment had agreed. He knew she now doubted that decision.

"There's a motel up here on the right. About four or five miles," she said hesitantly. Yep, definitely reconsidering. "You could just drop me off there."

Oh yeah, he was really going to do that one, he thought sarcastically. He kept it to himself, though. Sarah seemed to be riding the edge of panic right now, and he'd be damned if he could stand it if she started crying. The one time she had cried on him had broken what little had been left of his heart.

"Those beds are back breakers," he growled. "When I get inside you, Sarah, I don't want you sinking to the floor. I want you in place beneath me."

He heard her breath catch. Her breasts rose sharply, whether in shock or arousal he wasn't sure.

"This is so unreal." She shook her head on a disgusted sigh. "I just don't understand how this stuff always happens to me."

Brock glanced over at her with a slight frown.

"You and your husband need to schedule better," he grumped testily, wondering if he was insane.

What the hell was he doing messing with a married woman? They were trouble and jealous husbands could literally be a pain in the ass. Mark Tate wasn't known for his intelligence anyway, especially in regards to keeping his little wife tucked away at home while he dallied with the local talent. But first chance Brock had, what had he done? He went for her. Now he had her and he would be damned if he would let her go back to that son of a bitch. If Tate knew what was good for him, he would heed the warning Brock had given him weeks before to get the hell out of her life.

"He's not my husband." She surprised him by flashing him an angry look. "We're divorced. And why don't you have better sense than to be messing with a married woman?" She threw his thoughts in his face.

That flare of assertiveness, the flash of independence made his erection throb like a toothache beneath his pants. Damn, he bet she would be a firecracker in bed. Hell, he knew she would be. She had damned near burned him alive six years before. He hadn't even penetrated her with his cock and he had felt as though he were holding live fire.

"It depends on who the married woman is," he told her softly. He would have fucked her anytime, anywhere, no matter how many husbands she had. "You, Sarah-love, I would have had no resistance to, married or not. But remember the fact, I waited until you seemed receptive."

"Receptive?" She questioned him incredulously. "I was not receptive. I was minding my own business—"

"You were eating me up with your eyes." He grinned, remembering that shy, hungry look she had given him across the smoky bar.

"I was not," she gasped, shocked.

When he looked over at her, her soft, golden-brown eyes were widened in shock, her face pale in the dimly lit confines of the Jeep. The silken sweep of honey-gold hair was in disarray around her face, falling to her shoulders in tawny waves of splendor that begged him to reach out and touch.

"Oh yes, you were," he growled, fighting the need to touch. "With those lashes lowered just so much, and your golden eyes begging me to fuck you. I've stayed away from you for years, just because you were married and didn't seem willing. But you were more than willing tonight, baby."

So willing the pulse of her release to his oral ministrations flowed soft and sweet into his hungry mouth. The taste was addictive. Like nectar. Like the sweetest honeyed drug. He had spent six years trying to forget her taste and he still awoke with the essence of it in his mouth, his cock throbbing in response to the memory of her heat.

"You're insane." Anger lined every curve of her body and vibrated in her soft voice. "I refuse to go any further with you. Take me to the motel."

Flushed with indignation, he could feel the waves of anger pouring off her. He couldn't understand why she should be so angry. She wanted him. It was something he had waited on for a long time, so what was the problem?

"You'll come back to the ranch with me—"

"I refuse to go to bed with you now," she told him furiously.

Frustration had him casting her a frowning look as one hand raked impatiently through his hair.

"Okay, so we'll do it on a couch, the kitchen table, whatever. I'm adaptable."

Actually, the thought of either place was more than satisfactory. As long as he could hold her to him and take her in the ways he had dreamed.

"Kitchen table?" He wanted to smile at the amazement in her voice, but he had a feeling that would just invoke her ire once again.

He looked over at her again, barely containing a groan at the reluctant fascination in her voice.

"Yeah. We have a pool table, too." He grinned, wondering if she knew how pretty she was with that deep blush mounting her pale cheeks. Then a sudden thought hit him. "You are on the pill. Right?"

She shook her head. Disappointment raged through him. There was nothing he wanted more than to pound into Sarah until his cock exploded, filling her with his sperm.

"The motel," she breathed out roughly. "Just take me to the motel, Brock."

Brock frowned at the aroused rasp in her voice, versus the request. She wanted him. He knew she did. Why would that suddenly frighten her now?

"You don't want to go to that motel, Sarah," he told her gently. "You want to come home with me. Why not admit it?"

"Because. This is a mistake," she whispered. "A terrible, awful mistake. I told you before, you're way out of my league. I should have remembered that."

"The pool table scared you?" he asked her roughly. "Damn, Sarah, it's just a regular pool table. It's not like there are handcuffs or restraints on it. You act like I was describing a torture chamber."

He couldn't get the thought of that out of his head. Sarah bent over, lying against green felt as he lodged every hard inch of his shaft inside her body. He shifted in the normally comfortable seat. He'd be lucky if they made it to the ranch yard, let alone into the house.

"God. This is just not a good idea," she whispered, staring straight ahead. "Why won't you just do as I ask? Just drop me at the motel."

Brock's hands clenched on the steering wheel as the blood pumping furiously between his thighs made his patience exceeds its fragile limits. Why wouldn't he do as she asked? Because he had waited so long to fuck her that it felt like a lifetime.

"You want to know why I'm not listening to you?" he growled from between clenched teeth as he swung the Jeep to the side of the road. He pulled in behind an outcropping of boulders with a swerve of the wheel that had her gasping in surprise.

The Jeep rocked to a stop as Brock covered the distance between them, shoving her seat back, dropping the back to rest against the back seat, and ignoring her gasp of alarm as he kneed her thighs apart and rose over her.

She stared up at him in shock as he jerked her dress to her waist. His hand covered her mound, his fingers sinking into hot, wet flesh as the other hand hurriedly released the straining erection from inside his jeans.

"This is why, damn you." He took her hand, wrapping it around the silk-encased steel of his cock as he groaned roughly. "This, Sarah. Hot and wild. Me buried inside you while you scream out in pleasure. I told you, I wouldn't let you go again."

His fingers plunged deep into her melting vagina, invoking a shattered cry of ecstasy as he filled her. She moaned, a whimpering little sound as his thumb raked her straining clit, making her shudder in his arms as her fingers caressed him. His cock tightened at her small, stroking motions. So untutored, so hesitant, shy as she stared up at him in dazed fascination. It drove him crazy. He wanted to replace that inexperience with knowledge. He wanted to be the one to teach her, the one to replace the hesitancy with confidence and awareness. He wanted to steal her innocence, what little her ex-husband had left her, and it disgusted him at the same time that it made him wild with lust.

She whimpered, a small sound of longing and confusion.

"I'll take care of you, Sarah," he swore to her, his fingers moving sensually inside her body as he leaned down to touch her lips. "Trust me. Let me take you to my home. I've waited so long for you, love."

She jerked at his declaration, her thighs clenching on his hands as she fought to draw away from the seductive spell he was weaving around her.

"No." His lips covered her, his fingers moving deeper, making her hotter, wetter.

He needed to fuck her. To stake his claim on her here and now. To throw her into such pleasure that her climax drained her, left her unable to deny him. Unable to leave him. God help him if he lost her again. He couldn't risk it, not yet. Not while the fire was burning him alive, making him insane, making his body hurt with the need to touch her, claim her, hear her screams of release echoing around him.

"Feel how good it is, Sarah," he growled against her lips. "Tell me you want to go to that lonely motel room, rather than my warm bed. Tell me, and I'll do it, Sarah. Do you want to be empty and alone, or filled and screaming as you come around my cock?"

* * * * *

Sarah stared up at Brock, feeling his fingers hard and thick inside her body, his erection hot and hard in her hand. She couldn't even circle the broad length with her fingers. How full would he fill her? How hard could he make her scream in climax? The August men were rumored to be experienced, well-tutored lovers who could ride a woman well into the night. Mark had barely managed ten short minutes. She wanted him, but she was terrified of the strength of that wanting.

"Answer me, Sarah." His fingers thrust lightly into her, her vagina spilling its liquid into his hand as he groaned above her.

"Yes," she whispered, staring up at him, snared by his eyes, the intense sexual need in his expression. "I want to be filled and screaming. Please, Brock."

Strangled and tortured, a groan ripped from his throat. His fingers pulled free of her body, but he replaced them with the broad head of his erection. Sarah stilled, her breath nearly suspended in her chest as she felt the burning tip move against her.

"I swore not yet," he growled fiercely. "I was going to wait, Sarah. I swear I was."

Sarah felt fire, lightning arcing over her skin, between her thighs as the hard flesh began to invade her. Stretched, invaded, she gasped, her hips arching, the incredible sensations spreading through her as Brock slid deeper and deeper inside her body.

"Sarah." Her name was a harsh groan that sounded torn from his lips. "Damn. You're so tight. So tight, Sarah."

His hand tore at the buttons of her dress, several ripping from their mooring as the edges spread. Then his lips were covering one hard-tipped mound, his mouth suckling her heatedly as he pushed the last few inches into her body. She wouldn't survive it, Sarah thought. There was no way she would survive the lash of heat and need now searing her body.

That Brock August could do this to a woman didn't surprise her. The fact that he had her beneath him, moaning in pleasure, astounded her, though. Her—quiet, mousy Sarah— was making Brock August pant and whisper roughly as he pushed inside her. She tightened her muscles around him, crying out herself at the lash of pain/pleasure the action invoked.

"Oh hell. Sarah. Don't do that." His lips were at her neck, his teeth nipping at her skin as he fought for control. "Don't do that, baby, I won't be able to hold on."

Had he ever lost control sexually? She knew women who bemoaned over the fact that they could never make one of the August brothers lose control. She tightened around him further, her hips shifting as heat scalded her vagina, making her writhe in need beneath him.

His hips retracted then plunged harshly, and Sarah heard herself cry out as her flesh throbbed and pulsed around him.

Sensation after sensation tore through her, making her arch closer to him, tighten further around him.

"Stay still, Sarah," he begged her roughly, grinding his hips against her in short, involuntary jerks.

She couldn't help it. The feeling was too intense, the need riding her like a demon intent on satisfaction.

"Make me scream," she whispered, staring into his face as he rose above her. She was amazed at the husky sexuality in her voice. "Please, Brock. I've never screamed."

His eyes widened. For a second, long and intense, he watched her in surprise.

"Never?" He growled the question as his body seemed to tense, bunch for action. His arm wrapped around her hips as he moved her back along the seat.

The motion tore a cry from her. It made the flesh filling her shift, move, stroke and caress. She was desperate for more.

"Never," she cried out roughly. "I want to scream. Just once, Brock."

"Just once?" He levered over her, pulling back slowly. "No love, you'll scream more than just once."

A low, keening cry filled the interior of the Jeep as he plunged hard inside her. Sarah felt her vagina stretch with a bit of protest, but that small edge of pain made her want more. Always more. And he didn't stop with just one. One hand gripped her hip, his arm wrapped around her shoulders, and his hips began a strong, rhythmic thrusting that had her arching and crying out. The tension in her grew, the fire and heat filling her, stretching her on a rack of pleasure so torturous she began to fear insanity. She couldn't stand it. She couldn't. It was building harshly, always building, never releasing, never ending.

"Brock?" Fear was filling her now. It wouldn't stop. The tension in her body was winding tighter and tighter, with no ease, no release.

She strained against him, her head tossing, her hips fighting against his grip as they jerked in time to his hard thrusts. She could feel the invader, thick steel driving between her thighs over and over, making her body fill and gush with moisture but the tormenting grip of erotic fury never eased inside her.

"Soon, Sarah," he gasped at her ear, his lips caressing the lobe as she fought against the steady pace. "Just let it go, baby. Don't worry. Don't fight it."

"It's killing me." Her cry echoed around them, rising in intensity as the fire built in her body.

She couldn't stand it. She wouldn't survive it. She would die. It would kill her.

"Then it will kill us both." He arched into her, his cock pummeling into her like a flesh and blood jackhammer intent on driving her past the edge of frenzy.

The fierce impalement, the frenzy of lust and need made her gasp, cry out. The tension was winding tighter, fear threading through the haze of passion, making the sensations stronger, deeper. She wouldn't survive it. She couldn't survive it.

Brock jerked her legs back, holding them now as he rose above her, his face a mask of furious intent as he slammed his cock repeatedly inside her. The sounds of wet flesh, gasping need, and Sarah's pleas filled the interior of the Jeep. She writhed beneath him, her cries rising in crescendo now as the building inferno began to engulf her.

Fear edged her cries, her consciousness, but she couldn't halt his thrusts, couldn't halt her body's reaction.

"Now, Sarah," he cried out harshly, leaning over her, applying a pressure against her clit that sent her careening into insanity.

His pelvis stroked the ultra sensitive bud with one last hard thrust and Sarah felt herself dying. Exploding, lost in an inferno of sensation that threatened to destroy her. She heard someone screaming as she felt her flesh tighten around the pistoning cock painfully. Screaming, pleading as her body tightened to breaking point, arching so tight she feared she would break as wave after wave of shocking release tore through her body. It ripped through her vagina, burned past her stomach, and shredded her sanity as it wound over her, through her, seeming never-ending until finally, with one last brutal jerk of her body, she collapsed back to the seat, feeling the warm jet of Brock's semen against the soft flesh of her lower stomach.

"The pill," he gasped as he fell over her, breathing hard, sweat dripping from his face and hair as he fought to catch his breath. "Tomorrow, Sarah. Tomorrow you go on the pill. I want to come inside you, love."

Sarah shuddered at the thought of it. Feeling him pulse inside her would kill her. And why would the pill matter? It took at least a week to be effective. Did he intend more than the few nights the other women in his life had received? She shivered against him. Her eyes were closed, weariness stealing over her now. Her body was relaxed, the torturous needs of moments ago sated.

"Sleep, love," she heard Brock whisper gently as he moved away from her.

She felt him cleaning her stomach, running a soft cloth between her thighs to dry the cooling dampness there. Then her dress was lowered as he moved back to his own seat. The Jeep started once again, the soft hum of the motor lulling Sarah further into sleep.

Chapter Five

ဢ

"Do you know what you're doing?" Sam asked Brock curiously, drawing him out of the thick sleep he had fallen into after bringing Sarah to his bed.

Brock blinked drowsily up at his twin, seeing amusement edged with concern in his eyes. He glanced back at Sarah, making certain she still slept deeply before he untangled himself from her and slid quietly from the bed. She whispered his name, but didn't awaken. Making sure the blankets were tucked around her, he pulled a pair of sweats on and motioned Sam from the room.

His brother followed, but Brock was aware of the curious looks Sam had cast back at the bed before the door closed firmly on the view. Brock knew that Sam was more than aware of his desire for Sarah over the past years. Hell, they were twins; he couldn't help but know. But he wasn't ready to share her yet. Despite the heat that seared him at the thought of it, an edge of worry pulsed in the region that had once been his heart. He couldn't lose Sarah, and he was very much afraid that was the reason she had run the first time.

"I need coffee." Brock headed downstairs and the pot of coffee he prayed Cade had left before going out that morning.

"Cade's pissed," Sam said as he followed close behind him. "You were supposed to be in the barn at daybreak this morning. Remember?"

Brock grunted in irritation. He'd forgotten. Cade wanted him to help check some fences and move the cattle in the front pastures. He strode quickly into the kitchen and went straight for the coffee. Marly was still sitting at the breakfast table, her head rose as Brock went past her.

"Hey, sleepy head," she greeted him with a smile. "Cade was gonna pull you out of bed this morning, until he saw your friend."

Brock froze as he set the pot back on its warming plate.

"He came to the room?" he asked her carefully.

"Yeah, he did." Her voice was amused but he could hear the echo of strain beneath it. "Then he told me to let you sleep and he would talk to you later."

He picked up his cup, glancing at Sam's carefully controlled expression. For some reason, Cade hadn't wanted Marly to know just how angry he was. There was more to this than the work Brock had missed.

Picking up his coffee cup, he snagged several large biscuits and sausage and went to the table, followed closely by Sam.

"So who is she?" Marly asked curiously, watching him. "Anyone I know?"

Despite her amused expression, her blue eyes were dark with concern.

"Sarah Tate," Brock answered her, knowing his voice was edgy.

He caught the look between Sam and Marly. Sam's expression was mockingly amused and knowing. Marly's surprised.

"She's married." Marly frowned. "No wonder Cade was upset."

"She's divorced. The papers were signed yesterday," he told her tightly. "And since when did Cade think he could tell me who to fuck?"

Marly looked at him in surprise. Brock breathed out a rough sigh. He was on edge. He wanted to go back to the bedroom and waken Sarah. He wanted to hear her screaming out his name again. Begging him.

"You brought her home, Brock. You've never done that," she reminded him softly. "Cade's just concerned."

Was Cade concerned, or was Marly? The complications of this burst into the forefront of his mind. He hadn't thought; he had just reacted. And Cade had come to his room. He knew what Sarah meant to Brock, knew what having her there would come to mean. Just as Brock did; just as Marly should know. The edge of pain that she fought to keep hidden sliced his heart like a dull knife.

"Nothing to be concerned about." Brock shrugged, forcing the lie past his lips.

He wanted to keep Sarah; at least until he knew if the obsession he had always had for her went deeper than just lust.

"Is that why Dr. Bennett had a message on his machine this morning that you were bringing a patient in for an exam and a prescription of birth control pills?" Marly dropped her own little bomb, watching him carefully. "He called this morning to set up the appointment time. By the way, he said late afternoon would work."

Brock felt a stirring of lust and tamped it down ruthlessly. Soon, he would be able to take Sarah, to thrust into her and feel his own release shatter through him as it vibrated against the walls of her flesh.

"He's zoning out on us, Munchkin," Sam sighed with exaggerated patience. "He's a goner."

Brock flashed him an irritated look. He didn't need Sam's highjinks right now. He also caught the flash of fear in Marly's eyes and his chest clenched. He didn't want to hurt Marly. It was the last thing he wanted to do.

"Her ex was at her house when we showed up last night. It was late." He shrugged, keeping his eyes on his cup.

"So you're taking her home?" There was a measure of relief in Marly's voice.

Brock wanted to hit something. He could feel the pain boiling through his system, making him want to curse in fury.

"Yeah, soon as she's ready. Then I'll run the bastard out of her house and put the fear of Brock in him." He grinned crookedly, though he felt like howling.

He avoided Sam's look, knowing his twin would sense the emotions he was keeping carefully under control. He hadn't expected this, though he admitted he should have. He had hoped, no, he had believed Marly would eventually welcome any woman he claimed into the house. He hadn't thought she would feel insecure, hurt.

"Hey, Marly, you're gonna be late for your own appointment this morning," Sam told her laughing. "It's nearly ten. Didn't you schedule with Denise for eleven?"

Denise Lamont did the intimate waxing, plucking and toning of Marly's body.

"Damn." Marly swallowed the last drink of coffee and jumped to her feet. "You're right, and she'll kill me if I'm late."

She left the kitchen hurriedly, leaving Sam and Brock alone, the silence thickening harshly around them.

"What are you gonna do?" Sam finally asked him curiously.

Brock shook his head, hunching his shoulders as he sipped at his coffee. There was nothing to do but accept it. He hated it. The pain of it lay in his gut like acid. But what else could he do? He couldn't hurt Marly.

"I heard her and Cade this morning. She was crying, Brock. Cade's furious because she was upset. He's blaming himself." Sam kept his voice low as he leaned closer to Brock.

Brock grimaced, his own anger surging through his body. Dammit, it was his home too. His right. A right Marly's pain would steal away from him. There was no sense in arguing the fairness of it, or of bemoaning it. Marly hadn't been raised as they had been. She had been sheltered, loved during the years she had lived in their home. She didn't understand the bond they shared, the needs they had. Not fully.

"I'll take care of it." Brock shook his head.

Silence descended once again. It was strained, questions unsaid, explanations no longer important now.

"How will you take care of it?" Sam finally asked him quietly.

Brock flashed him a disgruntled look.

"I don't know, Sam, do I need your permission, whatever I do?"

Sam sighed again. He pushed his fingers through his hair, and Brock knew Sam was feeling his own frustration. Brock could only imagine how Cade felt.

"She won't handle Cade touching another woman, I don't think." Sam shook his head sadly. "It's what Cade's been afraid of."

"And I won't push her into it," Brock promised him, finishing his coffee. "I'll get Sarah up and head out as soon as I talk to Cade.""

He rose to his feet, feeling tired, lacking the enthusiasm of the day that he had felt when he first woke up. Damn. He didn't know what to do now. He would have to move out, at least until he knew what was going on with himself and Sarah. He wasn't about to do without her in his bed, in his arms, as long as he could keep her there. He would help her clear the trash out of her house, then come back and pack some clothes. The traveling between the ranch and her house would suck, but it beat the alternative.

"She isn't the type anyway, Brock," Sam told him sadly as Brock started to turn away from him. "She wouldn't ease into the family. You know that."

Brock wasn't so certain of that. She was untutored, innocent in many ways, but he had seen the spark of excitement in her eyes when he came to her in that damned bar. She knew the rumors, knew what was told about the

August brothers and the lover of the oldest. The rumors had been flying for years.

"Yeah. I'm sure you're right." Brock agreed with him anyway.

He didn't want Sam feeling guilty, didn't want Cade or Marly feeling that way either. Life just sucked sometimes. You had to accept it, or opt out of the game. Brock was no longer willing to opt out.

He left the kitchen, feeling the weight of it dragging at him. He loved the ranch, loved the house. Leaving it for even a little while wouldn't be easy. But he needed Sarah. The taste of her, so sweet and hot, was becoming addictive. He wanted more. He wanted her in his bed at night, he wanted to hear her scream out his name when she climaxed, but he also wanted to know that it was for more than just one night. He wanted her to be part of the family. His family.

* * * * *

Brock found Cade in the stables repairing a stirrup on his favorite saddle. He stood in the doorway to the tack room, silent, absorbing the scents of hay, sweat and horse as he watched his brother work to fix something older than all of them were. A piece of their history, yet one Cade had been unable to put away.

The saddle was old. Generations old. It had belonged to the first Cade August more than a hundred years before. Handed down from father to son, until Grandpa August had bypassed Joe and given it instead to Cade. The summer he died Joe had packed them off to the demon's house. Brock refused to even think that name. For days, months at a time, he could forget the horror of those months. Then it would swamp him again, rushing over him, boiling in his stomach like an evil acid, ready to devour him.

It never failed. It was the same for all of them. When they attempted to draw close to each other, to sense each other's pain, to attempt to make reason of the hell their lives would often become, the memories attacked. That had been the intention. The object of the lesson. They were alone. Just as that fucking bastard father of theirs had been. He had despised the bond they had as boys, so he had defiled it. Made it ugly and useless, made it something to fear.

Brock clenched his teeth, his jaw aching as he fought for control. He wanted to turn and walk away, to leave the sight of his brother, a man alone, fighting his pain. Cade had always fought so well. For all of them.

"You should put it up. You're always working on it." He stepped into the small room, ignoring the sense of oppressiveness, the demons raking at his soul with razor sharp talons.

Cade continued the delicate work, his tanned face tight and drawn as he concentrated on repairing the leather.

Brock leaned against the wall, as close to the door and escape as he could get. God, how did Cade stand it? Being closed up like this, enduring the small space and the memories he knew came with it.

"It endures, Brock." Cade shrugged, the harsh sound of his voice vibrating through the confined space.

And few other things do.

Brock crossed his arms over his chest, staring around the room. Saddles, ropes, bridles, the tools of any cowboy's trade lined the room. Sunlight filtered through a small, high window, but at no time of the day would the damaging rays of the sun be permitted to touch the leather. The damage would be irreparable.

"I'm getting ready to take Sarah home." Brock took a deep breath and exhaled slowly. Son of a bitch. He hated this fucking room. He could smell antiseptic, hear screams. He was breaking out in a sweat and only by force of control did he keep his body from shaking.

"Will you be back?" Cade didn't look up. Brock knew what he would see if he did. Pain, anger, blood.

"I'll be back in the morning for most of the day. I'll drive the distance for the time being." Brock shifted, watching Cade's hands work stubborn leather, his head down bent.

"Marly still crying?" Cade's voice reflected his torment now.

He couldn't bear Marly's tears. Never could. The sound of her sobs, or the whisper of tears over pale cheeks destroyed him. He would kill the man or woman who deliberately made Marly cry.

"No. I took care of it." Brock clenched his teeth. Cade's body tensed further.

"It's best." Cade finally nodded. "No sense in someone else being hurt by this, Brock."

Cade was alone. Brock felt betraying moisture prick his eyes and he fought it back. The time for tears was long past. But damn, seeing his brother drawing away, being separated from him, tore at him. He pushed his hands through his hair, exhaling with a fierce breath.

"She'll accept it, Cade. If you explain it to her." It was a heavy disagreement between them all.

Cade refused to tell Marly the details of the abuse, in even the vaguest form. He wanted her shielded, sheltered. His fury when he learned Tara, Marly's former bodyguard, had revealed part of it, had ended in a vicious, bloody fight between himself and Tara's brother-in-law, Rick.

Cade shook his head.

"Let me tell her, Cade," he urged him, unable to bear the lonely pain he knew Cade felt.

"No one tells her, Brock." Cade moved to lift the saddle oil from the bench beside him, and Brock felt a shaft of agony pierce his heart.

His brother's face was lined, rough with unshed pain, unshed rage. His eyes were bleak, and so damned dark they looked like violent thunderheads. Brock clenched his fists, sucked in a hard, silent breath. He could do nothing, say nothing. He could only watch as Cade tended a piece of their past that was forever gone. Like their innocence. Except shattered innocence was irreparable.

"What do I do, Cade?" he asked, clearing the emotion from his throat. No emotion. No need. He couldn't, because he couldn't bear the return of the nightmares, the horrible memories. "It's my home, too. Will you sacrifice us all without even trying?"

Shock bloomed through Brock when Cade faced him fully. God. He couldn't stand it. He couldn't look in those eyes, nearly black with memories, with pain, shame. They had no reason to feel shame. Yet, he knew Cade did.

"I will not take her sense of security from her, Brock." Cade's voice vibrated with all the shattered hopes and dreams of a man who had once been innocent. Young. "I won't do it, and neither will you. When I can control my need to be a part of that bond with you and Sam, you can bring Sarah home."

Brock looked around the tack room and thought of the large house. It echoed with Marly's laughter and sometimes with Cade's. More often with Sam's. And Brock knew that if this wasn't resolved, then as long as he had Sarah, he would never be able to return.

"Yeah. Sure." Brock straightened from the wall, avoiding Cade's gaze, avoiding more than just a look, and he knew it. "Just let me know, Cade." And he knew Cade never would.

He turned without giving his brother a chance to speak and left the room. He wasn't sure, but when he reached the wide stable doors, he thought he heard an animal's whimper of pain. That lonely, haunting sound burst over his soul with the agonizing force of time. A young man's whimper, his eyes black with shock, shame, his body —

He shook his head, pushing it back. Back. Far away where it couldn't hurt the man, where it could never destroy ever again. Back to the past, where the shame, regret and blood were forever hidden.

Chapter Six

๛

Sarah was showered and dressed when Brock returned to the room. She stood up from the bed as he entered, facing him with the knowledge that the night she had so longed for hadn't been nearly enough.

"I was hoping you would still be asleep." He paused as he closed the door, his gaze darkening as it traveled over the light, pale green sundress she wore. "I was looking forward to waking you up."

Her breath caught in her throat. He looked hungry, sexual. How in the hell was she supposed to ever get over this need crawling through her system if he kept looking at her like that?

"I need to get home," she told him softly, uncertain how she was supposed to act now.

She had never had a one-night stand, and she admitted that she knew very little about the rules that went with one.

"Yeah, I figured that," he sighed. "Come on downstairs, there's coffee and biscuits waiting."

"I'm really not hungry." She shifted nervously, clutching her purse with stiff fingers as she fought to keep her mouth from watering at the need to taste him just one more time.

She was lying through her teeth. She was starved, but not for food. She wanted to devour him, just one more time. Feel his hard muscular body coming over her, warming her from the inside out as his cock burrowed deep inside her pussy.

His eyes narrowed and Sarah glimpsed the control he was obviously exerting over himself. He wanted her again as well.

She could see it in the thick bulge in his jeans, the way his eyes darkend.

"We'll eat later then," he grunted. "Come on, we have an appointment to keep before I take you home. And trust me Sarah," the rumbling male purr sent shivers up her spine. "You really want to keep this appointment."

He moved to her, that slow sexy stroll of his making her heart hammer in her chest as he halted in front of her. One hand reached out, the back of his fingers smoothing over her cheek before he pulled her into his arms, cradling her to him. For a moment, she closed her eyes, willing back the tears of regret and the desperation she could feel moving through her. Or was it in his hold? She couldn't be certain. All she knew was at that moment, she didn't want him to ever let her go.

Sarah couldn't believe what Brock had done. The appointment at the doctor was bad enough. A thorough exam and blood test resulting in a quick shot into her forearm of a birth control medication. Dr. Bennett, pleased to learn that her cycle had just passed, was happy to begin the shots immediately. Then, to her immense mortification, with a nonchalant attitude, blithely handed her the report on Brock's last blood tests as well. Disease free. Her face flamed as she remembered the doctor's curious glance at her.

Normally, she would have balked at Brock's domineering attitude when he informed her of the appointment. But there had been something about him. Something broken and lost, an edge of desperation in his look that had halted her. The way he touched her cheek, pulled her to him, his arms tight, his breathing harsh as he held her. So she had given in instead. And she wasn't certain what she had glimpsed, or why it had hurt her to the soles of her feet.

"All set?" Brock stood to his feet in the outer office as she walked out of the examination room.

He ignored her blush. She was certain he had noticed it.

"Yeah, all set." She drew close to him, overwhelmed once again by the sheer maleness of him. He exuded testosterone. Hard and handsome, warm and strong, and if the bulge in his pants was any indication, more than ready to take her to bed.

"I just got a call from the sheriff," he told her as he led her from the doctor's office. "Mark and his little friend are gone, and the cleaning crew just finished cleaning the house. You'll have to replace most of the clothes he destroyed, but other than that everything seems in order. I also had your bed replaced."

Sarah sighed. He was taking over. Why was he taking over? What the hell was going on here? She brought a man home for a night of rough and tumble sex, and all of a sudden she had blood tests, a birth control shot, and a new bed. None of it made sense.

"Thank you, but there was no need to bother," she told him a bit desperately, aware that her one night stand could very well be turning into something that terrified her. "I didn't mean for you to be put out this way."

"That's okay, love, I haven't been put out." He placed his hand at the small of her back as he led her to the Jeep. "Mark doesn't seem to be real accepting of this divorce, though, Sarah. What's up with that?"

His voice was carefully controlled, but she caught the under-edge of pulsing anger flowing through it.

"What's up with you?" She kept her voice calm as she let him help her into the Jeep, meeting his gaze as though there was nothing out of the ordinary with their conversation. "I was unaware this was any of your business."

He stilled. Just like that. He didn't even blink as he watched her for long moments. Just watched her. There was no anger in his face, no determination, but there was tenderness. What was it about that one, almost non-existent light in his eyes that stilled her anger?

"I'm making you my business, Sarah-love," he told her softly. "All my business."

Sarah blinked. His gaze was, as always, hot and possessive, searing over her flesh as he watched her closely.

"You're supposed to wait for an invitation, Brock," she told him coolly. "The world does not belong to the August men."

"No, it doesn't, but you just may," he told her cryptically. "Now buckle up. I want to get you home so I can return to the ranch and get back here before nightfall."

Get back? The door closed on her question. Reaching behind her, she pulled the seat belt forward, clipping it with a jerky, tense movement.

"You are not moving in with me, Brock August," she bit out as he jumped into the Jeep.

She watched his hands tighten on the wheel, then they relaxed and he was closing his door, fastening his own seat belt and starting up the vehicle.

"I don't recall asking to." His voice was smooth as honey, but he couldn't hide the underlying edge of tension.

"I have a feeling you rarely ask for anything," she grumped, settling against the seat as he drove towards her small house. "I bet you just walk right in and take over when you want something."

She noticed the shuttered glance he gave her, despite the fact he appeared to be trying to hide the grin that tugged at the corner of his lips.

"Is there another way to do it?" he asked her as he navigated through the sparse traffic of Madison's main city street.

Sarah rolled her eyes.

"Why haven't I heard about this dominant streak of yours before now?" she asked him testily. "None of your other women complained about it."

He shot her a surprised glance.

"What the hell are you talking about?" His forced laughter was a bit strained.

Sarah looked at him mockingly.

"You think your other women haven't talked over the years?" she asked him softly. "Gossip makes the world go around, Brock."

"Hmmm. Cade says money does that." He stared straight ahead.

Sarah hid her own nervousness now. She could tell that the subject of gossip bothered him. It made her wonder how many of the rumors were really true. Were the ones that had caused her the most concern years before more than just talk?

He took a deep breath.

"Which rumors are you talking about, Sarah?" He seemed to clear his throat.

Nervousness didn't sit well on him, so it was easy to read as it crossed his expression. Sarah wasn't certain she wanted to go any further with this now.

She shrugged, staring out the windshield, wishing she hadn't said anything. There was obviously something Brock was concerned about her hearing. Did she really want to know the truth about the dark tales? She decided quickly that she didn't. There were some things a woman just couldn't handle after a night like the one she had spent with Brock.

"Nothing." She shook her head, refusing to glance over at him. "So why do you have to return to the ranch, then come back here?"

It didn't make sense to her. She thought she knew everything there was to know about Brock August, but the man sitting beside her in the vehicle was nothing like the man she thought she knew.

He glanced at her, his expression considering.

"You aren't staying the night." Sarah crossed her arms over her breasts. Enough was enough. "It's bad enough you kidnapped me last night, but this is ridiculous."

"Kidnapped you?" He grinned over at her, the sexy quirk of his lips making her heart race. "I didn't kidnap you, honey, I rescued you."

"Rescued me?" She harrumphed. "That wasn't a rescue, Brock, and you know it. You kidnapped and seduced me."

She fought the blush rising to her cheeks at the thought of the night she had spent in his arms. He hadn't just made her scream during that stolen hour in the Jeep. He had awakened her once again before reaching the ranch, his hot erection easing into her with a slow measured thrust, and within minutes had her screaming again. She had barely had the strength to walk into the ranch house and up to his room. He had carried her, though, his lips moving over hers, his tongue mating with her mouth as he stumbled his way to his room where he drove her higher, taking her breath, stealing her will as he forced the harsh cries of completion from her there as well.

Her throat was raspy this morning, her body pleasantly sore.

"Did you get the pills?" he suddenly asked her, his voice incredibly husky and hot.

Sarah's face did flush then.

"No," she mumbled. "I took the shot instead."

His body tensed.

"You're safe now then?" he asked her, and she could hear his battle to appear merely curious.

"I am not having sex with you in this Jeep, in broad daylight." She flashed him a hard, measured look. "Do you understand me, Brock?"

He grinned again. Damn, she hated that grin. It made her stomach all fluttery, her thighs weak. She wanted to spread her legs right then and invite him in. She was insane. If the rumors were to be believed, then the last thing she wanted or needed right now, was Brock August taking a serious interest in her.

"I understand you, Sarah-love," he said on a slow drawl. "Don't worry darlin', I won't make you scream again until I have you in that big new bed you have waiting on you."

She shivered. Damn she hadn't meant to shiver like that. And she knew he didn't miss it.

"I don't like screaming." She winced, wondering if lightning would strike her for that lie. It was a biggie.

He laughed now. No grin this time, she thought morosely, he knew better than that. But she liked that little, husky laugh. It was rusty, inexperienced, but a spark of enjoyment all the same.

"Sarah, darlin', why are you fighting this so hard?" He handled the vehicle easily as he pulled onto her street.

Her small house was farther down the lightly inhabited street, hidden by evergreens and elms from curious eyes. It wouldn't help her though. She knew the curious eyes that tracked the progress of the Jeep down the street. They would see it turn into her drive, then begin counting the hours before it left again.

"Because you're dangerous," she told him, twisting her fingers nervously as they lay in her lap. "I told you last night, Brock, I don't think I can handle this. I don't think I can handle you."

She expected him to argue immediately. When he didn't, she looked over at him worriedly. He was frowning a bit, his hands tense on the wheel as he pulled into her driveway and followed the one lane drive to her sheltered carport. He cut the engine, but rather than moving to get out of the Jeep, he sat there silently for long moments.

"I've wanted you for a long time, did you know that?" he asked her, his voice soft as he stared into the wooded backyard behind the carport.

Sarah's system went wild. The blood began to pump rapidly through her body, her stomach clenching and the moisture between her thighs building as it prepared her for his invasion. Dammit, she didn't have a lick of sense.

She took a deep, calming breath. It didn't help a bit.

"I didn't know." She shook her head.

"Yes you did," he told her, his voice sure and confident. "You were eighteen years old when you knew, Sarah. The night you ran from me, after the barbeque out at the ranch. You knew I wanted you. You married Mark Tate the next week. Why?"

Because he terrified her. Because she had known she would do anything he wanted, any way he wanted her to do it, and the thought of that had burned terror into her mind.

"I loved Mark—"

"You wanted me." He turned on her then, anger burning in his gray-blue eyes, vibrating in his body. "I know you did, Sarah. I felt it the minute I touched that hot little cunt of yours, you wanted me. You were drenched, begging for it. And you still ran off and married that pint-sized little bastard. Why?"

"Why do you care?" She shook her head in confusion. "You act as though I betrayed you, Brock. As though we were somehow committed to each other. We weren't."

"You didn't want him," he accused her, refusing to answer her question. "You wanted me, Sarah."

"I wanted Mark more—"

"God. Damn it, woman, at least don't lie to me. Tell me the fucking truth." His voice rose in frustration.

"Because I didn't want to be shared with your brothers," she cried out, horror spreading through her system the minute the words were out of her mouth. "Oh God. I'm sorry."

Panic burst through her blood stream. She jerked at the handle, threw the door open as she nearly fell from the Jeep, wanting to run from him, to run from the truth and the terrible, shameful thoughts she had once had. Thoughts she still couldn't get out of her mind.

"Dammit, Sarah!" Brock's voice echoed through the quickly closed back door of the house.

Frustration lined his tone, yet she also heard a bleak pain she wished she could block.

"Sarah, you have to let me explain," he said through the wood barrier. "Please, baby, let me explain."

She shook her head, as she lowered it, ignoring the need in her to let him in, to hear whatever he had to say. One night. That was all she wanted, all she could have. The doctor's appointment was a mistake. The hope inside her short lived. She couldn't share him, she couldn't allow herself to be shared. It was better this way, she promised herself. But she couldn't ignore the flare of lust or curiosity at the thought.

Chapter Seven

☙

He was gone. Sarah stood, her back to the closed door, breathing in raggedly. He had followed her, asked her more than once to let him into the house, but she had refused. She lowered her head, fighting the racing of her heart, the regret twisting in her stomach. She had wanted one night. Not a doctor's appointment and the implication of an affair she couldn't handle right now. Not with him. Not after seeing the truth in his eyes.

Rumors ran rife in Madison about the August brothers. Their father, old Joe August, had been a cruel man. Sarah remembered her father speaking often of the bruises the boys carried while they were younger, and how they had changed after old man Joe had sent them off to foster on another ranch one year. Not too much time had passed before the rumors started. How the men, young even then, would become attracted to the same woman. They would pursue her, seduce her, share her among them.

The women they chose were experienced enough to enjoy such play, but they were also gossips, relishing in the shocked gasps their tales brought. Sarah's father had been sympathetic, but she remembered several occasions when he had warned her to steer clear of their interest.

They were sinfully handsome. Dark, lusty, so sexy it made a woman's heart beat fast just to look at them. Sighing deeply, denying the tears that threatened to fall from her eyes, she looked around the dimly lit kitchen. She was home, and she was alone. Brock was gone.

"Goodbye," she whispered to the empty room, and she wondered if she were saying goodbye to the man, or to a young girl's empty dreams.

Straightening from the door, she dragged in a hard, deep breath before moving through the kitchen and into the silent living room. Or, it should have been silent. Tilting her head, she glanced toward the staircase that led to the upper floor and the muted sound of music coming from above.

Her eyes narrowed.

"Dammit Mark if you've come back I'm going to kill you myself."

She stalked to the staircase, moving up the steps quickly, anger pumping through her bloodstream. Wasn't it enough that she was forcing herself to give up the only man she had ever truly desired in her life? Did she have to deal with Mark's idiotic escapades on top of it?

Rounding the landing, she moved furiously into her bedroom and stopped cold. Her throat tightened with emotion, pain unlike anything she had ever known beating through her heart.

The curtains had been drawn snugly, blocking out the sunlight that would have poured through the windows. Candles by the dozen graced every surface and the new, white oak bed was turned down invitingly. Soft, romantic music poured from her CD player, lending an intimacy to her room that it had never known before.

"Oh Brock..." She sat down on the bed, her hand smoothing over the soft white comforter, the silk sheets and let the regret rock through her.

There was no hiding the truth from herself. She loved him. She had loved him when she was eighteen with a desperation that had nearly killed her when she had run from him. And she loved him now.

How do you love a man that you know would never stay faithful to you? A man who would take another woman, regularly, and expect her to not just accept it, but to condone it?

Her fist clenched in the blankets as a snarl of rage vibrated from her chest. There was nothing right or fair about what he would expect from her. How could he love her and still expect her to do the things she knew he would?

He would want her to allow his brothers to touch her.

And that was not desire that sped up the blood racing through her veins, she reminded herself. It was fury. Pure and simple. She didn't love the other two. She didn't want them. She wasn't going to do it, so there!

But for a moment, just a moment, her womb clenched in reaction to the sudden image that flashed through her mind. The August men, all tall and strong, their bodies honed from years of ranching. Warm, calloused hands as they surrounded her, touching her...

Her breath caught in her throat as she came off the bed. Within minutes the music was stilled, the candles extinguished and the curtains thrown wide to the late afternoon sun.

How do you love one woman and still fuck another? And on the other side of the coin, how could she love Brock and still grow wet, excited at the thought of his brothers touching her?

She wasn't going to allow this to happen, she assured herself as she stood in the middle of her bedroom, staring around at the effort Brock had gone to in his attempt to seduce her further.

She wanted the dream. One man, the children she would have with him, the life she would lead with him. Not three arrogant, impossibly horny ranchers intent on every man's sexual fantasy... And every woman's, her own arousal mocked her as she rushed from the bedroom.

She ignored the premonition that there was more to it than just horniness and fought the knowledge that perhaps it was that sexuality, that extremity about Brock that had first drawn her so long ago. She had wanted one night. She had it, it was over.

Simple.

Or was it?

Chapter Eight

Work. She worked because she wanted to. Because she enjoyed it. The inheritance her father had left her on his death had been hidden from Mark, thanks to her father's careful planning, rather than her own. Her mother's portion had been all Mark had known about. Unknown to her ex-husband, she wasn't as broke as he believed she was.

The library afforded her a peace, a solitude in what she did, and there were rarely any hassles. Until today. Brock August sat casually at one of the front desks, a newspaper spread in front of him, his eyes watching her possessively. His dark lashes lay at half-mast, the gray-blue orbs watching her with a hint of promise, or threat. She wasn't certain which. He was too handsome, with his long black hair laying almost to his shoulders, and disheveled from the repeated times his fingers had run through it. Each time she saw the gesture she was reminded of the countless times she had run her fingers through those silken strands as well.

He had been there most of the day. She refused to speak to him and he didn't speak to her. If curious patrons approached him, they quickly left. It made Sarah nervous, the way he watched her. He had seen her naked, had heard her screams, and it was there in every look he gave her.

Closing time came, and still he sat there. Everyone else was gone, the library deserted, the door sign posted.

"It's time to leave, Mr. August." Sarah kept her voice polite, low. "You're making me run late."

He folded his paper carefully.

"Have dinner with me." His voice was silky, carefully covering the underlying thread of sensuality. He wasn't fooling her for a minute.

"Not tonight. I have things to do."

"Like what?" He tilted his head questioningly.

"Oh, I don't know." She shrugged. "Walk my dog—"

She restrained her smile and fought to keep her expression blank as his lips quirked in amusement.

"You don't have a dog."

"Feed my cat—"

"Sarah, you don't have a cat." And his patience was wearing thin if the tone of his voice was any indication.

"Clean the basement?" She gave him a wide-eyed innocent look. She wasn't about to go anywhere with him, not until she was a little less weak. A little less needy for his touch.

"Why are you so scared of me? Do you think I'd hurt you, Sarah?" He leaned forward in his chair, watching her quietly.

His eyes. Shadows twisted in them, sadness a permanent part of their murky depths. Why couldn't she get past wanting to erase the pain in his eyes?

"I think you could destroy me, Brock," she answered him honestly. There was no point in lying. "I've spent six years paying for one mistake. I don't want to pay for another."

"And I waited for six years for you to admit to wanting me." His voice lowered, husky and filled with desires she didn't even want to guess at. "I don't want to settle for just one night, Sarah."

She couldn't hold his gaze. Pain seized her heart when she saw the wanting in his eyes, the bleak acceptance that she was turning him away.

"One night is all I had to give, Brock," she whispered, standing stiff. Still.

He sighed roughly, dragging his hands through his hair in a gesture of frustration. It was incredibly sexy, the way his jaw bunched as he fought for control, the way the strands of midnight silk caressed his fingers as he pushed them through it.

"I won't accept that. You won't even let me explain, Sarah. There are things you don't know."

There it was again. That dark loneliness in his voice that pulled at her.

"And they won't change my mind." She didn't want to know why she wanted to weep at the expression in his eyes. "I told you. It's more than I can handle. If I had known you waited for me. If I had known what you wanted from me. I wouldn't have gone to that bar."

"Then I would have come to you." He rose from his chair, stepping close, ignoring her when she stepped back nervously. "I was tired of waiting, Sarah."

"I was married. You didn't even know about the divorce." Censure edged her words, despite her determination to hold it inside.

He smiled, a small, crooked little quirk of his lips that broke her heart. That was his smile, and there was no joy in the gesture.

"It didn't matter," he whispered, coming around behind her, bending close so his breath feathered her ear. "I didn't care anymore, Sarah. I wanted you so damned bad I would have fucked you into that screaming orgasm you had even if you were wearing your wedding band. Need for you was killing me."

Her breath caught at the husky, ragged declaration. She could hear the hunger in his voice, echoing around her, sinking into her very flesh and igniting her nerve endings with a craving it was all she could do to ignore.

"And you've had me." She gasped as the clip holding her hair up was released, allowing the thick strands to fall to her shoulders. "Stop that, Brock."

"I haven't had enough, Sarah," he growled, his hands enclosing her hips.

Sarah breathed out in a harsh motion. His hands at her waist were hard and warm. His breath at her ear sent shivers over her skin. She wanted to turn to him so desperately she could barely stop herself from doing it.

"It has to be enough." She fought for breath, her hands clasping his. She intended on pushing him away in just a minute.

"Was it enough for you?" She felt his erection at her back as he moved against her. "Don't you want to scream again, Sarah? Explode around me while I thrust my cock deep in your tight little cunt. Feel me come inside you. I want to come inside you, Sarah. I want to feel you milking me, squeezing my cock as we explode together."

Her face flamed; her vagina ached.

"No," she lied.

He chuckled, the sound a velvet rasp at her ear.

"Lying to me or to yourself, baby?" he asked her, gentle, soft, his voice like a caress over her body as his fingers began to smooth over her waist.

Sarah hated the light, gray-blue silk of her dress that kept his fingers from touching her skin.

"This isn't going to work." She gasped for breath. Damn him, why didn't she have any resistance against him? "You know it won't, Brock. You know why."

"I know you won't let me talk to you." His teeth nipped at the skin of her neck in an erotic bite.

Sarah whimpered. It felt so good. She wanted more.

He bit her again, experimentally. A shudder wracked her body, her muscles weakened, flowing against him. That little flare of pain, of heat, was unlike anything she had known before.

"Sarah, I want you. Bad." He licked the small wound, whispering against her skin. "Let me inside you again. Let me show you how much I need you."

She could feel how much he needed her. His cock throbbed beneath his jeans, searing into her lower back. His hands moved along her waist as he pulled her behind the high counter separating her work area from the main library.

"Brock," she protested as he turned her in his arms, lifting her to the desk as he moved quickly between her thighs.

She stared up at him, wide-eyed, uncertain in the face of such strong sexual intent.

"You're so beautiful." His hands clasped her face, his head lowering, his lips sipping at hers. "You make me crazy, Sarah, remembering how hot and wet you get for me. How your screams echo around me."

"Brock, please." Her hands gripped his, her lips opening, seeking more of the light touches he bestowed.

"Please what, baby?" He licked her lips, making her heart stutter in excitement. "Tell me what you want."

He pressed his hips against her, grinding his cock in the vee of her thighs.

"You're taking me over," she cried out, her hands gripping his shirt now, fighting for strength.

"I want to take you, period," he growled. "Right here, right now, Sarah."

"Oh God. Someone will see." But she couldn't deny him as his hands pushed her skirt up her thighs, smoothing over her flesh, heating her.

His hands clenched at the bend of her legs.

"Ashamed of me, Sarah?" he asked her, his voice expressionless.

"Of you?" Surprise filled her. "Not you, Brock. Of being seen. Please, I don't do this. I don't want everyone seeing me."

She felt the heat in her face, knowing gossip would go wild. Sarah Tate, seen in the arms of Brock August, which wasn't that bad. The bad part would be if he were seen taking her.

He moved back fractionally.

"Let me take you home then. Let me make love to you, Sarah."

He didn't release her, didn't give her room to think. His voice pitched low, his expression filled with male arousal, a male plea as old as time.

She wanted to. She wanted to so bad it was a physical ache centered hot and sharp between her thighs, deep inside her body.

"It will only make it worse." She was desperate to make him see reason. "Don't you understand, Brock? I can't accept what you'll want from me. I can't do it."

"You don't understand, baby." He ran his fingers over her cheek, his thumb glancing her lips. " I just want to touch you. Hold you. That's all I want, Sarah. Just you and me. No one else."

"What about later?" She pushed away from him. If she didn't get away from him, she would have no resistance left. "What will you want from me next, Brock?"

She saw what he wanted in his eyes. They darkened at the thought, flaring with a heat that nearly seared her.

"Why are you so scared?" He leaned against the desk, crossing his arms over his chest as he watched her with those hot eyes. "It seems to me you're more scared that you'll want it, Sarah."

Sarah ignored the hot flare of guilt that surged through her. That wasn't it, she assured herself. She didn't want it. And she sure as hell knew she couldn't handle it.

"You're insane," she burst out in shock. "That's not true."

"I want you to remember one thing, Sarah, and remember it well," he warned her with pseudo-tenderness. "I didn't come looking for you. You came looking for me. You gave up the right to deny that you suspected what was coming."

"I wanted one night," she protested. "That was all."

"That's bullshit." His voice rose, his hand sliced through the air as he advanced on her once again. "You aren't a one night stand, Sarah. You never were. I knew that six years ago and I knew it the other night. Don't start pretending now."

He pulled her back into his arms, giving her no chance to fight, to protest. His lips came down on hers, his big body backing her against the wall, out of sight of windows or doors as he lifted her against him.

His tongue speared between her lips, tangling with hers as she moaned, nearly mindless with the addictive taste. Her hands clenched at his shoulders, her legs spreading willingly for the hard thigh inserting between it.

"You're wet," he accused, raising his head to stare down at her angrily. "So wet it's already sinking through my jeans, Sarah. Don't try to tell me you don't want me."

Sarah felt tears fill her eyes. Her emotions were in such chaos, her fears filling every part of her. He was forceful, dominant; he would destroy her life if she let him.

"I do want you," she whispered, feeling a single tear fall down her cheek. "I want you so much I ache with it, Brock. But I'm scared. I'm too scared to face what I know will happen."

He stared down at her, tormented, tortured.

"I can only give you who I am, Sarah," he whispered. "Everything I am. And everything inside me screams out for you."

Sarah trembled at his confession, at the hot desire in his look, the feel of his hard, hot body against hers. She wanted him, more than she had ever wanted anything in her life.

"Please, leave me alone," she begged him. "If you really do care about me, you'll just leave me alone."

She couldn't fight this, God help her. He made her weak, made her look for excuses, made her want to beg him to convince her. Would it really be so bad?

Her head instantly rejected the question. Fool! It screamed out. He would never be hers, not really, not completely. He would always belong to another woman as well.

He shook his head. A sigh heaved from his chest.

"For now," he whispered. "Only for now, Sarah. I won't be able to stay away for long."

He turned and walked away, leaving her the peace she pleaded for. But there was no peace. Her heart broke for him, for the lonely pain she saw in his eyes, for her own needs eating her up inside. But she knew; knew to the bottom of her soul, if she didn't stay away from him, then she would end up giving him exactly what he wanted.

Anything he wanted. Anything he needed to still the pain inside him. No matter how much it might end up hurting her in the end.

She pressed her lips together, tamping down the rising cry forming in her chest. The one that would beg him to stay. The one that would plead for him to make her understand. The one screaming out silently that he touch her again, that he ignore her protests and take her, hard and fast, wiping away her inhibitions.

Chapter Nine

ॐ

He was back the next day. Not at work, but coming up beside her as she jogged along the deserted sidewalk where she took her run every morning. She nearly stumbled as he came along beside her. He was dressed in sweat pants and leather jogging shoes. It was the first time she had seen him out of his boots and jeans. She had wondered over the years if he owned anything else.

His black hair was tussled, his muscular arms and chest bare.

She rolled her eyes, ignoring him, thinking he would give up or maybe run out of breath before long. But he didn't. He jogged easily beside her, not speaking, keeping a careful distance, only glancing at her occasionally.

She jogged past the little street she lived on, then headed along the concrete path that led through the deserted maze of juniper stands and dust covered dunes. The morning was warming up and she could feel the glaze of perspiration that began covering her skin. Not too much further ahead was a rest area, a few park benches and a water fountain.

She was panting when she reached it, but Brock was barely winded. He walked beside her as she paced around the shaded area, catching her breath, letting her body cool down.

"I bet you could fuck all night," he mused, his voice pulsing with lust. "You just jogged over three miles without stopping. Stamina, Sarah, means a lot." He flashed her a wicked look. He was pushing her on purpose.

"What are you doing here?" she rasped breathlessly, walking over to the water fountain.

89

She bent to the stream of water that came on a touch. The stream was cold, refreshing. After drinking, she held her cupped hand under the arched spray, then splashed it on her face.

"Courting you." The information had her turning slowly, rising to her full height and staring at him in shock.

He reminded her of a little boy who had finally found a way to get a much needed toy.

"Courting me?" she questioned him.

"Yeah. You know. Getting to know you, getting you used to me." He shrugged at the explanation, a sheepish little smile playing about his lips. God she loved those lips.

"Seducing me." She nodded. "That's not courting, Brock. It's seduction."

"Baby, I already seduced you. I keep trying to get you to remember that." He shook his head at her, his expression patient, tolerant. "Now, we're getting to know each other."

He gave her that boyish, endearing grin that set her heart to racing. The one that said he knew he was winning, but was willing to play it her way for a while. The one that made her entire body ache for his touch.

She looked around the secluded area, wondering if there would be witnesses if she decided to brain him out of sheer frustration.

"Brock, I know plenty about you. You're a local commodity, remember?" she said bitterly.

He crossed his arms over his chest, narrowing his eyes on her.

"So, you want to be the one that got away?" he asked her curiously. "I can understand that, sugar. Really, I can, but there's such a thing as cutting off your own nose to spite your pretty face. There are things I could do for you. Real good things." His voice lowered suggestively.

"I'm going to cut something off if you don't—" A gasp escaped her as he pulled her into his arms, his lips coming down on hers with all the power and erotic sensuality he possessed. And he possessed a lot.

Sarah was nothing if not susceptible to it. His tongue speared past her lips and hers met it heatedly. Her arms wrapped instantly around his broad shoulders, her breasts swelling, her nipples beading at the heated feel of those hard muscles. Her thighs parted as he bent, lifted her close and drove his swollen cock into the vee of her thighs.

"Damn, you're more addictive than drugs," he swore as he backed up, sitting on the bench then dragged her body over his, her thighs surrounding him, her cunt cushioning his erection through the layers of cloth that separated them.

She arched in his arms as his lips went down her neck, caressing the mounds of her breasts above the scooped neckline of the spandex running top. His hands were on her bare waist, his fingers teasing the waistband of the running shorts.

He held her close, his tongue delving into her cleavage, licking at her roughly as her hands speared into his hair, her hips grinding against him as he thrust toward her.

"Yeah, ride me like that, Sarah," he growled roughly. "Just like that, baby."

He was panting along with her now. His hands were work roughened and sensual along her bare back, his lips and tongue licking at the small beads of perspiration that dotted the upper mounds of her breasts.

"Don't talk." She lowered her head, her lips running over his brow, his cheek. "Don't talk, Brock, just kiss me."

His lips took hers. Her hair fanned around them as they ate at each other. Sarah rocked against him, feeling the secretion, the preparation of her body as his cock burned through her shorts and panties, his hand cupping her breast above the top, thumb raking the sensitive bead of her nipple.

She didn't know how much longer she could stand the torment. She didn't know if she could protest, or would even want to if he stripped there and drove into her.

His hands moved down her body, cupping her buttocks. They clenched in the smooth curves, lifting her closer as he groaned into her mouth. His tongue was like an invader, a conqueror. His cock was a steel hard spike of heat she was dying to impale herself on.

He was the worst sort of warrior. A seductive, addictive taste of lust in its purest form. He had no inhibitions, no lack of eagerness. He would give her whatever she wanted and more, then push her to the very edge of depravity. She knew it. She accepted it. And there didn't seem to be a damned thing she could do to fight it. She was drowning in him, on the verge of begging him to take her now, this minute. To drive hard and fast in her body, making her scream.

Her cunt clutched emptily, a pulsating plea leaking from between the lips as she moaned into his mouth. His cock pressed against her, teasing her, tormenting her. She wanted him. Wanted more and wanted it now.

"Enough," he growled, pulling back from her, staring into her eyes. "Not here, Sarah. I won't let you off that easy."

She breathed hard, fighting to drag enough air into her starved lungs as she stared down at him.

"What do you want?" she whispered, tormented with the needs of her own body. "What more do you want, Brock?"

"I want it all," he told her desperately. "All, Sarah. I won't have you for just one more night and then have the fight begin again. If I take you again, you have to understand, it won't end."

Shock entered her expression.

"Why do you want this?" Her whispered cry was dragged from the depths of her soul. "Why do you want a woman who's terrified of what you want from her, Brock?"

And she was terrified it. She admitted that, accepted it. Just as she knew that slowly he was eroding all her inhibitions, all her protests. If she didn't do something she would be his for the taking. His and his brothers'.

"Because she's the only woman I've dreamed of for six years," he rasped, pressing his cock against her again. "The woman whose image I jack off to on a nightly basis and I wake up searching for each night."

Sarah felt her face flush at his guttural admission. Her image of him, his eyes closed, his cock hard and straining, enclosed in his hand, became an image of her, leaning over him, taking the bulging head into her mouth. She wanted to taste him. Wanted to feel him thrusting past her lips, stroking clear to her throat as she laved the hard flesh with her tongue, felt him jerk, the hot release of his seed splashing into her mouth.

She groaned, staring into his eyes, seeing the same need, the same intense desires.

"I can't share you. I won't," she panted. "Give me that much."

She saw the need in his eyes, but saw his resignation as well.

"I won't lie to you." He gritted his teeth harshly. "I won't let you set boundaries on this, Sarah, when you know what it's coming to."

"That's not fair." She came off his lap, anger and lust vying for supremacy. "No other man touches me."

"By your own choice," he pointed out. "By your own choice, Sarah. That could be different, if you weren't so stubborn."

"I don't want it any different." She shook her head, fighting for control.

"Don't you?" he questioned her harshly. "You knew what fucking me meant, Sarah. You knew what I wanted six years ago, even though you deny it now. You knew the other night that it wasn't a one-night stand. You went to that doctor, you endured those tests and you took that shot with the clear intention of letting me fuck the hell out of you whenever I wanted to. You didn't balk until I refused to let you hide from the truth."

It wasn't true, she assured herself desperately. She wouldn't do that. Wouldn't hide from herself in the way he was accusing her.

"I don't have to listen to this." She shook her head furiously. "You ask too much, Brock."

"I don't ask for anything I know you can't give me," he told her, his lips thinning with his own anger now.

"Yes you do," she argued painfully. "You ask me to just accept. To just give in to what you want, ignoring how I feel about it. Ignoring my fears, and everything I am. I'm not like this, Brock. I can't be."

"Like what, Sarah? Hot enough to singe my skin every time I touch you? I beg to differ. I know better."

"This argument is pointless." She threw her hands up, desperate to get away from him, desperate to escape the temptations he presented her. "I'm going back home."

"Sarah, wait." He caught her arm as she turned to leave, staring down at her, eating her with his eyes. "What would it take to make you understand?"

Nothing. But she couldn't tell him that. She couldn't bear the haunting shadows she could see in his eyes now, let alone what they would be if she told him the truth.

She sighed roughly instead. "I don't know, Brock. I just don't know."

She pulled her arm from him, reluctant, hurting. But she turned away from him, running from him. She didn't jog, she ran, fighting to put as much distance as she could between him and disaster.

* * * * *

Brock crossed his arms over his chest as he watched her run. His eyes narrowed. He wasn't a fool, nor was he driven to possess someone who didn't want him. He knew Sarah wanted him. He knew if he could get her past her fears, he could get her to understand.

He raked his fingers through his hair. How could he get her to understand, though? How could he make her see that what he wanted wasn't the torture she had built up in her mind?

He needed a woman's opinion. Dropping his arms from his chest he started the jog back to his truck. The return drive to the ranch was a bitch. He had been hoping not to have to make it, but the situation was now growing desperate. Sarah was just stubborn enough to keep denying herself as well as him. She was scared enough to put as much distance between them as possible if he wasn't careful.

She had done that after her marriage. Making certain she was never within miles of him. Hiding from him, suppressing her desire for him and her own needs. The time for that had come to an end. He would have her, and by God he would do it without lies and without promises he couldn't keep. Sarah had no idea just how stubborn he could be and he was man enough to keep her in the dark about it.

Chapter Ten

෨

Sarah was fighting for breath when she locked her door behind her and grimaced at her own cowardice. She could have kicked herself for running. But it was run or rape him in the park and beg him to do whatever the hell he wanted to with her.

Mark was right years ago when he had caught her running from Brock's house after the episode in the bedroom. She was too weak-willed. Too easily influenced by the sheer dominance Brock wore like a comfortable shirt. She shivered at the thought of that. She should be insulted. Enraged. Outraged. She shouldn't be so wet her panties were sticking to her pussy.

Shaking her head, she stood a moment longer catching her breath before heading to the kitchen. As she passed the doorway, the phone rang insistently, making her growl at the intrusion. What the hell happened to her nice peaceful life?

"Hello?" she answered, expecting Brock on the other end.

"Sarah?" The smooth, quiet drawl of the woman's voice had Sarah's eyes widening in shock. "This is Marly McCall. Could you meet me in town for lunch this afternoon?" The voice on the other end of the phone had Sarah blinking in surprise.

"Why?" She was too surprised for politeness.

A soft laugh vibrated through the line. "Because Brock is stalking the house like a caged tiger and making he-man noises," she informed her laughingly. "It's just lunch. Not an orgy. I can meet you at Hampton's in an hour or so. I'll have the owner hold a nice quiet outside table for us."

Hampton's was one of the few restaurants in Madison to boast a garden dining area. It was extremely difficult to get reservations for and the food was sumptuous.

"Sarah, I just want to talk," Marly assured her quietly. "And I think you do as well."

Sarah drew in a hard, deep breath. "Fine. Hampton's in an hour," she finally agreed. "Alone. Right?"

The last thing she needed was all three August men at lunch with her.

"Alone." She could hear the agreement in Marly's voice.

"Fine. An hour." Sarah closed her eyes and shook her head, wondering if she had completely lost her mind.

But after getting off the phone she showered, fixed her hair and dressed in jeans, a light tank top and comfortable leather sneakers before picking up her purse and heading outside to her car.

Traffic was light in Madison. It was a small ranching town, with a few bars outside of town and a relaxed, comfortable atmosphere in the main city limits. Unlike many larger towns, the main street was still populated by the clothing and merchandise stores it had always maintained. Several streets down was a large grocery store, at the edge of the city limits were the feed stores. It wasn't hard to navigate and rarely too crowded.

Parking for Hampton's Grill was on the opposite side of the street, in an attractive, shrub-enclosed lot. Sarah pulled her car into one of the empty slots before stepping out into the heat of the day and tamping down the nerves determined to get the best of her.

She couldn't imagine why Marly had wanted to meet her for lunch. She knew the other woman fairly well, though several years separated them in age. Marly wasn't a malicious person, or one who would try to stand in the way of any relationship Brock would have with another woman. So what did she want?

Squaring her shoulders, Sarah loped quickly across the street and entered the cool, intimate atmosphere of the restaurant.

"Ms. Tate. It's a pleasure to see you again." Sheree Hampton was part owner of the establishment, a tall, striking dark-haired woman with an infectious grin and laughing, hazel eyes. "I understand Ms. McCall is waiting for you in the garden area."

"Ms. Tate," Sarah snorted. "Who stepped on your toes today?"

Sheree chuckled lightly as she looped her arm in Sarah's and led her across the restaurant floor to the back doors.

"Your brother was here earlier," she murmured. "With Kari Black. I swear, I'm going to pull every hair in her head out myself."

Sarah winced. Her half-brother, Dillon Carlyle, was one of the town's most unapologetic playboys. Kari Black was the bane of Sheree's existence, an annoying factor in her unrequited desire for Dillon.

"Want me to help you kill him?" Sarah's suggested with a soft whisper. "If he's with her again, he deserves it."

"Not yet." Sheree pouted as they reach the garden doors. "Let me get a chance to have my way with him first if you don't mind. Then we can kill him."

Sarah laughed again, moving through the doors as Sheree led her to the secluded, intimate dining area amid the sheltering trees and flowering bushes of the garden.

"Your waiter will be here in a moment," Sheree told them both as Sarah seated herself. "Can I have him bring you a drink, Sarah?"

Sarah glanced at the glass of wine Marly was having. She had a feeling she was going to need something a hell of a lot stronger.

"Just water for now, thanks Sheree," she said.

Sheree nodded before heading back into the main restaurant.

"She still hasn't forgiven me for Cade breaking Dillon's nose," Marly sighed as she nodded at Sheree. "I tried to tell her it only makes him look better, but she's not buying it."

Sarah restrained herself to a grin, despite the laughter bubbling in her chest at Marly's rueful expression.

"She's a little possessive of his pretty face," she admitted. "Though I think if she ever gets hold of him, she might do more than break his nose."

"I couldn't blame her much." Marly's eyes widened fractionally. "Can you believe Sam had the nerve to tell me once that all Dillon's exploits were merely gossip? Two months later, Cade and I got to see him and... Oops." Laughter rose to the other woman's lips. "You're his sister."

"Unfortunately," Sarah sighed heavily, though amusement filled the sound. "Doesn't protect me from the rumors making their rounds though."

With that, the laughter abruptly stilled. Both women were very well aware of the rumors that circulated about Marly, and had been since she was a teenager.

"Sorry," Sarah muttered.

"I'm getting used to it." Marly lifted her shoulders in negligent shrug. "There's very little in a small town as entertaining as the rumors. Especially when they concern sex."

Sarah opened her mouth to speak, but the waiter chose that moment to arrive with her water and take their orders. Long minutes later he was scurrying off, face flushed from one of Marly's dazzling smiles when she thanked him.

She was an exquisitely beautiful woman, Sarah admitted. A few inches shorter than Sarah, with long, riotous black curls that gleamed with a blue-black sheen. Wide, innocent blue eyes and a clear complexion. Exceptionally fragile looking in her build. She made Sarah feel like an elephant beside her.

"Rumor's are running rife about Brock this week it seems," Marly began casually, though her eyes were sharp with determination. "Are many of them true?"

Sarah tilted her head to the side. "It's depending on if the rumors involve me, or you, where Brock is concerned," she countered gently. She liked Marly, but she would be damned if she would be interrogated by her.

A light flush colored Marly's cheeks as she cleared her throat a bit nervously. "If they involved me, in any event that's occurred in the last several weeks, then they're wrong," she finally stated.

"Just in the last several weeks?" Sarah pushed back the jealousy that wanted to rage inside her.

Marly's look then was straightforward and direct. She leaned closely, her arms braced on the table as she watched Sarah.

"I'm not here to play games, Sarah," she said gently. "You know me better than that. You and everyone else in this damned nosy county are more than aware of Cade and his brothers' sexuality. I don't like them having that knowledge, but I'm stuck with it. As for the rumors, if you were Jane Doe on the street I'd laugh and lie through my teeth to you. But you're not. You're the woman Brock loves. That makes things a whole hell of a lot different."

Sarah breathed in deeply. At that moment she knew why she had fought so hard to stay away from Brock. If she didn't have to face it, then she didn't have to accept it.

"Will he still have sex with you?" She stared back at Marly, seeing the truth, as well as the sorrow in Marly's eyes.

"Sarah, I don't want to hurt you here today. That's not why I called you."

"Then why?" Sarah had learned long ago to hide the pain, to carry on, but she would be damned if it didn't hurt like hell.

"I don't know." Marly finally shook her head, leaning back wearily in her chair. "I love Cade until my soul would shatter without him." And there was no doubting the truth of that; Sarah could see it in her eyes. "I don't know why they are like this, but I know something happened. Something so terrible, so tragic, that this is the only way they can forgive themselves, and each other for it."

Sarah flinched. She had seen that pain, the remembered horror in Brock's eyes when he attempted to try to make her understand that morning. Each time the subject of his relationship with his brothers came up, a sorrow...no...it was horror, shadowed his gaze. So painful it was hard to glimpse.

"There's such a thing as enabling the victim, Marly," she whispered.

"Sarah..." Marly shook her head sadly. "This isn't enabling. It's accepting that they have so much more to give than any other man. Whatever was broken inside them, love alone can't heal. I've learned that. They're good men. Strong, dependable, and so damned loyal it makes you want to slap them sometimes. But they're more..."

"Or less..." Sarah suggested.

Marly smiled gently. "You don't really believe that Sarah. I remember the summer before you married Mark. I wasn't so young that I didn't know what was going on. You were wild about Brock, and he only marked the days until you turned eighteen. Then everything exploded around him when you married Mark. He spent months too drunk some nights to drag himself out of bed the next morning."

"I don't want to hear this." She shook her head desperately.

"Of course you don't," Marly sighed sadly. "But I didn't want to live it. And I sure as hell didn't like seeing someone I loved destroyed by a woman too young to know what she had thrown away. But..." She held her hand up when Sarah would have spoken. "But Sarah, even then, I knew the rumors, and a part of me knew they were true. And now..." She lowered her eyes to her wine for long moments before lifting them again, staring back at Sarah fiercely. "Now, I know it's true. I live it. And I'm telling you, this isn't lust. It's not sex. It's their survival."

Sarah pressed her lips together, fighting the arguments welling inside her. She leaned back in her chair and regarded Marly almost angrily.

"I don't understand you," she admitted. "You went nuts in school when the other girls mentioned their sisters fucking Cade, or even, heaven forbid, being part of an August ménage. Now, you're condoning it? Do you want him to have sex with other women, Marly?"

Blue eyes snapped with anger. "I think you know better than that, Sarah. Just as I think you're deliberately attempting to twist what I'm trying to explain. I thought better of you than that."

Was she? Sarah grimaced, realizing she was trying to do just that.

"I'm sorry," she forced the words past her lips. "But trust me, Marly, I would never, ever attempt to convince another woman to have a relationship with Sam if I knew it would mean she would be fucking Brock. No way, no how."

"What if you knew beyond a shadow of a doubt that what they share..." Marly swallowed tightly. "You don't understand Sarah. You think it's just the sex. Just lust. You haven't seen the three of them lately. Unable to connect, to support each other because this lies so heavily between them. I didn't ask you here to try to convince you to have sex with the man I love. I asked you here to see if you would at least listen to Brock. Let him tell you what Cade can't tell me, and see if it makes a difference. Stop denying Brock even the explanation."

Sarah grimaced, something shattering inside her at the pain in Marly's voice. She could see the genuine caring Marly had for Brock. The three men had raised her, and Sarah knew that even years before, Marly had protected the three men against rumors with a hellion's own temper and the ability to back it up. She loved them. All of them. But Sarah could see that Cade owned her heart.

"What if there's no explanation that could make a difference," Sarah asked her softly then. "What if I know, Marly, that I can never accept the man I love having sex with his brother's wife or lover? How do you know you can accept it?"

"Because I know Cade and I know my love for him." The simple, overwhelming honesty in her voice threw Sarah for a second. "I wouldn't know jealousy, Sarah, I wouldn't care, because I know I have his heart and his soul. The only thing another woman would have when he touched her is the pleasure he gave her. And trust me, it's no more or less than I'd get from Brock or Sam at any other time.

When I first learned you had spent the night at the ranch, with Brock, I was terrified. All I could think was that I might lose the man I love now. But I realized it's not Cade I'm afraid of losing." A rueful smile touched her lips. "It was the fact that I had grown used to having them all, to myself. And I realized the unfairness of that. I had to accept what you have to see, Sarah, whether you can accept it or not. The women they love will connect them, and eventually heal them. Or we can destroy them. Which would you prefer to do?"

"Oh, that was really fair," Sarah griped resentfully.

"I'm trying to be fair." Marly sighed. "Fair is not having the man I live for wake me up in the middle of the night after a nightmare that has his breath locked in his throat, his body saturated with sweat as he begs his brothers to forgive him." Tears glittered in her eyes then. "It's standing in the doorway of our bathroom as he stares at his hands, attempting to clean them of something that isn't there, avoiding me, too destroyed by whatever happened to share it, even with me. Fair is not hearing Brock and Sam's screams as they come out of their own nightmares and seeing the ragged pain, the torment that they keep hidden any other time. That's not fair, Sarah. And I will do anything, everything it takes, to ease that pain. No matter what it takes. That's love. Unconditional and direct. Nothing else."

The strength she saw in Marly's gaze, in the determined glitter of her eyes, assured Sarah that if Brock came to her, if he touched her, he would be welcome. But she couldn't manage to feel the anger she would have felt before. Or the jealousy. All she could feel was the pain and the fury that anything, anyone, could have hurt Brock in such a way.

"You've made your point," she said wearily, glancing away from her as the waiter approached with their salads.

They were silent as the young man set the shallow bowls and their accompanied dressing cups before them. He refilled Marly's wine, freshened Sarah's water and once again retreated. Sarah look at the leafy grilled chicken salad she had ordered and had never felt less like eating.

Chapter Eleven

🕉

"Sarah, I want to thank you for meeting me for lunch." Marly turned to her as they stepped outside the Grill, impulsively hugging her warmly.

Sarah found herself unable to rebuff the other woman. Before she could stop herself she had hugged her back, still feeling off-kilter, confused. The information Marly had given her still had her feeling dazed, uncomprehending. She wanted to see Brock. Needed to see him. But she knew if she did, then she would never be able to think all this through clearly. And she desperately needed to do that.

"Thank you for inviting me." Sarah sighed roughly as they parted. "Next time, hopefully, it will be under better circumstances."

Marly smiled in sympathy. "Sarah. You love him. I know you do. You can work through this."

She shook her head, wishing she were as certain as Marly seemed to be. "We'll see," she said, unable know right then, how she felt about anything.

"I'll see you soon." Marly's smile was confident, teasing. "You'll see. Give me a call sometime."

Sarah nodded, adjusted the strap across her shoulder before glancing along the busy street. As the light changed and the walk sign lit up, she started across the pedestrian marked street.

A motor roared at the light, a second later, Marly's scream had her twisting, turning, only to stare in horror at the car racing toward her.

Jumping back, she stumbled, landing heavily as the car brushed past with only inches to spare. Terrified now, she fought to find her footing, her ankle twisting beneath her as she struggled up, aware of the screams echoing around along the street as the car swerved and raced back at her.

He was deliberately trying to run her down! The thought flashed through her mind as she struggled to get fully to her feet, to race out of the way. Dear God! It bore down on her, the motor humming as her eyes widened…

With no room to spare, someone grabbed her, throwing them both across the street, holding her close and bracing her body against the lean, hard strength of her rescuer. Cursing a streak that would have caused her to flush at any other time, he rolled them out of harm's way, keeping her body protected by his own as they hit the sidewalk on the opposite side.

Just as fast, he jumped to his feet and jerked her into the sheltered parking lot as shop owners, customers and pedestrians alike began to crowd around her. Shaking, gasping for breath, Sarah tried to find the strength to stand on her own two feet but kept stumbling against whoever held her. Whoever had saved her.

"Stay still." A harsh voice barked at her ear as she was lifted from her feet once again and gently, protectively, lowered to a nearby bench.

She knew that voice. Horrified, her head raised, dizziness lashing out at her.

"Breathe, dammit." His voice was harsh, enraged, but the hard hands that pressed against her diaphragm was incredibly tender. "Come on, Sarah. You're safe now. Brock would kill me if you smothered yourself to death." He tried for a teasing smile, but she could see his eyes.

The stormy blue and gray orbs were dark, furious. She could see someone's death in those eyes.

"My God. Cade." Marly was suddenly there beside them, her face white as she knelt beside him, her hand touching a harsh scrape on his shoulder where his shirt had torn.

Sarah felt her breath rush out of her lungs with a whoosh. The voices babbling around her were chaotic while she stared in horror at his expensive shirt, ripped, blood marring it.

"I'm fine, baby." His voice was no less harsh as he glanced at his lover. "Did you get the plate number?"

His hands were running over Sarah. Her arms, ribs, legs.

"There was no plate," Marly snapped. "My God, if you had been a second less..."

Fear ricocheted through Sarah, terror bursting in her skull as she stared back at Brock's brother with shocked, horrified eyes.

"Why did you do that?" She gasped then. "He could have killed you too? Are you insane?"

He stilled, staring back at her in surprise. "You expect me to stand there and watch some asshole run you down in the street like that, Sarah?" he asked her.

She stared back at him, shock still washing through her system, unable to process the look she saw in his eyes. It wasn't lust. It should have been lust. But it was almost...affection? Possessiveness. Something deeper, stronger than any lust she had ever seen.

She shook her head, aware of another voice ordering everyone back.

"Here." Gentle hands lifted one of hers and a cool cloth was laid in her scraped palm.

She looked up, seeing Sam August, his gaze as filled with fury as Cade's.

"Where's Brock?" Marly questioned him quickly.

"On his way. I called him the minute I saw Cade roll across that fucking street. Son of a bitch, did you cut it close enough, bro?"

His voice was vibrating with his rage, but his smile was comforting as he glanced back at her. His hands were incredibly gentle as he cleaned her palm.

"Call Doc and tell him we'll bring her in as soon as Brock gets here." Cade's voice was clipped as he checked the scrapes along her arms then. "Then call Rick..."

"Get the fuck out of my way!" Brock's voice was like an enraged animal's as he cut through the crowd.

Sarah could feel the dizziness washing over her. Three August men had to be three too many. They were overwhelming her.

"Easy, Brock," Cade murmured as Sam suddenly jumped back and Sarah was staring into the face of a wild man.

"Sarah?" He lifted her as he came down on the bench, settling her in his lap despite her protests. "Stay still. God. Stay the fuck still."

He buried his head in her hair. She could feel his chest rasping for breath, the warmth of his perspiration soaked body. He was shaking. Why the hell was he shaking? But he was, his arms tight around her as he heaved for breath, holding her close to him.

"What the hell did he do? Run from the feed store?" Cade came slowly to his feet as Sarah stared up at him bewildered.

"Probably," Sam snorted. "He threw the phone. Damn near busted my ear drums when it landed."

"Sarah..." Brock finally came up for breath, his hands running over her, much as Cade's had done. "Are you okay, baby?"

"I'm fine." She would have shaken her head, but his was still damned near laying against it. "Really, I'm fine."

"Doc's waiting on her," Sam informed him. "I have one of the hands bringing the car around. Damned good thing Marly insisted on the limo today."

Limo? Doctor?

"I'm f-f-fine," she stuttered. She was stuttering. She never stuttered.

Only then did she realize how hard she was shaking. No wonder Brock was holding her so tight. She would have vibrated right off his lap if he hadn't been.

She swallowed tightly and tried again.

"B-B-Brock." She swallowed tightly, fighting to hold herself still as her gaze swung to him in horror.

"It's okay, baby," he whispered, picking her up in his arms as he stood. "It's just shock. It's okay."

She was freezing then burning up. She whimpered, horrified that the sound came from her throat.

"Here's the limo." He kissed her forehead as he carried her to the car that came screeching to a stop across from them. "Come on, baby. Everything's okay now. I have you. I have you, Sarah."

And if his hold was any indication, he had no intention of letting her go. Even more frightening was the way the others treated her as well. Cade kept Marly close to his side, but he watched Sarah and Brock. His voice was kind, gentle as he questioned her about the car. About Mark. Sarah was certain Mark would never do anything so stupid.

Sam sat beside her and Brock opposite Cade and Marly. Sarah faced him from where she sat on Brock's lap, still shuddering in reaction. It was a nightmare, she assured herself. This could not be happening.

Shock from the near death experience was nothing compared to the shock of the three August brothers at once, in such close confines. Brock held her, but none of them took their attention from her. Sam touched her cheek gently, wiping away a tear she hadn't been aware lingered on her face. Cade leaned forward, checking a scrape that her shirt revealed on her side.

His hands were calloused, but tender. Her eyes flew to Marly, but the other woman was checking the deep scratch closely as well. She didn't seem to think it unusual in the least that all three men were so totally focused on another woman.

It was no different in the doctor's office. Though Doc Bennett seemed more amused by their actions than anything else. Her scrapes were cleaned, bruises checked, a pain medication prescribed and she was given a clean bill of health. But did that stop the Augusts? Hell no!

"Enough!" She had enough when the limo pulled into her driveway and everyone made to get out.

They stared back at her in shock.

"I need a hot bath…" Interest flared in three sets of male gazes. "Alone," she snapped, pushing at Brock as he moved to follow her from the car. "Go home. Go away. Leave me alone."

Cade's brows snapped into a frown. "Sarah, someone tried to hurt you today."

"Someone who has surely left by now," she informed him. "Someone who likely was just too damned drunk to know what the hell he was doing. No one wants to hurt me, Cade."

"Mark…"

"Is too stupid for this." She could feel hysteria gathering at the edges of her mind. She had to get away from them before they overwhelmed her. "Please. Just go home. I'll be fine."

"God dammit, Sarah…" Brock began to protest furiously.

"Brock." Marly's voice was like a cool, patient salve to the situation. "Let her rest. Give her time to think."

"She thinks too damned much," he snarled as he exited the limo. "I'm checking the fucking the house out first. I'll come back later…"

"Brock." She stilled at his announcement. "Check the house out. But please. I need time. Just give me time…"

She wondered though, if there would ever be enough time to accept it all.

Chapter Twelve

ဢ

Time turned into days. Days that wore on him, that tested his resolve to allow Sarah the precious time she felt she needed. Time he knew she did need. But it was time that was killing him.

Brock knew only one woman to go to for advice on this. He needed to figure out quickly how to get back into Sarah's bed before he went insane with his need for her. The accident, and now Sarah's refusal to speak to him at all was making him crazy. He craved the sight of her, the taste of her. If he thought for a minute that she didn't want him, that she didn't ache just as hard for him as he did for her, then he could have left her alone. But he did know. He knew she needed. Saw it in her eyes, in the hard nipples beneath her clothes, the flush of arousal on her face.

She just needed to be seduced. She needed to be held and protected, cherished and loved, but first, she had to be seduced into it. Seduction had never been his forte. Cade had been the master of it. It had been he who had chosen their women before Marly chose him. But he wasn't comfortable going to his brother for this. For this, he went to Marly. To seduce a woman, he needed a woman's advice.

"You want to seduce her?" Marly asked him carefully from the depths of the large garden tub he found her in. "Brock, you saw the woman's determination. She's in no mood to be seduced."

Bubbles lay around her, caressing her skin, contrasting with the heavy mass of black curls she had piled on her head. She was young and sweet, and innocence still lingered in her eyes despite the sexual excesses she was often a part of.

111

"Yeah. I need to seduce her." He sat on the closed lid of the toilet and watched her, confused by the small smile playing about her lips. "Marly, I won't take this silence from her any longer."

"So she's still turning you away?" Brock didn't like the thread of laughter in her voice.

He knew she had met Sarah for lunch. Though he trusted her implicitly, he could still tell that Marly was holding a lot back from him.

His eyes narrowed. "You're making fun of me, Munchkin. That's dangerous right now."

He was hard and hurting and more than willing to drag her out of that damned bathtub without Cade's presence if she pushed him too far. He knew he had Cade's approval to do so. There would be no hard feelings, no anger. But neither would there be the bonding he needed when it occurred.

She rolled her eyes, settling against the back of the tub as she watched him.

"You can't seduce an unwilling woman, Brock," she told him, finally serious. "If she doesn't want you, then there's nothing you can do."

"But she does want me," he told her carefully. "She's just frightened, Marly. She's heard the rumors, she knows about us. Hell, most people do, we're just too damned rich for them to use it against us. That's what I have to fight."

Her face flushed. She wasn't comfortable with that knowledge, he knew. He wasn't comfortable with it, but he accepted it. He denied it when he needed to, admitted it when he had to, but he wasn't ashamed of it. He was alive, and reasonably sane for it, so he had no choice but to accept it. Cade fought his shame on a daily basis, and Brock understood that. The weight of the acts the older brother had been forced into had nearly killed them all. Sam, Brock was never certain of Sam. He appeared the least scarred inside, though the most scarred bodily. He laughed. He played pranks and seemed to be little more than a boy in a grown man's body at times.

He was hard to figure out, but Brock knew he hurt too. It was there sometimes, when Sam thought no one else could see. In the set of his shoulders, the shadows of his eyes, it was there.

"So if she wants you and you want her, and she knows the truth, then what's the problem?" Marly asked curiously. "She's not here and you are. Though I knew you intended to move out, so evidently she ran your ass off. Would she do that if she wanted you?"

Brock sighed. Marly was intent on being difficult today.

"She wants me. Bad. And you know it." He flashed her a confident smile. "It's Sam and Cade she's scared of, Munchkin. You have enough sense to know that."

Marly lost her smile. She frowned at him, a clear reluctance to discuss this subject evident in her expression.

"Marly," his voice was gentle, chiding. "Didn't you think Sam or myself would ever fall in love?"

The feminine growl, low and frustrated, had his lips quirking into a smile.

"He's still my lover, Brock," she declared mutinously. "I won't share him as long as he refuses to explain this."

"He shares you," Brock pointed out. "And don't try to say you don't enjoy it."

"That's not the point, Brock." She closed her eyes, sighing heavily. "Not one of you will explain this to me. Not in any way. Yet you expect me to willingly accept it. If Cade wants to continue in his stubbornness and not confide in me, then I can continue in mine."

"Even knowing how much it hurts him?" Brock asked her, trying to keep his voice gentle.

She looked up at him, her deep blue eyes shadowed, regret and resignation swirling in her expression.

"What about my hurt, Brock?" she asked him, her voice quiet. "He beat the shit out of Rick because Tara told me as much as she did, which was damned little. He becomes furious if I question him about it. He has nightmares and begs brokenly in his sleep and he refuses to let me help him. Do you think this is just about whether or not he fucks the woman you love?"

Brock's cock went to instant attention at those words. Damn. There were times he hated his more than willing flesh. It was causing him more problems than he needed.

"Look at you." She nodded at the erection straining his casual pants. "Just the thought of it has you hard as a rock, just as it gets Cade. There's more to this than the three of you finding your pleasures, or your little male bonding ritual or whatever the hell it is. Explain it to me. Make me understand it. I like Sarah well enough. If you love her, then so will Sam and Cade and I know...and accept...what that means. But not without explanations. Not without the truth."

He heard the conviction that rang in her voice and knew Cade had more of a battle ahead of him than he could guess. Marly could be stubborn as hell and she was planted tight in her determination now.

He would give anything if he could. But he knew the consequences, just as well as Marly did.

"And get my ass kicked?" he asked her carefully. "Rick spent a night in the hospital if I remember correctly, Munchkin. I like my bones unbroken if it's all the same to you."

Her eyes narrowed. A second later, Brock watched nervously at the grim light of calculation that entered her eyes. Marly was innocent in a lot of ways, but damn if she wasn't more woman than Cade sometimes gave her credit for.

"Then make Sarah understand it." Her voice hardened. "Listen to me, Brock, she wasn't raised with Joe's abuse. With the evil he stank of. She wasn't raised seeing the three of you alone, lonely, searching. She doesn't love all of you the way I did at one time or another, so she isn't going to accept it as easily. I can share Cade with her, because I can *see* and I've felt the connection the three of you share. But she won't. And for the same reasons I'm refusing to. If the three of you can't trust the women you love, then you can you suffer the same hell they do."

Brock tilted his head, memories washing over him then. Good memories for a change. The year she had her crush on him, then on Sam. Her teenage years had been more hormones than good sense as she went around rubbing on one of them at one time or another. Innocent touches, flirtatious glances. He shook his head, feeling a warmth he hadn't recognized where Marly was concerned.

"Wouldn't loving me be enough?" He had once thought that was her reason for giving into Cade's desires, and ultimately his and Sam's.

"God, you men are so dumb." Amazement washed over her expression.

"Would you sit quietly and let her ex-husband fuck the hell out of her while you watched? Would you join in with that?"

He frowned, jealousy filling him at the thought of Mark Tate touching her to begin with.

"See? Look how angry you are. Ready to kill him now," she pointed out.

"She's mine. She was mine to begin with," he told her stubbornly.

"Yet you'll expect her to accept you fucking me, right?" she asked him.

He narrowed his eyes, his teeth clenching.

"Right," she answered herself. "And you will expect her to let Sam and Cade touch her, whether you're with her or not when it happens. When you come into a room, realizing one of your brothers had just shot his cum inside her body, you'll feel pride, not fury."

"They're my brothers," he reminded her. "It's different."

Marly took a deep, fortifying breath.

"Love isn't enough for a woman who wasn't raised with you, seeing your interactions, loving you all to one extent or another." It was obvious she was growing irritated with him. "When a woman loves, it's possessively, Brock. She doesn't want another woman touching him, or another man touching her. The thought of it is abhorrent."

"It excites her. I saw it in her eyes," he denied, remembering the flare of heat that made her golden eyes sparkle.

Marly shook her head, her eyes flashing at him in impatience.

"I know Sarah, Brock. I went to school with her. If it excites her, it's because she sees and feels your excitement for it. That might make her fantasize. Make her wonder. Women do that. All the time. But the reality of it is a different matter entirely."

"So what do I do?" He pushed his hands through his hair then rested his elbows on his knees as he regarded her. "Marly, I need her."

He watched her wince. He knew she was aware of how that need would be transmitted to Cade. It was the only reason Cade would lust after another woman.

"Start by telling her the truth, Brock." She met his gaze, determined, fierce. "Don't lie to her. Don't try to trick her with it. Be up front with her. Sarah is an honest person and she hates liars. That would not have changed in the years since school. If you aren't honest with her, then no matter how she loves you, she will refuse to accept you or your family."

"I have to get her to listen first," he sighed. "Getting close to that woman isn't easy any more. She's like a damned skittish foal, all legs and big golden-brown eyes, and ready to run at a moment's notice."

Marly was clearly fighting her need to smile.

"Only you would compare a woman to a horse, Brock." She laughed, though the sound was tinged with sadness. "If she really wants you, then you'll find a way. She'll let you try because she's praying the rumors are lies and that you need her more than you need your brothers."

She watched him intently when she said that. Brock could see the unspoken question, the need to understand herself.

"And if she loves you, she'll understand that it's never going to be that simple. The day comes when you have to accept that jealousies and explanations will never fix what's broken." Cade spoke from the doorway, his voice dark, pitched with sexuality, desire, and haunting pain.

Marly's lips pressed together, a seductive little pout that had Brock recalling the feel of those tender curves sucking his cock. She flicked a sideways look at Cade.

"You weren't invited into this conversation," she told him, a pout clearly rising in her voice.

"If I waited for an invitation these days, then I would be taking care of myself in more ways than one," he reminded her, moving slowly into the bathroom. "I won't push you, Marly," he told her then, and Brock knew he was referring to seducing her into accepting Sarah into their family. "I won't ask for more than I can give you. But I won't let you go either. And I won't let you hold yourself from me."

His eyes flickered to the array of articles in the trashcan. The items used occasionally on her body to make it ready for her family's lusts were lying there, discarded. Brock watched as satisfaction edged Cade's mouth. His fingers went to the buttons of his shirt, his look becoming heavy-lidded, filled with desire.

"I'm not in the mood. I haven't finished my bath." But her voice had thickened, indicating otherwise.

Cade smiled. The powerful love he felt for Marly was reflected in the curve of his lips, but his expression was tinged with sorrow.

"Sure?" he asked her softly, shrugging the shirt from his shoulders as he glanced at Brock.

Brock glanced at Marly. Her face was flushed, arousal glittering in her eyes. She knew what her lover needed, even if she didn't understand why he needed it. She directed a sultry, inviting look to both men. Brock looked at his brother, seeing the question in his eyes, the unspoken hesitation in Cade. The dark shadows in the other man's eyes were more noticeable than before, the brooding intensity clearer.

Cade was his brother. Like he told Sarah, it didn't always make sense, but the bond was there. There was no way to break it. No way to break the need and the pleasure that came from it. Brock pulled his T-shirt from his body, then stood to his feet and loosened the soft, casual jeans.

"You're making me very angry, Cade August," Marly whispered as he helped her from the tub, tossing a towel to Brock. There was no anger in her voice, though, just hot, untamed arousal.

Brock knelt at her feet, hastily wiping bubbles from Marly's slender curves. When he reached her thighs, he parted them, his mouth going to the smooth, waxed flesh that tempted him. His tongue reached out, running down the small valley between the plump lips that shielded her secrets.

He heard her groan, tasted the sweetness of her cream. He let his tongue massage her clit gently, his hands holding her hips now as she cried out at whatever caress Cade was bestowing as well. Bending closer, he licked down to the entrance to her body, his tongue sliding in with a smooth, firm stroke. She jerked against him, and he lapped at the soft pulse of her nectar.

Her thighs widened further as Brock moved his mouth back to her clit, his fingers sliding up her thigh, two pushing into her vagina as she bucked against his mouth. She was crying out now, suspended between the two brothers, rocked by the pleasure, just as she always was.

This was what he wanted for Sarah. To know the pleasure, the incredible sense of sharing and love that welled through the experience. Marly lifted her leg, propping her dainty foot on the tub as Cade's fingers began to penetrate and stretch her nether hole, coating it with the lubricating gel he used excessively, thrusting in counterpoint to Brock's fingers in her cunt. He imagined it was his Sarah, her cries echoing around them as they drove her to her first climax.

Long minutes later, Marly lay stretched out over Cade's body, impaled by his erection, her head tossing as Brock moved behind her, inserting the head of his cock at the entrance to her anus. She was tight. So damned tight. He slid in by slow inches; tensing, growling with the pleasure as he felt her muscles relax, accept him.

He gripped her hips, bending over her, hearing Cade's whispered encouragements to her, the deepening lust in his voice, the need and the drive for release suddenly echoing in his voice.

"I love you, Marly," Cade cried out to her. "God help me, I love you."

Brock felt the hard thrust of his brother's cock into Marly's vagina, the retreat, then Brock thrust in to the hilt behind her, hearing her shattered cries of pleasure, feeling her tighten, merge with them, drawing them together through the acceptance, the rush of climax that began to fill them.

Brock closed his eyes, his hands gripping her hips as he found the familiar rhythm. He imagined Sarah, screaming for more, begging for release. His chest tightened with emotion, his cock swelled, pulsed. He groaned, surging inside the tight anus carefully, forcefully, sweat covering his body as he fought for control.

Then she tightened, shuddered, he heard Cade groaning, felt the hard slamming thrusts into the spasming cunt and let his body go. Two hard, quick thrusts and he was releasing the hot jets of his semen into Marly's body. But it wasn't her name on his lips, it wasn't her body he felt. It was Sarah's. Always, it was Sarah.

Chapter Thirteen

ဢ

Sarah was amazed at the incredible sixth sense that told a woman when a man had found release with another woman. She was never certain what it was that assured her of the fact. A look, a shadow in the eyes, perhaps the way they moved, but when she saw Brock days later, she knew he had. And she knew who it had been.

The same woman sitting at the table with him and his brother. His brother's woman. It wasn't just the rumors she had heard over the years, but a shadow in his eyes, the way Marly glanced over at Brock, the way his eyes flickered guiltily in Sarah's direction. Had he taken her today, Sarah wondered furiously? Had he relieved the lust he claimed he had for her with another woman?

Marly gave her a commiserating look, which only fueled the flames hotter. Marly knew how Sarah felt, she had to know how it would hurt.

She met Brock's eyes across the distance separating them, anger storming over her. She watched him sigh, a slow careful heave of his chest, a flash of pain in his eyes. Bastard. He was no better than Mark. There he sat with the woman he likely screwed on a regular basis, watching her like *she* had hurt *him*. Tears burned at her eyes, tightened her chest, and she wanted to scream with the unfairness of it.

"Sarah, you just dazed out on me." Dillon Carlyle sat across the table from her, lounging casually in his chair, watching her with an expression that clearly showed his amusement. "Are you sure you're over that accident?"

He was more handsome than he had a right to be, with his thick black hair and brilliant green eyes. He was almost as tall as Brock, but cockier, more cynical rather than shadowed.

"You knew he would be here." She turned back to him, almost shaking with anger as she picked up her wineglass and finished it off quickly.

Dillon lifted a brow then refilled the glass. She took a healthy drink of it as well.

"Actually, I wasn't certain," he told her, his lips quirking in a smile. "But I was curious about the rumors circulating."

If he wasn't her brother, she would kill him. She might just do it anyway.

"What rumors?" she snarled, trying to pretend they didn't exist.

His look chided her. He knew her too well and she had never appreciated how easily he used the information when he wanted something from her.

"Oh, the little ones that say you've joined the August family." He shrugged, watching her carefully. He seemed worried, though. Hell, she didn't blame him; she was worried. "Have you, Sarah?"

Sarah flushed. She felt the heat begin in her neck and work its way to her hairline. She couldn't get away from it; no matter how hard she tried she couldn't escape Brock or what he wanted. She felt pummeled from every direction and she was growing weaker by the day.

"No." She drank more of the wine, ignoring the once appetizing pasta that sat in front of her.

"Are you thinking about it?" He frowned now as he watched her. "You seem pretty upset over him."

"No." She wasn't even considering it. Damn Brock. Damn Dillon for bringing her here. Damn her aching, for wanting to give Brock August whatever he wanted in return for the pleasure that sang through her body at his touch. In return for the look of approval, the flare of emotion that came to his eyes when he touched her. Like he finally had all he ever wanted in her arms. A lie. It was all a lie, and she couldn't make herself accept it.

"I think you are." He was suddenly serious. "Do you know what you're getting into, Sarah?"

She glanced at him, then her eyes went back to Brock. He was watching her, his gaze hot and intense. God, she hated it when he did that. It made her ache, made her want what she knew she couldn't have. What Marly was clearly comfortable with.

"I'm a moron." She lifted the glass again, taking a healthy drink of more wine.

She was insane to be so aroused when she was so pissed off. She was insane to allow herself to be drawn into this. She knew what was happening, knew what he was trying to do to her. Why was she allowing it?

Her gaze flicked to Dillon's concerned one. His green eyes had darkened, narrowed on her.

"Don't look at me that way, Dillon," she snapped. "I'm not one of your puzzles."

"You've always been a puzzle, darling," he said softly. "I've wondered for years actually, why it hadn't happened sooner. Brock used an incredible amount of self-control to stay away from you until the divorce."

"God, did everyone know?" She rubbed her brow, trying to fight the tension she could feel gathering there.

"Not everyone, Sarah." He leaned closer, his elbows resting on the table as he watched her. "A few of us, though. A very few who are part of his circle of friends."

Fear leapt into her heart. Her eyes widened.

"No, Sarah." He shook his head slowly. "Just friends. The August men don't share their women. They are incredibly greedy."

Hah, that was a good one.

"Not greedy enough," she muttered.

She looked at him again. He was watching Dillon now, a harsh frown on his face.

"He's very angry with me." There was an edge of resignation in his voice. "I hope he doesn't break my nose too."

"Just what we need," she muttered, her gaze going to the small flaw in an otherwise straight, aristocratic nose.

"Cade broke it over Marly." He grinned, intercepting her look. "I wrecked the Harley with her on it while trying to make him jealous."

She kept her mouth closed only by sheer strength of will.

"Why did you wreck the Harley?" That one had always confused her.

He shrugged. "Doesn't matter now. She was on it. When he found us, she was hysterical, crying. Man, don't make Marly cry. That guy freaks out."

She grimaced. She had no desire to hear anymore about the other woman. She knew too much about her the way it was.

"Dillon, your life is too exciting to suit me," she said.

Glancing at Brock again, their eyes met. She frowned at the anger she saw there, the possessiveness. Ownership. She gritted her teeth. Turning her head she lifted the wine glass and drained it.

Dillon just looked at the glass when she set it down pointedly.

"You've had enough," he said softly.

"That isn't your call, Dillon," she told him firmly. "Pour another one or I'll do it myself."

He sighed heavily, reaching for the wine bottle.

"I'm sure glad you're a classy drunk, Sarah. I have a feeling you have high intentions of tying one on." He poured the wine, then sat back and watched as she sipped heavily from it.

"I'm not a classy drunk," she denied, casting him a hateful look. She sent Brock one for added measure, ignoring his surprised look, and the amusement on Marly's face as she whispered something to Brock.

Sarah's fists clenched at the easy familiarity the woman displayed with him. Cade was sitting beside her, his eyes dark, considering, as he watched Sarah. She wanted to ignore the flare of curiosity that look ignited, but she was just drunk enough to admit to it. God, she needed to be committed. She emptied her glass.

"Sarah, let me take you home." Dillon's voice was incredibly sympathetic.

"I'm pitiful, huh?" She sighed deeply, avoiding his gaze. "I can't keep my eyes off him, Dillon."

She wouldn't cry, she assured herself. She had known the rules going in, she just hadn't expected the pain.

"He hasn't been any better in the last six years, Sarah, he just never let you see it. I remember days I saw him outside the library, watching you leave. There were many times I sat with him, watching him try to drown the need with liquor."

Surprise filled her. She had never seen him, never knew he watched her, talked about her. What had he said? Why had he even cared?

"You never said anything," she whispered. "Does he know you're my brother?" Sarah knew Dillon told few people of their relationship. For reasons Sarah was never certain of, her parents had rarely spoken of the relationship to anyone.

He shrugged. "I never told him. As far as I know, he's unaware of it. But I didn't tell you about it because I knew why you ran from him. I knew what he wanted from you, Sarah, and I've never been certain it was what you wanted. Until now."

"It's not what I want." Her voice lacked the strength she wished she could put into it.

He covered her hand with his. He watched her, sympathy and understanding in his look.

"Sarah, they are tormented men. What they do isn't out of depravity. It isn't out of perversion. They're good men."

"Then why do they do it?" she whispered, sliding her hand back when she caught Brock's near violent look at their clasped hands. "Tell me why."

"That one would get me killed." He sighed roughly. "But I promise you this, if he doesn't tell you soon, then I will. You deserve that much. Now, are you ready to go home?"

Self-pity welled inside her. She played with her empty glass, her fingers running slowly up and down the slender base as she watched the motion. She wouldn't watch him, wouldn't die to have him. But she was. She knew she was.

"Okay." She finally nodded. "I'm ready to go anyway. If that woman keeps touching his shoulder I'm going to pull her hair out by her roots."

She ignored Dillon's amused chuckle. She stood to her feet as he came behind her, proud of her steady feet as he helped her from her chair. She smoothed her silk dress down her thighs and turned to him with a thankful smile.

"We should have brought the Harley," he told her with a smile as he put his hand at her back and led her from the room. "We could have gone for a ride."

"I like the truck more." She shrugged. "Remember when we used to go up to Uncle Chas's farm and race?"

Dillon laughed.

"Yeah, I remember." His reflective voice had her missing those years as she stepped outside the restaurant and felt the warm summer air.

"We need to do that again one night," she sighed.

"You say that every time you get tipsy, Sarah," he chided her. "One of these nights, I'm going to hold —"

"Dillon." Brock was suddenly standing there. Tall, fierce, frowning as he watched Sarah lean against him for support.

Dillon sighed. "She's not crying, Brock. I'd like to keep my nose in reasonable shape."

Sarah frowned as she watched a smile creep over Brock's lips.

"It's none of his business, Dillon," she sniffed. "Let him go find a girl of his own."

The irony of that statement had the men exchanging a telling glance.

"Deviants," she muttered, catching the look. "Go away, Brock. You're annoying me."

Surprise registered on Brock's face as Dillon smothered his laughter.

"Is she drunk?" he asked Dillon suspiciously.

"I am not drunk, I am just a shade tipsy," she informed him regally. "That's all."

"She's a very lady-like drunk," Dillon told Brock with mock seriousness.

"I am always lady-like," she told them both with a disdainful tone.

Brock crossed his arms over his chest, watching her from lowered brows.

They were standing in the parking lot, close to Dillon's truck, but closer to Brock's Jeep. Her face flamed remembering what had happened in the front seat of that Jeep.

"I'm ready to go home." She moved away from Dillon's support, very proud of the fact that she walked reasonably straight. "Come along, Dillon, maybe I'll let you tuck me in."

At first, the whacking sound of a blow didn't register in her mind.

"Dammit, you fucking hit me." She heard Dillon's outraged voice a second after the sound of flesh connecting to flesh.

"At least I didn't break your fucking nose," Brock pointed out furiously. "Keep your perverted ass away from her."

"Me? Perverted?" Dillon wheezed. "That's a low blow coming from you, you black-hearted bastard."

Sarah turned slowly. Dillon was resting against the back of a Suburban, gasping, his hand clutched over his waist. Brock was staring at him furiously.

"Neanderthal," she accused him roughly. "Why did you hit him?"

"What the hell are you doing offering to let him tuck you in?" he growled.

Sarah frowned. "He always tucks me in when I get drunk. He even sings to me if I ask him to."

Surprised fury registered on Brock's face, disgruntlement on Dillon's.

"Fuck, Sarah," Dillon moaned. "Keep your damned voice down."

Brock's face reflected surprise.

"Why the hell would he do that?" Brock was almost yelling.

"Because he's my brother, moron. My mother divorced his father, and he took Dillon away from her before she met my father. Happy?"

Brock angled his head, looking hard at Dillon.

"There's no family resemblance," he mumbled.

"Geez, you're pissing me off. Go back inside and let Miss Marly paw you some more. I have better things to do."

"She's almost a Mrs. Marly now, Sarah," Dillon reminded her breathlessly.

Sarah flashed him a killing look. She'd skin him alive if he didn't shut up.

"I'll tuck her in, just to be certain your nose stays intact." Brock patted Dillon's shoulder and moved around him.

"Brock." Sarah recognized the steel in Dillon's voice now. Evidently Brock did as well.

"What?" Brock frowned.

"It's Sarah's choice who she goes home with. I won't let you force her into one." Dillon stood straight now. "A playful tap here and there is fine. But you hit me over my sister again and I'll take you out."

Violence thrummed in the air between the two men.

"Sarah?" Brock turned back to her.

He wouldn't let her leave without him; she could see it on his face. She could leave with him, or he and Dillon would fight.

"Don't. Please," she whispered, staring up at his dark face.

"I swear, I won't do anything you don't want, Sarah. But we have to talk. We have to."

She heaved a hard, desperate sigh.

"Fine."

"Sarah, are you sure?" Dillon asked her quietly. "Be sure about this."

He would stand between her and Brock, she knew. But what would be the point? Brock was determined and she was weak. It would happen eventually, no matter how hard she tried to avoid it.

"Go away, Dillon." Brock turned to the other man, frowning.

Dillon merely watched her, ignoring Brock's defensive attitude.

"I'm sure," she mumbled. She wasn't, but what the hell? It was too late to claim maidenly virtue, and she was just relaxed enough to be dangerous. She hated being dangerous.

"Come on." Brock led her to the Jeep, unlocking the door and helping her in.

She watched through the rearview mirror as he and Dillon exchanged words, then he was getting in as well and starting the ignition.

"Can we go someplace and talk first?" he asked her.

"About what?"

"About us, Sarah. We need to talk about us." He glanced at her as he set the Jeep in motion, driving through the parking lot.

"There's nothing to talk about." She stared outside the tinted glass, watching his dark reflection within it. "You want what you want, I want what I want. They are not compatible wants, Brock."

"You act like I'm asking you to jump immediately into an orgy," he sighed.

"More or less how I feel." She shrugged, determined not to be hurt. She couldn't bear the hurt.

Brock was silent then and Sarah knew he was trying to figure out what to say, what to do to make her listen to him. She had no desire to hear it.

He cleared his throat.

"Women fantasize about the very things I'm offering you." He sounded as though he were reciting from a script.

She looked over at him cautiously, wondering if he had lost his senses.

"Excuse me?"

"You heard me." He frowned. "It's a favorite sexual fantasy for women. That of being with more than one man at a time."

Sarah blinked, wondering what catastrophic event had thrown him into insanity. He had never seemed crazy before. A bit intense, but not insane. What was his problem tonight?

"Look, Brock, I fantasize about fucking Dirk Diggler, but the actual man does nothing for me. Does this tell you anything?" she asked him with exaggerated patience.

"Size isn't everything, Sarah," he snarled, clearly offended. "I satisfied you plenty with what I have. I'm not exactly hot dog-sized, here."

Sarah shook her head. Where the hell had this conversation got off track? Hot dog-sized? Not unless he was talking about the whole pack.

"What the hell does that have to with anything?" she growled, exasperated.

"You think cock size is more important—"

"My God, can you get any stranger tonight?" She stared at him as though he were an alien species. What the hell was his problem?

"You know, as tight as your cunt is around me, I don't think you could handle a bigger dick." He was still clearly outraged.

Sarah shook her head.

"I'll figure that one out later," she sighed. "I think you finally lost your mind, though."

"Most likely," he grumped. "If I don't fuck you soon I expect to sprout fangs and start howling at the moon. Dammit, Sarah, I'm dying."

How could he be dying? He shared his brother's lover. He had been home most of the day, with Marly available, willing— She fought her bitter cry.

"You fucked her today. I know you did. Don't act frustrated and temperamental on me, Brock." Sarah was near tears now. How could he be so desperate for her after fucking another woman? His brother's woman.

Silence filled the vehicle.

"How did you know?" he finally asked her, his voice quiet.

"Because I know how you look after being satisfied." She gritted her teeth, fighting her anger.

"And I know how you look." He glanced over at her, his face suddenly intent, almost bleak. "And how you would look, Sarah, if my brothers touched you. I'm not asking for more than I'll give."

"You think that's enough, don't you?" she whispered as he pulled into her driveway. "You think that's all it takes to get me to agree?"

"No, I don't," he sighed raggedly. "But I'm not asking you to agree to anything or anyone but me. That's all. Just me, Sarah."

"For now?" she asked.

He stared at her silently.

She laid her head against the back of the seat and breathed out tiredly.

"You're killing me, Brock," she whispered.

"It's killing me, Sarah. I know you want me." He turned in his seat, his hand reaching out to touch her cheek. "I know you need me just as desperately as I need you."

And she did. She knew she did. Her body, her heart and her head were waging a battle she was afraid all would lose.

"Let me stay with you tonight, Sarah," he asked her softly. "I need you."

The throb of that need echoed around the Jeep.

"No." She threw the door to the Jeep open, nearly falling out in her haste. "I can't, Brock. Not yet. Not yet."

She didn't run, but she rushed. She was aware of him getting out of the vehicle, following her. As the key twisted in the lock, he flattened his body against her back.

"Think of this, Sarah," he whispered in her ear.

She moaned roughly as his hand moved up her thigh, one arm going around her waist as his fingers moved aside the leg band of her panties.

"Brock," she gasped, feeling his fingers tunneling through the lush curls to the saturated flesh below.

"Feel how wet you are." He pushed a finger deep inside her and she felt the walls of her cunt grip it, suck at it. "See how much you want me."

She opened her mouth to speak.

"Sarah, mention that damned fictitious alien again and I'll lose what little control I have."

She clamped her mouth shut. She moaned instead, then cried out when his finger retreated.

"I won't force you to ask me to stay, Sarah." He breathed against her ear. "I'll leave for now. But I promise, this isn't over."

He opened the door for her, standing still, hard, as she stepped weakly inside.

"Do you need me to tuck you in?"

She shook her head, dazed. She needed him to fuck her blind. She was already crazy.

"I'll see you soon, then." He kissed her lips softly, then turned and walked away.

"I'm insane," she whispered as she heard the door to the Jeep slam.

She closed the door, locked it, then leaned her head against the glass.

"Completely insane."

Chapter Fourteen

ᔓ

A day passed, then two. On the third day Sarah was convinced that Brock had finally given up on her. Dressed in a bikini she picked up her bottle of water and walked out to the pool out back. It wasn't as large as the August pool, but it suited her needs.

She swam for a while, working out the energy that seem to fill her, then pulled herself onto the deck and stretched out on the large foam pad that protected her back from the hard concrete.

Lazy, dozing, she allowed the heat of the sun to warm her body, ignoring the languid sexuality that pulsed just under her skin. She couldn't forget the touch of Brock's hands or his mouth. The seductive cadence of his voice or the dark promise in his eyes.

Her nipples beaded as the memories seared through her body. The flesh between her thighs heated and she felt the silky warmth of her body's need building beneath the swimsuit.

Her hands touched her stomach, moving over the skin as she thought of him. His touch. His hands, calloused and warm, fingers broad and experienced. She shivered, her own touch evoking the sensations she had felt beneath his. Her vagina clenched, her stomach muscles tightening as her fingers ran over them, her nails barely scraping, adding an extra edge to the sensation.

She wanted him; she didn't deny that. She couldn't deny it. She wanted until it kept her awake at night, tossing and turning as she fought the desperate emptiness of her body. Brock had filled her. He filled her to overflowing when he thrust inside her, so hard and hot she couldn't contain her cries. She needed it again. Needed his cock throbbing in her, making her mindless, unable to think, unable to listen to her fears.

The dual needs attacking her body, her mind, kept her in a constant state of confusion now. Her dreams were of Brock's face, his kiss, his touch. But there were other hands stroking her as well, heated encouragements, low male growls as she cried out her frustration. She swore she wouldn't think about that. She would think about Brock. Lust after Brock. It was Brock she had waited on, wanted so desperately all these years.

Her fingers moved to her lips. His kiss. She wanted to moan. His lips moving over hers, his tongue stroking the soft curves of her lips, sipping from her, nibbling at her. His kiss smothered objections, teased and cajoled, and whispered the sexy, hot words that left her panting for him. Explicit words. He hadn't been shy in expressing his needs or the desire he had for her.

Her neck. Her fingers stroked there, then down to the mounds of her breasts, tracing the soft flesh as they rose from the top of her bathing suit. The way his teeth scraped the skin. She glanced over her nipples, a whimpering moan exiting her throat. He had sucked her nipples with strong, sensual pulls of his mouth, his tongue and teeth scraping over them.

Her fingers wandered lower. She thought of the way his lips traveled over her stomach, his tongue licking, painting a portrait of sexual need along her flesh as he touched her. She bit her lip as her fingers paused at the waistband of her bikini bottoms. Did she dare? No one could see. The privacy fencing protected her from even the most curious eyes.

A breathy moan escaped her. She ached. She hurt for him. She needed what she couldn't have and this was all she had left. Her fingers dipped beneath the soft material moving closer to the wet, desire-slick flesh that pulsed at the memory of Brock's touch.

* * * * *

Brock almost groaned. He almost gave away his presence as he stood only feet away from her, watching her fingers travel over her upper body, moving lower. When they edged beneath the material at her hips, his cock jerked, his body tightening. Son of a bitch. He felt his mouth go dry, watching her slender fingers travel in agonizingly slow movements down the narrow slit of her cunt. He imagined how hot, how slick it was. How easily his fingers glided through it, drawn inexorably to the dark, honeyed depths of her vagina.

His teeth clenched as he thought of the fiery heat those fingers moved towards. How she gripped him, tight and hot, her muscles like a velvet fist fighting to hold him inside her as he thrust against her.

She moaned his name and his fists clenched. He watched her fingers, covered by the material of her swimsuit, move lower still, her fingers curving. Her hips arched and he knew she was filling her tight cunt with her fingers, thrusting, filling the empty flesh as she thought of him. One hand cupped her breast, the firm mound spilling from the cup of her bikini as her fingers pinched and pulled at the hard tip. Those weren't light touches either. Her fingers were rougher than he would have expected, pulling at the hard flesh, tightening around it as the fingers between her thighs drove her closer to climax.

Oh, no. No climax. Damn her to hell. She whispered his name as she touched herself, drawing closer. *Oh baby, not without me, you won't.*

"Sarah," he groaned her name as he drew closer.

Her breath hitched in her throat, her head twisting on the foam pad as her fingers thrust harder into her body.

"Sarah, stop that before I fuck you on this damned deck," he growled, his voice harsh.

Her eyes flew open—wide, dazed. She blinked, then her hips jerked hard and he cursed as he watched her shatter, climaxing despite his intrusion.

"Oh, God," she wailed, embarrassment and heated satisfaction washing over her expression as her fingers finally stilled.

He moved to her as her fingers came from between her thighs. He went to his knees, capturing her wrist before she could wipe the betraying evidence of her satisfaction from them.

Her fingers were slick, coated with the soft cream of her release. Holding her eyes, daring her to look away, he brought them to his mouth. She jerked, moaning low as he sucked one finger into his mouth, licking it clean. Then the next. Then the third. He groaned at the taste of her, so sweet and warm, more addictive than any drug he knew. He hungered for her. Ached like a man in a fit of withdrawal.

"You shouldn't be here," she cried out as his fingers went to her bared breast.

He held the hard point between his fingers then applied pressure. Her eyes closed, her body arched when he tightened around it to the point of pain. He rolled it between his fingers, watching her face flush, feeling her nipple grow harder. She liked the pressure, the edge of pain. He could see it in her face, in the too-quick breaths, the way she bit her lip as though she could contain her cries.

"You're mine, Sarah," he told her harshly, pressuring the little nipple further, watching her hips raise, her eyes dilate. "Do you understand me?"

"Just yours?" she whispered as his hand went to the material of her suit bottom. "Am I just yours? Or will I be theirs as well?"

His hand halted, the pressure on her nipple eased as he dropped his head. He wanted to lie to her. God help him he wanted to lie, but he couldn't.

"Whichever you want it to be," he finally whispered, knowing he would never be satisfied but one way. "I won't force you. Neither will they."

Her eyes flared. She read the message in his, read the intent behind his words.

"But you'll try to convince me?" She jerked away as he moved his hands back.

Rising quickly to her feet, she adjusted the bathing suit, staring at him as he came to his feet as well.

"You'll use my body against me, won't you, Brock? You'll try to seduce me into it."

Brock breathed in raggedly, wanting to wipe the hurt from her expression, wanting to assure her she would never have to face the darker side of his sexuality. But he knew she would. He wouldn't be able to control it, eventually. The ache would become too strong.

"You can't seduce someone, Sarah, if the desire isn't there to begin with," he said, his voice gentle. "If you don't want it, then you won't be forced, at any time. If you don't want it, then you can't be seduced."

Her eyes widened. She had wanted him to lie to her, he could see it in her eyes.

"I have no desire to be a camp whore for the August brothers." Her fists clenched, tears filling her eyes. "Why don't you just leave, Brock? Just get the hell out of my life and leave me in peace."

She turned on her heel, rushing for the door. She had to get away from him. Get away from the need, the pain in his eyes, before she gave in. Before her body forced her into promising him whatever he wanted.

Chapter Fifteen

ဆ

He caught her at the door that led from the carport into the house. Half inside it, breathing harshly from an anger she couldn't understand or define, she lashed out at him in fury as his arm wrapped around her waist, bringing her to a halt just inside the kitchen.

"Stop it, Sarah." His voice was tight, but incredibly gentle as he avoided her hands as she slapped at him, pinning them to her waist as he pushed her into the house, and kicked the door closed.

"Let me go, damn you." She was crying. She hated crying.

She knew she was weak, knew she needed him, had wanted him for too damned long. It was the height of insanity to need a man so desperately. Especially this man.

"I can't let you go, Sarah." He turned her in his arms, holding her close, pinning her against the door as she struggled against him. "Stop fighting me, darlin'. We can't get through this if you refuse to talk to me."

"I can't do this." Her hands gripped the front of his shirt, her face pressing into his chest as she fought for breath. "Oh God, Brock. I can't do this. You don't understand."

She couldn't fight the passion, the need. The terrible overwhelming fear that she would do anything this man asked of her.

"Shh, Sarah-love." He kissed the top of her head, his hands running over her back in slow, even strokes. "It's okay."

"I'm sorry." She trembled against him, feeling his erection against her stomach, achingly aware of the big, powerful body

139

that controlled hers so easily. "I shouldn't have said that. I shouldn't have started this."

"If you hadn't, I would have," he sighed roughly. "Don't you know how bad I've wanted you? Dammit, Sarah, the taste and feel of you tortured me for years. Remembering it, needing more."

She shivered at the harsh sound of his voice. Tortured, needy, tormented by the same desires that had haunted her through so many lonely, aching nights.

"You married Mark to hide from me." He pulled her head back, staring down at her, his gaze accusing. "You ran from me, Sarah, and you hid from me. We could have worked through this. You could have given me a chance."

"Worked through it?" she questioned him in bemusement. "You wanted me to fuck your brothers. You didn't want me, you wanted a toy."

She still remembered the look on Sam's face as he stood in the connecting doorway. Dark, his eyes filled with lust, with need as he watched his brother between her thighs, listened to the sounds of Brock licking at her hungrily.

"I wanted you," he growled, his hands clenching in her hair. "All of you, Sarah. Every damned hot, wet inch of that pretty body, I wanted. You were mine. Mine. And you ran from me."

Panic was welling inside her. She could feel tension thickening the air, and in his eyes, in his avoidance of the subject, she read the truth.

"It's true," she whispered, fighting for breath. "That's what you would have done. You would have tried to share me. I was eighteen years old, Brock. I loved you. I loved you until I wanted to die, and you let another man watch—" She shook her head, her body shuddering with reaction, with needs and desires and emotions she could no longer hide, even from herself.

"Sarah." His voice was achingly tender, but his eyes flared hot and wild at her words. "You have to let me explain."

She swallowed hard, fighting the fear and her nerves, not to mention the tight knot of panic forming in her throat. She shook her head. She didn't want to know. She didn't want an explanation. How could he ever make any of it acceptable?

"Marly," she whispered the name of the woman gossipmongers talked about the most. "She's the reason the three of you don't do that together anymore, with other women. What your ranch hands say is true? You share her and you expect me to join your little party."

She watched his eyes, saw them darken as his hips pressed against her in an involuntary thrust. She didn't scream, she couldn't. She didn't rage; she didn't fight. She rested her head on his chest and she let her tears fall. She had waited all this time, fought the need for so long. How was she supposed to walk away now?

"It's not like that," he finally whispered, his voice dark and quiet. "It's not the way you're thinking, Sarah."

"It doesn't matter." She pushed out of his arms, surprised that he let her go, and turned and walked through the kitchen and into her living room.

She walked to the wide, bay window that looked out over the prettily landscaped yard. Colorful summer blooms were everywhere, birds and butterflies and even a squirrel or two played through the yard. Brock followed her, but she knew he would. She shivered with reaction. She had promised herself six years ago that she would never let this happen. Never give him a chance to destroy her again. And yet here he was, doing exactly what she had married Mark to avoid.

"I want you to leave." She fought to swallow past the lump of pain threatening to strangle her. "This won't work."

The problem was, she didn't want him to leave. She wanted him to make it better, to swear he could change for her. That he could heal for her. And she had a feeling that would never happen.

She watched the bleak anger that twisted his face. So much pain. How could he be hurting so badly, so terribly that it seemed like an aura around him? She couldn't forget what Marly had told her about the nightmares, the horror in the eyes of the August men. She could barely stand to see the shadows, how did Marly survive the rest?

"I won't leave, Sarah. I won't let you go now." He stood behind her, staring at her through the reflection of the glass. "You have to at least give me the chance to explain."

"How could you ever justify watching another man touch me?" She turned to him, frowning, fighting past the betraying quiver of lust, to the betrayal the thought brought her. Sure, she could fantasize as well as other women, but it didn't change the fact that he could not share her and still care for her.

He was silent for a long moment, and Sarah had to forcibly still a gasp of protest as his eyes darkened in agony. The pain was so deep, so raw, she wanted to scream for him. He swallowed tightly then glanced away from her as he took a deep breath.

"How do you justify complete silence?" She flinched at the grating tone of his voice when he turned back, but still didn't understand until he continued. "How do you explain that the only time you were allowed to be a brother was when you shared a cup of rice or a drink of water from the same cup or plate? That to save your brother, you were forced to give up your pride, your self-respect and your manhood?"

His body was strung tight. He stared down at her with rage glowing in his eyes. His fists clenched with the agony of whatever memory boiled in his soul. Never at any time had Sarah seen pain, the likes of which was reflected in his eyes.

"What are you saying?" she gasped, horror filling her as his words sank into her mind.

And then she saw agony. Soul-destroying, intense…agony. His eyes reflected it, dry, no hint of tears, but a pain that bled from his very soul.

"It's the way we were trained," he sneered, his voice raspy, so rough, she wanted to scream at him to stop. "We were sent away during our late teens, to a friend of our parents. For training, my father said. We were forced to share everything and always in silence. Our dinner, our glass to drink from, the fork to eat from, and…" He swallowed tightly, his gaze never leaving hers despite the shame that filled his eyes. "Our bodies. If we didn't do as we were ordered, then one of us was beaten. Never the one who refused, but the one who was innocent, the weakest one. The one who had already suffered too much. We weren't allowed to speak to each other, and we were monitored constantly. Forced to hurt each other, Sarah, trained to hate each other."

Sarah flinched at the fury, the indescribable pain in his expression. There was no sense of having done wrong, just acceptance, and an aching fury mixed with it. And pain. Dear God, the pain she could see radiating in his body, in his heart. He stared down at her, so tense, so wary. Expecting another blow. Expecting disgust. She could see it in his face, in his tormented eyes.

"Don't, Brock." She couldn't bear it. Couldn't bear to see him hurting like this.

"We swore to each other, we wouldn't let him make us hate. So we shared willingly, everything, no matter how angry it made that bastard. When he held the whip at Sam's back, Cade and I touched each other; we fucked each other, no matter how much we hated it. Then we did the same to Sam, knowing it was the only way to survive. Knowing we loved each other enough to get through it. But it hurt us, Sarah. It scarred us. When we came out of there, there was no sense of affection, of closeness left in us. Despite it all, he had taken it from us. We were alone inside and it was slowly killing all of us."

She could hear the proof of it in his voice. His tone was guttural, the words ripping from his chest as his hands moved to her waist, his fingers holding onto her as though she alone could save him from sinking into the pit of despair his memories held.

"Please, Brock." Her stomach was tight, nausea building inside her at the thought of such pain, such incredible abuse.

How had he survived it? His dominant male sexuality was so much a part of him that no one could mistake it. His male confidence, his arrogance, all of it was deeply, strongly ingrained in him. How had he survived such horrible conditions.

"For a long time, we weren't even sexual," he continued as though he hadn't heard her. "Then Cade brought home a woman. A prostitute he said would help us get it back. We were so fucking young. He was barely twenty, Sam and I were only eighteen. But as we started touching her, sharing her, it brought it back, Sarah. We were close again. Without pain, without fear, with no shame, we were together again. We were giving pleasure rather than pain. Increasing the pleasure each of us gained. We survived, we could fuck a woman and enjoy it, and we were brothers again. I don't understand it. I can't ask you to. But it's something we've had to have to survive."

No, it didn't make sense. They should have been warped, broken men, instead they were sexual, smiling, productive men. Sarah shook her head. It didn't make sense, but she understood.

"I can't—" She shook her head.

"Sarah, I want you, not just for a few nights." He laid his hands on her shoulders, his eyes meeting hers in the reflective glass of the mirror, filled not with a demand, but with simple truth. "I don't want to let you go."

She trembled under his touch.

"It's wrong," she whispered. "If you love someone, you don't share them."

"I know it's hard for you," he said gently, his eyes incredibly sad. "I don't blame you, baby, not at all. All I'm asking you for right now is to be with me. Just me, Sarah. Give me a chance."

"A chance to convince me?" Her laughter was nearly hysterical.

God, he didn't know. She could never let him know. If it would wipe the memories and the pain from his eyes she would fuck whoever he wanted her to and never regret it. How could anyone be so cruel, so soulless as to torture anyone in such a terrible manner.

"To seduce you. To show you how good we can be, how much I need you. The rest will come in time." He rubbed his chin against her hair, his hands moving slowly against her back, pressing her close.

"You'll still fuck Marly." She knew he would. She wanted to cry when she saw the knowledge in his eyes.

"Marly is a part of my brother. I love her, as surely as I love him. I can't stop that, Sarah. Please don't ask me to. Because you're not asking me to not fuck Marly, you're asking me to turn away from my brother. If Cade needs me, if he needs that to still his demons, then I will. I won't refuse him. Don't hurt us all by demanding that I do." He was vulnerable and she had never imagined he could be. She didn't like the power it gave her, or her inability to use it.

"What do I do?" she whispered achingly, her heart breaking for him. For her. "You're asking me to let go of all my dreams of happiness to sustain yours, Brock. It's no different from my marriage to Mark."

"I'm different Sarah, because I offer you everything I am. Inside and out," he pleaded with her to understand. It was in his eyes, the throb of his voice. "I don't just offer myself, but my brothers, their love for me, given to you. Their only aim in life to provide for you, to care for you and protect you, just as we do with Marly. Just that, Sarah. That's all. All we are and all the love we have left in us."

Sarah wanted to cry. She wanted to reach into his soul and wipe away the loneliness, the ache, the torment he had endured and replace it with laughter. Had he laughed, in all the years she had known him? Had she ever seen laughter in his eyes? Amusement. Self-mockery. But never laughter. Never joy. Did he even know what joy truly was?

"What if I can't give you what you need, Brock?" she questioned desperately, agonizingly. Fantasizing was one thing. Reality was another. "What makes you think I can share you, let alone let you share me?"

"Because you're curious, aroused," he accused her, though his voice was gentle, understanding. "That's why you ran six years ago, Sarah. That's what scared you so damned bad. Sam told me he was there. That you saw him. You were afraid you wanted it, so you ran and married Tate to escape it."

"No!" He was lying. She hadn't. Had she?

Sarah moved away from him, needing distance between him and the vibration of needs, arousal and pain emanating from him.

"You did, Sarah." He stalked her slowly through the room. "Lie to me if you have to. I don't blame you. What I'm asking has to be hell on a woman. But don't lie to yourself. Not now. Not after all this time. The thought of it arouses you. Just as it does me. Admit it."

"Stop." She shook her head desperately, ignoring the ache between her thighs, the plea in his voice. "That's not what I want."

He jerked her to him, his body drawn tight, pulsing with demand, pressing his erection into her stomach as he bent her head back.

"Don't you?" he growled, his mouth going to her neck, his teeth rasping roughly, making her body shudder with

146

longing. "We could seduce you, Sarah. No one would force you; no one would ask more than you could give. But you know damned good and well you think about it, fantasize about it. I could give you the reality in ways you've never imagined."

"I won't do it." Her voice was weak, her body wilting against his as his hands pushed under the bikini bottoms, dragging her against him, pressing her crotch against his straining arousal as he ground himself against her.

"Then I won't force you." He shook his head, staring down at her, his eyes so heartbreaking in their sadness, were also tender. Aroused for her, wanting her. Fighting to reassure her. "But I won't let you go either, Sarah. I can't. Don't you understand, baby? You stand between me and the nightmares. You always have. Your taste, your touch. All of it. I've lived for it for six years. I can't stop now."

How was she supposed to deny him? She could see his emotions, his hungers, his needs in his eyes. Shadowed from nightmares, yet lit with a flame of hope that he saw in her. A love… She wanted to scream out at the love she saw there. A love she had run from six years before.

He lifted his hand gently, touching her face, and she saw his joy in touching her. A joy she knew only when he touched her, when she touched him.

"Just let me love you, Sarah…" he whispered. "The rest we can get through as we have to…"

He broke her heart. He drew her. In that second, Sarah knew she was lost.

Her skin was too sensitive, her body too aroused. When his lips took hers, his hands guiding hers to the front of his jeans, she had no resistance left. She was quaking inside, a fury of desire racing through her system, making her crazy for him. Crazy to have him buried hard and deep inside her. Her hands released the metal buttons, then pushed the material desperately from his thighs, dragging his underwear with them, going to her knees, hunger invading her.

She wanted his cock filling her mouth. She wanted to taste him, clean and hard, his need for her in the hard pulse of his flesh. She was desperate to taste him, hungry for the hard jets of semen he would reward her caress with.

"Son of a bitch." His rough groan followed the swipe of her tongue over the swollen head of his cock.

His hands clenched in her hair, pushing the length of his erection toward her mouth. Sarah wrapped her hand as far around the base as her fingers would allow. There was still an impressive amount of flesh left uncircled. One hand gripped his hip and she stared up at him, mesmerized by the demonic need reflected in his eyes. She licked him again, slow, her tongue curling around the thickly flared tip of pulsing flesh.

He growled at her. The sound rumbled from his chest as his teeth clenched, his jaw bunching in his effort to control the raging desire arching between them.

Sarah opened her mouth, watching his eyes, moaning as slowly, so slowly she enclosed the hot, demanding head of his cock in the moist heat of her mouth. His hips jerked, his chest rising and falling harshly, his breath rasping in the dim light of the room as she slowly, so slowly allowed the hard length to sink into her mouth.

"Sarah." His voice was rough, demanding.

He tore his shirt off. Buttons flew, muscles rippled as he shrugged it from his shoulders then his hands returned to her hair, bunched masses of it in his fingers, his hips moving with short, controlled thrusts against her lips.

He filled her mouth, stretching her lips over it, pulsing against her tongue. He tasted of male heat and a shade of musk, hot passion and overwhelming demand, and she loved it. She licked the underside of his cock, hearing him groan, watching his eyes droop sexily as she moved back and forth, allowing him to fuck the shallow depths of her mouth as she sucked at the head timidly. She had never done this before, refused to allow Mark's fickle flesh in her mouth. But she wanted to devour Brock. She wanted to keep his rigid cock against her tongue forever. And at the same time, she wanted to suck him until she heard his harsh shout of surrender and felt the hard jet of his seed filling her mouth, shooting down her throat.

"There, baby," he whispered as her tongue stroked just under the head of his swollen flesh. "Right there, sugar, tongue it. Let your tongue rub it real good."

She flattened her tongue, keeping the firm suction of her mouth in place as he bared his teeth in a grimace of raw pleasure. She kept her eyes firmly locked with his, drawing back, seeing his eyes flare as she balanced the tip of his cock on her tongue, then slowly swallowed as much of his length as her mouth would allow. All the while she kept her tongue on the underside, rubbing, rasping against the sensitive area that seemed to bring him such pleasure.

"Oh, yeah, Sarah," he growled, his voice rough and low. "There you go, sugar, make it feel real good. So damned good, baby."

His voice was like an aphrodisiac, spreading through her body, drenching the flesh between her thighs, making her burn with the desire to please him.

She drew on him slow and easy, then fast and hard, eliciting strangled gasps from his heaving chest, causing his hands to clench in her hair until she was moaning with the sensuous tug of pleasure/pain it brought.

"You like that?" He could barely breathe as he groaned the words, tugging slowly at her hair again.

Sarah could barely keep her eyes open, the sharp bursts of pleasure were so intense.

"Yeah, you like that don't you, baby?" His smile was strained as he thrust against her mouth, his hands then pulling slowly at her hair, drawing her head closer, his cock nearly to her throat before he pulled back.

Sarah was burning alive. She could feel the wet, flaming need drenching her thighs, swelling her breasts. She was empty, tortured with the ache of her body, and the need, overwhelming, making her insane to feel his cum spurting into her mouth. She needed it. She wanted to taste him so bad she felt starved for it. At the same time, the sharp tugs at her hair, something she had always found painful before, had her nearly climaxing with the forbidden sensations.

"Suck me harder, Sarah," he whispered deeply, his hands clenching deeper in her hair now, pulling her closer, releasing her, closer again, the tempo increasing as his cock seemed to swell, pulse, heat within her mouth. "Harder, baby. Suck me harder."

She tightened her mouth on him, moaning as he pulled her hair harder, his hips pushing, pulling back, penetrating her mouth with quick, hard thrusts.

"Son of a bitch. I'm going to come in your mouth, Sarah. You have to stop if that's not what you want." The thrusts increased. Short. Hard. As deep as the hands gripping his cock would allow. "God. Damn, baby. I'm going to come."

Once. Twice, he thrust harder, then he moaned, low and hard as Sarah felt his erection tighten, jerk, then the fierce, hot jets of his creamy semen began to shoot into the back of her mouth, flowing down her throat as she fought to swallow every erotic drop of the hot seed he spurted into her.

She was gasping, moaning around his jerking flesh as his hands pulled at her hair, released, pulled, like a cat digging its claws in pleasure into her scalp. The sensation was so arousing she hovered on the edge of climax from it.

"Damn you." His voice was harsh as he dragged her from the floor, pushing her onto the couch as he came over her. "Did you like that, Sarah? Did the pain make it better, baby? Hotter?"

Sarah shook her head, wanting to deny the charge, but unable to as he jerked her thighs apart, kneeling between them as he stared down at her.

"Tell me you like it, Sarah. No lies, baby. I won't let you lie to me about this." He leaned over her, his lips within inches of hers as his eyes dared her to deny him. "Tell me you liked it."

"Yes," she gasped out, her hands clenching his forearms, her hips rising in desperate need as his still-hard cock kissed at her wet folds. "I liked it, Brock. I liked it. Please."

"Please what?" He dragged his hips against hers, his erection lodging in the open lips dying to embrace it. "Please what, Sarah?"

"Please fuck me," she begged harshly, fighting to take him, furious that he would edge away, denying her the feel of him inside her.

"Is that all you want, Sarah?" He pierced the tight slit, just as he had that night so long ago, only the head of his cock penetrating her. "How do you want it, baby? Slow and gentle—" He pushed into her, separating her grasping flesh inch by slow inch, then retreating with the same excruciating manner. "Or hard and fast?"

Sarah screamed. Her body arched, her muscles quivering as he thrust hard, burying the full length of his cock into her desperate, achy flesh. She couldn't control it. She couldn't stop the bone-tightening, muscle-ripping pleasure from destroying her. She climaxed, exploding harshly, screaming his name as he began to pump hard and fast, slamming his flesh almost brutally into her as she pulsed around him. She melted, her juices flowed, her vagina rippling around his flesh until his own cries joined hers, his semen flooding the tight channel as he gave one last hard lunge into her body, and came with a shout of male pleasure.

He collapsed over her, dragging air into his lungs as though he had been deprived of it for too long, then turned and rolled over as he dragged Sarah over him. Like a sweat-sheened, human blanket she lay limp and exhausted, her head pillowed on his chest as she fought to catch her breath. She had never known such intensity, such soul-destroying pleasure. She felt possessed, taken over by a creature of need that had no care for humility, no shame in her desire. A woman on the verge of destruction.

Chapter Sixteen

ᔟ

Hours later Sarah lay naked, sprawled over Brock's body as they dozed on the couch. What was it about him, she wondered. It wasn't just his sexuality, his dominance. There was something so elementally male about him, that she knew she had been lost six years before but just hadn't realized it.

As she lay there, the near hit and run played through her mind. The three men as a whole were overwhelming, but they had been protective. Caring. She had seen, though not understood, as far as they were concerned, she was already a part of Brock. They'd had six years to accept what she was only now facing.

"Can we go to bed now?" Brock growled at her ear, drowsy and replete.

Sarah sighed softly. "I go to bed. You need to go back to your own bed, Brock."

There was a moment of silence as he stiffened beneath her.

"Shit, Sarah. I'll be damned if I'm driving back to that ranch just to begin this fight again tomorrow. It's not happening."

There was no plea in his voice now. No asking. He had staked out his claim and she could hear his determination to fight for it.

"I'm not ready yet, Brock." she said softly. "You're asking a lot from me. Give me time to let this sink in. To come to terms with it."

"Why don't you want me to stay?" Brock asked the question long minutes after she asked him to leave for the night.

Sprawled on the couch, naked, his body behind her, holding her against his broad chest, Sarah sighed.

"I need to think," she whispered. And she did.

She needed to accustom herself to the decision she had made. Not about his brothers, but with him. She couldn't deny Brock, and she didn't know how much longer she could hold out against what he needed. The only question was, could she ever forgive herself if she gave in.

She glanced back at her lover, the closed eyes, the thoughtful expression on his face as he considered her request.

"Do I get to come back?" She could hear his determination to never leave if she answered negatively.

Sarah took a deep breath, turning her eyes to the ceiling and studying it as though it held the answers to all her questions.

"Yes, in a day or two," she whispered. "I can't deny you anymore, Brock, but just you. I need to understand what I'm doing here."

She felt his body tense, his arm move, his hand cupping her breast.

"You can't decide this while I'm gone tomorrow?" he asked her softly. "I'll leave in the morning, Sarah. Come back at night." He wasn't pleading, merely stating another alternative.

She shook her head.

"You're asking a lot of me, Brock. Is this so little to ask for?" She questioned him, keeping her voice quiet, reasonable.

A part of her had calmed. As though Brock's revelations earlier had stilled the agonizing thrust of betrayal that seared into her heart. She didn't understand, but she needed to. She needed to think about it. She needed to be certain of this next

Sarah's Seduction

step in her life. She needed to be certain she could handle the passion and the pain Brock would bring with him.

He sighed deeply. "I hate sleeping without you, Sarah," he revealed with weary male patience.

She shook her head. Give a man sex he thinks is good and he's a bigger baby than he was to begin with. Or at least more determined.

"You're a big boy, Brock, you can handle it." She smiled. "Just for a night or two."

"One night," he bargained. "That's all I can handle, Sarah."

She looked over at him as he opened his eyes, stretching, moving that large, muscular body until he was leaning over her, staring at her stubbornly.

Sarah rolled her eyes. "I'll call you when I'm ready," she told him firmly. "That's my final word."

"Then you better open your mouth and decide on another one," he assured her softly. "I will not stay away from you for an undetermined amount of time. I won't spend all this time getting past that prickly pride of yours again. Next time Sarah, I'll just strip your damned clothes and take you. I won't give you a choice."

"You gave me a choice this time?" Mockery lay thick in her voice. "Why, Brock, I never noticed. Maybe your subtlety lacked something. I would work on that if I were you."

She didn't raise her voice, didn't argue, didn't demand, but she knew her tone was noted when his eyes flared with lust. What was this? Defy the man and instead of getting angry, he gets horny. It made no sense. At least not to Sarah. But she felt his cock rising, long and hard at her thigh, its heat tempting her to urge him into her one last time.

"I'm going to work on something all right but it won't be the least bit subtle," he warned her. "When I come back, Sarah, I'm going to work on broadening your horizons a bit."

155

Sarah swallowed nervously. "My horizons are plenty wide enough to suit me, Brock," she promised him carefully.

"Too fucking bad." He pulled her over his body, settling himself into the cushions as he arranged her thighs to straddle him intimately.

Sarah gasped.

"Don't tell me you've never done this." His look was wickedly sexy.

"Well, Mark and I never experimented much," she gulped. "So, no. Straight missionary. That was enough."

"He never ate that sweet pussy?" he asked her, his voice deep, husky. "Never lapped the honey from between your thighs?"

Oh hell, she was in some deep trouble here. She shook her head.

"No. Just you. No one else."

The beginnings of a smile shaped his lips. For the first time since she had known him, Sarah saw a measure of joy reflected in his eyes.

"Oh Sarah, you have a lot to learn," he promised her. "What about dildos? Surely you've used one."

She shook her head, her face flaming, then she gasped as he lifted her, lodging the head of his penis between the hot lips of her hungry cunt.

"No dildos, huh?" he asked her, considering, though his voice was husky and tight as he slid slowly into her. "I'll get you one."

"That's okay." She breathed harshly. "Who needs one with you around?"

"I do," he growled, his hands gripping her hips as he filled her, grinding against her. "I want to teach you how to use it. Watch you fuck yourself with it."

Sarah whimpered, her womb contracting almost painfully at the erotic words.

"That's so perverted, Brock." She was shocked, aroused at the thought.

"So much pleasure, Sarah," he promised her. "I would watch you, tell you how, let you find the ways of pleasing yourself. "

Her head tossed, her hips jerked as she fought to ride him harder. He held her still, the hands at her hips keeping her locked to him.

"How could that be better..." she gasped, "than this?" She clenched her muscles around him, hearing him groan in pleasure at the small movement.

"It's a different pleasure," he promised her, watching her from beneath lowered lids, his eyes glittering with sexual promise. "I promise, baby, you'll love it."

His hands loosened on her hips, his thighs bunched as he pulled back, then drove into her. Sarah lost her breath. Her hands braced on his chest, her head tossing in an agony of need and fiery sensations.

"Ride me, Sarah. Like this." He stilled, his hands moved on her hips again, teaching her how.

She lifted her hips, feeling the glide of silk-enclosed steel along her vaginal walls. He stopped her an inch from total retreat.

"Now, lower yourself slowly," he whispered. "Ride me like that, Sarah, slow and easy until you get a feel for it."

A feel for it? The feel *of* it was slowly killing her. She rose by slow degrees, her breath heaving from her throat at the forced reduction in the pace she so loved. She wanted him driving into her, throwing her into climax. This was too much; too many sensations rioting through her body. The slow steady impalement as she lowered herself had her tossing her head, moaning brokenly.

She felt the slow pinch of his thick cock stretching her, filling her. The bulging head flared, pushing past sensitive tissue. It slid slow and easy through the natural lubrication of her body until it lodged, tight and hard at her womb. There, it throbbed against such sensitive flesh that she wanted to scream at the pleasure.

"Oh, Sarah," his moan sounded awestruck.

She opened her eyes, staring down at him. His face was flushed, his eyes glittering with emotion. So much emotion. So intense, so filled with—adoration?—that it made her heart clench. Did she really do this for him? Make him as wild for the building explosion as she became?

"You like this?" She was surprised. More than surprised, actually.

She rose on him again, watching him grimace as her flesh gripped him, suckled his straining cock.

"No, baby. I don't like this. I fucking love the hell out of it." His teeth were clenched hard, the muscles of his neck and shoulders bulging as he fought for control. "You're killing me with pleasure, and I promise you, I'm a willing damned sacrifice."

His voice was strained, gasping.

She lowered herself again. A keening wail of excruciating sensation had her nails digging into his hard chest muscles. His hands flexed on her hips, his thighs bunched, lifted, driving his flesh deeper, harder inside her.

"Sarah, baby," he gasped. "Find that fucking rhythm soon, sugar, before you kill us both."

She lowered her lids, fighting the need to ride him hard now. Her lips lifted.

"You don't like this?" she asked him, her voice soft, wondering as she watched him.

"Hell no," he growled. "Oh shit, Sarah." She rolled her hips above him, moving languorously as she twisted on the thick intrusion of his cock.

Her stomach clenched, her womb vibrated with shudders of impending orgasm.

"You sure you don't like it?" she panted, rising up again.

He didn't give her a chance to torment him further. With a lurch of his hips, a swift motion of his hands on hers, he drove her body onto his, his cock like a battering ram, tearing through her with such a mind numbing intensity of pleasure that she exploded the minute it struck the back of her throbbing pussy.

She screamed, jerked and began to thrust against him mindlessly as she felt his cock explode, spewing his seed deep, deep inside her body, flooding her with the hot release as his arms wrapped around her, dragging her to his heaving chest.

"God. Sarah." His voice was tortured, emotion spilling through it as his arms spasmed around her body.

Her body continued to tremble, shudder. Small explosions shaking through her as she fought for a measure of control now. It was the most sensual, erotic experience of her life. She was still gasping for breath, still enjoying the small, brutal pulses of orgasmic delight.

Minutes, hours, days later, he shifted her body and allowed her to collapse beside him once again.

"Let me stay and I'll let you ride my cock again first thing in the morning," he bargained with a drowsy sigh.

"Get dressed, cowboy." She yawned, tucking her head more comfortably against the couch cushions. "You're out of here until I personally call you and ask you to return."

He sighed deeply.

"Sarah, you forget to call and I'll tan your hide when I get you naked again," he promised her, his threat followed by a slow caress over her rounded buttocks.

"I promise. I'll call, Brock." She smiled lazily. "Now go home."

He grunted with grouchy emphasis and rolled until he could find a sitting position.

"Never seen the like, Sarah. Running me off this way." He snagged his pants from the floor and began to drag them over his legs.

Sarah sat up on the couch, pulling the afghan from the back and wrapping it around her shoulders. Brock dressed in silence, his expression quiet now, thoughtful. When he had his shirt buttoned over his broad chest, he turned to her, watching her out of somber, dark eyes.

"You going to be okay?" He touched her cheek gently. "Don't worry over the things from the past, Sarah," he whispered of his abuse. "It's over."

Sarah took a hard breath.

"It won't be over until you can live with it normally, Brock," she told him gently. "Until then, the bastard has won. Because he's stolen that from you."

Brock shrugged. "We survived. We're sane. He's dead. That counts as winning to me."

He rose to his feet, then pulled her up behind him.

"Go onto bed. I'll lock up as I leave." He nodded to the stairs. "Don't wait too long to call me, Sarah. My patience isn't at its best these days."

She smiled up at him. Standing on her tiptoes, she kissed his swollen lips with a soft movement.

"Go home, Brock. I'll call soon." Her hands tightened on the afghan and she moved to the stairs.

She was almost to her room when she heard him leave. He closed the door soundly and long minutes later she heard his Jeep start and pull from the drive. She shook her head, lowered it, and headed for her room.

Chapter Seventeen

80

It was still dark when Sarah awoke, groggy, uncertain what had disturbed her. She blinked, staring in confusion at the ceiling when she heard it again. The stairs were creaking. Slow, measured steps, but the creak of the wood in the silent house was easily heard.

Her heart jumped in her chest, nearly strangling her with her fear. Brock? Would he attempt to sneak into her bed after she had asked him to leave? It didn't seem his style. He would be the one pounding on the door, demanding that she let him in. That she make the choice to allow him to enter. He wouldn't try to steal in on her while she was asleep. Defenseless.

After the attempted hit and run the day before, Sarah felt terror wash over her. What if it hadn't been an accident as she assumed? Or a case of someone drinking too much? What if someone really did want to hurt her?

It wasn't Mark. She knew the sound of him sneaking up the stairs. She had lived with it for years. She swallowed, nearly strangling on her fear as they creaked again.

She slid silently from the bed, grabbing the cordless phone from the cradle and crept across the room. She dialed 911 quickly, knowing the call would go directly into the sheriff's office.

There was no time to question or to wonder. A sudden overwhelming sense of fear was strangling her with the knowledge that whoever was on those steps meant to do her serious harm.

"Sheriff." Joshua Martinez answered the phone on the first ring.

It took long seconds for her to speak. Panic welled in her chest, made her stomach boil with fear. She was shaking, naked and fighting to hold onto her control

"Joshua, it's Sarah. Sarah Tate." Her voice shook. Another step was breached. Nearly to the top.

"Sarah. You okay?" Joshua was instantly on the alert, his voice cool, precise.

"I need you over here, someone's in the house." Her teeth were nearly chattering as she heard the last step reached. "Hurry. Hurry."

Oh God. He was never going to make it on time. They were almost at the top of the stairs, it was a simple matter to get into her room. Seconds. She had only seconds.

"Sarah, I'm on the way. You stay on the line with Mary here." She heard him lay the phone down, the rush of feet. She heard a footfall outside her bedroom door.

"Sarah, hon. Give Josh five minutes. He'll be right there. Do you know who's there, Sarah? Sarah, talk to me honey. Is everything still okay?"

Sarah couldn't speak. The steps paused outside her door. Clutching the phone to her stomach, she crept across the floor, sliding quickly beneath her bed as the door began to inch open. She couldn't breath. She could barely hear Mary's frantic voice yelling through the phone pressed to her breast. She clearly saw the black sneakers that entered the room. She heard sirens in the distance, and knew Joshua was coming. What if he didn't make it on time? She was within the city limits, but still, it was going to take the Sheriff time to get there.

"Sarah, you're in here." The voice was mechanical, distorted. "Come out, come out, sweeting, wherever you are."

She couldn't breathe. She was terrified he could hear her heart pounding in her chest, threatening to smother her with terror. She shook with dread; with the impotence of realizing she was totally at the mercy of a stranger until the sheriff arrived. A stranger intent on causing her harm. She could feel the sick premonition of danger in the pit of her stomach, the stench of her own fear. Her hand covered her mouth as she fought the screams building in her chest. Dear God, why hadn't she let Brock stay?

"Sarah, I'm gonna get you." He didn't move from the door but his voice wrapped around her with sinister threads of malice. "Come on out, bitch, let me see the August boys' new plaything." The voice was soft, amused, yet filled with hatred. "Do you enjoy it Sarah? Letting those nasty boys share you, shove their dicks up you?"

He spoke the August name as though it were a curse. A vile, tarnished word that he had to force past his lips. Tremors of terror shook her body. She clenched her teeth hard to keep them from chattering, her eyes closing tightly as she fought the reality of this danger.

No, this wasn't Mark. It had nothing to do with Mark. Someone was trying to hurt Brock.

"Come on, whore. I know he's fucked you. Let me show you what a real man can do." Sarah heard the sneer, the growl of obsessive loathing in his voice.

The sirens were getting closer. Josh would be here soon, she assured herself, fighting the screams welling in her throat. Just a few more minutes, that was all.

"Whore, did you call the cops on me?" Fury filled his voice now as the sounds began to fill the night. "I bet you did, didn't you? That's okay, bitch. You'll pay for that too. Get ready, whore. To die."

She screamed as the shots blasted through the room, the vibrations to the bed, the maniacal laughter as feet pounded down the hall and out of sight. The phone fell to the floor as she felt a burning pain across the top of her shoulder, felt the fear explode in her head like dynamite. She pushed her way out from under the bed dragging the comforter from the bed around her body. She shook so hard she couldn't stand; she could only scoot in jerky movements to the opened door. She hid behind it quickly, her hand clamped over her mouth as she fought her hysterical screams. The shriek of the siren was in her yard, in her head. Raised voices, curses, the sound of gunfire echoing around the house.

She pressed herself closer into the corner, clutching her shoulder, wondering why it hurt so bad. She was cold. Or was she hot? She knew for a fact she was on the verge of hysteria.

"Brock," her whimper shocked her. The need for him terrified her. She wouldn't be safe again until Brock found her.

* * * * *

The ringing of the phone brought Brock from a restless sleep, lending ire to the growling curse that escaped his throat. Hell, he had hardly closed his eyes and already the damned phone was ringing?

"What?" He pulled the phone to his ear, checking the hands of the clock blearily.

"Brock August." The official voice asked without hesitation.

"Yeah." He frowned, hearing raised voices, imperative shouts.

"This is Sheriff Martinez. Josh." He and Josh had been friends in school. A long time ago.

Then it hit him.

"Sarah? Is she okay?" He was out of the bed and jerking his jeans from the chair before the words were out of his mouth.

"Hell if I know." Frustration edged the sheriff's voice. " She won't let anyone check her. She's been shot, though, I can tell you that much. We're at the house. She's refusing treatment and damned near hysterical. I need you to get here as soon as possible."

"I'm bringing the chopper. I can land in her back yard." There was no question of it. It more than an hour's drive away. He would kill himself before he made it there.

"So I figured," Josh informed him. "Just get here. She needs treatment and she's in shock. And I don't know if there are any other injuries."

Brock's heart jumped to his throat.

"Meaning?" he asked.

"Meaning all she's dressed in is a comforter she has wrapped around her body and she refuses to let any of us near her. I don't know, man. But she keeps asking for you, so I called you."

"I'll be there." He disconnected. "Cade!" He threw open the door, yelling his brother's name as he jerked on his boots.

Seconds later both Sam and Cade were in their doorways.

"Someone attacked Sarah. I'm heading to town." He rushed down the hallway.

"Sam, get the Jeep ready. Marly get dressed," Cade called back to Marly.

"I'm taking the chopper."

"Then you'll wait on one of us." Cade caught him as he made to pass.

"Think, Brock. Five minutes. That's all. Sam can go out in the chopper with you and Marly and I will follow in the jeep. Don't be a fool."

Cade's expression was savage, imperative. Brock knew Sarah was his soul, and he knew that made her more than important to his brothers as well. They had no choice but to fight to protect her now, for it made her their heart.

"Get going then," he growled. "Hurry up, Sam, I'll have the chopper warming."

He didn't want to spare five minutes but, hell, he knew it would take that long to get the helicopter ready to fly. He ran from the house, his heart pounding, fear clogging his throat.

She was hurt. It was all he could think about. He had to get to her, and he had to get to her now.

Chapter Eighteen

ॐ

Brock wanted to kill when he saw her. She was huddled in the corner of the bedroom, a bloody comforter wrapped around her, surrounded by enough damned men to send his possessive instincts into overdrive.

Her head was lowered, her silken honey-colored hair falling around her, mussed and tangled, stained red on her left shoulder.

"This is how we found her." Josh stood back as Brock entered the room. "She only shakes her head and cries when we try to treat her, Brock. We have to find out how bad she's been hurt."

Brock ignored him. Fury, raw and ripe traveled through his body, made him want to scream out in rage.

"Get a handle, bro. Doc's on his way here." Sam laid his hand on Brock's shoulder warningly. "Cade was calling him as we left the ranch. Just help her pull it together."

Brock shrugged his hand away.

"Get the fuck out of my way," he growled at the EMT's and various deputies huddled around her. "Dammit Josh, why are you letting them crowd her this way?"

Her head came up. Son of a bitch. He was going to kill someone. He could feel the rage traveling through his system, heating his blood. She was white as a sheet, her whisky-colored eyes nearly black with shock, dark circles lying thick beneath them. She was on the verge of hysterical collapse and all the fucking morons around her could do was try to get closer to her.

"Brock?" Husky from her tears, her fear, her voice shattered him.

"Get the hell out of my way." He pushed at a reluctant EMT, going to his knees in front of her huddled form.

"God, Sarah-love," he whispered desperately, his hand touching her white cheek. "Are you okay, baby?"

"Bastard shot me." She tried to smile, but her lips trembled in violent reaction to the attempt.

"Is that all?" His hands went to the comforter at her shoulder, pulling it back enough to see the long, jagged gash in her shoulder.

A flesh wound. He wanted to close his eyes in relief. It looked bad, but it would heal.

"That's all," she whispered. "I was under the bed. He shot at the bed. He knew where I was." The tears were falling down her cheeks now.

"Was it Mark, Sarah?" Brock fought to keep his voice gentle as he moved her hair back to get a better look at the wound.

He knew if Mark had done this to her, the man wouldn't live out the night.

"No," she whispered, her eyes flickering to the impatient men behind her.

The thread of wariness in her voice had him narrowing his eyes on her, watching her carefully.

"Who was it, Sarah?" he asked her softly.

"I don't know." The helpless fear in her voice had him fighting to contain his rage.

"What do you know, baby?" He knew Josh and Sam were listening carefully.

She did too. He saw it in her face, in that spark of nervousness in her eyes. She looked at him pleadingly. What did she want to hide?

"Sarah?" he questioned her softly. "You have to tell me what happened."

Her glance went to the men gathered around her, shame and pain reflecting in her eyes.

"Josh, get these fucking men out of here." He cast the sheriff a hard look. "Now."

"They need to check her out, Brock," Josh argued. "And I need a statement."

"Evidently you didn't hear him well enough, Josh." Sam's voice was a low, warning growl.

Brock glanced at his brother, seeing the untamed violence that rarely came to the surface in the other man. Josh saw it too. The sheriff paused, winced, then turned to the men crowded behind Brock.

"Outside, boys, before these two cowboys decide to piss us all off." Frustration lined his voice.

"Doc Bennett will be here any time. I want him brought up here. He'll check her out and see if she needs to be taken to the hospital." Sam continued to direct the action behind Brock.

"Come on, baby. Let's get you off of the floor." Brock eased her into his arms, his chest tightening at the little sob that escaped her lips as he picked her up in his arms.

"He shot my bed," she whispered, her voice forlorn as he carried her toward it. "He wanted to kill me, Brock."

Brock knew if he found out who did this to her, the man wouldn't live five minutes after he got hold of him.

"Damn. New bed too, hon." He tried to keep his voice light. Tried to keep the violence out of it. "I hadn't even got to share it with you yet."

He stood aside while Sam grabbed pillows from the floor and propped them against the headboard.

"Here you go, sugar." He settled her against them, sitting beside her. "Now, it's nice and quiet in here. I want you to tell me what happened."

She stared up at him, misery filling her expression.

"I think he wanted to hurt you," she whispered bleakly. "You and your brothers, Brock. How would killing me hurt your brothers?"

Because she was a part of him, just as they were. Brock knew why. He had learned that lesson at the hands of a madman. He listened carefully as she told him what happened, her voice tear-filled, stuttering at times as she fought the shock and the pain.

Violence filled him, tore through the control he kept built carefully around his emotions. His hands were gentle, though, as they smoothed over her hair, his voice comforting, as tender as the ragged emotions escaping him would allow it to be.

"Brock, Doc is here." Sam stood behind him, speaking softly. "He's outside. You want me to let him in now?"

The words were no sooner out of his mouth then the bedroom door was pushed open to admit the doctor and his more than irritated nurse/wife.

"Sam August, you don't hold us up like this when one of our patients is hurt." Elizabeth Bennett pushed open the door, determination filling her lined face as her husband followed her.

Small, fierce, her dark brown eyes as sharp as an eagle's went over Sarah where she huddled in the bed. She was an excellent nurse and a good friend to the August family. Brock was more than thankful that she had come along.

"Sorry, Beth." He swallowed tightly. "Guess I wasn't thinking."

"Knothead." Her voice was affectionate, but worried. "Now get out of the way and let me and Doc check our girl here. She doesn't look so good at the moment."

Brock moved aside, standing close in case Sarah needed him and watching as the couple began to take over. Sarah had made an impression on the couple the few times she had been to the office, he could tell. Beth was as fierce as a mother hen, and Doc was plain goofy he was so gentle with her.

"Cade's coming into town now." Sam moved to his side. "He wants her ready to bring to the ranch if she doesn't need hospital care."

Brock sighed. He doubted she would go.

"I'll see what I can do." He crossed his arms over his chest as Sarah glanced up in confusion while Beth worked at her shoulder, questioning her gently.

"Did he touch you, Sarah?" The older woman's question had Sarah looking at her in surprise.

"No. I was under the bed," she answered the older woman; her voice still carrying the dazed confusion Brock knew was running through her head.

"Good. Then this is our only problem?" Beth held Sarah's hair back, tilting her head as Doc moved in to treat the wound. "This ain't too bad, hon. Doc can fix you right up with it. Won't even need stitches. Just a nice bandage."

Sarah winced as antiseptic was applied. Doc worked on the wound gently, a soft lullaby humming from his lips as he cleaned and patched the wound. A lullaby? Brock shook his head glancing at Sam, sharing his confusion at the sound. He would have never imagined it. The big, rough doctor was all thumbs and needles when he treated them.

"She's okay. Shocky, but fine. Flesh wound, shallow at that. Bullet just grazed her." Doc stood back a long while later. "I want to leave her a sedative. She needs to rest, take it easy for a day or two."

"She can come to the ranch." Brock had been unaware of Cade entering the room until he spoke authoritatively.

His brother stood with a concerned Marly at his side watching Sarah with brooding eyes. Cade was clearly pissed; it showed in the utter stillness of his body, the darkening of his eyes.

"No." Sarah's voice was firm, nervous now. Her expression mutinous. "I'm not going to the ranch."

Silence filled the bedroom as all eyes turned to her.

"Sarah, someone tried to kill you." Brock heard the throb of fury in his voice, even as he fought it. "You're not safe here."

He couldn't get it out of his mind. The vile, vicious words the man had said to her before firing the gun.

"I'll get security added to the house. I'll buy a dog. I'm not leaving my home." Hysteria mounted in her tone.

"Brock, leave her alone." Doc frowned over at him. "If you're that worried, you boys stay here with her until she's in better control. Now is not the time to hassle her."

Brock dragged his fingers through his hair roughly, worry and fear building inside him.

"Fine," he bit out. "We'll talk about it tomorrow."

"There's nothing to talk about," Sarah whispered desolately as the sedative Doc administered moments before began to hit her. "I'm not a plaything, Brock. I won't go."

Brock flinched, watching as her eyes slowly closed, her head finally relaxing against the pillows. He sighed roughly, his gaze meeting his brothers'. He saw the weary acceptance on their faces.

"I called Rick on the way here. He'll be here with his team tomorrow. I'll have a guard put on her if you can't convince her to come to the ranch." His voice was cold, hard. "This time, we'll find the bastard."

But that wouldn't change Sarah's fears. It wouldn't change her feelings towards the family. Brock sat down heavily beside her, his fingers touching her hair, her cheek.

"We have to," he whispered, staring down at the woman who had held his heart for so long that she was as much a part of him as his brothers. "Because I don't think I can live without her, Cade. I just don't think I can."

172

Chapter Nineteen

✍

It was dawn before the house cleared out. Cade and Marly were in another room, Sam was sitting up downstairs with plenty of coffee and a slightly illegal rifle that Cade had brought along. The lethal Russian AK47 was loaded and waiting for anyone stupid enough to try to get into the house with Sam on guard. And he was pissed enough to kill. Sarah was family now and they all accepted it, except Sarah.

The mattress had been flipped and remade until a new one could be bought, and Brock laid next to Sarah, holding her against his chest, his heart still thundering even now. He had almost lost her. Some maniac intent on destroying the August men had almost taken her from him. He buried his face against her hair, fighting the agony rising from his soul. What was it? The hard knot of brutal pain that clogged his throat. How did he ease it?

Along with sedatives, Doc had left pain pills. The wound at her shoulder wasn't bad but it would be sore, he had assured Brock. She was sleeping comfortably now, resting against him. As long as his arms stayed around her, as long as his body shielded her, she didn't become frightened.

"Brock." Sam opened the door, his voice soft enough not to awaken if everyone slept.

"Come on in." He was used to his brother knowing when he couldn't sleep, knowing when the demons haunted him. It was the same for Brock; he knew when Sam was tormented as well.

"She doing okay?" Sam moved to the chair beside the bed, the rifle held loosely in his hands.

"She's sleeping. That's what she needs for now." Brock sighed.

"Dillon showed up earlier, madder than hell," Sam sighed. "Seemed to think we should be able to force her to the ranch."

There was a question in his twin's voice.

"She's not ready, Sam."

"We have to get her to the ranch, Brock." Sam's voice was imperative.

"She won't go. Not yet." Brock smoothed his hand down her arm. "It will take time."

"We may not have time," Sam said, his voice hushed. "What if the bastard strikes again?"

"Then I'll be here." Brock's voice hardened. He would kill the bastard himself.

"I'll have security added to the house as soon as I can get someone out here. Get her locks changed." Sam planned. "It won't be easy to protect her this far from all of us."

A guard would be watching the house as well, Brock knew. They would keep her as safe as possible until they could convince her to come home.

"We'll see," Brock finally said softly. "I know what I have to do, Sam. I just know she's scared right now. All the way to the bone scared and not just of the attacker or of us. She's scared of herself."

He had seen that the day before. The shocking excitement, the pleasure from the edge of pain he gave her. He hadn't expected that from her and it added to the growing desperation to bind her to him. She met his needs and fired others he had no idea he had.

She shifted in his arms, a soft, plaintive moan that he clearly recognized easing from her lips. He saw Sam's grin of amusement. She shifted her buttocks against the erection lying along the tender separation of flesh. He had been hard ever since crawling into the bed beside her.

"Would she let me watch?" Sam asked huskily.

Sarah moaned deeper, rubbing against Brock now, her buttocks clenching on his cock.

"Not yet." Brock gritted his teeth at the sensations racing along the sensitive flesh.

He couldn't do that to her. Not while she was unaware, reacting on instinct rather than common sense. She moaned again, pressing against him.

"Shit. I gotta get out of here before she makes me come anyway," Sam sighed. "Lucky bastard."

He rose from his chair, leaving the room quickly as Brock slid his fingers to the soft, curl-covered flesh of her cunt. She was nearly unconscious, in no shape for what she was begging him for. But she was hot, her honey dripping from between her thighs, soaking the thick curls that covered the little mound.

"Brock," she whispered his name as his fingers slid into the saturated slit, touching her clit with the lightest touch as his other hand moved between her legs, his finger playing there, teasing the narrow entrance into her body.

Her head turned, her eyes glittering from beneath lowered lids.

"Fuck me," she whispered, moving against his hand, her legs shifting. "Please, Brock. Now."

"Sarah, you're hurt," he groaned, amazed that she was even awake. When Doc gave a sedative, he usually did it right.

"You're hard," she mumbled drowsily.

"And you're sore and drugged." He gritted his teeth at the warm grip of her cunt around his fingers as he slid them slowly inside.

"Fuck me and then I'll go to sleep." She moved against him again, lifting cautiously, angling her body until he removed his fingers from her soft heat and gripped her hip with his damp fingers. Groaning with his need, Brock let the head of his erection lodge between the silky lips of her cunt.

"God, Sarah," he groaned as he pushed in slow and easy. Her inner muscles gripped him, drew him in, suckling at his flesh with such heat he didn't know how long he could stand it.

It was like this every time he got his cock inside her. Like a furnace of lust, burning him alive with such intense desire he could barely sustain control. She was so damned tight he wanted to howl at the excruciating pleasure building from the grip of her body.

"Brock," she moaned his name, her hips moving languorously, thrusting against him, taking by slow degrees until he filled her, his shaft buried to the hilt inside her.

"Easy," he gasped, moving against her, holding her hips, not wanting to hurt her as he thrust against her. "Oh, Sarah, it's so good, baby. So hot and tight." His chest labored for breath, his stomach tightened with the fight to hold back his climax.

He moved his hand, his fingers delving between their bodies until he found the slick opening to her anus, coated with the lubrication of her cunt. His finger pressed gently, moving against her, slipping inside her to the first knuckle.

She stilled. He felt her breath halt, the tension that filled her.

"Relax," he whispered at her ear. "Your body's already relaxed, Sarah. It won't hurt at all." He slid his finger back, gathering more of the lubrication then sliding back in.

Her moan was harsh, her breath panting from her chest as her cunt tightened on the thick length of his cock, her anus gripping his finger with a hot bite.

"You like that?" Her breathless cry whispered through the room.

176

"Do you?" He pushed his finger deeper inside, his hips flexing, grinding his penis harder into her as she took him to the second knuckle.

"I think so," she panted, the muscles easing around his finger.

"There you go, just relax, baby," he soothed her, moving gently, easily inside the tender entrance of her body as his hips stroked his cock inside her vagina.

Her panting little cries told him she was eager, ready for him. Her inhibitions were lowered, her desires coming to the fore as he introduced her to the new experience. Her vagina gripped his cock tighter as his finger slid fully inside her. Small, light little thrusts of the digit had her breath hitching, her cream spilling over his cock as she accustomed herself to the new sensation.

"I want to get you a butt plug," he groaned at her ear. "You wear it for a set time, daily, stretching the muscles there until they learn to loosen. I want to fuck you here, Sarah. I want to slide my cock deep inside while I fuck you with a vibrator. I want you to see how good it feels, baby. See what I can do for you."

He moved his finger, his hips thrust his cock against her, gaining speed as the excitement became too much for him to bear, and the breathy moans coming from her throat only drove him higher.

"Seducing me..." she panted. "You're trying to seduce me."

"I already have, baby," he gritted out, driving himself deeper inside her, feeling the familiar tightening of his cock, the sensation of her cunt gripping him harder. She was close to orgasm but no closer than he was.

"No. For them," she trembled as he thrust harder into her, her cunt beginning the tiny spasmodic shivers that heralded her climax.

"For me," he corrected her. "Not for them, Sarah, just for me. All for me baby, because the pleasure is more than you can know."

He drove himself deep, unable to hold back, unable to control the desperate flight into burning release.

"For this, Sarah." He held her close, cushioning her shoulder, driving his cock hard and fast inside her as his finger mimicked the movements in her anus, the burning grip on his finger increasing as she shattered.

He exploded to the wash of her climax over his cock. The gripping, grasping muscles tightening, her creamy release soaking him, making him lose his last shred of control.

When the last tremors shook their bodies, he eased his finger from her and rose from the bed. He collected a warm, wet rag and a towel from the bathroom. As she watched him, silent, thoughtful, he cleaned her thighs, then dried them gently.

"Sleep," he told her, crawling back in beside her, a tired breath escaping his throat. "You killed me, baby. No more sex for you tonight."

Her husky laughter had him smiling. When he looked into her face once again, her eyes were closed, her breath slowly evening. He settled his head on her pillow, took a deep breath and joined her in the darkness of exhaustion.

Chapter Twenty

ॐ

Sarah awoke the next morning, tangled around Brock like a living vine. One of her legs rested between his, her head on his chest, her shoulder resting into his body. The wound throbbed painfully now and her head was groggy, her mind dazed from the painkiller the doctor had injected the night before.

She remembered waking once, hearing voices only to realize it was Brock and Sam talking.

Would she let me watch? She remembered Sam's question as heat blazed through her body. But she remembered even more. Her instant, shocking surge of lust at the thought.

Thankfully, Brock had murmured that she wasn't ready yet, sent his brother on his way then proceeded to drive her into an orgasm that even now had the power to make her tremble in memory of the pleasure.

"Now this is how a man is supposed to wake up." His voice was edged with drowsy amusement as she felt his hand move caressingly over her hip. "With his woman snuggled tight enough against him to make him remember why mornings are supposed to be so damned nice."

A mocking unladylike snort left her lips at that declaration.

"I need to get up," she said, rather than replying to his comment. "I need a shower and the bathroom. Urgently."

He sighed with mocking patience. "Leave it to a woman to forget the romance."

Sarah smothered her laughter, then winced as he moved, leaving her to support her shoulder alone.

"Hurt?" He touched her hair gently.

"Sore," she muttered, accepting his help as he eased her up the bed.

He pulled on his jeans, zipping them carefully over his erection before he picked up her robe from the chair. "Let's get this on you then you can take one of the pain pills first. I'll help you shower when you're ready."

"I don't want pills," she tried to snap as he shoved one past her lips and held a glass a water of her to lips.

She swallowed it resentfully, casting him a look of retribution.

"I won't watch you hurting," he told her darkly then. "It's bad enough you were hurt because of me."

"They make me too groggy," she sighed then, seeing the pain edging into his expression once again. She couldn't bear it, that bleak, dark misery. Not now, not while she was so weak.

"You can handle groggy for a day or two." He sounded uncompromising. Determined. "Come on, I'll let you use the bathroom alone before your shower. But you get in the shower without me and your backside will regret it."

"Brock, you're entirely too interested in spanking my rear," she muttered self-consciously. "This has to stop."

"Baby, I have a feeling you'd love the hell out of it," he chuckled, arousal thickening his voice, not to mention his cock. "I know I would."

Sarah rolled her eyes at that one, but kept her sarcastic reply to herself as he helped her ease to her feet. She was wobbly, but reasonably steady, she assured herself. Though she still allowed him to help her to the bathroom.

"Cade and Marly are here," he told her quietly as he opened the door and stood aside. "Sam should be back from town anytime for breakfast."

She drew in her breath sharply as he stared down at her, his gaze dark, resigned.

"I'm not going to the ranch." She knew what was coming.

"Sarah, you're too damned stubborn," he growled. "Let me know when you're ready to shower and we'll talk about it later. Sam should be back with breakfast soon and we'll see about how to deal with this then."

"I didn't ask you to deal with it," she snapped back, cranky now from the pills and his determination. "This is my home. I don't want to leave it."

She didn't want to be at the August ranch, weak, dependent. She couldn't imagine a place harder to say "No" to what she knew they wanted than in the den of carnality she knew that place would be.

She entered the bathroom, closing the door effectively in his face and locked it. Damn man. She could feel him taking her over and making her like it. It was disconcerting to realize it, and she wasn't ready to accept it. She needed to put her foot down or he would make her independence a thing of the past.

But she couldn't help but smile. At least she wasn't bored. She had spent the past six years bored out her mind, always reaching, always wondering what was missing. Now she knew. She was afraid she had known six years ago when she had raced from his room. Brock had been missing.

She used the bathroom, brushed her teeth, then adjusted the water in her shower before unlocking the door and opening it slowly. Brock was standing patiently in the hall, watching the door unblinking, aroused. He stayed aroused. Hard and hot and ready to pleasure her at a moment's notice. What woman wouldn't love that? A smile quirked his looks as her eyes narrowed in response.

"Go ahead and shower," he drawled as he pushed inside the small room, taking a seat on the small bench next to the door. "I've already made use of it."

She sniffed disdainfully at his amused response. "I didn't want you in my shower anyway."

He chuckled. The sound was rusty, as though it wasn't used often, but it was there all the same. Shaking her head, Sarah stepped beneath the warmth of the water, thankful for the tight fit of the adhesive bandage on her shoulder.

The water pounded on her head, not completely clearing the grogginess, but helping. Minutes later, washed, rinsed and reasonably awake, she shut off the water. And there was Brock. The glass doors slid open slowly as he shook a towel out, holding it out for her, his expression so gentle it made her throat tighten with emotion. Did he know he was breaking her heart by something so simple as his protectiveness? His determination to care for her?

"You don't have to wait on me," she muttered, though she stood still while he dried her hair, carefully rubbing the strands between the material as her breathing became ragged from the emotional and sensual pull he exuded.

"I'm not waiting on you," he growled. "You're hurt. I'm taking care of you."

She snorted at that. If she left it up to him she doubted she would manage to lift a limb to do more than fuck him on a continual basis.

He dried her off quickly, effectively. He knew his way around a woman's body and she didn't doubt that he had plenty of experience doing just this. It should be criminal to be so damned sexy, she thought.

"Sam's back with breakfast." He handed her a clean gown and robe as he tossed the towel in the laundry basket. "The new diner in town finally started serving 'To Go' orders."

Sarah snorted.

"They did not. I talked to the owner last week. Who was, by the way, bitching ninety miles a minute over Sam's determination to get breakfast to go."

"Well, Sam has the food, that's all I care about." She could hear the smile in his voice as he pulled the gown over her head.

"What did he do, seduce the daughter?" She demanded, incredulous. "Juarez is going to get pissed," she warned him, speaking of the father and owner Juarez's Bar and Café.

"No. He didn't seduce the daughter." He grinned. "He spent the last week ordering then placing the food in the go boxes he bought from the diner down the street. Which incidently had the name of said diner on it. Juarez nearly had a stroke from what Sam said."

Sarah groaned in resignation. "He's going to end up dead."

Sam's high jinks was nearly has gossip worthy as the family's sexual practices. He was a devil-may-care, smiling temptation. Or so they said. Sarah didn't think so though. There was something about Sam that warned her that the smiles and fun-loving hilarity was only superficial."

"Most likely," Brock agreed as he helped her get the robe on then buttoned it quickly. "Come on, let's feed you, then we'll talk..."

"It's not happening." Sarah faced the combined efforts of Marly and three determined August men over the breakfast table an hour later. "You guys may as well pack up and head for home, because I'm not leaving."

"You have got to be the one of the most stubborn women I've ever met in my life," Cade growled, his eyes darkening a near, true blue as he frowned at her, then his wife. "What the hell is it going to hurt you? Do you think for a minute that whoever tried to shoot you is just going to go away, Sarah? This makes two attempts on your life. You really want to risk the third time?"

She pressed her lips together tightly, refusing the answer. The more she argued, the more frustrated, and aroused, these men were becoming. The testosterone was so thick she could cut it with a knife.

"It's my life…"

"Wrong," Brock snarled then.

"Sarah, if something happens to you, it will affect all of us," Marly pointed out then. "It's a weight that it's not fair to expect us to carry."

Genuine concern filled all their expressions, especially Marly's.

"Look, I admit I have a problem," she finally sighed roughly. "But I can't leave. I have a life here, and one I like. I won't be forced into hiding."

She tried to keep her voice steady, determined. It was really hard to do that with the August men.

"I swear we won't touch you, Sarah," Cade finally said softly, drawing her shocked gaze.

To this point, none of the men had even mentioned that aspect. Sarah felt her nerves shudder at the comment.

"We don't want to go there," she snapped in reply, shooting him a silencing look.

A crooked smile touched his lips.

"The subject has to be broached eventually if that's the reason for your reluctance," he pointed out. "I promise you, there will be no pressure. We just want to protect you."

"I don't need your reassurance," she replied sweetly. "I know how to tell you to kiss off, Cade. Unlike the rest of the female population of Madison, I don't think all the August men have dicks of gold."

Marly seemed to choking, but her eyes were glowing with laughter.

"Damn," Sam muttered across from where she and Brock sat, casting Brock a woebegone expression. "I'm the only one with a gold dick? Are you sure we're brothers?"

Brock dropped his head, his expression a grimace of incredulity as he glanced at Sarah's frowning face. She didn't like the amusement glittering in his eyes either.

"You're all insane. And I don't need insane people cluttering up my house and my head. I'm going back to bed. Go home or something. Just leave me alone."

She could tell it was rare, if ever, they were given their walking papers. All three men watched her with varying degrees of shock, and unfortunately, arousal, as she stood up and made her way carefully out of the room. She was praying that if she went back to bed and back to sleep that she would wake up and it was all a dream. Yes, a dream would be much preferable.

Chapter Twenty-One

ဆ

Sarah dragged herself out of bed several mornings later, stumbling to the kitchen with a wide yawn as she headed for the coffeepot. Filling the machine, she walked to the fridge, pulling out a cold can of soda and popped the lid as she sat down at the kitchen table.

Sam, Cade and Marly had left the day before, disgusted by her steady refusal to run away to sin central also known as the August Ranch. Sam she knew would be returning sometime today, supposedly to watch the house while Brock went back himself to pick up more clothes. At this rate, he might as well change his address to hers. He almost had more clothes in her closet than she did.

The house was silent. Almost too silent. The television that she usually kept playing low in the living room had not been turned on the night before. There had been no need to fill the house with sounds; her screams had filled silence instead. She would have blushed if she weren't so damned tired. Her body ached pleasantly, the flesh between her thighs more sensitive than it had ever been. Her breasts were tender and she knew from her blurry perusal in the shower that they were marked with the proof of Brock's passion.

Pulling her robe tighter around her body, a grin tilted her mouth. He had been like a madman after his family left. He had barely made it into the bedroom before he had her on her back again, throwing her into one climax after another then building her up again. She doubted he managed more than a few hours sleep before he left that morning.

Her shoulder was healing well and it was barely sore now thanks to the doctor's salve. The wound hadn't been that bad;

the experience had been horrifying, though. The security system was now installed and Sam was waiting on special locks for the doors just in case someone managed to bypass the system. And Brock was practically living with her.

She had told him he wasn't staying with her. But she was more than aware of the suitcase under her bed, the clothes now hanging in her closet. Not a lot, but enough to assure her that he had no intentions of leaving anytime soon. That thought brought a frisson of worry to her mind. He was moving in and taking over, ignoring her attempts at self-preservation and making love to her until she begged him to stay. And she had no idea how it had happened. She knew he was worried, knew he had been upset by the attack as well, but she couldn't let him take over like this.

Honestly, all she had been looking for was one night. She hadn't expected a new roommate and a lover that kept her exhausted. But she had to admit that this new roommate more than satisfied her. Sarah had never been so well loved, so well satisfied. The rumors about his stamina weren't lies. If anything, they were understatements.

Hearing the last pop of the ancient coffeemaker, she set the remaining cola in the fridge and went for that first cup. She was just tilting it to her mouth when she heard the back door open.

"So what did you forget?" She turned to face a returning Brock and found her ex-husband instead. "What the hell are you doing here?"

Mark Tate was a handsome man, if you could get past the overbearing, sulky expression on his dark, tanning booth-tanned face. His hair was a light brown, cut almost military short, his eyes a soft hazel. His body was toned from hours at the gym and his clothes were always tightly pressed and the height of male fashion. He had drained damned near every last drop of money she had keeping himself attired.

"Checking to see what a crazy woman looks like," he grunted, moving to the coffee pot and snagging one of the cups from the cupboard as she moved out of his way. "Why the hell did let August sic the sheriff on me for, Sarah? That was low. Hell, its not like I have a place to really live yet. And who the hell attacked you the other night? Haven't you figured out you're messing with trouble with the Augusts?"

Sarah saw the signs of his building anger. They were easy to read. The pouty look around his mouth, the surliness in his eyes. He could carry on for hours, his comments like serrated knives tearing at the skin. Over and over, hour after hour until she gave in, did whatever he wanted, just to make him shut up. Just to get him off her back and to find the peace she needed so desperately. The divorce was supposed to facilitate that. He wasn't supposed to return as though he still lived there.

"I'm not in the mood for your irrational tirades, Mark," she told him firmly, sitting back down at the table. "So you can just mosey on home to Lolita and leave me the hell alone. You should have never brought her here to begin with. This is my home."

"Her name's Jackie," he reminded her sullenly.

"Whatever." Sarah raked her fingers through her still damp hair and covered her yawn.

"When's August due back?" he asked her suddenly, snagging a chair and taking a seat across the table as he sneered the question in her face.

Sarah looked up at him in surprise, wondering at the attitude.

"That doesn't concern you, Mark," she told him firmly. "Nothing I do concerns you anymore. Get used to it."

"The whole damn town's talking about your little spectacle at the bar the other night, Sarah." His lips twisted into a grimace. "It's making me look like a fool."

Sarah blinked at him in surprise. After six years of his public infidelities, he had the nerve to say that?

"We're divorced," she pointed out. "It can't make you look like anything."

She watched his face twist in anger. He looked not quite rational, she thought with an edge of worry.

"You're still carrying my name," he threw back at her.

Sarah watched him carefully, wondering if he had been drinking this morning.

"Not for much longer," she assured him tightly. "So why don't you just leave. Brock August, or what I do, is none of your business."

She controlled her flush of embarrassment as she remembered what he had done to her beneath that table, promising her no one could see. But she knew, most likely, no one had seen what his fingers were doing to her. Merely speaking to another man was enough to shame her in Mark's eyes. What was good for the gander was definitely not good for the goose.

"Hell, Sarah, if I knew you wanted to play the whore, I could have accommodated you." Mark smiled maliciously. "I have brothers. They liked you well enough to fuck you."

Sarah set her coffee cup down on the table carefully, watching her ex-husband with mingled amazement and anger.

"You're insane," she rasped out furiously. "Why don't you take your coffee and just get the hell out of my house. I didn't ask you to come here."

"Like you asked August?" He followed her when she rose to her feet and stalked to the sink. "Dammit, Sarah, I thought you learned your lesson the night him and his brother nearly had you at that barbeque. What, did the thought of it turn you on as you got older?"

"Get out!" She was shaking with fury now. Fury and fear. She didn't want to hear this, didn't want to hear the truth of what she was trying so hard to walk blindly into.

"Sarah, I don't hate you. I don't want to see you hurt." His voice was soft, edged with faux confusion. She didn't understand this game or its rules. "Dammit, we were married for six years."

"Six cheating, lying years for you," she reminded him, rounding on him. "We weren't married, Mark. You just lived here."

"Doesn't change the fact that I always liked you, Sarah," he breathed out roughly, trying one of his charming, shy grins on her. They didn't work anymore. "Dammit, you're not like his other women."

"Look, Mark, I don't want to discuss this with you," she told him again, shaking her head as she tried to get away from him. "I want you to leave. This is none of your business."

She made to move around him, to stalk from the room and pray he would just leave. Surprise shot through her system when he grabbed her arm painfully, jerking her around. Sarah stared into the flushed, more than furious face of the ex-husband who had never shown any violence towards her, until now.

"Let me go, Mark." She tried to jerk away from him, then cried out painfully when he pushed her against the kitchen wall. Hard.

"Dammit, you will listen to me, bitch," he snarled in her face, his nose inches from hers.

Sarah was in shock. She had never seen this side of Mark. She had been aware it existed, knew of his barroom brawls, but he had never brought it home.

"Mark, you're hurting me," she .whispered, straining against the hard hands that held her arms to the wall. "Let me go."

He was breathing hard, his hazel eyes glittering with his anger as he watched her.

"Do you bend over and let him give it to you up the ass like the other bitches did?" he growled harshly. "Bend over and let me have it then."

Sarah nearly choked on her incredulous fear. She couldn't believe the rage reflected towards her. He acted as though she had somehow wronged him, instead of the other way around. Then fear drove sharp and deep as he ground his hips against her.

"God. Mark, don't do this." She pushed against his chest, feeling the erection against her stomach, seeing the anger-driven lust in his eyes. "What the hell has gotten into you?"

"Your ignorance," he lashed out at her. "You think I want my friends telling me about that bastard shoving his fingers up your pussy at that bar? Did you think no one would check what he was doing for me?"

Her face flushed in embarrassment. No one could have seen, but they could have guessed.

"It's none of your business." She shook her head, fighting the fear washing over her.

His abrupt fury, the violence surrounding her made her choke on the words. She wanted to push away from him, escape the flushed, contorted features staring down at her, but he wouldn't let her go. He held her hard and fast to the wall, his body, not as muscular or as strong as Brock's, yet still more than enough to control her.

"You stink of him," he accused her roughly. "I can smell him on you, Sarah, and you stink."

"Then get away from me." She shrank back from him, turning her head aside as his face pressed closer.

She struggled against him, fearing the irrational anger that seemed to have a hold on him, driving him to want to hurt her. He hadn't gotten this angry when she had slapped the divorce papers in front of him.

"You had the sheriff drag me out of my home," he sneered. "My home, Sarah."

"It's my home," she argued uselessly. "It always was, Mark."

191

"My fucking home, my fucking wife." He jerked her arms, pulling her forward then flinging her across the room.

Sarah caught herself on the kitchen table, backing away from him, her eyes flickering around the room, searching for an escape route. The back door was the closest means of escape. It was still cracked open and would be easy to get past. If she ran to the neighbor's or if they heard her, they would call for help.

She watched his eyes narrow, reading her intentions. Before he could jump for her, she turned and sprinted for the door. She flung it open, then came to a hard, bouncing halt as something blocked her way. Before she could regain her senses, she was set aside with a gentle touch and Mark screamed out in pain.

Sarah pushed the hair from her face, blinking in amazement at the madman gripping Mark's throat, lifting him from the floor then throwing him from the kitchen out the back door.

"Want to die today, gnat?" White teeth flashed in a snarling grin as the enraged man faced her ex-husband.

"You bastard, Brock," Mark screamed at him from a safe distance. "She'll pay for what she's done to me. You wait and see."

"Evidently you do." He started for the door.

Mark let out a furious curse before Sarah heard him run for the front of the house. Seconds later, the sound of a vehicle starting then roaring away echoed through the room. She stood still, quiet, watching the large man as he turned to face her with a charming smile.

"Mornin', Sugar." He made to reach down and kiss her, but Sarah moved quickly out of his way.

"Where the hell is Brock and why are you here?" she asked Sam August, an edge of hysterical fury working its way into her voice.

192

Sam grinned, a soft tilt to his lips almost identical to Brock's. It was the eyes though that warned her of the difference. Sam's, though, crinkled with laughter. His lips, edged with a smile, were shadowed and saddened worse than Brocks.

For a horrifying second she remembered what Brock had told her. The painful acts they had been forced to inflict on each other and her heart broke for this brother as well.

"How did you know?" he asked, closing the back door and walking to the coffee pot. "We're usually hard to tell apart if we aren't together."

She didn't know how anyone could miss the differences. Brock's brooding intensity was there on his face, in the small lines at his mouth and eyes. Sam's was carefully hidden beneath a cheery false front. That deception worried her.

He poured the last cup of coffee, then turned back to her, watching expectantly.

"You do not live here." Sarah felt like stomping her foot. What the hell was going on? Men were going crazy today. "You don't live here and you have no right to act as though you do."

He lifted a brow in a gesture of curiosity.

"I just saved your virtue. Surely I deserve a cup of coffee?" he groused good-naturedly.

"I didn't have any virtue left to save," Sarah snapped, shaking now in reaction and anger. "Your brother took care of that already." Horror consumed her at the words coming out of her mouth. But she couldn't seem to stop.

"Where was I?" He frowned in mock bemusement. "Surely he would have invited me for the last scrap of virtue. Brock was never a greedy person before."

Shock held her immobile, her mouth open, her eyes rounded. She felt like a fish gasping for air. She shook her head, her hands gripping the sides of it as she felt reason wash away on incredulity. He was admitting to it. As though it were

193

no more than a kiss on the cheek, admitting to a lifestyle she could not comprehend, no matter the reason. And acting as though it were already a done deed. A forgone conclusion that she would participate.

"Get the fuck out of my house!" She kept her voice low, calm, despite the fury overwhelming her. "Get out and don't come back and tell that moronic brother of yours not to come back. God. Damn it, I don't need this."

Sam leaned against the counter, smiling in that crooked way that so reminded her of Brock.

"It's okay, Sarah. I didn't come here to jump your bones. Brock had some stuff to take care of at the ranch that's going to keep him a few hours longer than he expected. He asked me to come over and stay with you instead of cramping my legs in that damned truck across the street."

Sarah frowned at that information. Her jaw tightened, her fingers fisting in her robe.

"Marly?" she asked him, her voice sounding strangled. She knew, saw it in Sam's eyes, felt it in the tightening of her heart. It was this that she couldn't accustom herself to. This knowledge, the acceptance Brock needed that he could bring another woman pleasure with her acceptance, her approval.

Sam shrugged. "Cade's in a fit over this shit, Sarah. You won't come to the ranch and we can't stay here and still take care of things at home. He's worried about Brock, and about you."

"What does that have to do with Brock fucking Marly?" Tears came to her eyes as her hands shook, her body trembled. "Why didn't you fuck her instead?"

The anger was nearly overwhelming. The years she had spent, humiliated by Mark's infidelities surged through her mind. It didn't matter that it was just Marly. Knowing why didn't ease that terrible, first flash of pain. It didn't ease the flash of curiosity either, and that one was the hardest to deal with.

"Sarah, that's enough." Sam's voice firmed, somber concern filling it now. "I'm not the one with a woman in danger and up to her neck in stubborn. This isn't about sex. I know Brock told you that."

"But he's having sex with her," she pointed out incredulously. "He went back to fuck her. How can he fuck her? He spent all night coming inside me."

Sam grimaced with a flash of amusement.

"Damn, Sarah, stop making my own hard-on worse." He grinned with easy humor. "You think I didn't want to stay? Instead I'm here with you. The least you could do is go easy on me."

She threw the coffee cup at him instead, barely missing his head and turned to rush from the room. Sam caught her in the doorway, his arms wrapping around her, his head bending to her ear as she stood in frozen surprise at the feel of his erection at her back.

Sarah stilled. She felt heat rock her body, felt her vagina tremble in awareness of his arousal for her. It wasn't supposed to be like this, she protested silently. She wasn't supposed to want another man. No other should arouse her; no other should draw her. She loved Brock. Knew she did, deep in her soul. Just as she knew how desperately Brock needed exactly what she was feeling.

She stifled a moan. The images Brock had painted in her mind rushed over her. Sam and Cade touching her, taking as he watched, reveling in her cries of pleasure. She bit her lip, fighting the wickedness, the depravity of the desire.

"He told you he would do this, didn't he, Sarah? Did Brock lie to you?" he asked her softly, compassionately.

"No," she whispered, knowing he had told her of the complicated relationship he shared with his family. Knowing he had begged her to come back to the ranch that day, if not for her own safety, then so she could understand the

195

implications of that relationship. He had known, she realized, that he would be fucking Marly when he returned without her.

She couldn't halt the whimper that escaped her throat. But not of pain as it should have been. The insidious tendril of curiosity that weaved through her body had her pussy tightening, weeping in shameful anticipation of pleasure.

"It's hard as hell to accept," Sam whispered, his warm breath caressing her neck as he leaned closer. "Hard to make love all tidy and easy on the heart when dealing with this. I know that, Sarah, and so does Brock and Cade. Brock would cut out his own heart before he would betray you. But you have to understand, this isn't a betrayal of you. It's an acceptance of his brothers."

Unfortunately, she did understand that, and that bothered her more than anything else. Coming to grips with the reality of it though was harder. How do you break a lifetime of beliefs and morality in the space of a few weeks? It wasn't possible. She didn't know if it would ever be possible.

Sam's lips were at her neck, whispering over her flesh as he spoke. One hand was flat against her abdomen, the other just under her heaving breast. Sarah could feel her breasts swelling, her nipples hardening. The fire wasn't as intense, as white-hot and brilliant as it was with Brock, but it was there just the same.

She shivered as his tongue touched her neck. He licked her softly and Sarah found she couldn't halt the small moan that escaped her throat.

"Let me go, Sam." She swallowed tightly. She shouldn't let him touch her. Shouldn't think of what Brock was doing now, of what he wanted her to do. She knew, knew to the bottom of her soul that if she fucked Sam, he wouldn't care. He would find pride, pleasure in the act. He would look at her, his eyes glowing with warmth, with lust at the knowledge. That thought seemed to fuel her own heat. She felt the warm cream of her arousal sliding delicately from her vagina, coating the lips of her cunt.

"Your heart is beating out of control, Sarah," he told her softly. "You can't tell me that if I touched your pussy it wouldn't be wet and hot."

She fought for breath. Why had Brock done this? Why was he pushing her this way? Why was she letting him?

"I asked you to let me go," she gasped, feeling his fingers flex at her stomach.

"Is your pussy wet, Sarah?" he asked her, his warm breath caressing her ear. "Do you see what Marly feels when we touch her?"

Sarah fought to breathe. Her chest was rising and falling with harsh breaths, her flesh weakening. She fought the insidious arousal. She wasn't this weak, this vulnerable. She couldn't allow herself to be.

"Let me go before I kick your ass, Sam August," she bit out then, her nails biting into his arms where she gripped them. The words were tough, the voice behind it weak as his teeth scraped her neck.

"I won't take you without Brock here, Sarah," he promised her, then a strangled cry erupted from her throat as he took one hard nipple between his fingers, pressuring it firmly.

Fire lanced from her breast to her womb, tightening her stomach. It was the edge of pain, she told herself desperately. That was what sent that erotic thrill heaving through her body, made her cunt spasm, her juice to spill along the thick curls there. The edge of pain was all it took. Her vagina trembled, pleaded for surrender.

"Stop," she whispered pleadingly. "Please stop, Sam."

"He's not just fucking his brother's lover, Sarah," his voice was gentle, but the words cut at her like a knife. "He's reassuring his brother. He's giving him a hug. He's promising him he'll be careful. He's shedding tears for Cade's sacrifices for him. Do you understand that?"

The pain of the act Brock was committing was suddenly gone, replaced by the agonizing lance of grief. The reminder of the pain, the scars inflicted on his soul. Not just his soul. Cade's, Sam's. And now hers as well.

"I understand." She whispered, trembling, terrified of the emotions, the arousal pulsing through her body."

"He's with Cade and Marly," Sam whispered again. "And I'm here with you. Protecting you, holding you. I like holding you, Sarah..." She didn't like the soft, almost boyish sound of pleasure in his voice as he rubbed his cheek against her hair.

She wanted to deny the emotion that his tone of voice evoked in her. For a moment, one insane mad moment, she wished Brock were there, watching them, experiencing whatever it was he needed so desperately, with her at the center of it.

"Sam..." That wasn't a moan, she assured herself, it was a protest. Yes, that was what it was. A protest.

Sam stilled behind her. His fingers flexed on her nipple again, drawing a hard breath from her lungs as she stared sightlessly ahead of her.

"Sometimes, it's that little bit of pain that feels best," he told her gently, his teeth scraping over her neck. "That biting heat. The thrill of the unknown. The forbidden, curling flames that wash over you when it comes."

His teeth pressed against the sensitive muscle of her neck, making her shiver with the pleasure that rushed through her system.

"Enough," she rasped, her hands gripping the arm wrapped around her upper stomach.

"Are you sure?" He whispered silkily. "I can show you how good it can be Sarah. How hot..." his voice was curiously tender, not pleading, yet not demanding either.

"I'm sure." But she wasn't, not really, and that scared her more than anything else.

He released her slowly. Sarah took a hard, relieved breath, then moved quickly from the room. Away from Brock's brother, away from his grief and his lust. But she knew she couldn't forget it. She couldn't escape it. The silky slide of her own arousal on her thighs would ensure that.

Chapter Twenty-two

ဢ

"Your brother does not belong in my house." Sarah's surprising greeting was his welcome into the house that evening.

Brock paused for a moment, seeing the agitation in her body, the shade of guilt in her eyes and hid his smile. His heart swelled with emotion as he watched her, the way her gaze held that shade of remembered pleasure, arousal. There was a curiosity in her expression that he knew she was unaware of. It made his cock swell, throb.

"Neither does Tate, but I hear he made a nuisance of himself anyway," Brock told her, carrying the intimate purchases he had made earlier to the counter. "Why didn't you leave the door locked after I left?"

She shrugged. "He has the key. I never changed the locks."

Brock stared at her in surprise. For a moment, he couldn't actually believe she had said that.

"Why not?" He fought to hang onto his control.

"Just didn't get around to it." She walked over to the bag, opening and peeking inside.

Brock was distracted from his anger at her easy acceptance of Mark walking in whenever he liked. He watched her eyes widen, her face flush as she glimpsed his purchases. Her lips opened as though to speak. Closed. Opened again. Finally, she clamped them shut and turned her gaze to him hesitantly as she swallowed tightly. His anger over the locks dissolved. Fuck it, he could fix the locks himself.

"What's for dinner?" He wasn't about to give her the chance to refuse him. "What's in the bag is for later."

She blinked, a little shocked. A little confused. "Chicken from KFC. I don't cook much."

He smiled. "I'll take a breast and thigh, hon. My favorite pieces."

Sarah gave an unladylike snort. "Not the piece I was thinking about, but whatever."

"I have to shower." He patted her rear in payment for her remark then headed for the shower.

* * * * *

Brock watched Sarah stomp around the house early that evening. Her angel's face mutinous, her curvy body stiff and tense as she washed the few dinner dishes, cleaned off the table, ignored the innocent-looking paper bag in the center of it, then swept the floor. He leaned against the doorframe; his arms crossed over his chest, his brows lowered into a frown that he knew could intimidate the strongest adversary. But Sarah only ignored him. Him and the contents of the bag.

Not that he had expected her to accept this without a fight. Hell, he may even end up on her shit list for all time, but he didn't think he would. He had seen the flare of curiosity in her eyes, the spark of arousal before her body stiffened and she became queen bitch for the evening.

He hid his grin. She could put the stubborn on better than any woman he knew or heard tale of. But he could be just as determined; she would find that out quickly.

"You should have got the locks changed after you got home from work."

Brock worried about this Mark thing. Her ex-husband didn't seem too willing to let her go.

"I'll get it done." She washed her hands in the sink after sweeping the non-existent dust into a dustpan and tapping it into the garbage can. "I'll call in the morning."

"Sam will take care of it in the morning instead," he told her. "I trust him to take care of the job right with those locks he ordered this morning."

She frowned at that; evidently she didn't care much for the thought of Sam coming out again. She was nervous around him, his brother had reported, nervous and expectant, as though she expected him to jump her at any second. She was displaying those same signs now.

"You were with Marly today," she whispered the words without heat, surprising him with the change of subject.

Brock stared at her for long moments. There was no anger, no recrimination, just a quiet fight for understanding. He didn't know what to say to her, didn't want to hurt her.

"I was with Marly," he agreed sadly. God he wished he could make it easier for her. Make her understand.

"You fucked her." He watched her take a deep, steadying breath.

She looked vulnerable, so damned uncertain of herself that he wanted to scream out in pain. His Sarah was confident, strong, and knowing he had done this to her broke his heart.

"I fucked her." He nodded. He wouldn't lie to her, he wouldn't apologize, no matter his pain, his regret. He was who and what he was. She had to accept him as that. She knew before she came to that damned bar what he was and what he would want. He wouldn't make excuses now.

She was silent for long moments, as though expecting something from him. He knew she was expecting him to mention Sam. To mention how his brother reported their confrontation, how he touched her. Brock didn't fight his rising erection at the thought of Sam touching her, or her pleasure in it. Sam had smiled with a reckless pleasure that had been missing in him since Marly's attack the year before.

"Brock." She licked her lips nervously. "Sam—" Her gaze flickered away, her face flushing in guilt.

"Sam what, Sarah?" He was more than aware of what had happened.

She bit at her lip.

"Sam touched you today, Sarah?" he asked her softly. "I know that, baby."

He didn't know if he imagined the little whimper, one filled with arousal that escaped her lips.

"Did you tell him—" She was fighting fear and desire. He could see the shy hunger, the confusion that filled her.

"No, Sarah, I didn't tell him to touch you," he assured her, his chest tightening as she watched him, on the edge of discovery and so frightened to trust him to cushion her fall. "Did he hurt you?"

She shook her head, staring everywhere but at him.

"Did it feel good, Sarah?" he asked her softly, tilting his head as he watched her hands twist nervously at her waist.

She took a hard breath, merely shrugging her shoulders as she turned away from him.

"Sarah." He stopped her, pulling her against his body. "Did you want him?" Brock's cock was throbbing at the thought.

"I was angry with you. He touched me." She was fighting for an excuse, a reasonable way to explain the flare of heat she found in his brother's arms.

"And you got wet. Your pretty little nipples got hard for him and Sam would have touched them, maybe made them feel good the way you like."

Her nipples were beaded now, but he'd be damned if he would touch her, take her too soon. She shrugged, clearly uncomfortable. He let it go for now. It was enough that she acknowledged the pleasure.

"Do you work tomorrow?" Brock moved away from her. He wanted to hide his grin as he caught her nervous glance toward the bag once again.

"Not tomorrow." She shook her head, standing by the sink as though she didn't quite know what to do with herself. "I only go in a few days a week now."

"Good." He nodded.

He walked over to the table, holding her gaze the whole way. He picked up the bag he had placed there earlier and moved it closer to the edge of the table.

"Take care of this now, Sarah." He watched her eyes widen.

Brock's body tensed. Arousal flowed through his system as her face flushed heatedly and those big golden eyes widened in surprise as he lifted the items from the bag that he wanted to keep downstairs with him.

"It's been a long day, Brock. I think I'm just heading to bed." She made to do just that.

Brock caught her at the doorway, his arm snaking around her waist, drawing her against his body. He felt her gasp and knew she was more than aware of the erection beneath his jeans.

"Sarah, I won't let you run away. You'll enjoy this, I promise." He bent and kissed her neck gently, feeling the hard throb of her pulse just beneath her skin. "It's okay baby, I promise I won't hurt you."

"I'm not ready for this." Her nails pressed into the skin of his arm as his teeth raked over her sensitive flesh.

"Yes you are, Sarah. You've been ready for years." He licked the lobe of her ear, feeling her tremble beneath his touch.

Her skin was so soft. She tasted of peaches and heat and made his mouth water, his body pulse in demand. She drew in a quick, hard breath as he pushed the paper bag in her hand.

"Go to the bathroom and get ready now, Sarah. I'll be waiting down here for you. And don't take too long, or I'll have to come up there and help you." He injected an edge of warning in his tone. She shivered, but the heat coming from her body had nothing to do with fear.

She took the bag from his hand, glancing up at him nervously, then walked through the house. Brock stood still, his eyes on her the whole time, keeping his expression implacable as she glanced back at him time and again. Her eyes were wide, excitement and fear glittering in the dark depths with equal intensity.

Finally, she disappeared and he breathed a sigh of relief. Going back to the table he picked up the articles he had taken out of the bag. A large tube of lubricating jelly, a mid-sized butt plug and a long, thick gel-filled dildo. He picked them up and walked back into the living room.

He laid the articles on the oaken coffee table, and moved to close the window shades throughout the room. Next, he dragged a large blanket from the linen closet and spread it over the wide couch. Upstairs, he could hear the shower running. He closed his eyes, anticipating Sarah's return. She would prepare herself for him, just as he intended. Tomorrow, she would go even further. Her appointment with Denise Lamont would see to the removal of the soft curls between her thighs. He could hardly wait to see her smooth and soft there, those silken lips spreading around the thick length of his cock. He breathed out a harsh breath. His cock was steel hard, throbbing beneath the material of his jeans.

Tamping down on the lust rising in his body, Brock took a deep breath, then lit the large, fat candles he had placed around the room. Turning the lights off, he surveyed the effects of the soft glow and smiled in anticipation. He pulled his clothes off, throwing them over the back of a chair and sat back on the couch, knowing Sarah wouldn't be much longer.

The instructions in the note he had included in the bag had warned her to come downstairs naked. He couldn't wait to see her, fresh from her shower, her skin glowing in the candlelight. His hand massaged his hard cock as he thought of her, pink and ripe, juicy and wet, coming to him, knowing what he would prepare her for. She wasn't being tricked or lied to. She would know because he would tell her. He refused to lie to her about the plans he had for her.

"Brock?" He turned his head at the sound of her voice.

Brock rose to his feet, his eyes narrowing at the sight he beheld. Just as he knew, skin so pretty and pink, a flush of arousal staining her breasts and cheeks. She was naked, not entirely comfortable with it, but standing before him, excited.

"Come here." He held his hand out to her, fighting the need to throw her to the couch and pound into her mercilessly.

She came into his arms, her eyes locked with his, flashing with uncertainty and heat. Her skin was warm against his hands, against the sensitive flesh of his throbbing cock. He inhaled the smell of peaches and warmth and closed his eyes as he fought for control. Tonight. Tonight he would know if she had the strength to satisfy all his needs, or just the most immediate. God help him if she didn't, because he had a feeling he needed her too much to ever let her go.

"What are you going to do, Brock?" She was trembling against him. Brock could feel the small, almost imperceptible shudders that racked her body.

"I'm going to love you, Sarah, the only way I know how," he whispered against her hair as he drew her to the couch. Sitting down, he pulled her to his lap.

She curled into his arms, fitting him perfectly. Her head lay on his chest, her hair, still just a bit damp, caressing his flesh. He tangled one hand in the honey gold mass as the other smoothed gently from her knee to her ankle.

She didn't question him, though Brock had expected her to. The fact that she wasn't showed him the lingering fears she was holding. He had tonight to convince her that she could do what he needed.

"You're so soft, Sarah." He nudged at her chin. "So soft and warm. And all mine."

Her face rose, her eyes dark and somber in the soft glow of the candles. Brock couldn't resist kissing her. His head lowered, his lips settling on hers as they opened to admit the firm stroke of his tongue. He swallowed her low moan as she relaxed in his arms, turning to him, her tongue tangling with his.

She tasted as sweet as sugar, like nectar, fresh and dew kissed. He lowered her against the arm of the couch, her body stretched across his like an offering to some primeval god of lust. Her thighs shifted, parted as his hand swept up her leg. She was already wet for him, already soft and needy.

His lips sipped at hers slowly, his tongue washing over the gentle curves. He loved her mouth, had dreamed of it for years. He sucked lightly at the bottom curve, hearing her moan, his heavy lidded eyes watching the emotion and arousal that crossed her face. She was beautiful. So damned beautiful it hurt.

"Brock," she whispered his name, her neck arching for the lips that trailed over it.

Skin so sweet, so soft he could devour her. Brock took a gentle nibble, then soothed the little bite with a lingering movement of his tongue. He felt her breath escalate, heard the hot entreaty in her keening moan. She arched in his arms, tilted her head to allow him greater access.

His lips moved across the expanse of skin, feeling the throb of blood beneath the living silk, pounding through her veins, rushing through her system. He could feel it echo in his own body, in the hard erection cushioned by her hip and the thump of his heart in his chest.

Brock's lips went to her breasts; one hand cupped the full mound as she arched over his arm, his mouth covering the turgid tip. She twisted against him sensually, pushing against him harder as he licked and sucked with slow, light movements. She needed more, needed harder. She had a taste of the pleasure that came from a minute bite of sensual pain. He knew she wanted more.

Brock made her wait. Deliberate, hesitant licks of his tongue had her crying out in a fever of need. He wanted her like this. Arching and crying beneath him, begging for the pleasure he could give her.

"What do you want, Sarah?" he asked her as he ran his tongue around the flushed, reddening pucker of flesh. It tightened further, pouting out at him in need.

"Please, Brock." Slender fingers clenched in his hair, trying to draw him closer, to make him give her what she needed.

"Tell me what you want, sugar." He blew a whisper of breath across the damp flesh. Sarah trembled with a panting moan.

"Harder," she begged him, her voice breathless. "Please, Brock. Harder."

His head lowered again. He took the hard flesh into his mouth, suckling it deep as his teeth nipped and his tongue stroked. She nearly arched out of his arms as her back bowed, her hands pulling his head closer.

He nibbled at her, knowing the quick little flares of heat would drive her crazy. She cried out for him, her legs twisting, thighs tightening. Perspiration dotted her skin with a sexy glaze, making the slide of his hand over her stomach smooth and silky.

Sarah's thighs fell open as he neared them, but Brock wasn't ready to take her there yet. He wanted her hotter, wilder. He wanted her willing to do anything he asked, go to any lengths for the climax he could bring her. Brock kept his hand above the damp flesh, his fingers playing at her hips, her heaving abdomen, or plumping her firm breasts as he suckled first one, then the other, his teeth nipping at them, his tongue soothing the little ache.

"It's too much," she cried out, breathless, tormented. "Please Brock, please do something."

He raised his head, staring into her eyes, feeling her nails biting into his shoulders and loving the little sting.

"What do you want me to do, Sarah?" he asked her as his thumb ran over her swollen lips. She had bit at them, fighting the need. The proof of it marked the reddened skin.

"Anything, Brock. Whatever you want." She shook her head, her eyes wild as his hand smoothed to her hips once again.

"Anything, Sarah?" he asked her intently. "Anything I want?"

She hesitated, breathing roughly, knowledge and a very small measure of fear reflected in her eyes now. She knew he would push her. Knew it was time to face the demons that pushed him.

"Anything, Brock," she said the words he had to hear. "Anything. Just please, do something."

Brock nearly lost control in that single moment. He fought, baring his teeth as he gritted them harshly. His hands moved her, laying her back on the couch as he moved over her, his mouth taking hers fiercely as two fingers plowed into the tight heat of her cunt.

Her hips came off the cushions as her juices gushed over his fingers like hot cream. Her hands tangled in his hair, her moan filling his mouth, his tongue filling hers.

She twisted against the impalement, pushing her hips harder against it as she begged for more.

"Not yet, Sarah," he panted huskily, feeling his control slipping dangerously. "Soon baby. Soon."

His lips wandered down to her neck, taking frantic, biting kisses as his fingers moved in and out of her tight flesh, sinking in slow and easy, pulling back, relishing her pleas.

He attended to her breasts once again. Suckling hard and deep at the reddened nipples, then licking his way down her heaving stomach. Heat and need pulsed from between her thighs, drenching his hand as it flowed from the depths of her vagina.

"Easy, Sarah," He groaned, lying between her thighs, the sweet smell of her arousal driving him insane. "Easy, baby. Let me show you how good it can be."

He reached over to the coffee table and she stilled. Brock stared up at her as, one at a time, he picked up the articles he had laid out. The lubricating jelly, the medium sized plug that would stretch her tender back hole and prepare her for him. The large, gel-filled dildo nearly as thick and long as his own cock. Her breath stilled, a ragged moan escaping her throat as Brock felt her cunt grip the fingers still lodged there. It pulsed, flowed, her rich cream washing over him as he maintained the stare, letting her know that the time for running was now at a halt.

Chapter Twenty-three

જી

Fire seared Sarah's body as Brock stared up at her. He brought the articles from the table slowly, laying them between her splayed thighs as he watched her carefully. At the same time, he kept his fingers inside her vagina, moving them only slightly, only occasionally, keeping her on edge, keeping the wet, sticky warmth flowing there.

"You need to be well lubricated to take the plug," he whispered, his voice rough as he pulled his hand back from her now. "It will stretch you there, make it easier for you to accept my cock."

Sarah couldn't control the whimper that escaped her throat. Soon. Would that be when he shared her as well? She hated the betraying pulse of arousal that filled her body.

"The dildo is firm, but not too hard," he promised her as he kissed her thigh, licking the skin there briefly. "I want to use it on you, Sarah, while you suck my cock. I want you prepared, ready. I want you to know what's coming."

Sarah wanted to close her eyes, but the instructions in the note he gave her forbade that. She had to watch. If she didn't watch, then he would punish her. She wasn't certain what the punishment was, but she had a feeling it just could involve extreme arousal and his refusal to satisfy it.

"Tomorrow, you have an appointment with Denise Lamont. She'll wax your cunt for me." She jerked at that bit of knowledge, an instinctive protest on her lips. "I'll take you," he continued. "I want you smooth and naked here, free to feel every touch of lips and tongue on your flesh. You'll keep a regular appointment with her to keep it smooth. Do you understand?"

Sarah nodded hesitantly. He looked hard, determined.

"Listen to me, Sarah." He stared up at her, his blue eyes glittering fiercely, darkly. "You aren't going to hide from what I want from you. We'll experiment, see what's best for you, but you won't hide from it. From what I take from Marly, do you understand me?" Sarah flinched at the other woman's name.

"Please, Brock." She could handle it, she could. But she didn't know if she could bear hearing about it.

"No. I won't let you hide, Sarah," he denied her. "I don't want to just fuck that pretty cunt of yours. I want to hear you cry out in pleasure when I thrust inside you anally. I want to watch you masturbate. I want to fuck you in a million different places, a million different positions. Understand me. I won't let you balk just because you fear the unknown. And if the time comes, Sarah, I want to watch you as Cade and Sam touch you, as they bring you pleasure, as they fuck you. I will never force you, but I won't let you deny your own pleasure either. I fuck Marly, I do it regularly while Cade participates. While Sam participates."

Sarah wanted to look away from him, but she couldn't. While he spoke, his fingers were touching her, dipping into her cunt, drawing the thick juices down to her anus, then dipping his finger into the tight little hole.

"I'll watch Sarah, while Sam pleasures you. While Cade touches you. Just as you'll watch soon while I take Marly. It has nothing to do with how much I love you; do you understand that? Just as the pleasure you gain from what my brothers do to you has nothing to do with your feelings for me. You have to get that in your mind."

"You did that," she gasped. "Today."

She knew he had now. Had known it when he walked in the door that evening.

"I did," he whispered. "While Cade watched, encouraged her, drank in her screams of pleasure, just as Cade and Sam will take you later."

212

Sarah couldn't halt the rough groan that tore from her throat as that teasing finger finally breached her anus, spearing deeply into the tight little hole. His words weren't lost on her, the image of it had her body pulsing in traitorous arousal. He thrust into the little hole again, slow and easy, the slide of her own juices and the lubricating gel making the penetration effortless.

"God, Sarah, look at you," he whispered then. "Your eyes are so dark, so aroused. Your little nipples hard, your cunt is so wet I could drown in it."

Sarah whimpered, arching to his lips as he drank from her, his tongue spearing into her gripping vagina as he continued to thrust his finger easily into her anus. Stretching her, God, was he using two fingers now? She felt so full, invaded, penetrated, on the verge of a climax so explosive she wondered if she would survive it.

"Easy now," he growled, moving back from her, pulling his tormenting fingers from her greedy body. "I need you to relax as much as possible, Sarah."

Sarah stared at him, dazed beyond belief as he uncapped the lubricating jelly. Seconds later, the cold gel touched her flesh, causing her to flinch.

"It's cold. But it will get warm quick." His smile flashed, wicked and hot.

Sarah shook her head, fighting the need to close her eyes as he began to push his fingers into her tight hole once again. One finger, sliding easy inside her, spreading the gel. Then two, easing into the passage as he spread the cooling lubrication deep inside her. She cried out, but not in pain as she felt three invade her, stretching her. The sensations tore through her, leaving her gasping as he continued to stretch her slowly, his tongue running through her slit as he did so, caressing her clit, keeping her on the edge of release.

"Ready now?" he asked her, raising his head as he lifted the plug from the couch.

Sarah shook her head, her mind fogged, her body lethargic despite the blood surging through her.

"Yeah you are, sugar," he told her, his tone so gentle, so approving her lashes fluttered. Only at the last second did she manage to keep them opened.

Then she felt it. The tip of the plug was inserted into her tight butt hole. Brock spread her legs wide, one bending, placed over his shoulder, the other over the back of the couch.

"Oh God. Brock." She couldn't stop the arch of her body as the thick device began to fill her, stretch her.

Tingling fire shot up her spine, then back down. She could feel her cunt pulsing, leaking her own natural lubrication, preparing itself for what was to come as he pushed the plug deep into her. She writhed beneath him, her hips arching, then a high, startled cry escaped her lips as she felt the flared base lodge past the tight ring of muscles there.

It stretched her impossibly, leaving her gasping, nearly pleading for him to take her now. Right now. But she couldn't speak. The breath strangled in her throat as pleasure washed over in wave after wave.

"Sarah." Brock's voice sounded as strained, as violently aroused as she was now. "Baby. Oh baby. Yes, let it feel good for you."

His head lowered and he was lapping at her cunt like a starving man. His tongue plunged inside her, his hands holding her legs in place as he drank from the well of hot cream her body pulsed into his mouth. Yet, he still refused to let her climax. He brought her time and time again to the edge, only to pull back before she could go over.

Then he lifted the thick, gel-filled dildo from the couch. Sarah cried out as he looked at her. His expression a tight grimace of arousal, his eyes glittering with a raging lust that made her own rise.

"I want you to know the fullness of it," he whispered as he lodged the bulging head of the dildo at her slick entrance. "I want to watch your face, your eyes and know you like it. I want to see your pleasure, Sarah."

Her eyes widened as she felt the sexual toy slowly enter her, part the flesh of her vagina, burning, stretching her. Her head shook in short, jerky movements, her hands fisted in the cushions of the couch. She couldn't stand it. She couldn't. It was too much. Too much and yet not enough. Each slow, thrusting inch being buried inside her made her more aware of the plug lodged in her anus, it made the fiery pleasure sear her body with lightning streaks of arousal so hot she expected blisters.

"Ah, Sarah, how pretty you are," he whispered when she finally cried out, her body bucking, driving the dildo those last inches, lodging it firmly against her cervix. "You're stretched so tight around it, just as you'll be stretched around me."

He pulled the dildo back, then pushed it home again. He did so slowly, his strokes firm but not too fast. Sarah arched desperately to him, an agonized haze of lust burning her alive. Her cunt was stretched as it never had been, and still the dildo was only just a bit smaller than the width of Brock's cock. And how she needed him now. She needed to climax, but the unfulfilling strokes used kept her only poised on the brutal edge of her release.

Through it all, Sarah watched Brock. Their eyes were locked, their needs, their arousal feeding from each other until Sarah could stand no more. She bucked against the slow thrust, lifting to him, her hand gripping his wrist, halting the movement inside her body.

"Fuck me, damn you. Stop teasing me like this." She had to grit her teeth when that small, wry smile tilted his lips.

Then he was removing the dildo, tossing it aside, his eyes darkening, purpose hardening his expression.

"Now, come here." He lowered her legs, then took her hands and pulled her to her knees.

Laying back on the couch, he helped her over him, positioning her over the straining, pulsing head of his cock. Sarah felt the moisture between her thighs increase, knowing he would impale her on the thick length.

"Slowly, Sarah." He gripped her hips, lowering her.

Sarah's head fell back as the head nudged her inner lips, then spread them wide. She was gasping with desire and an edge of fear. The plug filled her, stretched her, and she knew it would make her vagina smaller, tighter. Would it hurt? He was a bit larger than the dildo, harder, hotter. So hot and thick.

He slipped in only marginally. Sarah shuddered. His cock felt like a brand. A thick, hard, incredibly arousing piece of hot steel sliding past her gripping muscles. She tried to impale herself more fully on it, but his hands gripping her hips held her back.

"Slow, baby," he growled, his voice thick, so rough it rumbled from his chest. "Slow and easy."

Inch by excruciating inch he pushed into her. Sarah groaned, her lashes flickering as she fought to keep them open. She was dying; stretching on a wrack of desire so intense, she knew she wouldn't survive it.

"Sarah." Brock bucked against her, lodging another inch of the incredibly thick flesh inside her. "God Sarah, you're so tight. So damned tight."

He slid the last inches into her, seating himself fully inside her as his head tossed on the cushions and Sarah cried out in desperation. She was stretched fully, burningly aware of every inch of hard flesh buried inside her. The tight ache was making her mad for his cock. She wanted him driving inside her, throwing her into madness as she screamed out her release. Instead, he held her still, one hand at her hips as the other pulled her upper body to his, holding her head against his chest.

The position pushed her buttocks higher and placed her clit in direct contact with his pelvic bone.

"Stay still," he ordered, his voice harsh as she tried to thrust against him.

She couldn't. She was mindless with need. She writhed upon the shaft impaling her, her hips twisting desperately.

"Stop." He smacked her ass. Not an easy, light tap. It stung. It sent her into a mindless realm of pleasure that would kill her. Her hips bucked again.

He smacked her again. Sarah cried out in humiliation and a desire so deep and desperate she could no longer control it. His hand landed again on the other cheek. Sharp, loud. Sarah bucked, moaning, nearly crying now the pleasure was so intense. Her buttocks were on fire and she knew she wanted more. The humiliation of it was deep, intense. It was a part of herself that she didn't know if she could handle.

"Sarah. God, Sarah." His hands gripped her hips hard, holding her tight as his body tightened. "Not yet, baby. Not yet."

"Please, Brock," she cried out against his chest as he held her close, her hands gripping his shoulders, need rocking through her as she pleaded with him.

"Stay still, Sarah." His voice was hard now, determined. "I want you to feel, baby. Just feel it. See how good it is? How hot it is to be filled like this?"

"The feeling is killing me, Brock," she cried out into his chest. "I can't stand it. Please let me come."

"Not yet," he groaned. "In a minute. I promise. This is what it will be like, Sarah. What it's like for Marly. Hot and full, stretched and held. It's like that, Sarah. Do you understand?"

She understood. She understood from the first what this lesson meant.

"Yes," she gasped. "Yes, Brock. Now please. Please fuck me."

She twisted against him now, grinding his cock inside her as a shattered cry tore from her throat.

He gripped her hips harder. Slowly he drew back, then pushed into her once again. Easy, lingering strokes that had her nearly screaming out her need for more. Her hips twisted against him, her body bucking as her back arched.

"Damn you," she cried out hoarsely. "Fuck me. Do it now."

"Will you accept it, Sarah?" His voice was tortured. "Tell me now. Now, Sarah. Will you accept their touch?"

"Yes," she screamed, delirious with arousal. "Anything, Brock. Anything, damn you. Just fuck me."

The growl that tore from his throat sounded feral. He gripped her hips then, hard and tight and began to thrust. Sarah lost her breath. Deep, hard thrusts. They speared through her tight cunt, surging through the gripping muscles as he seemed to spear into her very soul.

She lost her sanity. Her back arched as a scream tore from her throat and she shattered. The explosive climax tore through her body with the force of a tidal wave, washing over her, drowning all humiliation, shame or regret. On and on, it pulsed through her body, tightening her cunt around the cock plunging harshly inside it. Until she felt the thick erection jerk, felt Brock shudder then flood her inner recess with spurt after spurt of his thick, hot cum.

Sarah collapsed on his chest, breathing harshly, her body still trembling, her vagina gripping him, pulsing around him. She couldn't move. She could barely breathe. Sweat dripped from their bodies, and the scent of sex and satisfaction wrapped around them with heated remnants of desire.

"God. Damn." Brock's voice was hoarse, astounded as he continued to fight for breath.

He eased Sarah gently to his side, tucking her against the back of the couch as she drifted in a haze of completion, awake, but not really aware.

"Leave me alone," she mumbled, feeling the gentle hands as he brought her to her back and spread her thighs.

She whimpered as she felt him pull the plug free of her body. An echo of her earlier climax pulsed through her body. What had happened to her? She had been mindless, begging, in the grip of something she couldn't understand and didn't want to look at too closely right now.

"It's okay, baby." He soothed her gently as he picked her up in his arms and headed for the stairs. "Come on, I'll carry you to bed."

"You aren't staying tonight. I need to sleep." She laid her head on his chest, sleepiness sheltering as warm and light as Brock's arms.

"You'll sleep," he promised, and Sarah knew she heard a smile in his words. Evidently, he intended to ignore her, just as he had last night.

"Bossy," she muttered as he laid her in the bed then began to clean her thighs gently. The soft warmth of the cloth he used lulled her tired body into settling closer to sleep.

"I have to be," he told her as he kissed her forehead gently. "If I weren't, you wouldn't be so tired right now, Sarah.

Sarah sighed. Was he right? He probably thought he was. She blocked the thought from her head, slipping into the sheltering arms of sleep as she felt the blanket being tucked about her shoulders. He was tender. He kissed her forehead, smoothed his hands over her hair, then darkness enfolded her.

* * * * *

Brock sat at the edge of the bed and watched Sarah sleep. She looked innocent and sexy at the same time. It tightened his chest, made his throat ache with emotion to see her like this, curled close to him, exhausted from satisfaction. The silken, honey-gold strands of hair were tangled around her face and shoulders, the long, light lashes lay like soft shadows on her cheeks. One hand was tucked beneath her cheek, the other lay on his thigh.

He lifted the hand on his thigh, his fingers rubbing over hers lightly. They were soft, long and graceful with short, pink nails. Her palms were so soft, like satin. He brought her hand to his face, holding the warmth of her palm to his cheek as he closed his eyes.

He had waited for her. For six long years he had waited, knowing that eventually, sooner or later, married or divorced, he would have her. The taste she had given him when she was eighteen had driven him insane at times, making him almost desperate to rip her away from the cheating bastard she was married to. The nights he spent at the bar, listening to the braggart running his mouth about his frigid little wife had been hell. But he had endured. He knew better and he knew that to make his move, to show his hand to Mark Tate before the time was right would be a mistake.

He knew Tate too well. Much better than Sarah did, and he knew her ex-husband wasn't about to let her go so easily. How Sarah had managed to get him to sign those divorce papers he had no idea. How she had escaped the marriage with no scars, he was even more uncertain. One thing he did know for sure, after this morning, he was going to have to keep a careful eye on the bastard. From what Sam had told him, he had come in just in time to keep Sarah from being hurt. First the unknown assailant, and now Tate. The danger was growing and he knew he couldn't allow her to stay here much longer.

Brock sighed wearily. He wished he had her at the ranch where he knew she would be safe at any given time of the day. He had a bad feeling about this situation. A feeling Sarah had yet to escape from the bastard.

Chapter Twenty-four

છ

Sarah was furious, embarrassed and intimately bald. The latter directly related to the former and she hated it. She couldn't wear panties; Denise had strictly forbidden it for up to six hours after the waxing. Her flesh smarted, despite the cream the other woman had rubbed onto the flesh of her cunt, and further back to her anus. She had waxed it all. Every tiny hair was gone, and it had hurt.

Not that Brock seemed to care. When she left the house, he had jumped from the Jeep, anticipation filling his expression. She wanted to shove him into the house and let the demonic, wax-happy bitch have a go at him. She changed her mind just as quickly. Denise Lamont appeared like a woman who would be more than happy to ply her trade on Brock's sensitive flesh.

She sat now in Brock's Jeep, silent, her eyes narrowed as they drove back to the house. Brock appeared entirely too smug, the lustful glances he kept casting her way heating her blood despite her determination to not allow it. She didn't want to get wetter. It might sting. It was stinging enough.

"You okay?" he asked her softly, glancing at her once again.

"Fine." She stared mutinously out the windshield. She wasn't ready to forgive him just yet.

"I'm sure it wasn't that bad, Sarah." He frowned, correctly interpreting her anger. "Hell, Marly has it done all the time."

She cast him a controlled glance. She did not want to hear about Marly right now.

"How would you know?" she asked him coolly. "Last I saw, you had all your hair."

He laughed. Damn him, she didn't need his laughter.

"Let me see it." His words had her head swinging around, her eyes widening incredulously at the question.

"Let you what?" she gasped.

"Raise your dress and let me see it." His eyes were heavy-lidded as he glanced over once again. "Come on, Sarah, no one will see."

"That's what you said at the bar," she reminded him. "Evidently someone did see it. Mark knew about it."

She did not need the good gossips of Madison speculating about her riding in Brock's Jeep, flashing her privates. Her face flamed. It was bad enough already. All her old friends were filled with questions. The damned phone had rung off the hook before they left the house. She hadn't been this popular since — her teeth clenched — since the week after the episode six years earlier. Terrific. Just what she needed; everyone knowing about her sex life. She knew about it, she considered that bad enough.

"Mark knew about it?" The question seemed posed very carefully.

"Well, evidently he did. One of his friends was there and kindly informed him of the fact," she related stiffly, remembering the way he had flung the information at her.

"He was laying on the floor to see it then," Brock growled. "I'm not stupid, Sarah. I knew what I was doing."

Jealousy, possessiveness, two emotions she hadn't expected from him, colored his voice.

"Maybe he just guessed." She shrugged. "It doesn't matter. I'm not flashing you in this Jeep, in public. So you can forget it."

Brock sighed, regret radiating from him.

"Can I touch it?" God, he sounded like a little boy wanting to play with a new toy.

"No, Brock." She shook her head, flashing him an exasperated look. "You can't see it and you can't touch it."

"Let me touch it and I'll spank you later," he bargained smugly.

Sarah felt her body heat, her face redden further and her heart jump with excitement.

"Forget it." There was no way in hell she was going to let him touch her.

"Let me touch it and I'll spank *it* later." His voice lowered as he upped the stakes.

God, she was so depraved. The thought of that was actually making her wetter. And she was right. It stung. Damn him.

"No." She knew her voice was strangled with her own excitement.

"I'll spank it if you don't let me see it," he threatened darkly, flickering a glance at her.

Sarah rolled her eyes. "I get spanked either way, so why should I give in?" She tingled at the thought of that. She needed help. Serious psychological help, because she was getting used to the arousal, the needs he inspired in her. She didn't consider it a good thing.

Brock shook his head, his lips tilting in that sexy, knowing grin. That grin made her nervous. He was up to something; she knew it. She trembled at that knowledge. She had promised him anything he wanted last night. His deepest desires if he would just fuck her. The memory of that had hit her the moment she awoke that morning.

"I get to look when we get home. Even if I can't touch for a while." He grinned at her. Evidently he knew exactly how long it would be before she should have sex.

She narrowed her eyes on him.

"I'm not as easy as you think I am, Brock." She nearly winced. Oh, she had really proved that one.

"Sarah, I never imagined you were easy." His voice was suddenly serious, his touch firm as he reached over and gripped her hand. "Anything but. I've waited six years for you, that's long enough for any man."

It was hard for her to imagine that he had been waiting for her, or wanting her all that time. She had assumed years ago that he would have forgotten about her.

Brock's fingers caressed hers; running slowly from base to tip before he raised her hand, then took one into the warmth of his mouth. Sarah's strangled moan filled the interior of the Jeep. He glanced at her from the corner of his eye and she felt his tongue wash over the digit, curling around it seductively.

Sarah watched his profile, seeing the flush on his cheek, the way his other hand gripped the steering wheel tightly. His jeans were bulged and a groan rumbled from his throat.

"I love feeling your mouth wrapped like that around my cock." He gave her finger a last, lingering lick. "All hot and silky, drawing the life out of me as surely as you do my cum."

Sarah swallowed hard; the memory of him filling her mouth took her breath. Then it strangled in her throat as he took her hand and cupped it around the cloth-covered bulge between his thighs.

"Brock, you are a dangerous man," she whispered, breathing out with careful deliberation. "You should seriously be outlawed."

He grinned, then groaned as her fingers tightened around his girth, caressing, her nails scraping over the rough cloth. He was hot, and so hard it made her mouth water.

"Thank God I almost have you home," he growled. "You'll pay for that later, Sarah." The silky promise caused her thighs to tighten in need. The slight stinging of her sensitive flesh was now more erotic than painful. God, she thought desperately, she was so pathetic.

He pulled into the driveway and drove into the carport. Parking beside her small Corolla, he slammed the Jeep into park and threw open his door.

"Let's go, I want to see." His voice was tight, anticipation lacing the tone.

"Geez, Brock, you're so romantic." She laughed as she got out of the Jeep and headed for the door. "You act like it's Christmas."

"Damn. This has to have any Christmas present I ever got beat." He stuck the key in the lock and opened the door with a quick flick of his wrist.

Brock grabbed her wrist, pulling her in behind him, then came to an abrupt stop. Sarah's eyes widened at the destruction that greeted her. Her kitchen had been destroyed. The table lay in pieces, glasses and plates shattered on the floor. The refrigerator had been emptied, its contents staining the walls, counters, and cabinets.

"Oh my God." She couldn't believe the destruction.

She tried to push past Brock, but his body blocked her, tense and dangerous as he pushed her out of the house.

"Get in the Jeep." His voice brooked no argument.

"No, I have to see—"

"Dammit, Sarah, get back in the fucking Jeep." He threw his door open and pushed her inside before jumping in himself. "Don't you dare try to get out of that door or I'll tan your hide with my belt."

The heavy violence in the warning had her sinking back in her seat, her eyes wide as she watched him. He started the Jeep, backing up and pulling out of the driveway as he jerked his cell phone from its case at his waist.

"Sam, where are you?" he barked when the call was answered. "Forget the locks. Meet me on the street outside Sarah's house, someone's destroyed her place."

He disconnected then called the sheriff. Sarah sat stiff and quiet as he parked on the tree-shaded lane, listening to him talk. She wrapped her arms around her chest, fighting the shock that wanted to take over. Someone had destroyed her home. That knowledge lay like a hard, heavy weight in her chest.

Who could hate her that much? And if it were the same man who tried to kill her, what made him think this would hurt Brock? It made no sense to her. She stared through the trees at her home, watching it, wondering if he was still there. Was he still destroying everything she had while she sat, helpless, unable to stop him?

"Sarah? Are you okay, baby?" Brock wrapped his arm around her, leaning close as he tipped her head up to look into her face. "Damn, you're white as a sheet."

Sarah shook her head. She didn't want to be cuddled right now, she didn't want to be bothered. She wanted to sit there and try to make sense of what happened. Her well-ordered, fully structured life had just gone to hell. And she couldn't figure out how.

"Sheriff will be here in a minute," he promised her. "We'll get this taken care of, Sarah. Don't worry."

How, she wondered, did he intend to take care of this? So far, she had been attacked, her house destroyed and her life ran roughshod over by the August men. It seemed to her that her problems had begun the night she brought him home with her. She wouldn't change the time she was spending with Brock, but God help her, she was at a loss as to how to deal with this. From the looks of her kitchen, someone hated her with an all-consuming fury. Hated her enough to risk exposure to break in during the light of day to destroy her home.

Brock's hands rubbed up and down her arms as he spoke. His voice soothing, low and deep as he tried to comfort her. Sarah lay against him, absorbing the heat of his body, still trying to reject the reality she had seen within her home.

"I'm ready to wake up now," she told him, fighting her tears as she turned away from the house. "Wake me up now."

"Oh, Sarah." His voice was pain-laden, harsh with worry. "If I could just wake you up and make it all go away, then I swear I would, darlin'."

"Who's doing this? Why are they doing this?" She couldn't understand the reasoning behind such actions. She wondered if there even was a reason.

"I don't know who or why, baby," he sighed against her hair. "But I promise, we'll find out. That's all I can do."

As he spoke, the flashing light of the sheriff's cruiser reflected in the rearview mirror. Sarah looked over at her house once again and had a feeling she had spent her last night in it.

"Sheriff's here with Sam." He eased her up minutes later, frowning as he lifted her face once again. "I know you're scared, Sarah. We'll get this taken care of. Come on, let's talk to the sheriff."

Chapter Twenty-five

ஐ

The sheriff wasn't the only one arriving. Pulling in behind him was Sam and behind him the elder brother, Cade August, and his petite lover, Marly. Cade was tall, stern looking, with steel hard gray eyes, and a finely tuned muscular body. He resembled the brothers in looks, though Sarah could tell the man would be a much more dangerous adversary than his brothers. If you got on his wrong side. She knew he had been at her home the night of the attack, but she didn't remember seeing him. And he and Marly had left before she awakened the next day.

Marly was another story. She was small, delicate, with expressive deep blue eyes and a very worried expression. The minute she caught sight of Brock she ran to him, throwing herself in his arms. His arms went around her in a swift hug, his big body wrapping around her in a protective manner. Much as he did with Sarah while having sex.

Releasing her, he stepped back to Sarah, wrapping his arms around her again as he looked at Cade questioningly. Sarah could smell the delicate scent the other woman wore on him how. A scent she smelled on him often. God, she couldn't believe what she was allowing herself to get sucked into. Did she have no resistance to this man?

"You're all right?" Marly questioned him, staring up at him in concern. "We were on our way out here when Sam called. You scared the life out of me, Brock."

"I'm fine, Munchkin, we both are," he promised her, frowning as his brother watched them from shuttered, cool eyes.

"Why were you headed out here?" Brock frowned at his brother. Cade's eyes flickered to Sarah, before returning to Brock.

"We have trouble," Cade informed him quietly, keeping his voice low as Sam took care of the sheriff and led them to the house. " Get Sarah some clothes, you'll have to bring her to the ranch. Rick refuses to even consider that a guard outside her house is enough now."

Shock held Sarah rigid. What guard? And who was he to insist she go anywhere?

"Excuse me, but Brock isn't my keeper, Mr. August," she informed him sweetly, ignoring the flash of trepidation that his spearing look sent through her stomach. "I don't need to come to the ranch."

Marly bit her lip as Cade's body seemed to tighten dangerously. Sarah watched that telling sign. Why would her defiance be a source of worry?

"Ms. Tate, I understand your reluctance to do so. But there's more going on here than you know. The attack was bad enough, but it won't stop. And it endangers not just your life, but Brock's," he warned her, the color in his eyes shifting, swirling.

"What happened?" Sarah didn't like the suspicion or the throb of concern in Brock's voice.

"I received an envelope of pictures in the morning mail." Cade's hard glance sliced into Sarah once again, almost making her shiver. "Evidently, we didn't get the right man last year."

"Pictures?" Brock asked carefully.

Cade glanced at Sarah and she felt bile rise in her throat.

"A candlelit room and a very willing woman," Cade told him carefully. "Get your woman home, Brock. Until we can find out what the hell is going on."

Sarah stared in shock at the elder brother. Pictures? A candlelit room? Her face flamed. He had to be talking about her and Brock and the previous night when they spent in the living room. She opened her mouth to pour out a torrent of questions when the sheriff chose that moment to step forward.

"Brock, I need a statement from you two," he told him, his voice brisk, official. "Let's get it taken care of so Ms. Tate can find a place to stay tonight. We won't be finished with the house until late."

Sarah turned to the sheriff carefully.

"It was just the kitchen," she said, though she somehow knew better.

"I'm damned sorry, Sarah." Joshua Martinez shook his head carefully, pulling the sheriff's hat from his head, watching her with sympathetic eyes. "Whoever it was got the whole damned house. Clothes, furniture. Looks like he took an ax to just about everything."

Sarah gasped, her knees weakening. She knew if Brock hadn't been holding onto her, she would have fallen to the ground in shock. Everything? She didn't have much, but damn, it had been hers.

"Easy, Sarah." Brock's voice wrapped around her, gentle, supportive.

She shook her head, pushing away from him, desperate for enough room to think.

"Who would do this?" She shook her head, finding it hard to understand such destruction.

"What about Mark, Sarah?" The sheriff glanced back at Brock shortly, his suggestion loaded with implications.

"Why?" She shrugged. "The divorce was final weeks ago, Josh. There's no reason for him to do this."

"He's been running his mouth about you and Brock a bit. Seems pretty put out over how easy you've put it behind you," he told her. "Have you seen him lately?"

Sarah shrugged, remembering Mark's last visit to the house. He had been enraged, something she had never seen from him before. The violence he had shown had scared her, but she couldn't imagine him doing this.

"A couple of days ago," she said uncomfortably. "He came to the house."

"Was he angry?" Joshua asked her, understanding, sympathy emanating from him.

"Yes. A bit."

"A bit nothing. He was furious. I walked in to find him throwing her across the room." Sam stepped in now, his voice a low growl.

Sarah frowned at him, wishing Brock would keep his brothers in line. She didn't need three men trying to take over her entire life.

"Sarah, I need you to be honest with me." Joshua ran his fingers through his short brown hair. "It won't help if you try to hide things from me. I can't help you that way."

She sighed impatiently.

"I don't think Mark did this," she bit out, shaking her head. "But I don't know, Josh. I can't believe it's even happened, let alone that someone I know could do it."

"Cade?" Josh looked to the elder August, causing resentment to flare in her chest.

"It's not Cade's house, Josh." She drew the sheriff's surprised attention back to her. "Why ask him?"

"Sarah," Brock whispered, his voice low at her back as he tightened his arms around her. "Josh and Cade can only help, baby."

"Well I don't need your brothers' help. Either of them." She pushed away from him, turning to stare into his worried eyes. She hated throwing his concern back in his face, but they were running over her. Making her feel like the helpless little woman she swore she would never be again.

Something flashed in his eyes. A flare of arousal. A hidden pulse of some inner excitement, answered by the sudden flare of heat between her thighs. Dammit, she didn't need this right now. It confused her, excited her, the way he turned all male and forceful when she defied him. She didn't need him doing this to her, in the middle of such chaotic events.

"Ms. Tate," Cade began.

"Are any of my clothes salvageable?" She ignored Cade August's warning protest.

Joshua sighed wearily, watching her with a disgruntled male expression.

"I don't know, Sarah. I say you go buy a few things until tomorrow. I can let you in then. Until then, I want to give my men time to go over the house, get what evidence they can and get out. You might want to call Bucky back in too, to clean the place up for you."

Bucky Leddingham and his wife had cleaned it last time. Sarah gritted her teeth. At this rate, every penny she had would go out on cleaning fees.

"Fine." She closed her eyes, fighting for patience. "What about my car? Can I have it?"

"Sarah," Brock's voice dropped, the vein of warning heavier now. "We'll get you some clothes. You can come back to the ranch."

"Maybe I don't want to go to the ranch," she told him, nerves and anger rising inside her as the three August men watched her carefully.

"Sarah?" Marly stepped forward, laying her hand on Sarah's arm, watching her with an unspoken message Sarah fought to understand. "Can I talk to you a minute? Alone."

Sarah looked at the expressions on the men's faces. Male disgruntlement filled them all, a flare of dominance, of sexual suggestion lurking on their expressions.

She allowed the other woman to lead her to the front of Brock's Jeep. Turning back, she watched as the men huddled together, their voices low as they talked to the sheriff.

"Sarah, I don't want to frighten you, but staying alone isn't a good idea right now," Marly told her, her voice soft as they stared at each other. "I know the men can get pretty forceful, but Brock will go crazy with worry. He'll stay with you, and that will make Sam and Cade crazy. Please don't force me to put up with all that male concern alone."

There was a slow smile, a flash of laughter in her eyes. But Sarah also saw the feminine worry. She knew as well as Sarah did what each man would want if she went to the ranch. There lay the problem. Sarah didn't want to face the complications, the inherent suggestion of agreement should she do as Brock wanted. And she knew that was uppermost in each man's mind. It was there, that sexual knowledge, the edge of satisfaction in their eyes.

"You don't want me there, Marly." There was no sense in beating around the bush.

Sarah glanced at Brock. His raised his head to look at her, his light blue eyes zeroing in on her by instinct. Affection, worry, lust, she read each emotion in his expression. It terrified her.

"Sarah, I want you safe, for Brock's peace of mind. If Cade is right then you are seriously in danger." Marly's declaration had her turning back to the other woman in surprise.

"What are you talking about?" she asked her, confusion filling her.

"Last year, Cade found pictures of me and him together. We thought it was my stepfather stalking me. After he tried to kidnap me, we were certain it was. But he swore it wasn't. Even the bodyguards we hired weren't certain after all the evidence came to light. Now Cade is convinced it's something more. Something aimed at the brothers. Now, after your attack, and the pictures of you and Brock he received this morning, there's no way we can ignore the threat."

Sarah flushed, then paled. Her knees weakened, her stomach churning with an edge of fear.

"He saw the pictures?" She couldn't look at Marly. A fury of embarrassment washed over her.

"Sarah, come to the ranch." Marly gripped her arm in an effort to convince her. "It doesn't matter who saw the pictures. They exist. That means you're in danger. Don't let Brock be hurt because of your stubbornness. Cade couldn't bear it. Please."

Sarah trembled. She looked in Marly's eyes and saw acceptance, resignation.

"I will not sleep with all three of those men," she bit out, ignoring the surprise Marly showed at her declaration. "I won't do it, Marly."

Bitterness edged the smile shaping the other woman's lips.

"Has he told you why?"

"Brock told me. And I won't do it." At least, she hoped she wouldn't.

"They won't force you, Sarah," she sighed, in relief or disbelief Sarah wasn't certain. "You'll come to the ranch then?"

"Do I have a choice?" Sarah asked her, knowing she didn't.

"Not a safe one." Marly glanced over at the men then, smiling at Cade.

Sarah caught the edge of adoration in the man's gaze. It shocked her. How could a man love a woman that much and still touch another?

"We'll talk at the ranch." Marly caught the question in her eyes. "If you like?"

"I think we need to." Sarah squared her shoulders. As far as mistakes went, she knew this one would be a doozy.

"Come on then, let's relieve their minds. We'll stop at Claire's and you can get some new clothes. We'll all come out tomorrow and see how much damage has been done."

Marly led the way back to where the men still talked in low voices, their tones vibrating with an edge of violence.

"Sarah?" Brock pulled her into his arms as she neared him. "Is everything okay?"

Her eyes locked with Cade's as he pulled Marly into his arms. Hers narrowed, his crinkled with amusement.

"Fine," she sighed. "I guess I'm going to the ranch."

Brock's hands tightened at her stomach and she felt the almost immediate swelling of his cock as he pressed against her back. She shivered at the feeling, her heart beating in a fierce, hard rhythm at his instantaneous arousal.

"I'll call when we're done here," Josh promised. "I'll pull Tate in, see where he was this morning, how pissed he really is."

Sarah lowered her head. She couldn't believe Mark would do this. Despite the anger he had shown days ago, this just wasn't like him.

"Come on." Brock led her back to the Jeep, opening the door for her and helping her inside.

Sarah sat still, watching him pull the seat belt across, leaning over to buckle it. He was hard, vibrating with arousal.

"Brock?" She whispered his name.

Slow, hesitant, he raised his head, his eyes meeting hers. She saw his fight to contain his pleasure, his anticipation.

"Yeah, Sarah?" he whispered back.

"Only you, Brock." She fought her fear. She didn't want him expecting what she couldn't give. She didn't want recriminations later.

Disappointment flashed in his eyes for a brief instant. She watched him fight it back, watched the smile that finally tipped his lips.

"Whatever you want, Sarah," he promised her. "I'll give you whatever you want."

She took a deep breath, nodding sharply at his promise. She could ask no more of him.

Chapter Twenty-six

ஐ

Sarah hung her new clothes in Brock's closet. Filmy dresses and soft skirt outfits for the most part. She put new underclothes in a drawer in his dresser and placed several pairs of shoes in the shoe port at the end of the large walk-in closet. She wore one of the new outfits. His begging had been pathetic. The skirt was filmy, soft and short. The sleeveless top she wore with it didn't accommodate her bra. Thankfully, her breasts weren't too large and they were firm and full.

She sighed deeply, staring around the masculine room with its heavy, dark furniture and the large four-poster bed. There was a sitting area at the far side of the large room. A couch, chair and corner entertainment center with a large television set in it. It lacked no comforts. The whole house lacked for no comforts, from what she had seen.

Large, airy, with high ceilings and wide windows, the house was beautifully arranged and comfortable. The bit Brock had showed her after their arrival left her gasping. The unassuming façade of the house did little to prepare a visitor for the beauty inside.

"Everything okay?" Brock stood in the doorway, lounging comfortably against the frame as he watched her.

He was aroused. He stayed aroused. Sarah wondered if other men were as virile, as sexual as Brock August. If they were, she hadn't heard of them.

"Yeah." She closed the closet door, facing him fully. "Everything's put away. But I don't intend to be here that long, Brock."

"At least until it's safe." Determination thickened his voice.

Sarah sighed. She knew coming here would be a mistake. She stood still, watching him straighten from the doorway. He stepped into the room, closing the door carefully behind him. She felt her heart speed up in excitement. He hadn't touched her all day and she knew from the look on his face that touching her now filled his mind.

She licked her lips nervously. He always made her nervous, made her too aware of her body, her femininity. Her thighs tensed, the bare flesh of her cunt becoming slick and warm within seconds. The quickening of her blood in her veins, the beat of her heart, she could feel it all in the empty portal awaiting him.

"You look good in that skirt, Sarah," he whispered, not touching her, merely watching her.

He stepped close to her, almost touching, the warmth of his body searing her. Sarah swallowed, cleared her throat, her eyes trained on his hands. He unbuttoned his shirt with careful deliberation before shrugging it from his shoulders. He tossed it carelessly to the padded stool at the end of the bed.

She breathed in hard when his fingers went to the buttons of his jeans. They were dealt with efficiently, leaving the front open, the hard flesh of his cock rising from between the parted fabric.

Sarah felt her breath slow, her heart beat harsh and heavy in her chest. She laid her hand against the taut flesh of his abdomen, staring into his eyes as he watched her intently.

"I want you in my mouth," she told him, her voice soft, the husky, needy sound surprising her.

His cheeks flushed with a dull, dark red. His eyes darkened as his chest heaved hard.

"I want to be in your mouth," he told her, his head lowering until his lips could caress the bare skin of her neck. "I want your hot little mouth wrapped around me, your tongue stroking me."

Sarah almost released the whimper building in her throat.

She gripped the waist of his jeans, pushing them down as she lowered her body. On her knees before him, she looked up, seeing the savage, naked need reflected on his face. His cock strained toward her, heavy and hard, the thick head pulsing, releasing a small pearl of liquid. That droplet tempted her, made her hunger for more.

Gripping the base in her hands, she leaned forward, her tongue running over the broad tip, licking the pearly drop of liquid that collected there. Brock groaned deep, his hands going to her hair to pull her forward. Sarah enveloped the first few inches, groaning as he filled her mouth. Hot, steel-hard, he pushed into her mouth with a slow, measured thrust, until she could take no more.

Sarah raised her eyes, watching him, loving the vulnerable pleasure she saw reflected in his expression. He watched her, his gaze never leaving hers. His hands tightened in her hair. She whimpered, feeling the tiny bursts of the tugging sensation, almost pain, heightening her pleasure.

"Your mouth feels so good, Sarah." He pulled back, then eased into her mouth once again. Each thrust, slow, measured, as his breath sawed from his chest. "Tight and hot, wet and silky; watching your lips part for my cock makes me crazy to take you."

The husky-voiced words had the flesh between her thighs weeping, clenching tight in agonized need. Her body heated, flushing as she drew him deeper, suckling at his flesh hungrily. The soft slurping sound filled the room as she sucked the hot shaft, her hands running over the base, cupping his scrotum, her nails scraping sensitive skin to the tune of his rough, sensual growls.

"Enough. I want to come in your tight little cunt. I won't let you drain me with that soft mouth of yours." He pulled away from her, shedding his jeans in a quick, controlled movement before reaching down and drawing her to her feet. "God, Sarah, I've waited all day to eat your sweet pussy."

Brock jerked the zipper of her skirt down, pushing at the soft fabric until it fell from her hips and pooled on the floor. Stepping out of her sandals, she stood still as Brock pulled the shirt over her head, his hands going to her breasts as she sighed in heated pleasure.

His lips captured the sound, covering hers, his tongue pushing between her lips. His arms went around her, his big body bending close, protective, sheltering. She weakened at the surge of passion that raced through her. The way her body leaned into him instinctually, flesh meeting flesh, heat and fiery need bonding them together.

Sarah leaned into him, into his kiss. Her lips opened for his tongue, hers twining with it, a willing captive to his seductive kiss, his dark desires. Her body ached, her hips pressing into his, the flesh of her stomach pillowing the erection that throbbed between them.

She gasped, feeling him move. He swung her into his arms and the emotion that action sent surging through her terrified her. Had she ever felt more a woman? Had she ever needed anything as desperately as she needed Brock?

"I won't last long." He laid her on the bed, bending over her, his lips hot and fierce as they bathed her neck in kisses.

Sarah gasped, her hands going to his head, her fingers spearing through the night-black hair. His lips caressed her neck, his tongue licking at her skin, making her shiver, making her hips arch to the hard male thigh that pressed between her own.

Oh. That felt good. Her eyes opened in startled awareness, only to be caught by the heat in Brock's. He knew, damn him. She rubbed the bare flesh of her inner lips against his thigh, her breathing now an audible series of short little cries. The sensitive flesh, so slick and hot, pulsed, tingled. It spread as she pressed against his thigh, her clit meeting no interference in pressing against the hard male muscles of his upper leg.

"Feel good?" The slow smile tilting his lips fascinated her.

She rubbed against him again, her thighs tightening on him, sensations racing through her body at a speed that defied her ability to grasp and hold onto them long enough to decide if she could bear them. She could only cry out, arch and grind against the hard male thigh, seeking more.

"Not yet, Sarah." His chuckle sounded rusty. Unused. Happiness, not amusement lit his eyes. It lightened them, even as the arousal fought to darken them.

"Oh God, Brock. Don't stop." She gripped his hips, stopping him from moving back from her. "It's so good. Don't you dare move."

She ground herself against him, feeling the moisture seeping from her vagina, coating sensitive flesh, his leg, making a perfect base for the exquisite tingles of heat and building urgency between her thighs.

"You'll come on my leg," he whispered at her lips, pressing harder against her. "Wouldn't you rather come in my mouth?"

Sarah lost her sanity at the sound of those whispered words.

"Will it feel as good?" she demanded, her breathing harsh. She couldn't imagine anything this good. Her bare slick flesh in perfect touch with his hard thigh. She wanted to come and she could, if he would only let her.

"Better, baby." He eased back from her, ignoring her cry at his desertion.

He moved down the bed, spreading her thighs, lowering himself between them, watching her, his eyes hot, hungry. The insatiable light in those light blue eyes sent her pulse careening. The way he licked his lips, watched her, his smile filled with knowledge an instant before his tongue licked over the smooth lips of her cunt.

"Oh, Brock." Her hands clenched in his hair as fire sped through her body.

He licked her again, his tongue dipping into the narrow slit, raking over her clit, unhindered by the curls once growing there. Sarah's head tossed on the pillows. His caresses slid over her flesh with soft, smooth motions. Nerve endings she never knew she had were suddenly sizzling to life. Wanton, gasping, she was on the verge of begging for more when she felt that diabolical tongue circle her clit, an instant before his suckling mouth covered it.

Sarah's hips came off the bed, a strangled cry erupting from her throat. At the same time, she felt his fingers, knowing, experienced, wicked in their quest to drive her past the edge of sanity, slide deep within her gripping vagina.

She exploded violently. Her cries echoed around the room as she felt the shudders wracking her body. Deep, intense, tightening her muscles, sending her careening into a climax so strong, it left her gasping for breath.

Brock moved over her as the last vibrations tore through her body. Before they could ease, he pushed his cock swift and deep inside the greedy depths of her body. Sarah's head tossed, her hands gripped his shoulders, her eyes staring in dazed fascination at the man by the bedroom door.

She couldn't speak. The look in his eyes, so like Brock's, dark, intense, hungry, ate into her. Her nails bit into Brock's shoulders, her hips pushing against his in desperation, her eyes locked with those of his brother.

"Brock," she cried out his name, unable to control the building lust rising inside her. She should be shocked, horrified, not so excited she was nearly demented in the grip of a carnality so wicked, she could do nothing but scream out the climax tearing through her.

Brock's hips drove her through the violent shudders of release, then his harsh male groan sounded in her ear and she felt the hard, rapid jets of his semen spurting in her. Pulse after pulse as he trembled against her, whispering her name as he shuddered one last time. Sarah watched, barely able to keep her eyes opened, as Sam slipped from the room.

Chapter Twenty-seven

ঞ

Rick and Tara Glaston weren't married, as Brock explained the next day. Rick was Tara's ex-brother-in-law, a tall, muscular ex-Special Forces Commando and part owner of Security Unnamed, a private protection business. Tara was tall, with red hair and green eyes, and a light scattering of freckles across her nose. Rick was taller, with brown hair and hazel eyes. Both were well acquainted with the August family. With them, was Tara's sister, Heather James. She was a bit shorter than Tara, standing close to five feet four inches rather than her sister's five feet six. She was slender, compact, with her long dark auburn hair falling in a thick braid down her back, her darker green eyes solemn as she watched the group.

Also in attendance to the little meeting was Dillon. A more than furious Dillon who listened to the proceedings with a dark frown. He had shown up early that morning, threatening to kill every August man that breathed if anything happened to his sister. Sarah rolled her eyes. He was acting like an overprotective father rather than a sometimes brother.

"I brought a team with me this time, I have them scattered along security points where the house can be accessed by a weapon." Rick pointed to several areas on a makeshift map. "We don't want a repeat of Sam's little accident."

Sam and Cade had been shot two years before by a stalker, possibly intent on getting to Cade. Sarah watched the men, listening to the bodyguards, and fought the reality of the situation. She felt too overwhelmed and on the edge of an abyss she was afraid of entering.

Watching Brock, seeing his concern, his determination to protect her, frightened her. He would stand between her and danger and she knew it. The proof lay in his determination to keep her at his side.

"I want everyone to learn from the mistakes made the last time we were here." Tough, no nonsense Tara spoke up, eyeing each man individually.

"Yeah, remember, we're cowboys not green berets this time, huh?" Sam rolled his eyes at some private joke.

"Be careful, Sarah. Brock and Cade like to play cowboys and stalkers with madmen." Marly grimaced. "Cade has the scar to prove it."

"Hey, I have a scar too." Sam pouted. How a grown man with features as bold and nearly savage as his could actually pull it off was a mystery to Sarah. But he managed.

"Yes, you do, and you were such a big boy about your boo boo." Heather grinned at him, drawing a round of chuckles from everyone but Sarah.

Sam cast her a bold, sexual look. "Wanna kiss my boo boo again, baby?"

Heather flushed, her eyes narrowing on him with promised retribution.

"That wasn't your boo boo she had in her mouth, Sam," Tara reminded him tartly. "If it was, then you're in some major trouble."

"Okay, boys and girls. Remember, stay inside or just in the ranch yard, no riding off for midnight rides." Rick gave Sam a hard look. "And no sneaking out to play cowboys and stalkers." Brock and Cade were next. "Maybe we can catch the bastard this time."

"Last shot, Rick." Cade stood to his feet, all humor wiped from his face. "I want to at least know who it is this time. Get your people on that."

"We've had them on it for two years, Cade," Rick bit out, his hazel eyes cool, hard. "Our people and a PI firm. There's no trace of evidence linking anyone."

"Only one person could be behind it," Cade told him carefully, flickering a look at Sarah.

"He's dead, Cade." Rick shook his head. "I checked that myself. ID was positive. It can't be him."

"Then it has to be someone close to him, who knew." Cade wrapped his arms around Marly instinctively as she moved to his side. "Find out. Concentrate there. It couldn't be coming from anywhere else."

Rick sighed roughly, dragging his hands over his short, spiky hair. "I'll try a few other angles. But I swear, that line is pretty much exhausted."

"Just find the bastard, I don't care where you have to look." His voice, harsh and cutting, sliced through the room. "I'm sick of having to lie awake at night worrying about the women in this house. I pay you damned good. Now make your fucking money."

He stomped out of the dining room, the heels of his boots beating out a harsh rhythm on the hardwood floor.

Marly sighed, looking at everyone apologetically.

"It's okay, Munchkin, we understand and so does Rick." Sam leaned back in his chair, sighing with a rough breath. "Give him time, he'll settle down."

Marly nodded, then turned and followed Cade. Her petite body, dressed in clinging white silk gave her the appearance of an innocent seductress. She was soft-spoken, gentle and too damned sweet for the life Sarah knew she lived. She wondered how the other woman did it and kept from being bitter, cynical.

"Miss Tate, we'll be checking your ex out as well," Rick told her, turning to her now. "Make certain he's not a smoke screen."

"The sheriff is doing that," she protested. "He knows what he's doing."

"I'm sure he does." Rick nodded. "But this way, I know it to the bone. It's best for all of us."

Sarah shrugged. He could beat a dead horse as long as he wanted to.

"I need to go home soon, get my clothes." She turned to Brock. "If there are any left."

"Let one of our employees handle that instead," Tara requested. "Make a list of anything else you want right now and we'll have it brought here. We need to keep everyone together for now."

Sarah pressed her lips together in irritation. She was beginning to feel like a prisoner.

"It won't last long, baby," Brock promised her. "Whoever the bastard is, once he starts, he doesn't take long to show himself."

"And I want him this time," Rick said, his voice hard. "Last shot boys, let's see if we can't get it right this time."

* * * * *

Sam slipped from the house as darkness was edging over it. He ignored the edge of nervousness in the pit of his stomach, the anticipation that had his dick throbbing. He was horny, he assured himself. That was all it was. He could handle one little spitfire long enough to find out why the hell she had come back. He moved quickly across the backyard, heading for the small van parked past a cluster of shoulder-high boulders about two hundred feet from the kitchen door. He had waited as long as he could. His curiosity, his lust wouldn't allow him to delay the confrontation another moment. As he neared it, the side door was pushed open, and Rick came out of it growling.

"Tara finds out about this and she'll kick your ass, cowboy," he snarled. "I'll watch out here, but you won't have long."

Sam grinned, tipped his hat and jumped into the van. The door was slammed shut then locked behind him.

The dim light from the camera monitors at the side of the van spilled a tenuous, soft glow through the darkened interior, enabling him to catch sight of Heather as she watched from the back.

"Rick's not going to cover for you again, Sam." Heather was sitting on the small bed at the side of the van, one slender, jean-clad leg propped on the thin mattress as she leaned back against the van wall, her grin mocking. "And if I had known ahead of time you were coming, then I wouldn't either."

Her slender face, with her small pouty lips fascinated him. The slightly tilted green eyes, and slender arched brows all combined to create a fairy tale image that should have been dressed in gauzy silk, not jeans and a rough cotton blouse.

He wanted to tear her clothes from her body. He wanted to stroke her satin skin. He wanted to rage at her for making him feel again.

"Why the hell didn't you come back?" He faced her, furious. A year. A damned year and he hadn't seen hide nor hair of her.

She quirked a slender brow mockingly. Sam felt the blood begin to heat in his veins, his cock hardening to the point of pain.

"A blowjob does not a relationship make, cowboy," she said sarcastically, her gaze flickering to the bulge that had grown beneath his jeans.

He remembered that sweet mouth, so small, so damned tight and hot. He clenched his fists as he stared down at her, fighting his needs.

"If I remember correctly, it was a hell of a lot more than a simple blowjob, sugar," he bit out not wanting to remember, to ache for her mouth. "I do believe you screamed pretty damned loud while I ate that sweet pussy of yours."

Hell yes, she remembered. Her nipples beaded instantly. She wasn't wearing a bra beneath that damned shirt again. Did the woman ever wear a bra?

When he glanced back at her face it was to see the shy flush that stained it. She didn't back down, though. Her eyes met his, the forest green color darkening with her arousal. He remembered exactly what she looked like aroused, needing. His teeth clenched at the memory. He should have stayed away. He should have never come out here to her.

"Are you still a virgin?" He wanted to bite the words back the minute they were out of his mouth.

"Are you still fucking your brother's lover?" she snarled back, anger brightening her eyes now.

She was a prickly little thing. Quick with her mouth, hot with her passion, and driving him crazy with her female stubbornness. Sam took a deep, hard breath then went to his knees in front of her. He had to touch her. She was temptation and one he didn't understand, yet couldn't resist. Her eyes widened, then she blinked when he did nothing more than watch her. He loved watching her. The shift of her expression, the anticipation in her eyes.

"I don't know how to fuck a virgin," he whispered, shaking his head, confused by the overwhelming need he had to touch her in gentleness; confused by the tremble in his hands. "And I want to fuck you, Heather. I want to fuck you bad."

He watched her breasts heave on a hard breath. He clenched his fists in an effort not to touch them. He tamped his grin as she frowned fiercely, the evidence of her fight against her arousal telling in her deepening flush, the rapid rise and fall of her breasts.

"You should really wait on an invitation, big boy. And I don't remember protesting how rough you became before,"

248

she bit out, but he heard the breathy indication in her voice that the idea intrigued her. Just as she had been intrigued before by the small taste of pleasure/pain he had introduced her to.

And it intrigued him. The memory of her pleasure, her unmasked lust as he pulled that long hair, or erotically nipped at the plump lips of her perfect cunt made him insane with his growing lust for her.

"Invite me, Heather." He moved closer, unable to deny himself. He was weak, he admitted. Damned weak where this fiery little redhead was concerned.

She bit her lip, her eyelids lowering, her breathing fast and uneven now.

"Do I look like a fool, Sam?" she asked him, though her voice lacked conviction.

"Naw," he whispered with a grin. Damn, she could lighten his heart when nothing else could. "You look like cinnamon candy, baby. Sweet and hot on my tongue, blowing my mind with your taste. "

She watched him carefully, her lips parted now as she fought for air. He knew just how she felt. He was smothering with his desire for her.

"And you look like trouble." She trembled, though, despite her objection as he pulled her leg from its propped position, then moved closer to her.

"Unbutton your shirt," he whispered as her hands gripped his wrists.

"What?" Surprise flared in her eyes.

"Do it," he growled almost wincing at the roughness of his voice. "I want to watch you, Heather. Unbutton your shirt, then spread it apart. Let me see your hard little nipples. Touch them."

"I'm still a virgin," she reminded him, her bitterness heard and understood.

Sam winced. His last words to her before she left the year before were to lose her virginity before returning. He wasn't an easy lover and he was terrified of hurting her. Evidently, she hadn't heard that part.

"Not for much longer," he promised her. "Now unbutton that fucking shirt, Heather. Don't play coy, baby. You knew what would happen when you came back."

Her nails bit into his wrists, biting into his skin as her tongue ran over her lips nervously.

"I didn't expect anything, Sam," she told him, and he was surprised at the honesty he heard in her voice. "There were no promises between us. How could I have expected anything?"

Sam took a deep, rough breath as he watched her. She didn't try to hide her arousal, didn't care to let him know he would be first. Even knowing what he was, the life he lived, she wanted him. How much more would she want?

"I won't be easy. I warned you, Heather." He fought to keep his voice hard, but he heard the vein of need in it. "Now unbutton that damned blouse before I rip it off your body."

He was almost shaking with the need to taste those hard little nipples beneath the cloth. To suck them into his mouth, nibble at them; hear her cries of passion as he drove her crazy with his mouth. Then his mouth went dry as her hands went to the buttons. One slid free, parting the material minutely. A moment later, the second came undone. His cock jerked in anticipation.

Her fingers went to the third, was slipping it slowly from its mooring when the van door was suddenly jerked open. Without thought, Sam pushed Heather to the floor in a quick movement, his body bracing for danger as he turned to meet the person stupid enough to interrupt him.

He stopped within a second of a blow to the intruder. Tara Glaston stood watching him, her eyes narrowed, her hands propped on her slender hips, her green eyes glittering with anger.

"Heather, do you have any idea what the hell you're getting into here?" she bit out.

The soft chuckle behind him surprised him. He turned back to Heather, wondering at the knowing glint in her amusement filled gaze.

"Maybe that's a question you should be asking him, Tara." She was sitting back up, re-buttoning her shirt and watching Sam with a knowing glint.

"Get out of here, Sam." Tara's anger slowly simmered as she watched him. "I think they need you at the house for something."

He wanted to argue, but he knew Tara, and knew well she was as mean as a blind rattler.

"This isn't over, Heather," he warned her. "Don't think it is."

She bit her lip again. Damn her, he wished he could do it for her.

"For now it is, Sam," she sighed, watching him warily. "Maybe we can talk later."

"Talk isn't exactly what I have in mind," he bit out as he jumped from the van. "And next time, I'll make sure Big Sis here is locked out."

He flashed Tara a hard look before stomping away from the van and the woman slowly driving him to complete madness with his lust for her. His cock throbbed painfully, his veins pounded with the surge of blood. His mind was a mess, though, and he knew it. Memories, dark and fragmented, stirred within him as he navigated the dark landscape around the house. Damn her, he cursed. Damn her to hell for making him feel and in turn, for making him remember.

Chapter Twenty-eight

Sarah stared out in the darkness, sitting quietly on the patio, watching the pool ripple beneath the faint light of the moon. The evening's events played through her mind, the reality of it finally sinking in. A madman stalked her because she slept with one of the August men. She sighed. The last damned time she decided on a one-night stand. This one seemed never ending.

"You shouldn't be out here alone." Sam stood in the shadows of the patio, watching her, the moonlight casting a pale, eerie glow over his face. He looked tortured, tormented, not the easygoing cowboy she had glimpsed before.

"Doesn't look like I am any longer." She sat back in the padded chair, her feet propped on an ironwork planter filled with blooming moonflowers. The sweet scent washed over her, adding a breath of sensuality to the air.

Sam moved forward, roughly masculine in jeans and boots, a T-shirt stretched over his broad shoulders and flat stomach.

"You should go back in." He hunched down by her chair, in front of her, too close for comfort. He looked too much like Brock and the sexual interest in his eyes was much too heavy. "It's safer inside, Sarah."

"Maybe, but I doubt it," she sighed, watching him carefully.

Would it matter where she was, she wondered. The brothers seemed to surround her. Their eyes shadowed, their expressions more relaxed than she had ever seen, yet the marks of the past were still there. The faint lines of bitterness alongside sensual lips, on their broad, sun-darkened foreheads. Worry and pain had scarred them in more ways than one.

"You act like I'm going to attack you." Sam smiled faintly. "I wouldn't do that, Sarah. Brock would kill me if I tried."

"But you want to." Her heart sped up. There was something about Sam that didn't mesh with the laughter and amusement he usually portrayed to the world.

"No, Sarah." He shook his head, his voice gentle. "I don't want to hurt you."

There was weariness in his voice, the same sadness the others carried. He lowered his head, then glanced back up at her. The smile was back in place.

"Too late," she told him softly.

He shook his head. His hand reached out, running over her smooth ankle before she could jerk away from him. The touch left a fiery impression that unsettled her.

"You remind me of a friend," he said regretfully. "A very good friend, Sarah. She's easy to talk to. Easy to be open with."

"Then why aren't you with her, Sam?" she asked him, wrapping her arms across her breasts. "Why are you here?"

"Because I owe them," he whispered. "I owe them everything, Sarah, including my life."

"What about your happiness?" She tilted her head, watching as a finger ran softly over the side of her sandal.

"If they want it." He shrugged.

"What about what you want?"

"I want to know my brothers love me again," he whispered darkly, secretively. "I want to know some demon from hell didn't take it all, Sarah. I want to lie with you, touch you, see Brock watching me take you and know he loves me. The same as I do with Marly. I want to find my way out of hell, if only for a little while."

Sarah's heart clenched. Her hand covered her mouth, she didn't jerk away this time when his fingers circled her ankle.

She did nothing to wipe away the tear that drifted down her cheek.

Sam seemed more than surprised by that bit of moisture. A finger moved, lifted the drop from her cheek. He looked at it, seeing the glistening dew settled on the tip of his finger.

"I haven't cried in over twelve years, Sarah, and no one else has cried for me." He looked in her eyes, and Sarah knew if this man didn't cry soon, then there would be no hope for him. Cade and Brock would lose a part of their souls as well.

"Sam." She shook her head, hating the pain she saw in his eyes. "This doesn't work for you."

"For a little while it does, Sarah," he told her, his voice rough. "It works for a while. For as long as I can forget that I'm the cause of it. That my brothers knew hell because of me. Will you help me forget?"

His hand was at her knee, his voice turning sensual, heated with arousal. Sarah came to her feet with a deep breath.

"I need to find Brock." She went to move around him, but he was too fast. He stopped her, not forcing her to stay, his hand on her arm warm, not hurtful.

He stared down at her, his hand soothing, smoothing over her skin.

"Just a kiss," he whispered, his lips tilting in a smile so similar to Brock's it broke her heart.

She trembled, desperate to get away from him, wondering why she wasn't running from him. She stared up at him, wide-eyed, shivering despite the heat of the night as his hand cupped her cheek. Nerves tightened the muscles of her stomach, made her suck her breath in roughly.

His head lowered. He watched her, his eyes dark, lonely, need whispering through the night. His lips were a breath from hers, his eyes narrowed, arousal pulsing in the air around them when she found the strength to jerk away.

"Brock," she gasped out, moving jerkily around him, rushing for the door.

"Brock wouldn't care, Sarah," his voice was soft, so somber it tore at her soul. "You're a part of him now. He loves you. Return it to me."

"No." she gripped the door handle, shaking her head desperately. "I can't. God help me. I can't."

She pushed the door open, rushing into the family room, past Brock and Cade, Marly and Tara. She hid her tears, fought her overwhelming fears, and ignored the damp need collecting between her thighs.

Chapter Twenty-nine

ЮŊ

"Sarah?" Brock followed her to their room, concern edging his voice and his expression.

She stood at the large window, knowing it was bullet proof, knowing the precautions that had been taken two years before in case the family was ever threatened again. Good precaution she thought, because it appeared they knew nothing but the fear and disquiet of evil.

She looked out at the night, fighting tears, sadness, needs. Needs she shouldn't have. They were getting to her, each of them. Slowly, insidiously, their needs, their pain was wearing away her resistance, tearing down the fabric of her objections. She didn't care much for the fact that she was so weak in the face of it.

"How did it happen?" she asked as he closed the bedroom door. "How did your father get away with sending you to that madman?"

She watched the pain twist his expression at her reminder. She hated bringing that expression to his face, hated hurting him. But she needed to know. She needed to understand before she made the biggest mistake of her life. She loved Brock. She knew she did. She always had. Now she just had to figure out how to live with it.

"He was our father. We thought we were going to work for another rancher for the summer. We found out better when we got there. When he locked us in cages after drugging us during our first meal. We understood, though, the first time one of us was dragged out and raped."

His voice was cool, his expression tortured. Sarah closed her eyes tight, fighting the overwhelming fury that something so terrible could have happened to him.

"Sam was first." He glanced away from her, swallowing hard. "He tortured him for hours. He still carries the scars from it on his body. And in his mind. He was just eighteen. We both were. "

Sarah trembled violently. God, how had they survived? How had they managed to ever survive such horror?

"He blames himself," she told him. "Why?"

He seemed surprised by that.

"I don't know." He frowned worriedly. "It wasn't his fault. Not at all. It was Joe's decision to send us there. He swore he didn't know what was going on. But he did. We all knew he did."

Sarah wrapped her arms over her chest, unable to turn to him, watching his reflection in the glass. He stood still, straight, tense. His body vibrated with sorrow and pain.

"I feel like I'm drowning here, Brock," she whispered tearfully. "The three of you are killing me. It's too much pain, too much need. Too much pressure."

He pushed his hands into the pockets of his jeans, a sigh heaving from his chest as he watched her. He watched her with warmth, with love. She knew it was love, she had seen Cade watching Marly with the same expression, knew she often carried it in her own eyes.

"In what way?" he asked her, tilting his head, watching her curiously.

"The three of you and your desires," she groaned, dragging her hands through her hair. "It's like being in the middle of a sexual soup, the tension is so thick."

"It arouses you." There was no heat in his tone, he was past arguing with her. He had given her the choice, just as they had given Marly.

257

"It arouses me," she admitted starkly. "And it terrifies me too, Brock. He's almost broken. You and Cade are little better. Sharing Marly hasn't helped, how will sharing me help?"

Surprise lit his features.

"That's not true, Sarah." He shook his head. "We were worse before Marly. Frozen inside. Everything bleak and dark. Sharing didn't help, because there was no love for the women we shared. I knew what it was the night Sam found you and me in my room. I knew he was there. I knew the difference then."

Sarah closed her eyes.

"I want this over," she told him quietly. "I don't like being closed up like this. I don't like feeling helpless, Brock."

She took a deep, hard breath as she felt his hands on her shoulders, pulling her against his chest.

"I want to always hold you, Sarah," he breathed against her hair. "Every night, in my bed, close against my body. I don't want to lose you."

"And I don't know what to do." She laid her head against his back. "Love isn't supposed to be like that, you know?"

Sarah couldn't stop the tears that drifted from her eyes. She loved him. Loved him so desperately, always had. How was she supposed to survive the hell they lived in, seeing everyday the scars of it in the three men who knew no other way of life.

"I know that, baby. And it won't always be. Just sometimes. Just when the memories are too bad. Usually in the spring. That's when it happened Sarah, in April. It's usually only then, because that's when the memories are the worst, when the demons strike in nightmares and fears we can't control. It's our bond. Our survival. And letting go of it would mean letting go of each other forever."

There was bleak agony in his statement, a plea for acceptance, for understanding. This big, strong man, so sexual, so determined needed her so desperately that he would plead for her understanding. She closed her eyes, stemming her tears. She loved him. She loved all of him. Even the wounded warrior Brock was, who knew the only way to love the brothers who had survived with him.

She opened her eyes, staring at him as she sighed, shaking her head.

"I knew you were trouble years ago. I just didn't know how much."

That rusty smile tipped the edge of his lips once again. She loved his smile. Loved the hesitant light of it in his eyes that pushed away the shadows of remembered pain.

"Come back downstairs. Have a drink with me while we watch TV with Cade and Marly?" he asked as he kissed her cheek with endearing hesitancy. As though he were unused to the tenderness he felt for her.

"Just watch TV?" she asked him with a smile.

"Well, unless you want to do more, baby. It's all according to what you want." Amusement filled his eyes, lightening the color, lifting the haggard expression he carried.

"Hmmm, it's all up to me then?" she drawled. "Somehow, I think the three of you are a hell of a lot more calculating than you let on."

Mock surprise filled his face as he took her hand and led her to the door.

"We're just simple men. How could you say that?" he asked incredulously.

"Can the act, cowboy." She shook her head, following him, a prickle of unease skating down her spine.

She turned back to the bedroom, stopping Brock as he paused, looking at her questioningly.

"Brock, when did you take that stuff and put it out?" The dildo and plug were lying on the bed as though dropped by a careless hand.

Brock walked into the room, staring at the objects. She felt the dangerous tension that gripped him then. His body tightened with fury, with rage.

"Fuck." His harsh exclamation was preceded by a hard grip at her waist as he forced her from the room.

"What?" She gasped.

"Rick. Tara." His voice echoed through the house, demanding, infuriated. "Cade, get the fuck up here."

He pushed her into the hall as everyone began running up the stairs. Rick and Tara and several of the other members of their team came with weapons drawn. Cade and Sam had converged on Marly, keeping her carefully between them as they followed.

"The bastard's been in our room." Brock turned on Rick, his hands reaching out, gripping the other man's shirtfront and throwing him against the wall. "How did he get in, Rick?"

Violence pulsed through Brock's body, a killing rage that terrified Sarah.

"That's not possible, Brock." Rick stayed calm, matter of fact. "I have every entrance into this house monitored as well as a security system. He couldn't have got in."

"Mother fucker, he got in. Go look on the bed and tell me what the fuck you see, Sam?"

Sam moved cautiously into the room, followed by Tara. There was complete silence for long, long seconds. No one moved in the hall. No one spoke. Finally, they stepped back, their faces were pale and Tara was on the verge of shaking.

"Tara?" Rick asked.

"Someone did a little work on Sarah's dildo, Rick." She breathed out roughly. "There are half a dozen needles driven through it, only the sharp edges poking through. If he hadn't messed up and left it laying out, it would have shredded her." Her voice was rough, edged with anger and horror.

Rick paled; Marly's cry was smothered by Cade's chest. Sarah felt her knees going weak; a whimper escaped her throat. Instantly Brock was at her side, pulling her against him, staring at Rick, his expression livid.

Rick wiped his hand over his face.

"Son of a bitch." He jerked the two-way radio from his belt. "Report in, all posts."

"Marshal here."

"Clive here."

"Kensington here."

There was a brief silence as they waited for the last female member of the team to answer in.

"Sorry boys, Miss James is a bit under the weather right now. She sends her apologies."

Mechanical, amused, the evil voice held them all suspended for precious seconds.

"That's him," Sarah whispered as the guards burst into action. "The guy who shot me."

"Heather," Sam's scream shocked them all. It vibrated through the hall as he took off after them.

"Let's go." Brock pulled Sarah behind him as they rushed through the house. "Where was the girl stationed?"

"Back of the house. She was watching the kitchen door." They rushed for the kitchen, fear pulsing through them all, the shattered fury in Sam's voice still throbbing inside them.

* * * * *

They found Heather in a secluded area, hidden behind brush and boulders. She was unconscious, naked, bloody. Where the blood originated from Sarah couldn't tell. But she saw the effect it had on the three men. They were pale, furious. Violence throbbed through the air, in their voices.

"Brock is readying the chopper. Get her prepared to fly." Cade stood aside, holding Marly close. "We'll meet you at the hospital."

Rick motioned to the men standing around and they positioned themselves around the August family. Tara was calm, cool, but you could see the fear that pulsed just under the surface.

"I'm going." Sam was kneeling beside the small woman, his hands gentle, tender as he touched her pale cheek.

"Sam." Cade's voice held a warning thread.

Sam shook his head. A tight, fierce movement that seemed to threaten his self-control.

"I'll be fine. I have to go." His voice was broken. There were no tears and Sarah wondered if after twelve years Sam would find the tears he had lost? His shoulders were slumped, though his body was rigid. He stared down at the bound, nude body, jerking his shirt off his back, then laying it over her as Rick worked to cut her ropes loose.

"Let's move." The shirt was wrapped around her now, but she still hadn't regained consciousness.

As Sam picked Heather up gently and rushed with Rick and Tara to the helicopter, Sarah looked at Brock questioningly. His face was haunted, his eyes bleak and pain-filled.

"He hurt her," Brock whispered.

"Did he rape her?" Sarah asked hesitantly.

"I don't know." Brock shook his head. A slow, careful motion. "But she'll carry Sam's scars now. I noticed the work." He turned to Cade and their eyes met. "He's not dead after all."

Chapter Thirty

ဢ

It was Brock's nightmare that woke her up the next night. His cry shattered the night and her security in one bleak instant.

"No! God, No!" He jumped from the bed, crouching on the floor like an animal, his face white, his eyes so dark they terrified her as he stared around in dazed horror.

"Brock." Sarah came to her knees, fear washing over her as he jerked to his feet, his hands shaking, his body shuddering from the remembered terror as he raked his fingers through sweat dampened hair.

"Fuck. I have to go outside." He acted like a man with claustrophobia, stuck in a small room rather than the cavern-sized bedroom he inhabited. "Go back to sleep."

He pulled his sweat pants on, nearly tripping in his haste, then grabbed cigarettes from the dresser and rushed from the room. Oh yeah, she was really going to stay put. Sarah donned her short, silk robe and moved after him. She didn't rush, giving him a chance to realize he was no longer trapped in the dream. She went to the family room first, poured them both a drink and then walked out the open front door.

He sat in the large, cushioned lounge chair at the end of the porch, deep in the shadows. His long legs were braced over the side, his elbows propped on his knees, his hands covering his face. A lit cigarette was clamped between his lips and he drew on it with the desperation of a man dying for ease.

"Here." She set the stiff whisky and ice on the table beside him.

263

Her brows raised as he tipped it to his mouth, draining it, then went back to the cigarette. She set her glass beside him then.

"Go back to bed." His voice was rough, savage. "I'll be up later."

"Would you leave me alone with such demons, Brock?" she asked him, sitting at the end of the lounger, pulling the robe over her thighs as she watched him.

"I don't want you to know my demons, dammit." He drew on the cigarette with a harsh motion. "You'll suffer enough for them. Get back to bed."

Sarah couldn't imagine suffering for him, as bad as he was suffering with it. His muscles were so tight and bunched she hurt just seeing it. His eyes were dark, his face creased with bitterness.

"I already suffer knowing you hurt, Brock." And she was. It was breaking her heart, seeing him, so strong, so alone, his eyes bleak and hopeless.

"You'll suffer worse before it's over with," he growled, tossing the filter to the yard, then lighting another cigarette. "Just like Marly suffers."

And yet, in no way the amount he was suffering right now. Sarah felt tears come to her eyes. If he were a weaker man, he would be rocking in misery. Instead, his body was tight, corded with tension and despair, his eyes bleak and hopeless. It was breaking her heart, tearing a piece of her soul from its mooring to see him like this, hurting so desperately.

"Brock, don't shut me out," she whispered. "If you shut me out, how am I supposed to understand?"

She could barely suppress her cry of rage when he looked up at her. His eyes were hollow, his face ravaged by pain.

"You don't want to know, Sarah," he denied her, his voice gentle, heart-breaking in its agony. "I wish I didn't know."

"But you do," she told him, touching his face, her fingers easing over the lines sorrow had edged into it. "I love you, Brock. Very much. You can't shut me out like this."

He turned his head away from her. He drained the second drink, breathing harshly as the whisky burned a path down his throat.

"I told you what happened," he reminded her. "I won't go over it again."

He couldn't go over it again, Sarah knew, and she didn't know if she could bear it if he did. Her heart would shatter from his pain.

"What's the nightmare about?" She edged closer, relieved when he pulled her desperately into his arms, holding onto her as he braced her back against his chest.

"Cade." He buried his face in her hair. "It's always about Cade."

"What about Cade?" She felt his lips in her hair, a dampness that shouldn't be there falling from him. Sweat, or tears? She was terrified to turn back and look.

"How that bastard hurt him. How he made Cade hurt us, or watch him do it. It was always Cade's choice." He held onto her, a lifeline, Sarah thought. He held onto her as though she alone were keeping him sane.

"Which did you prefer, Brock?" His arms tightened around her, his breath was harsh at her back. "Would it have mattered which it was?"

He drew in a shocked breath.

"Cade tried to protect us."

"But the abuse was done in a way that destroyed your trust in the one person you knew you could depend on. If you didn't depend on him, you could depend on no one. And Cade knew that. Just as he knew he was sacrificing that trust in an effort to save you the physical pain," she guessed.

"Yeah," he whispered, seeming to breathe easier. "That was it. The bastard knew what he was doing, didn't he, Sarah?"

Like a man lost, searching desperately for an innocence forever denied him, but resigned to the cost. Sarah breathed in deeply.

"I would take your pain if I could," she told him. "If it would ease you, Brock, I would take the pain myself."

"God no." He pulled her tighter to him. "No, Sarah, never wish that. I'm sane now, but if such a thing happened to you, it would kill me. Do you understand that? I couldn't survive it."

"Tell me how to help you then, Brock," she said, fighting to keep her voice soft, tender. "Tell me how to ease you."

The front door opened and Cade stepped onto the porch. He was dressed as Brock was, in sweats and nothing else. His dark eyes found them, his pupils flaring, his pants bulging.

"You okay, Brock?" His voice carried little emotion, but Sarah glimpsed a raging pain in his eyes.

"Yeah." His hand moved, cupping Sarah's breast with a slow, deliberate movement. "I'm fine."

Sarah gasped, her eyes widening as she watched Cade's gaze center on that hand and the plump flesh Brock cupped. She blinked, not just at the arousal in Cade's eyes, but a softening of the agony and easing of his own lines of grief about his mouth and eyes.

"Brock?" She gasped as the other hand released the belt that held the robe together. "Oh God, I don't think I can do this."

"You don't have to do anything, baby," he promised her, desolation echoing in his voice. "He won't fuck you, I swear. Just touch you. Sarah please, just try baby. Just try."

Brock drew the edges of her robe from her shoulders, down her arms. Cade went to his knees beside the lounger, watching her, his expression so tender she wanted to weep.

266

There was love there. A gentle, abiding, heartfelt emotion that she knew wasn't reflected to her.

"You tie us together, Sarah," he whispered, his hand reaching for her breast as her head fell back to Brock's chest. "Do you understand that?"

"No," she whimpered, her eyes closing as his hand cupped her breast, his head lowering.

She jerked as his lips touched her. Her breathing became laborious, matching Brock's, her body responding to the hard length of his cock rising along her back. She tilted her head back to the side, resting it on his shoulder, eyes opening, her breath halting for long seconds at the look on Brock's face as he watched his brother suckle at her breast.

"You're beautiful." His gaze flickered to her. "So damned pretty, Sarah, it breaks my heart."

She arched into the caress, whimpering as she felt male fingers, not Brock's, smoothing along her thigh, inching closer to the flesh between.

"Don't look away." He turned her head back to him when she would have looked away. "Look at me, baby. Let me tell you something."

She jerked violently as Cade's fingers met the throbbing, slick lips of her cunt. His fingers ran through the narrow slit, circled her clit, retreated, then advanced. Each touch a whisper against flesh, an electrical charge of lust.

"What?" she gasped, confused, fighting to hold onto her sanity as she felt the dual pleasure of those experienced fingers between her thighs, the hungry mouth at her breast.

"I would die for him, Sarah," he whispered, staring down at her, the fingers of his hand tweaking the nipple Cade had yet to administer to. "I would give my life for him, and him for me. And this is the only way I have of proving it. The only chance we both have to feel any affection, any love for each other. Through you. Through Marly. This is all we have, Sarah. Let him pleasure you, just for a minute. Let me watch, knowing the woman I love binds us together. Just let him touch you. That's all."

"Marly," she groaned, her head tossing as the pleasure rioted through her system. "This will hurt Marly."

She couldn't bear it. She couldn't escape it. Cade sucked at her nipple, his tongue flickering it heatedly as his fingers traced every bare inch of her cunt. Through the narrow slit, circling the entrance that wept in emptiness, then back to her clit. Slow, sure strokes that destroy any chance of rational thought.

"Shh, I promise, Marly won't hurt. We would never hurt Marly, Sarah." Brock's lips were at her neck, his tongue stroking, his voice whispering over her flesh. "Do you know what it does to me, to see you dazed, helpless in your pleasure?" he asked her deeply. "It eases my soul, Sarah. It eases a part of my heart that never knows light. Never knows warmth. To see you, accepting, loving me enough to give the ultimate sacrifice to my brother. Do you understand that, Sarah?"

God, did he know what he was saying? Did he know he was sacrificing her body on an altar built of lust? Aroused, soothed, knowing he was showing, finally, ultimately, that he could love his brother? Rather than disgusting her, confusing her further, it began to make a strange sort of sense. Then nothing made sense.

"Brock," she nearly screamed his name as Cade's fingers penetrated the entrance to her body.

She felt the muscles of her pussy grip him. Hold him. Her juices flowing around his fingers, easing his way as he groaned against her breast. She was gasping for breath, moaning like a demented sex goddess as she felt her body being lowered along the lounger, Cade's mouth following the movement, his tongue licking down her stomach, growing ever closer to the soaked, slick flesh of her cunt.

"Yes, Sarah." She looked into Brock's face as he arched her back over his arm, his head bending to her breast, his tongue laving, then covering the nipple as Cade's mouth covered her clit.

She couldn't hold on. She fought her release, fought the ultimate pleasure they were giving her, but she couldn't fight forever. The feel of long fingers thrusting deep inside her, Brock's mouth at her breast, the utter depravity of the act was too much for her. Her body arched, her head tossed. She was only vaguely aware of Brock stroking his erection with his free hand, as Cade did the same to his own. Then the world rocked around her, stars exploded before her eyes, her hips arched, her cry shattered the night, joining two harsh male cries as they climaxed simultaneously, caught in a web of mutual desire, passion, love and fear.

* * * * *

Marly closed the front door, careful to make no sound. She didn't want to disturb them, didn't want to take away from the bond being re-established, the pleasure pulsing between the three. Her heart was beating a symphony of pain, jealousy and arousal. She knew what Sarah was feeling, knew the incredible eroticism of the act, the sheer lust that pulsed through her body. She also knew that Cade was her lover.

She trembled, tears seeping from beneath her closed eyes as she listened to Sarah's climatic cries. Her fists clenched, her heart aching. Her little whimper lost in the darkness.

"Hey, Munchkin." Sam's arms wrapped around her, strong, warm, pulling her against his bare chest, his head resting on hers. "You okay with this?"

Sarah's moans were building again. Cade and Brock wouldn't leave her with just one climax, though Marly knew the actual sex act would not be completed. Not tonight. Not like that. It was a seduction, a well-intended easing, a bonding. Sarah was too wary, too frightened of what was coming. And

Marly hadn't been able to tell Cade that he could complete the act. She was terrified.

"He loves me. Right?" she whispered as his lips feathered her neck. His erection at her back proved that he was not immune to what was happening on the porch. But then again, Sam stayed hard. And since Heather James' attack, he stayed seeped in pain.

"He loves you, Marly. You and Brock. But you're his soul." Sam assured her, and she knew Sam wouldn't lie to her. She knew Cade wouldn't lie to her, but she was scared of this change. She was terrified of losing the security she had come to cherish.

"He loves you too, Sam." She leaned her head against his chest as he moved her away from the door.

The sounds of pleasure from the three outside were arousing, primal. Marly shivered, knowing well the ecstasy the other woman was experiencing.

"Yeah, me too." Sam sounded tired, weary.

She opened her mouth to speak but was interrupted by the sound of Sarah's scream of release from the porch. Marly shivered and bit her lip as arousal flooded her body.

She glanced up Sam, seeing the flush on his cheeks, feeling the taut sexual tension that invaded his body.

"Coffee?" she asked breathlessly.

Sam breathed out roughly. "Tranquilizer." He shook his head as he grinned down at her. "Hell, Marly, at least you can't say you and Sarah will live boring lives."

Marly snorted. Boring now. But she admitted, until she learned why their lives were so intertwined, it would be more than frustrating.

Chapter Thirty-one

ॐ

Sarah was desperate to forget the night before. The sight of Cade August, his cock in his hand as he stroked himself to completion while his mouth threw her into orgasm, Brock behind her, finding his own relief, his mouth at her breast, was too much. She couldn't forget it. She couldn't stop the pulsating echo of lust from trembling over her body as she thought about it. And neither could they. Breakfast had been strained, Sarah and Marly were quiet, the men tense. Sarah had no idea if Marly knew what Cade had participated in the night before, but she didn't want to ask, either. The sexual tension was thick in the air, emotions were charged and Sarah felt as though she were slowly drowning.

Desperate to escape the suddenly stifling atmosphere of the house, she put on the skimpy two-piece bathing suit Brock had bought, a wrap, grabbed a towel and headed for the pool. The men were supposedly working in the stables and barn that afternoon, so she hoped for a couple of hours of peace. A chance to clear her head.

The pool was cool, the water rippling over her seductively as she floated on a thin, foam, floating pad. Her eyes were closed to the sun, her body relaxed and warm when she felt the disturbance to the water, indicating another body had entered. She rose, shielding her eyes, watching as Marly pushed a matching pad towards her, her body stretched out on the soft foam, evidently intent on enjoying the summer sun as well.

"Everything okay?" The other woman's eyes were dark, sad.

"You looked so peaceful, I thought I would join you," Marly said softly, propping her head on her crossed arms as Sarah turned over as well.

Peaceful? Not hardly, Sarah sighed.

They faced each other now. Both wary; both uncertain. Sarah could see the questions in the other woman's eyes, a need to understand, a need Sarah felt echoing inside her.

"I checked before I came out. The men are still working." Yet, Marly kept her voice low. "I needed to talk to you."

Sarah watched her, wondering at the pain in the other woman's eyes.

"So, talk." Sarah shrugged, uncertain now that the time had come to do so.

"I know what happened last night, Sarah. I'm not angry at you."

Sarah flinched. Marly's voice was too gentle, too understanding.

"I'm glad one of us is fine with it," she muttered in frustration. "Because I'll be honest, Marly. I'm having a hell of a time here."

"I didn't say it doesn't bother me, instinctually," Marly sighed. "It was the nightmare. Cade won't stay away when one of them has the nightmare. He knew you were with Brock. I knew something would happen."

Sarah's heart beat sluggishly in her breast. Panic threatened to engulf her. A panic born of her own confusion, her own conflicting emotions. None of this made sense to her, especially her own arousal.

"How much has Brock told you about this?" Marly couldn't meet her eyes now.

Marly wasn't ashamed, she wasn't frightened, but Sarah could tell she was uncertain. That uncertainty made her vulnerable and Marly August wasn't a woman noted for vulnerability. Sassiness, daring, even a measure of pride, but not vulnerability.

"I would like to think I know everything," Sarah sighed. "If I don't by now, I'm going to be pissed later."

Sarah knew that more would likely be too much.

"Their lifestyle?" Marly's eyes met hers fully now. Sarah saw the incredible strength it was taking for her to face Sarah's knowledge head on.

Sarah lowered her eyes, watching her fingers play nervously through the water. She shrugged.

"I know about the lifestyle and the part you play in it. I know Brock refuses to stop." Sarah remembered his flash of pain when he asked her not to make him. As though she had control of what he did.

"Do you know why?" There was the edge of pain. But it was rife with confusion, with sadness.

Sarah raised her gaze until she met Marly's once again.

"Cade hasn't told you?" she asked, checking the yard again to make certain there were no ears to overhear their conversation.

"He won't tell me, Sarah. And I have to know. Whatever's going on is killing the only man I've ever loved and I can't stand it anymore." Despair edged her words, and filled her eyes. "The attack the other night and what happened outside last night, has only made him worse. "

Sarah sighed roughly. "I need a drink."

Dammit, she didn't need this. She moved from the foam pad, wading through the waist deep water to the wide set of steps that led to the concrete patio. There, sitting in icy splendor beneath the table umbrella was the pitcher of southern tea she had made early. Sweet, with an edge of whisky, it was created to calm even the worst of maidenly jitters. She was getting those a lot lately.

Marly followed her, watching her, needing something Sarah wasn't certain was her place to give. Pouring two glasses of the tea, Sarah sat down in one of the cushioned chairs, shaded by the umbrella above. Marly was only seconds later joining her.

"Sarah. I know these men," Marly whispered. "They're good men. Strong, honorable men. What they need from the women they love isn't natural. It's not painful, it's filled with love, and often a beauty you would never expect, but it leaves whatever is broken in them unmended. I want Cade whole. I need him healed."

"I haven't agreed to what they want." She couldn't look Marly in the eye. She hadn't agreed, but she knew the pressure was on. She wasn't certain how long she could resist, as long as she was in this house.

"You will." Marly smiled, showing no jealousy, no remorse. "They're exceptional men, Sarah. But I can't accept it until I know why."

And Cade obviously didn't want her to know. This placed Sarah in a position of knowing, of seeing Marly's pain, her inability to understand in the face of him touching another woman. It was a touch Sarah had been unable to deny. Why should she deny this woman understanding in return?

"Cade acts like a dangerous man, Marly." Sarah breathed roughly. "I'm not certain if I want to be the one to tell you anything."

"He won't hurt you," Marly promised. "I swear, Sarah. Please, just tell me."

Sarah gazed into those wide, pleading eyes. Marly was younger than she by a few years. Two perhaps. Younger, but already accepting more than Sarah could have believed possible.

"Men are assholes," she muttered.

Marly's return smile was bitter, accepting.

"I know they were abused. Somehow. I know something terrible happened, Sarah. But none of them will tell me what. I need to know what happened." Marly leaned close, staring at Sarah in determination.

Sarah took a long drink, tasting the liquor in her drink and praying for courage. Where was Brock and his sexual itch when she needed the distraction? Oh no, he had to go out and play cowboy.

She set her glass on the table, breathing deeply.

"I don't know specifics," she told Marly, remembering the pain, the haunting echo of agony reflecting from Brock that night. "I know it was a friend of their father. Mr. August sent them away when they were young, teenagers. The man chained them, abused them." She swallowed tightly past her own pain. "He forced them to abuse each other. From what Brock said, Cade took the worst of it, to spare his brothers."

Marly's face was white. She stared at Sarah, unblinking, almost dazed.

"How long did it last?" It was the voice of horror, speaking in a whisper.

"Months, I know that." Sarah breathed deeply. "The result was that it destroyed their ability to be brothers. To show affection to each other. Especially the twins. Brock called it isolation. They were mentally and emotionally isolated from one another after they escaped. The only thing that brought it back was when they were with a woman. Together."

Her hand trembling, Marly pushed back the stray strands of curls escaping from her braid. Tears filled her eyes, but she didn't let them fall.

"When Brock told you about all this," she whispered. "He told you about me? About being with me?"

Sarah's heart softened. She was well aware that the men had raised Marly, and each loved her in some sense. She could see Marly's fear of censure, her fear of hurting any of those men.

"Brock told me it was an extension of his love for his brothers. That through you, through your bond with them, he can be close to them again," she told the younger woman. "He cares for you, Marly."

"But he loves you," Marly replied, her voice just as soft. "In essence, Cade needs to be with you, to express his love for Brock. His bond with him. That's why he wants you."

It wasn't a question. At least not the kind that required an aye or a nay.

"I don't lust after Cade, Marly. I love Brock. I always have." Sarah fought to explain, even though she didn't understand.

"Sarah." Marly laid her hand on her arm, her eyes too understanding. Too sympathetic. "I know. I know, because I don't lust after Brock either. But neither do I refuse him."

Sarah took a deep, nervous breath.

"I'm scared, Marly," she could admit this to the woman, but not to Brock. "I'm terrified of this."

There was no anger now, no sadness in Marly's expression.

"Because you know you'll enjoy it. Because you know you want to take that sadness from his eyes, that pain, if only for a while. And the acceptance he has of it, makes you wonder at his love." She knew.

Sarah bit her lip.

"I love Cade, Sarah, more than you know. But I had to know why, before I could bear the thought of him being with you."

Sarah shook her head desperately. She wanted to deny it would happen, but couldn't force the words past her lips.

"Oh Sarah, you don't know the August men very well." Marly smiled sadly. "They are seductive, dominating. When you least expect it, when you are at your weakest, they'll be there for you. Once they touch you and you look into Brock's eyes and see his pleasure, his joy, you won't be able to resist. Just as you couldn't resist last night."

"How do you stand it?" Sarah whispered.

"You've accepted that Brock has sex with me, haven't you Sarah? You saw his need when he told you, and you let it go. That's all I can do. I can't let Cade be destroyed by this."

"And I'm supposed to just give in?" Sarah asked her incredulously.

"When the time is right, and it happens, you won't want to stop it." Marly shook her head, her expression resigned. "I know where Cade's heart is. I know who fills his soul. I can handle this, if you can."

"And if I can't?" she asked Marly with exaggerated patience. "Marly, they want to share their women. That isn't natural."

Marly shook her head.

"It's not natural for normal men. But they aren't normal, Sarah. They are strong and brave and they've survived where others would not have been able. If this is what it takes for them to survive, then I won't deny them."

"You talk as though you want me to do this," Sarah burst out, incredulous. "He's your lover, Marly."

"And I'll have to leave the room and let my lover be a brother, through your body," Marly pointed out fiercely. "But do you know what? I love him with everything that's in my soul and if this is what he needs to survive, considering the pleasure I get from it as well, then I won't deny him."

Sarah stood to her feet, trembling, hating the curiosity in herself, the knowledge in Marly's eyes. Hating the acceptance slowly building within her. None of it was natural. None of it should be acceptable. And yet, in some small way, she was beginning to understand, and that terrified her.

"Sarah." Marly stopped her as she turned away. "Loving Brock won't be easy. But I do know he's loved you, ached for you for years. Can you just walk away from him? And if you stay, can you bear to see this need eating at him, day after day? Can you do that, knowing you can wipe it away? Knowing that in one act, one that will bring you no pain, only pleasure, you can take his pain away? Don't you understand why I can allow this? That I would love Cade enough to give him this?"

She walked away from the other woman. Walked away from the questions, and the knowledge. But her fears pounded inside her head. Not fear of the brothers, but her fear that she couldn't resist, and soon, too soon, she would give in.

Chapter Thirty-two

ဢ

"You told Marly about the abuse." Cade stood in the doorway of Sarah and Brock's bedroom, his expression furious, the color in his eyes shifting like thunderclouds.

Tense, vibrating with his anger, he watched Sarah and Brock with an intensity that should have flayed the skin from their bones. Brock glanced at Sarah with a frown of disapproval.

"You didn't," he said with a heavy sigh. "Did you make her cry, Sarah?"

Sarah's watched them, mingled anger and confusion filling her. She had known Cade would be furious. Had known it would hurt him for Marly to know the truth, but she was sick of these men expecting her and Marly to carry the brunt of their pain.

"What difference would that make? She's a grown woman, not a child, and she deserved to know why her lover was on the porch last night with his head buried between my legs."

Her statement had Cade's eyes narrowing on her.

"That's not a good enough reason," he snarled.

"Oh, it isn't." She crossed her arms over her chest, watching him with mock incredulity. "Excuse me, Mr. August, but most women would have done more than cried a little bit. They would have killed you anyway, and me with you. They would have cut your damned tongue out so you couldn't use it on another woman."

Cade raked his fingers through his hair, frustration and fury evident in his expression and the tense set of his shoulders. He was enraged with no way to expend the fury.

"She wasn't supposed to know," he growled, still furious, unrepentant at the secret he had been holding.

Sarah saw more than that in his eyes, though. She saw shame. Cade had not accepted the past as Brock had. The helplessness of whatever actions he had been forced to take still haunted him.

"No one told me one way or the other," she told him, refusing to back down. "She asked, I told her what I knew. Period."

"It was none of your damned business." His fists were clenched at his side now, watching her stand up to him, making her nervous, more than aware of the strength of the man facing her so furiously.

"I beg to differ," she argued. "You forget, Cade, the men of this house are doing everything they can to drag me into the little love nest they've created. That makes it my business."

Sarah could feel her own anger edging into her voice. The dominant streak in these men was becoming more than aggravating. Irritation was setting in on her fast.

"Sarah." Brock's voice held a warning edge.

She turned to her lover, frowning. His carefully controlled expression sent a frisson of unease down her spine, but not enough to make her back down. She wasn't about to back down. She hadn't asked to be drawn into this, she would be damned if she would allow them to run over her.

"Don't 'Sarah' me." She rolled her eyes in irritation. "What's the big deal anyway? Didn't Mr. High-And-Mighty August over there expect that his lover would want to know why he wanted to fuck another woman? I sure as hell would."

Was it just her, or had the sexual tension in the room risen dramatically?

"You don't know what you're doing, Sarah," Brock told her, his voice low. "Let it go for now."

Sarah rolled her eyes. She cast both men a disgusted look, impatience filling her.

"Fine. Let it go, Sarah," she mocked. "I'll be more than happy to let it go. Now excuse me while I go find lunch."

She stalked across the room, more than expecting Cade August to step aside when she reach the doorway. Instead, he stood still, watching her from eyes building with anger, emotion.

"Brock?" Cade's voice pulsed with arousal.

Sarah heard a heavy sigh behind her. She looked over her shoulder at her lover, sitting in the chair to the side of them. His eyes were heavy-lidded, aroused, his body tight with sexual tension. Sarah felt a small tingle of apprehension work its way through her body.

"How?" Brock asked Cade, his voice throbbing now with intensity.

"How what?" Sarah stepped back from Cade, her eyes widening as he stepped completely into the room, closing the door behind him.

"What about Sam?" Brock ignored her question as they both watched her.

"He's gone again." Cade's voice was brooding, still angry, but darker, more sexual now.

"Brock?" Sarah wondered why she wasn't completely terrified. Cade August looked like a man intent on fucking, and Brock appeared more than willing to let him have at her.

"Come here, Sarah," he said, his voice gentle, though filled with the hot throb of lust.

"Why?" she questioned him, almost frantic now.

Cade watched her, his expression filled with anticipation, sexuality. Dark determination defined his body, and his erection bulged the loose jeans he was wearing. Brock wasn't in any better shape. As a matter of fact, he had risen from his chair and was unbuttoning his jeans as her eyes widened.

"Come here, Sarah." He held his hand out to her.

"Why?" she whispered, trying to find her voice. Oh God, what had she gotten herself into this time?

She could feel her heart speeding up, sexual tingles of awareness raced over her skin, making her too aware of the intent in their expressions. She could feel her nipples hardening and that sent a flare of exasperated self-disgust through her. She had no self-control. It was pathetic. She wasn't frightened, but she admitted to being more than wary at the moment.

"Because I told you to, Sarah." His jeans were pulled off, his shirt falling to the floor, his swollen cock rose from between his thighs, thick and hard.

In an almost absent gesture, she watched as his hand circled his erection, his fingers stroking beneath the bulging head as he watched her. Pleasuring himself, totally comfortable with the act.

"What are you going to do?" She stepped back again, watching as Cade began to undress as well. " Brock. Tell me what you're going to do first."

He moved to the table by the bed. Pulling out the drawer, he lifted the erotic toys he had replaced for her, checking them carefully, laying them on the table, his eyes never leaving hers.

"I don't want to be punished like this, Brock," she whispered, her body trembling, preparing itself. She was already wet, aching.

"This isn't your punishment, Sarah," he told her, a small grin tilting his lips. "The spanking will be your punishment. The fucking will be your pleasure."

He walked to her then, his cheekbones flushed, his eyes holding hers. Moving with relaxed confidence, he went behind her, stopping at her back. His hands lifted to the zipper on her dress.

"Make him leave then." She was breathing hard, too fast. Fighting to draw air into her lungs.

"No. He stays. He gets to spank you, Sarah." Shock rippled over her in waves.

"Brock, please." She was almost frantic now as his hands went to her shoulders, the dress inching down her body as he pulled the small straps over her arms.

Where was her strength? She couldn't find the will to run. They wouldn't rape her; she knew they wouldn't. If she wanted to leave, she could go. Why couldn't she go? She whimpered as her dress fell to the floor. The silk thong she wore went next, Brock's hard fingers pushing them over her hips, down her thighs until they pooled at her feet.

When Sarah looked up, Cade was sitting on the bed, his cock stretched along his abdomen as he stroked it, much in the same manner that Brock had stroked his own.

"Sarah, when you showered, did you do as I told you?" Brock whispered in her ear.

The daily ritual he had laid out for her, for staying prepared for his pleasures, was burned into her mind.

"Yes," she whispered. She had just showered less than an hour earlier. She shivered, knowing her body was more than ready for whatever they wanted.

"I want you to go to Cade. He'll tell you what to do, Sarah." The hands at her back urged her forward.

Sarah swallowed, fighting the trepidation washing over her body, the lust pulsing through it. She walked slowly, Brock urging her nearly every step of the way towards Cade.

"I'm scared." She hated admitting that. Merely feet from Cade's big body, she whispered the words to Brock.

He stopped. She stopped. She felt him sigh deeply.

"Would I let anyone hurt you, Sarah?" She felt his lips at her neck, watched Cade's eyes darken as he too watched the caress.

"No," she admitted, the breath heaving from her chest.

"It's unknown. You're aroused, more so than ever before. It's not fear, baby, it's anticipation. You know that."

She knew that, but she couldn't control it.

"Cade won't fuck you this time." He breathed hard at her back. "At least, not with his cock. This time, he'll just play with you. He would never fuck you while he's angry with you. But he would never hurt you either."

He urged her into Cade's arms, then turned from her.

"Where are you going?" She turned to him, terrified as he started to leave the room.

"You aren't the only one in trouble, Sarah," he told her softly. "Cade won't do anything until I return with Marly. She knew better than to draw you into this. So she can share in your punishment."

She went to stop him, but suddenly hard hands shackled her wrists. Cade was on his feet now, staring down at her, his body too warm, too close.

"This is insane," she gasped as Brock left the room.

"Do you know what it will do to me, to watch Brock prepare Marly to take her plug? To watch him spank her, then fuck her with the dildo I bought especially for her?" His voice was tight, growling with his arousal.

"It should kill you," she gasped, hating the way her breasts swelled, her nipples hardening further at the thought. She was as insane as the rest of them were.

"It kills me with pleasure," he told her, his voice rough. "To know he loves me enough to do that for me. To know he finds the same pleasure in it. The same bond I feel as well." His voice gentled. "The sexual dominance inside us can't be explained away, Sarah, or governed rationally. It just is."

It just was. The implication was clear. Her love of Brock would extend to his brothers, or his pain would only intensify.

Chapter Thirty-three

ဢ

Brock chose that moment to re-enter the room, tugging a reluctant Marly behind him.

"Cade August, I'm going to kick your ass," she snapped as she caught sight of Sarah and Cade.

Sarah didn't like the flare of heat in the other woman's eyes as she glimpsed Cade shackling Sarah to him.

"Are you darling?" he asked her silkily. "You may very well do it, but your little ass will be spanked first for defying me."

"I needed to know." She should have stomped her foot. Sarah could clearly see her desire to. "You're my lover."

"You had no need, Marly, to share my shame." There was the fury, the anger he had been fighting to contain. "I chose to protect you from it. It was not your choice to go behind my back if you were not content with my decision."

"I needed to understand," she yelled at him, pulling against Brock's hold. "I had to, Cade."

"Had I decided to fuck her, Marly, then I would have told you myself," he informed Marly as he sat down on the bed.

Sarah cried out in surprise when he pulled her across his lap after him, holding her there effectively.

"Instead," he continued. "You can watch Sarah's punishment before receiving your own."

His hand landed with stinging force on the right cheek of Sarah's butt. She squealed out, jerking against him. Her body began to hum. Why couldn't she be normal? A kiss should excite her, not a hard hand slapping her ass. She felt it again.

Not hard, but with enough force to make her skin flush, she knew. Enough force to make her vagina tighten in anticipation.

His hand fell again, leaving a burning impression of force. Tears came to her eyes; pleasure flooded her senses. She had never known she could be like this. That she could be so depraved. He slapped her again. She cried out, her eyes locked on Brock, watching his eyes darken in a haze of arousal as his hands moved to cup Marly's full breasts. Her lover was holding another woman, caressing her hard nipples, and Sarah couldn't find the outrage she knew she should feel.

Bright burning blows continued to rock her body. At least a dozen landed to the full globes of her rear. Each one sent the juices pulsing in her cunt until she felt as though the slick essence frothed along the intimate lips.

"Your skin is soft." Suddenly, the hand was caressing rather than punishing. "So pretty and red now, Sarah."

His fingers, hard and calloused separated the full mounds, a finger running down the little valley that separated the flesh. His finger paused at her tight rear hole before continuing to the bubbling heat of her cunt.

Her hands clenched in the comforter, her eyes tracking Brock's hand as it smoothed down Marly's heaving stomach to the saturated flesh between her thighs. Sarah whimpered, then cried out when Cade pushed his finger deep inside her.

"I'm going to lubricate you, Sarah, then insert the plug up that tight little hole," Cade's voice was guttural. "I want you to stay still. Very still, Sarah."

She felt him reach for the tube of lubrication. She heard Marly cry out harshly, watched her body arch as Brock pushed two long fingers deep inside her vagina. The other woman's legs were spread and Sarah couldn't help but watch as Brock pulled back, then thrust forward again. The sight of his fingers disappearing into the other woman's body sent varying warnings shattering through Sarah's brain. She shouldn't enjoy it.

Her breath lodged in her throat as she felt the cool sensation of the lubrication, followed by the gentle insertion of a thick finger up her anus.

"Are you watching them?" Cade asked her, stretching her, pulling out, then apply more of the slick gel as his finger thrust smoothly inside her once again.

"No," she gasped, watching Brock, his arm around Marly's waist, lifting her against him as he slowly pulled his fingers from her, moved up to smooth over her clit, then back down to thrust quickly inside her once again.

"Don't lie to me, Sarah." A hard hand came down on her buttock, the force firmer than before.

Sarah cried out, jerked, felt her cunt pulse, spilling her essence along her thighs.

"Are you watching them?" he asked her again.

Sarah cried out at the biting pleasure as two fingers slid into her anus now, moving with smooth, stretching thrusts against the tight hole.

"Yes," she wanted to scream out at the pleasure, the sinful decadence washing over her.

"Marly's watching you too, Sarah," he told her, his voice filled with approval. "Her eyes are all big and dark while she watches your flesh separate for me. Stretch for me."

Sarah's cry echoed Marly's. Unfortunately, neither of them sounded as though they were protesting. Over and over his fingers pulled back, applied more of the gel, pushed in again, stretching her, easing inside her until she wanted to scream out at the deliberate teasing being inflicted on her.

"Are you ready yet, Sarah?" Cade's voice was dark. Growling with sexuality.

"Yes. Yes." She tossed her head, almost, almost understanding the men now as she watched the pleasure washing over Marly.

There was something so forbidden, so darkly erotic about watching the man she loved pleasuring another woman, as she was pleasured in turn, that broke through the normal barriers of sexuality. A sharing. She knew that she and Marly would both share this forever, and knowing the other woman knew her lover so intimately, wasn't nearly as abhorrent as it should have been.

Finally, she felt him move away again. She imagined him picking up the thick plug, moving back to her. Then she felt the tip of it lodge against her tight hole, causing her to tense instinctively.

"Relax for him, Sarah." Brock's voice was filled with desperate yearning. "Please, baby, do this for me."

Her eyes locked with Brock's. She allowed her muscles to relax, breathing harshly as she felt Cade begin to push the device firmly into her body. Brock's eyes were nearly black now, his face heavily flushed, his expression absorbed, centered on Cade's action.

Seconds later she felt the thick base lodge inside her, stretching her, filling her. Then stinging force was applied to her rear once again. She jerked, cried out, tensing as Cade slapped her ass harder this time, his hand falling in rapid succession until the fire spread across her rear, making her squirm on his thighs, rubbing her inner flesh against his hard thigh, screaming out with the duality of the pain and the pleasure.

The harsh slaps stopped just as fast as they began. Then Cade was moving, pulling Sarah to her feet, wrapping his arm around her as Brock took his place, Marly took hers.

The other woman was clearly excited, already moaning, already prepared for the pleasure to come. Her eyes locked with Cade's and Sarah was confused, surprised by the love glowing in them. Adoration, complete and heartfelt glittered in the dark blue depths. Pleasure, excitement, complete acceptance reflected in her expression.

Sarah watched as Brock smoothed his hand over the other woman's buttocks. Then he raised it, high. The resounding smack had Marly jerking, crying out, grinding her hips against Brock's thighs jerkily. A total of eight sharp blows, until the flesh was bright red, and Marly was crying out in both pain and pleasure.

Brock's cock jerked along his abdomen. A pearly drop of fluid collecting on the tip as Marly moved against him. Sarah licked her lips. She wanted to go to her knees, run her tongue over the near to bursting flesh and take it into her mouth.

She watched as Brock then separated Marly's buttocks, preparing her. His eyes raised to hers and she barely contained her cry at the look there. Like Marly, complete love, complete devotion. Approval washed over her. There was no pain in his eyes now, no shadows of sadness. There was joy. It made Sarah willing to do anything, give anything to keep that look in his eyes. She now understood how Marly accepted.

"Sarah," he whispered her name as his finger sank between the cheeks of Marly's rear.

He prepared the other woman carefully, just as Cade had prepared her. Stretching her, using the lubricating gel in large amounts, then pushing the thick plug slowly into her.

Marly was almost screaming, pleading. She begged for Cade to allow her ease. Perspiration covered the other woman's skin, lust and love in equal measure filled her eyes.

Then Brock was pulling her up, standing, looking at Cade. He picked up the dildo he had brought with him when he went for Marly. Cade picked up Sarah's as she whimpered, feeling Cade pull her to the couch, stretching her out on the thick cushions as Brock moved Marly to the bed.

"Don't do this, Brock," Sarah cried out as Cade settled himself between her thighs, holding her open, his eyes dark, intense. "Please, Brock. I need to be fucked. Now. Not like this."

Cade lodged the head of the dildo at her grasping, wet entrance.

"If we gave you what you needed, where would be the punishment?" Cade asked her a second before the dildo plunged home.

Sarah's back arched. She no longer had the ability to watch Brock and Marly, or the sense to understand anything but the incredible fullness, the stretching, driving pleasure erupting between her thighs. Then, hot, destroying, his mouth latched on her clit, sucking it in time to the smooth strokes inside her clutching cunt as lust slammed through her system so hard, so fast, she wondered if she would lose her last grip on reality. She shuddered, cried out, her flesh tightening on the thrusting device as he rode her through such torturous pleasure she felt she was dying. Yet she couldn't climax. She cried. She begged. She twisted on the driving device and still it only built higher.

She heard Marly. Screaming. She was coming. The other woman was exploding, screaming Cade's name, her climax throbbing in her voice. Sarah's head tossed. She was dying. Dying to come.

"Brock," Sarah gasped out his name as Marly's cries began to subside. She jerked, her head tossed as she fought for release.

Then he was there. His hand took the dildo as Cade strode to the bed. He drove it in hard, his head lowering, his lips latching onto her clit, hot and hard as he sucked it with a steady pressure. One thrust, a flick of his tongue. A second hard thrust, a firmer stroke, and she exploded. Over and over, her hips raised high, her orgasm tearing through her.

As it eased, Brock pulled the device from her, then moved to her head, his cock, huge, thrusting towards her mouth.

Brock didn't ask. He went to his knees, his eyes meeting Sarah's, then he was pushing the head of his erection past her lips with an agonized groan. Sarah enclosed the thick head, her hand going to grip the base, turning to her side, taking him hungrily as he watched her, his eyes bright, filled with promise as she drew on his flesh, matching the hard, quick strokes into her mouth.

He came with a shout. His body jerked, his semen exploding from the tip with hard, hot jets into her mouth. His hands clenched in her hair, his back arched and her name was a harsh, brutal shout of satisfaction.

Chapter Thirty-four

♊

Brock and Cade were sitting on the patio that evening when Sam returned from the hospital. He walked onto the sheltered concrete area, a fifth of whisky in his hand, his face haggard.

The vine-draped iron and wood enclosure provided a measure of protection from anyone with a binocular or rifle scopes, but as Brock looked into his brother's eyes, he realized there were other ways to kill a man.

Sam sat down heavily in a padded chair, staring up at the vine-covered opening as though the pattern of greenery twisting about the thick wooden beams required concentration to decipher. He lowered his head long enough to bring the bottle to his mouth, drink deep and grimace, then go back to the perusal.

"How's she doing?" Cade's voice was as haunted as Sam's eyes.

Sam shrugged. "Tara says she fine. She won't see me. She won't talk to me."

Brock took a deep breath. Rick returned earlier, rage glittering in his eyes when he reported her injuries. She had been tied and gagged, the clothes cut from her body. Then the knife had sliced small, hairline cuts into her thighs and the flesh of her genitals. As far as pain went, it was tolerable. The mental and psychological damage was great, though. The bastard had recounted how Sam had been similarly cut and the abuses he had suffered through. She had been warned she would suffer the same if she came back to the ranch. She had been told that she was paying for the lust Sam felt for her.

They hadn't even known Sam was attracted to her. Had no idea their brother had been slowly courting her, seducing her. The woman was a damned wildcat. Or at least, she had been.

Sam was alone. Isolated in silence and liquor, staring into the evening sky as though searching for answers. There was no laughter in him now, no wise-assed comments, no sense of joy. The very qualities Cade and Brock had sacrificed everything they were at one time, to preserve a part of, had been snatched away as though it had never existed.

Sam took another long pull on the liquor. His body was tense, wired. He almost vibrated with the rage and pain swirling inside him.

"Don't get drunk, Sam," Brock warned him quietly.

"Why shouldn't I?" Sam asked him, his tone unconcerned, cool.

Brock glanced at Cade.

"Sam—"

"I want your woman, Brock." Sam looked in his eyes and Brock almost winced at the shattered look there. "I need her."

Brock shook his head, he wouldn't tolerate Sam touching her while he was like this. "You should have gone to her before now."

Sarah would accept him, Brock knew. She was slowly accustoming herself to Cade's touch. Brock knew she would grow used to Sam's as well. The idea of it. Once, she had warned him, only once. And only for him. But he saw the excitement in her eyes, the same excitement he felt at the thought of it.

"I frighten her." Sam lifted the bottle, his glance surprised as though he should have drank more, or hadn't drank enough. Brock wasn't certain which. "I don't blame her for being frightened."

Brock frowned.

"What do you need, Sam?" he asked him carefully.

Sam swallowed tight, grimacing.

"Fuck it," he growled. "I need to leave her the fuck alone."

He tipped the bottle to his lips, the amber liquid draining further. He breathed in harshly when he lowered the bottle.

"Have you ever wondered what we're doing to them?" Sam finally asked quietly.

"Don't, Sam." Cade's voice was dark, rough. "We don't hurt them. We love them."

Sam shook his head. He wiped his hand wearily over his face, leaning forward in the chair, staring at the floor now.

"She likes the pain doesn't she, Brock?" Sam didn't look at his brother.

They all knew Sarah liked the edge of pain. Cade had discovered that earlier, Brock had known it since the first. There was no disguising her screams, her pleas in the dead of night, the sound of his hand slapping her ass.

"Sam, you don't have to ask my permission." Brock felt helpless, uncertain of what his brother needed.

"You would," Sam whispered.

Surprise flared in Brock's chest. Sam's head raised, his gaze tortured, glittered with agony, haunted with the past.

Brock shrugged. He glanced at Cade, feeling as uncertain as his other brother looked.

"Sam—" Cade started to speak, his voice low, vibrating with concern.

"Forget it." Sam fell back in the chair and drank again.

He was taking long, hard pulls of the liquor. Sam had never been much of a drinker, so it worried them both that he was hitting the bottle so hard now.

"I want to forget," Sam whispered, staring at the leafy ceiling once again.

His voice was agonized. It seared their brains, their souls with the memories. Brock shook his head, his fists clenching, unable to look at his twin. He could feel his rage, Sam's rage, beating at his heart. The bond they had shared when they were younger had been nearly destroyed in those nightmare months. Now, Brock only knew it again during sex, or during the overwhelming grief that often gripped Sam.

"That's enough." Cade came to his feet, his voice hard, final. "We can't change it and we can't forget. And there's no sense in allowing the bastard to win. We survived, Sam, it's better than many would have done."

Cade turned his back on them. He propped his shoulder against the patio support, his head lowered. Brock took a deep, hard breath.

"Where's your woman, Brock?" Sam asked him, his voice easing into a low, slow, drawl after drinking heavily from the bottle once again.

"You don't touch my woman drunk, Sam. You know we don't do that. Sarah can't ease this demon and I won't make her try."

The demon, rage. Rage so all-consuming, so bitter and soul-worn that Brock knew Sam would never find the softness within himself to touch Sarah with any tender emotion. He wouldn't allow his brother's demons to destroy the fragile balance they were building within their home. The pleasure Sarah received from their touch could be tainted for all time if Sam took her in anger.

"I wasn't going to fuck her." Sam rose slowly to his feet now, his shoulders slumped, his voice broken. "Just wanted to make sure I stayed out of her way. I know I'm not fit for a whore, let alone a good woman."

Brock had a feeling Sam wasn't talking about just while he was drunk.

"Sam." He came to his feet as his brother stumbled to the study doors.

"I'm heading to bed, Brock." Sam waved his hand back. "Maybe I can sleep it off."

There was a better chance of the nightmare leaving him screaming in broken rage. Brock glanced at Cade, who was now watching the weaving twin as he entered the study. Absolute worry creased his face; pain wearied it.

"She meant something to him. More than just a friend." Cade sighed deeply. "Fuck. He should have told us. We would have tried to protect her."

Brock thought of the redhead wildcat sister of Tara Glaston. She wouldn't have accepted protection. She was too busy trying to give it. He sighed wearily, shaking his head at the pain and grief that surrounded Sam now. It would ease, when the three of them came together with Sarah. It always did. It didn't make sense and hell, a psychiatrist would have a field day with them. But it worked for them. They had survived and they were still a part of each other. That was all that mattered. They had won. The Monster had lost. Or had he?

Chapter Thirty-five

ဢ

The house was quiet, the television set at low sound in consideration for Sarah who sat at the far side of the family room, engrossed in a book. Television had never been her thing.

The men were in their normal loungewear, sweatpants and bare chests and feet. Marly was dressed in one of Cade's long shirts and dozed comfortably. Sarah wore one of the nightshirts she preferred. It went past her knees and was loose enough to allow for the lack of a bra. Not that wearing one did any good in this household. The men here thought they were made to hide. Every one she owned had disappeared.

She didn't know how long she had sat there, and paid no attention when Sam walked into the room. She definitely took notice when he went to his knees before her, though.

Sarah looked up, blinking, her heart pounding at the sheer, undiluted agony in his eyes.

"I need—" He swallowed tightly, regret and remorse thick in his voice.

Sarah's eyes went to Brock. He was watching his brother closely. When his eyes met hers, there was in a plea in them. Her breath stuttered in her chest. Sam needed. He needed her. His only connection to his twin. Just as Marly was his only connection to Cade.

He lifted the book from her hand, carefully marking her page then laying it on the table beside her. Sarah trembled. She had never seen lust in a man's eyes like she saw in Sam's. No love, no affection, only lust, tortured and desperate. Brock was sitting on the couch now and she saw his thick erection tenting his sweat pants. There was the love she needed. Love and approval shining bright and pure in his eyes.

She looked at Sam, watching as his hands went to her legs, curled in the chair, tucked beneath the nightshirt. He gripped her knees, pulling them from their bent position until her feet were flat on the floor, one leg on each side of him.

Her hands fluttered, then settled on the chair arm, gripping it desperately as his hands went to her thighs and began smoothing the shirt up them. She could feel her body warming, arousal building. She didn't want it to, she still couldn't believe it could happen, but it did. And Sam looked so much like Brock that it was easy to allow herself to slip into the desire he needed.

Brock didn't approach Sam. He just sat on the couch watching, breathing heavily, entranced with the sight of another man preparing to pleasure his woman. Sarah allowed herself to relax in the chair, to lift her hips as Sam drew the shirt over them. Then he was pulling it from her body and tossing it aside.

"I know what you like," Sam whispered as he leaned forward, his lips touching hers as she watched him, wide-eyed with shock and desire. "Will you let me give you what you need, Sarah?"

He whispered the words then licked her lips. Sarah's eyelids fluttered, her breasts heaved with the need for air. She felt her thighs weakening, her cunt moistening, preparing her body for her lover's brother.

His lips drifted over hers, his fight for control tightening his muscles, making his body tremble. She could feel the drive for domination in his body, his desperate fight to stay gentle, to touch her with tenderness in spite of the fury raging inside him. He didn't want gentle, he didn't want easy. She nipped his lip. Hard.

Sam jerked, his eyes flaring with surprise.

"What's the point, if it doesn't help you?" she asked him. "I'm not Marly. I don't need your love."

Sam's eyes narrowed.

"I could hurt you." She could see the fear in his eyes that he would.

Her hands rose from his shoulders, going to his thick hair and fisting in it tightly.

"And I could hurt you."

She watched his eyes flare, his lust rising, but the shadows lessened. A hard smile tilted his face. He jerked her to him, his lips mashing down on hers, driving her lips into her teeth as his tongue speared into her mouth. And Brock was watching. Sarah gave herself to Sam, to the violence he was more than willing to spend on her body, her arousal deepening at the thought that Brock watched. That he approved.

Sam groaned into her mouth as her nails pricked his scalp. His hands were at her back, his blunt nails scratching over her skin, his mouth eating at her, the violence of the kiss throwing them both into a maelstrom of pleasure.

Sarah was breathing hard, rough, when Sam ended their kiss. There was a smear of blood on his lip where her teeth had nipped him. He licked over it experimentally, then grinned. A true grin. One filled with promise.

"Sarah?" Brock was standing beside the chair, concern marking his face, and he wasn't alone.

Cade was there, his eyes narrowed on them both. Sarah was breathing roughly. Her breasts were swollen, her nipples hard, on fire with hunger. As she watched Brock, her eyes heavy-lidded, she felt Sam's mouth cover one of the turgid tips. She moaned harshly as she felt the edge of his teeth, a sharp nip, a rough lave of his tongue. She bucked against his him, her body catching fire as Brock's eyes seemed to glitter with knowledge, with intent as he bent to her free breast.

She screamed out with the searing sensations. Two mouths, equally hot, teeth equally sharp, hard male groans vibrating against her flesh as both breasts were tended to. It was too much. She didn't know if she could handle more. Her head fell back, one hand burying in Brock's hair, her fingers clenching tight and hard in the strands, the other repeating the action in Sam's. They were killing her. Their fingers plumped her flesh, mouths suckled hard, teeth nipped while tongues stroked. Sarah's moans shocked even her. Deep and harsh, hungry.

A sense of movement had her eyes opening. Sam and Brock drew away from her as Cade pushed the central table out of the way and dragged the mattress from the futon couch in the corner of the room. Each man was naked now, cocks hard and throbbing, swollen with anticipation and lust.

"Are you sure, baby?" Brock bent, his tongue soothing her swollen lips. "Be sure it's what you want, Sarah."

She was breathing so hard it nearly hurt. Her hand fell to her heaving stomach, her fingers gliding slowly to the heated flesh between her thighs. Her fingers dipped into the valley of her cunt, sliding low, to the entrance of her vagina. There, they dipped into the narrow channel as each man watched in fascination. She lifted her hand, her fingers glistening with the slick essence of her want. She brought one finger to her lips, coating them with the glistening juice, then sucked her finger languidly.

"Son of a fucking bitch," Brock growled, his eyes dazed.

Sam wasn't nearly as vocal, he used actions to show his approval. He jerked her from the chair against his chest, picking her up and carrying her to the mattress.

"She's using the plug," Sarah heard Cade growl. "Take it out before we go any further."

Sam flipped her onto her stomach when he laid her down, jerking her hips up, her knees automatically catching her weight. The position lifted her buttocks, giving each man a clear view of the bottom of the device.

Sarah growled as she felt Sam grip it, then with steady pressure pull it from her body. Her muscles gripped it, sending a flare of heat through her anus, contracting her womb. A hard hand fell on the cheek of her ass. Her hips bucked. She wanted to beg for more. She stayed silent instead, her head lowered, submission vibrating through her body.

The hand fell again on the other side. She jerked, her head tossing. The flare of heat, the provocative position, the acts she knew were coming sent her spiraling into a lust that frightened her. Her head lifted. There was Brock, on his knees before her, stroking his cock slowly as he watched her carefully.

She saw the rising heat in his eyes, but also concern.

Sam slapped her again. She arched her back, the pleasure/pain zinging through her body. None of the blows were hard enough to seriously hurt, but she knew her flesh would be blushing now, her buttocks slowly reddening beneath the ministrations.

"I love you, Sarah," he whispered deeply.

" —love you—" she groaned as another blow landed.

Her head tossed. This was for Sam. Sam and Cade. She somehow knew Brock would partake of Marly. The other woman was on the couch, her eyes wide, flared with arousal and surprise.

Sarah met her look; she saw the arousal, the acceptance and even pleasure in Marly's eyes. The other woman knew what was coming, knew she would soon be feeling Brock's cock slamming inside her cunt while her lover fucked another woman.

And Sarah felt no resentment. She felt a kinship with Marly, an understanding she never thought she would reach.

"Sarah." Brock was still worried.

Sam's mouth went to Sarah's buttocks, his teeth scraping the sensitive skin, his groans a husky growl. Sarah didn't answer her lover, her hand wrapped around his bulging cock and she drew him to her, ignoring his surprise. Her lips wrapped around the purpled head, sucking it into her mouth, her cry a strained groan as she felt Sam's teeth and tongue caressing her flesh harder. Deeper.

His hands went to her hair. The feel of them bunching in the strands, pulling her closer, sent her to another level of heat. She could feel the moisture leaking from her cunt, coating the lips and her inner thighs.

He drew back from her, glancing at his brothers, then at her with a small smile.

"You're sure, baby?" he asked her. "Be positive."

"Will you still love me? Always?" She needed to be sure. It was his love that gave her the courage. His love that gave her the need. She couldn't bear to lose him now.

"Forever, Sarah," he swore, his expression so tight with lust, with love, that it appeared savage. "With everything I am. Everything I have. With my heart, my soul, and my brothers."

The declaration was followed by his slow retreat from her, watching her, gauging her reaction as he went to Marly. Sam's hand landed on her ass again. Her eyes closed, her cry echoing through the room as she allowed the pleasure to build inside her.

She was turned then to her back, given no time to think before Sam went between her legs, his mouth latching hungrily at her aching, weeping cunt. Cade was at her breasts, his teeth nipping at her. Did they all know she liked the pain? She felt the edge of Sam's teeth as he raked the pulsing inner lips between her thighs. She arched. Ached. His tongue drove deep into her dripping vagina, his fingers, coated with slick lubricating gel slid firmly, deeply into her relaxed anus.

Cade's mouth was going crazy at her breasts. Licking, sucking, biting. She felt fire racing through her blood stream, lust raging through her body. She cried out at the sensation, shaking in the midst of such intense pleasure she felt faint.

"Sarah," Sam's guttural cry was in retaliation for the fingers pulling at his hair. It didn't sound like much of a protest, though.

And Sarah was tired of passive pleasure. Her muscles tightened with the need for her own domination. The need to give as well as to receive. As Sam rose to his knees between her thighs, intent on impaling her with the swollen cock rising from his body, she moved.

She came to her knees, her teeth bared in a grimace of sexual lust. Sam and Cade seemed more than surprised. Sarah didn't explain, her mouth went to Sam's cock, enveloping the near bursting tip, her teeth scraping along the fine scars that marred it. The growl that erupted from his throat was guttural, wild, animalistic.

His hips surged against her. Driving his flesh deeper into her mouth while he circled the base in his hand to keep from choking her with it. Cade moved behind her. She felt him taking up where Sam had left off at her anus. Cold gel stroked into her, her teeth nipped at Sam's scrotum, her mouth moving back to suck him deep, then retreating again to lave and nip lower.

His hand was in her hair. It bunched tight, making her cry out with the sensation. She nipped the side of his cock. He jerked.

"Again." His voice wasn't even his. It was wild, jerky.

She nipped again, her teeth torturing, tormenting. She enclosed the head in her mouth, allowing her teeth to scrape gently along the hard pulsing shaft stretching her lips. Her tongue laved the mild hurt, her nails bit into his thighs.

"Son of a bitch." Sam pulled her hair again, his groans growing hotter. "Oh yes, Sarah. Make it good, sugar. Make it so good."

She felt Cade part her buttocks, felt the tip of his cock lodge in her anus. She screamed out as Sam's cock thrust to her throat at the same time Cade slid deep inside her back entrance.

She was wild. She sucked and nipped at Sam's cock, bucked at the driving hips behind her, screamed out her need to climax as perspiration coated her body. She felt Cade stretching her, driving into her. The tight grip around his cock made the bittersweet pinch of each impalement drive her higher. The driving thrust of his cock, his hands hard, smacking at her buttocks, his harsh voice encouraging her in her lust, pushing her, driving her deeper into the combined lusts of the men she pleasured.

She felt Sam's cock pulse in her mouth. He was near. He was gasping, his hands hard in her hair as he pulled the strands, his body quivering with his impending release. Cade was thrusting harder inside her anus, his hands holding her hips, his penis driving smooth and easy inside her tender flesh.

"Sarah, not yet. I have to fuck you," Sam cried out, holding her head still now, easing his thrusts, gasping for breath. "I have to fuck you, Sarah."

Cade increased his pace. He groaned, harsh, violently as he drove harder into her. She felt his cock pulse one, twice. She screamed around Sam's erection as she felt the hot, harsh blasts of his sperm deep inside her anus. Then he was sliding away, his hands smoothing over her buttocks.

Sam moved from her mouth. He pushed her to her back, grabbing her legs as he raised them straight up. Holding her ankles at his left shoulder, he positioned his swollen flesh then drove deep, hard, penetrating her soaked, grasping pussy in one hard lunge.

Sarah screamed out at the pleasure. Her head tossed, her body bucking at the incredibly tight fit, the angle of penetration stroking nerves she never knew her body possessed. She couldn't thrust back, she couldn't halt the driving thrusts into her. Not that she wanted to. She screamed for more. She begged him to fuck her harder.

Her head tossed, her eyes opening, then widening as she caught sight of the couple on the couch. Brock had Marly on her back, her legs raised, her feet held at his far shoulder. His cock tunneled into her pussy with deep driving strokes, and Sarah glimpsed the base of the plug that she knew stretched the other woman's ass.

Marly was screaming, bucking into the strong motions of Brock's hips as he drove the thick shaft home repeatedly. Sarah knew how it filled the other woman, knew the pleasure driving her higher. Just as Sam was driving Sarah higher.

At that moment, Marly's head tossed, eyes opening, meeting Sarah's gaze. Dark blue eyes glittered with lust as the woman glanced at her lover watching as he watched Sam fuck Sarah now. There was trust there. Trust and understanding. Sarah fought to answer her look, but Cade chose that moment to come over to her, his lips latching onto her breast, his teeth nipping at her nipple.

Sarah lost what little sanity she may have possessed at that point.

She was poised on a pinnacle of absolute sensation. Every inch of Sam's fiery erection sent needles of agonizing pleasure straight to her womb, contracting it, making her beg, gasp, plead for a release that wouldn't come.

She was dying. Sam was sweating, the warm moisture dripped from his hair and fell to her body as he groaned, harsh, desperate sounds erupting from his throat as he fought to throw her over the edge. Her body wouldn't fall. The climax hovering on the edge of reason would drive her insane.

"Brock," she screamed his name.

Her body was tight, her orgasm was so near, promising to explode in such pleasure she would die from it, if only it would happen.

"Can't — can't hold on —" Sam gasped.

"No. No. Sam. Please —" she screamed out as she felt his cock twitch, pulse, then he was driving it deeper, harder, his release spurting hot and hard inside her as he cried out his own pleasure.

"No," she begged, near tears, so close. "No. No. Not yet."

He moved away from her quickly as she reached out for him. Then Brock was there. He was still spike-hard, throbbing. He slammed his cock inside her as he lifted her legs as well, pulling her hips to him as he buried his flesh to the hilt. So deep. Oh God. So deep he pierced her soul. He was hotter than a brand, harder, deeper than anything she had ever known. He didn't pause after entering. He threw himself into her, thrusting mindlessly, chanting her name.

Her eyes widened. Her mouth opened in a soundless scream. He pierced her womb; her flesh quivered then erupted around him. She screamed his name as she felt the orgasm shatter her. It tore through her, every bone and muscle in her body, each individual cell exploding in such chaotic pleasure that she wondered if she would survive it.

She felt Brock's heated release, the hard jerk of his cock inside her, and still her orgasm didn't ease. It echoed along her body, pulsed in her cunt until she felt a sharp tearing release deep inside her womb.

Shuddering, gasping for breath, her arms fell weakly to her side as her eyes closed. She was soaked with sweat. Hers, Sam's, Cade's. Brock's. She felt it dripping on her body as he moved over her, as hot as tears.

She looked up at him, dazed, blinking at the moisture that fell slowly from his eyes.

"I love you." Brock lowered her legs as Cade moved back, then came to her, catching himself on his elbows , burying his face in her neck.

His body shuddered. Not sexually, not in climax. Emotionally, desperately. She felt the hot wash of his tears at her neck, his whispered love words.

"I can't live without you—" she gasped, fighting for breath. "I can't, Brock. Not now."

"And you won't have to," he whispered at her ear, and she knew he was hiding his emotion, his tears. "Because I couldn't either, Sarah. I couldn't. And I won't."

She closed her eyes, her arms lifting to hold him close as he wrapped her protectively in his arms.

"Marry me." The words were more than a surprise to her.

"What?" She looked at him as he raised his head, watching her tearfully, though no more moisture fell.

"Marry me, Sarah." He touched her cheek, wiping away her own tears. "I can't lose you, baby. I can't. Please."

She smiled, kissed the fingers that glanced her lips.

"I'll marry you," she sighed. "But tomorrow. Tonight, I'm really tired, Brock."

She gasped as he moved, then he bent close, lifting her in his arms, holding her close.

"We're going to bed," he told the others.

Cade and Sam were still gasping, collapsed on the floor at the edge of the sofa. Marly looked asleep. Weary, worn. Brock had obviously driven her past her limits. He had been doing that a lot lately.

"You fucked her unconscious, Brock." Cade frowned. "She'll be pissed at you."

"She'll forgive me." Brock chuckled, a rusty, rarely used laugh that lifted Sarah's heart.

He didn't wait for a reply.

He carried her quickly upstairs, her body tucked against him, her breathing still labored, wearied. He was drained. The explosive release he poured into her had come from his soul. There were no other words to describe it.

"Bathe," he told her as he sat her on the wide rim of the large garden tub. "Then bed for you, my little sex goddess."

Sarah watched him prepare the bath. He was tired himself, yet he was caring for her. The tenderness, the adoration in his expression warmed a part of Sarah that she had never realized was cold. A part of her she hadn't known existed. At that moment Sarah realized that her soul had never been free. She had been missing something, something essential, something she found only with Brock.

"Okay?" His fingers touched her cheek, his expression was clear of pain, the shadows gone from his eyes.

She smiled, tired, at peace.

"Perfect," she answered, her voice soft as she gazed up at him. "Never better."

Chapter Thirty-six

ॐ

A routine of sorts developed in the next few days. The sexual tension that had once been a part of the house, eased. Sarah breathed in relief, unaware until then just how tense she had been herself. The plans Brock put in effect for their upcoming wedding blew her mind. She had thought he would try to rescind the offer, she hadn't expected him to surge forward at such a quick pace.

"We could always lock him in his room until he slows down," Marly told her as they sat at the kitchen table, tired from the frantic pace they had kept in getting a gown and arrangements together for the small church wedding Brock promised her. Unfortunately, he refused to wait longer than a month to marry her.

Sarah grinned and shook her head. "Probably wouldn't work. He'd talk me into untying him."

"You're so weak, Sarah." Marly shook her head, laughing.

"Yeah, like you're any different," Sarah grunted, glancing out the kitchen window as a spark of light reflected from the trees in the distance.

She frowned, squinting against the sunlight to see if one of the men was working the deserted pasture.

"Marly, is this window bullet proof—" A large crack appeared, as Sarah blinked at the bullet suddenly lodged in the glass.

She heard Marly scream. Sarah jumped away from the table, falling, scrambling away from the window as several more shots fired and suddenly glass was raining down on them as they scrambled across the room.

"Marly, are you okay?" Sarah screamed as she grabbed the other woman and jerked her back along the wall toward the pantry.

Shots were still echoing around the house, dishes shattering, wood and cement flying around them.

"Where are the men? Cade. Brock," Sarah screamed out desperately as a bullet sent wood flying from the cabinet across from them.

"They're away from the house," Marly cried out, clutching her arm, shaking in shock and fear.

A trickle of blood oozed from the other woman's arm.

"Sarah, he shot me," Marly whispered, blinking down at the blood.

"It's a flesh wound. That's all, Marly." They ducked as another bullet shattered the toaster on the cabinet. "We have to get out of here. Where the hell are Rick and his men? They should have that bastard by now."

"Unless he got them." Marly turned wide, terrified eyes up at Sarah. "What if he got Rick's men, Sarah?"

"Then we're sitting ducks," Sarah said, breathing harshly. "We have to get out of here. We have to get upstairs, Marly. Brock's gun is in his room. We have to get something to defend ourselves. If he gets into the house and we're pinned down here, then we're sitting ducks. We're dead."

Another bullet whizzed through the room.

"We'll have to crawl out." Marly was pale, but pulling together fast. "If we're careful, we should be able to avoid the worst of the glass."

Evidently, the bulletproof glass in the kitchen wasn't so bullet proof. It had shattered into millions of sharp pieces after the second bullet.

"Belly crawl," Sarah muttered. "Let's get it the hell over with, before the bastard gets any closer."

"Cade's going to be really pissed over this one," Marly sighed as they began to crawl across the room.

The bullets didn't stop. The glass over the sink shattered as they crawled past it, sending a shower of glass spraying over them. Sarah couldn't scream. She was terrified and evidently Marly was in the same shape. She felt the glass cutting into her arms, her bare legs, but moved quickly across the tile until they reached the door.

"Come on." She jumped to her feet, helping Marly up behind her. "We have to get upstairs, Marly."

"The men are hurt, Sarah," Marly said, fear thickening her voice. "They would have been here by now if they weren't."

Sarah knew that. Brock would have been there by now if something weren't holding him up. She couldn't even consider he was hurt. If she did, she would lose it. Panic would destroy her, and she couldn't panic right now.

She eased the kitchen door open, her heart pounding so hard and fast she could hear nothing but the blood rushing through her own veins. The gunfire had ceased, which meant he was likely trying to get to the house. There was no return gunfire. Brock , Cade, nor Sam were rushing into the house, which meant it appeared they were screwed for the moment.

Staying close to the wall Sarah and Marly eased through the dining room until they came to the foyer. Taking a deep breath, Sarah peeked around the wall, seeing the front door open, giving anyone a clear view into the house. Why was the door open—

"Hello." Sinister, evil, the sound of the mechanically distorted voice whispered from the shadows of the staircase.

Sarah froze. She felt Marly stiffen beside her. She watched as the black clad figure moved from the end of the staircase, his eyes glittering wildly from behind the holes of the pullover mask he wore.

"Sweet Sarah, innocent Marly. Where are your men, I wonder?" He sounded gleeful, smug and confident.

"They'll be here." Sarah raised her head, refusing to let the bastard see her fear. "And when they get here, they'll kill you."

Damn, there had to be a dozen security guards out there too. What the hell had happened? One man couldn't have taken them out.

"I believe they are all safely napping, along with their guards," the stalker sighed, the sound hollow and echoing in the silence of the room. "Tranquilizers are an amazing thing sometimes. If you move carefully, you can take out a whole team of men, and none of them know what happened."

Marly sagged against the wall beside Sarah.

"So kill us." He intended to anyway, she wasn't about to beg him.

He moved closer.

"What's wrong with sweet little Marly?" Despite the cruel voice, Sarah gained the impression he was suddenly hesitant, concerned.

"You shot her," she replied breathlessly. "What do you think is wrong with her?"

There was surprise in the dark eyes, in the way his body jerked.

"No. I was aiming at you."

"Then you fucked up, big boy," Sarah informed him, her voice harsh.

What the hell was Marly up to? It was just a damned flesh wound. A deep one, she admitted, but it looked worse than what it was.

Then Marly whimpered. A pain-ridden, bleak sound as she started to fall. Sarah jumped in surprise as the assailant jumped for the other woman.

"Run," Marly screamed, suddenly moving quickly.

Her leg shot out in a karate move that would have done Jackie Chan proud as she swept the man's feet out from under him. His gun went flying as he screamed out in rage.

Grabbing Marly's arm, Sarah ran for the door, careening past it and turning the corner as hard arms grabbed her from behind.

"No!" She was being dragged around the house, a hand clamping over her mouth.

"Sarah, shut up." Brock. Oh God. His voice, furious, enraged, but his voice hissed in her ear.

She saw Cade then, sweeping Marly back away from the doorway as the black clad figure went running out of the house, still clutching the rifle, searching for a target.

The men moved swiftly. The guns they held in their hands rose, leveled as bullets suddenly pelted the side of the house.

"Fuck!" Brock cursed violently, dragging Sarah on around the house as the sound of a motorcycle fired up.

Brock and Cade kept them moving until they were able to push them into the back door, back into the kitchen.

"Stay." The order was direct, furious as they rushed from the house again.

Sarah looked at Marly with a frown.

"Do they do that often?" Sarah asked Marly with a frown.

"Often." Marly slid down the wall, her pale face gleaming with perspiration as she collapsed on the floor.

"Are you okay, Marly?" Sarah flung a drawer open, grabbed a dishrag and wrapped it around the wound on the other woman's arm.

"Yeah. Just tired." Tired and terrified. Sarah completely sympathized with her.

Sam stumbled into the house then, dazed, shaking his head.

"Asshole put us the hell to sleep." He shook his head, took one look at Marly and paled. He turned and rushed back out of the house again.

"Uh oh." Marly leaned her head against the wall. "All hell will break loose now."

Cade's demented scream echoed around them, causing both women to wince. He rushed into the house at a dead run, nearly falling on the glass as he slid to a stop. He stared down at the bloody rag wrapped around Marly's arm, then paled alarmingly.

"Marly?" He went to his knees in front of her.

"You faint and I'll clobber you," she told him harshly. "Big, tough man can play cowboy and stalker but can't handle a little blood."

Sarah snorted. Cade could only shake his head.

"Marly, how bad is it?" Brock seemed to be the only sane one. He knelt beside Sarah, touching Marly's cheek gently as he watched her.

"It's a scratch. Might need a stitch or two, though. I'd appreciate it if you would call Doc. I could sure use one of those pain shots he's always pawning off on everyone," she sighed.

Cade unwrapped the makeshift bandage and it was then that Sarah saw the tears that covered the man's face. Marly ignored them, but her face was ravaged by the pain the sight of it caused.

"Cade, she's fine," Sarah assured him. "What about the bastard with the gun?"

"He got away. He drugged Rick's men, knocked Rick out. We were lucky this time. He thought he got Brock and me but we were able to fool him. We tried to get here sooner."

"Call Doc, Sam," Cade rasped. "I'm taking Marly upstairs. Get the sheriff out here and see if Rick and his men are able to walk yet. I want everyone in the fucking house, now."

He picked Marly up in his arms, cradling her close, his body trembling with tiny shudders barely discernable in the dimming light.

"That man needs a relaxer," Sarah sighed, leaning wearily against Brock. "Hell, I think I need one."

Brock was silent. He lifted her into his arms, much as Cade had Marly and moved swiftly through the house to his room.

"You're bleeding." His voice was rough as he sat her on the toilet and began to run water into the tub.

Sarah looked down at her legs, her arms.

"Scratches, I don't even feel them." Then she gasped.

Brock was kneeling in front of her, jerking her to him, his lips covering hers desperately.

* * * * *

His control shattered. Brock knew he was losing his grip on his sanity. Damn her, she was so cool, so controlled, but he could see the fear in her eyes, the shock and terror and it was too familiar, reminded him too well of the horror he sometimes saw in his own eyes when he dared to look in a mirror. He had to wipe it away. He had to take the pain away. Erase the fear.

He kissed her in desperation. His tongue licked at her lips, his hands tore at her dress until he had her naked, his hands stroking her until he heard her moans of pleasure. He looked in her eyes, saw them darkening with passion, felt the heat of her body, the pleasure replacing the fear.

"Bath," he whispered.

He drew her to her feet, then helped her into the large garden tub, sinking in with her, drawing her over him until his cock slid easily into the tight heat of her vagina.

"Ride me," he growled.

315

He watched her face as she moved over him, her eyes lowered drowsily, her face flushed, sweat and blood rinsing away as he drew her into the water, his body laying back against the tub, his head twisting in pleasure as he let her set the pace, let her find their pleasure.

Then he felt the small tremors in her cunt. Felt her flexing around him, milking him, burning him alive. He groaned, harsh and deep as he began to come, spurting his semen deep inside the wet velvet recess of her cunt.

She collapsed against his chest, breathing heavily. Fighting for his own breath, he grabbed a cloth and soap and began to wash her. He checked each scratch, kissed as many as he could find, and when she was laying relaxed and drowsy against him, her head cushioned on his chest, he let his own tears fall. For the first time in twelve years, he felt the salty moisture easing over his cheeks. But rather than tears of pain, they were of thankfulness. She was alive. And that was all that mattered to him. All that would ever matter.

Chapter Thirty-seven

ဢ

Sarah sat beside Brock in the kitchen the next day, the others gathered around the table, surrounded by Rick and his deal of guards. All eyes were centered on the paper lying in the middle of it.

Time to go. Yet I shall return. Precious children, the future is mine.

Lock your doors, cover your windows well. The past has returned, and now tis time to die.

You shed the blood. You took the life. But your sins were never hidden.

Cade and Marly. Ahh, the perfect pair. Brock and Sarah, safe within the lair.

Sam I ask, is precious Heather near?

Until you seek again, to mend a fractured soul. I shall rest in ease, for none shall be whole. As long as one aches, twists in nightmares and screams in pain. Then I shall have my pleasure, until the last, the final shall be slain.

"Heather stuck his own knife in his gut the night he attacked her," Rick told them all. "We found blood with traces of DNA that doesn't match hers. A good puddle of it, so I suspect she got him good."

"But he'll be back." Sam stared at the paper, his eyes haunted, his voice hoarse. "If I seek again."

His fist clenched on the table. They all looked at him, all knew he was blaming himself, not just for Heather's attack, but Sarah's and Marly's as well.

"Sam, he'll come back anyway," Tara told him, her voice soft, but filled with anger. "We know this. This isn't about you. It's about all of you. We have to figure out who he is. None of you are safe until we do."

Sam rose to his feet. He shook his head, turning and walking quickly from the room.

Tara looked at Cade. No one knew what to say now, how to go on. The danger wasn't over, and they all wondered if it ever would be.

"He had to have a son. One no one knew about." Rick stepped forward, talking about the bastard who had nearly killed the men years ago. "I'm sending out a team to Utah in the morning. We'll get a complete background on him, see what we can find out."

Cade rose to his feet, sighing deeply.

"Find him quickly. What about Heather?" His voice was hard, cold.

"She's healing. She'll be out of the hospital next week. Doc says a month for recovery," he told him. "Why?"

"I want her back here, if she's willing." The look he gave Rick was filled with cold purpose. "She belongs to Sam and I want her here."

"What about Heather and what she wants?" Tara asked him, her eyes narrowing.

"The bastard knows what he's doing. If Heather hadn't cared for Sam, it wouldn't have happened. And if she cared for him before the attack, then she cares for him now. She didn't look like a woman who scares off easy."

Tara exchanged a glance with Rick, then sighed.

"She's fighting to come back now," she told them wearily.

"She can recuperate here. We'll take care of her." Marly came to her feet, her face drawn, her eyes hard. "Bring her here. Sam doesn't need time to build a defense against her. Get

318

her here, Tara. Then get every man you can find here. We'll put them on as cowboys, no one will know the difference."

Sarah leaned her head against Brock's chest, feeling his arm tighten around her. They still weren't safe. As long as that bastard was out there, they were all in danger.

"We'll get through it," Brock promised her, holding her close. "And we'll get Sam through it."

"Sam is the catalyst," Rick told Brock softly. "Sam knows it. Find out why, Brock. Until we know, we're helpless. We have to know why this guy has fixated on Sam."

Brock sighed. He rose to his feet, pulling Sarah up with him.

"Sam won't talk about it. But I'll do what I can."

"Brock," Tara stopped him. "Heather won't give Sam what he needs from a woman. Are you sure you want her here?"

Brock glanced down at Sarah. When his grin came, it was slow, easy.

"Yeah." He nodded. "I'm sure, Tara. Maybe she's just what Sam needs."

Sarah shook her head. Brock sometimes had a strange sense of humor, she had learned.

"When she's released, we'll bring her here." Rick nodded. "I've pulled in more men, they'll work the ranch, blend in better than the others. We have to get him soon, Brock. This is becoming more dangerous each time he attacks."

"I agree, Rick. Get your men here. We'll do whatever we have to, to catch the bastard." Brock nodded.

He turned, drawing Sarah from the dining room, heading for their bedroom. Rick's arrival had disturbed his play and he was eager to return.

"Do you think Sam suspects he's in love with her?" she asked him as they entered their room.

"Sure he does. He's no fool. But he'll fight it." Brock closed the door behind him, then began removing Sarah's clothes quickly.

"But does he *know* he loves her?" She slapped his hands away as she continued to worry about the despondency Sam had sunk into since reading that letter.

"Not yet." Brock grinned. "But he will, Sarah, when the time is right. Just like we did."

* * * * *

Marly sat alone on the patio hours later. The words in the poetry-style letter haunted her. She knew them. Knew the style. Surely it wasn't an uncommon style of composing such poetry, she thought. Random phrases, a blending of sounds. She knew herself from her college classes two years before that it was common. But she also knew that each writer had his or her own style. Each one did it differently.

She licked her lips, staring into the darkness. She was wrong. She knew she had to be. No one she knew could be so cruel. No one she cared for could be so deceptive. She prayed she was wrong. She couldn't say anything, because Cade would kill without proof, his rage would become so all-consuming. Yet, if she didn't speak out— Her hands fisted, her teeth clenched. It could mean the end of her family

Enjoy an excerpt from:
MEN OF AUGUST:
Heather's Gift

Copyright © Lora Leigh, 2003.
All Rights Reserved, Ellora's Cave Publishing, Inc.

Prologue

⟨⟨

The night was soft. A gentle, early summer night, thick with the scent of honeysuckle and the rain that had passed hours before. The glow of the full moon shadowed the land, leaving secrets hidden, scars unseen and the gentle mystery of the land left to soothe the soul.

Sam slid through the shadows cast by the stables and the thick brush that led to a sheltered grove. He was adept at hiding in the darkness, at using the shadows to slip and hide and make his way to whatever destination he had chosen. He had been doing it since he was ten. Finding adventure, finding peace within the open land he called home. There had been times when it had saved his sanity, that peace, the wide-open freedom, the smell of juniper, honeysuckle and a cleansing rain.

He wasn't a kid now, or a tormented young man. He was an adult, and though he fought the shadows in his own mind, he knew the demons weren't far behind. He hid behind careless laughter, teased his brothers, played childish pranks. Even at the age of thirty, he made certain to find a way as often as possible to break the bleak sadness that filled Cade and Brock.

The sadness was lifting a bit now, and Sam found as their happiness began to bloom, the darkness within himself began to grow. Marly helped. Bright and filled with laughter and a compassion and acceptance he would never fully understand, she lightened the hell they all lived within.

He paused beneath the spreading limbs of a thickly leafed oak and glanced back at the house. She would be sleeping now, held close by Cade, and possibly even Brock, unless he had headed back to town and Sarah, while Sam was showering.

Marly wasn't the first they had shared, but she was the most important. She was Cade's soul. She was his and Brock's heart. They had helped raise her since she was twelve, had endured her teenage years as she flirted and rubbed against them like a frisky foal, and they now shared in the passionate, heated love she had for Cade.

"Bad Sam, sneaking out of the house like that." He jumped as the amused, feminine voice brought him out of his thoughts.

He turned quickly, watching as a dark form separated itself from a nearby tree. His lips quirked in humor. Heather March was going to break his heart. He couldn't help the thought as he watched the petite redhead stroll slowly toward him.

"You're following me again." He tried to sound disapproving, stern, but it was hard when she made him feel so damned light inside.

"It's my job, Sammy." He winced at the nickname she had stuck on him. Marly's mother used to call him Sammy. He didn't like it then, and he didn't like it now. "I'm supposed to follow your bad ass."

A soft ray of moonlight speared through the trees, glistening in her red hair, glowing against the soft creamy skin of her pretty face. Her green eyes reminded him of a cat, softly tilted, inquisitive. Her pert nose was just too cute for words, but her pouty little mouth was a work of art. The curves glistened with moisture and made his cock thicken and harden beneath his jeans with abrupt need.

As she came close he reached out, jerking her against his chest as she gasped in surprise. He held her close, letting her feel the erection straining beneath his jeans.

"Sam," he reminded her softly, inhaling the soft scent she wore. It was romantic and soft, and undeniably hot. "Not

Sammy, Heather. I'm going to get you for that nickname you're trying to pin to my ass."

A grin stretched her lips as her body softened against his. "My sister catches you holding me captive like this and she'll kick your ass," she snickered. "Better let me go."

He turned until he could back her against the tree, holding her there with easy strength. "Your sister just likes to think she's all bad," he whispered, the fingers of one hand playing with the long braid that fell down her back. "I'm not scared of her."

Her hands smoothed up his chest and he fought himself, fighting for breath and for control. Damn, he shouldn't be this horny, this hot. Not after the hour he had spent with Marly, her lips wrapped first around his thick cock, then the tight, velvet heat of her ass gripping him. But Heather could make him hot when no one else could. She was soft and sweet, and so damned smart-mouthed she could make him crazier than hell.

"You better be scared of her. She's mean." Her hands paused at his heart, and he knew she could feel the hard throb of his excitement there as easily as she could feel his hard-on pressing against her abdomen.

Silence lengthened between them then as sexual tension thickened in the air.

"You were with Marly tonight," she finally whispered softly. "Tara cleared us away from the house. She always does."

He wanted to look away from her, but he could see the questions in her eyes. Why did he go to his brother's woman, when he could have her? And he could have her. He knew she got just as wet for him, as his cock got hard for her.

His finger ran over her cheek gently. "Would you want to watch?" The thought of it was almost enough to make him crazy with arousal.

"I don't think so, big boy," she sniped with a fierce frown. "You're a real interestin' man, Sammy. But watching you fuck another woman wouldn't be the highlight of my day." Jealousy shimmered in her voice along with a thread of anger.

He sighed deeply. "It's not like that, Heather." He moved away from her, shaking his head as he crossed the short distance back to the stables.

She was silent, but he was aware of her following him, keeping up with his longer stride until they entered the dimly lit haven of the building. The horses were all in the pastures, and the building smelled of sweetly scented hay and leather saddles.

"You shouldn't be sneaking out like this, Sam," she said as she closed the door behind her. "With the stalker's return, it's hard telling..."

"I wish he would come after me." He turned to her, rage surging through his body. "Son of a bitch thinks he can get away with attacking our women and trying to destroy our lives. He's a fucking coward, Heather, and one day, one of us will get our hands on him."

"If he doesn't kill you first," she snorted, watching him with that bright, sharp gaze that sometimes seemed to pierce his soul. "You need to be more careful. All of you do."

She leaned against one of the stalls, her arms crossing under her breasts as she watched him with that militant look in her eye.

"Keep looking at me like that, and one day I'll take you up on the fight you seem to be wanting," he told her softly, unable to keep from going to her again.

His hands settled on her hips, and he marveled at how small she was, how delicate her bones seemed. But she was tough as hell. He had watched her practice her martial arts moves with Tara, as well as Rick, and he knew she was a hell of a lot tougher than she looked.

"If you have the energy left, you mean?" She arched a fiery brow mockingly.

He sighed deeply. "Do you want to know, Heather, why I haven't taken you? Why I haven't come after you with every weapon I can think of to get you into my bed?"

"Because you know I can kick your ass?" Her hands ran up his arms until they lay against his shoulders. Soft, graceful fingers that he was dying to feel on his bare flesh.

He shook his head. She was good, damned good, but he wasn't the least bit intimidated by her. He could take her, eventually.

"Because I know that eventually, I would need to see you beneath my brothers as well," he told her softly, warningly. "We survived hell together, Heather. A hell unlike anything you could imagine if you hadn't lived through it. And I don't think you're ready to consider the thought of being part of that."

"And how does the sharing help you, Sam?" She tilted her head, frustration lighting her eyes. "How can sharing something that should belong solely to you heal any part of that?"

He shook his head, wondering how to explain. It was complicated, difficult. At times he couldn't make sense of it himself, so he struggled with how to make her understand.

"We gave our souls for each other in that hell hole." He fought the blinding pain that the thought of it, the shadowed memories of it, brought. "We were forced to betray each other, to brutalize each other, Heather. And we swore we wouldn't let it break us. It changed us though. It forged a bond that can never be broken, but it destroyed another part of us in the process. A part that kept us together as brothers, the love that was between us as brothers, he destroyed that. Destroyed it, Heather. It's gone. Now we fall back on the only thing we had before it happened. It's not just a desire, or a need. It's a bonding that reaffirms we didn't lose everything to that bastard's cruelty."

"Sam, it's unnatural." She shook her head, and though her voice was gentle, it lacked any understanding. "You love each other more than you love those women."

"That's not true." Shock filled his system, traveled through his body. "Heather, that's not the way it is, baby. It's not. It's because of our love for them, don't you see? The fear that one of us alone can't protect them, can't care for them. We know our limits; we know the horrors out there and the monsters who live to destroy. We know how easily one of us can be destroyed. It's our love for those women, our need to see them always protected, always cared for, always loved, Heather. It's to prove to each other that we trust the other to do this. And Heather, the heat..." He broke off, his cock throbbing, thinking of her sharing in that, screaming out in the pleasure. "The heat and pleasure is like nothing you've known. Marly connects us again, she reaffirms that we're alive and that we can still function and love. That we're not alone."

She stared up at him, a frown darkening her brow. "But Sam, you aren't alone," she stressed. "You shouldn't need to share your lovers to reaffirm this."

"No, we shouldn't." He sighed heavily, hearing his own doubts, his own guilt in her words. "But it's always been that way, Heather," he whispered, knowing it was true. "Cade glories in Marly's pleasure. You can see it in his eyes, in his love for her. Her pleasure and her happiness are everything to him. He gives her in return the only thing he knows how. More love. More pleasure. His brothers. And it will be the same for Brock and Sarah, if she agrees to come to the ranch. It's all their love, Heather. All our love."

He watched as she licked her lips nervously, nibbled on the lower one as she thought, then she sighed deeply, regretfully.

"And if the woman you eventually love can't accept it?" she asked him softly. "What if she can't bear your touching another woman, or one of your brothers touching her?"

He was quiet for long moments, sadness filling his soul, because he had a feeling he held the woman who would very well hold his heart. The woman who would refuse.

"Then she would hold only half a man," he whispered painfully. "I worry, Heather, and I agonize that we're hurting Marly, that we'll hurt Sarah. The guilt eats at me in ways you could never understand. But I also know if I didn't have it, or one day share in it, then a part of me would be lost forever. A very important, very vital part of me."

"Or," she whispered. "A part of you would be healed…"

* * * * *

It was a question Sam couldn't answer. As one week turned into two, and the attraction progressed, thickened, Sam couldn't reconcile his needs with those he felt were Heather's. A kiss progressed to two. He tasted her breasts, brought her to climax with his mouth and felt the overwhelming pleasure of her mouth enveloping his cock.

When he learned she was a virgin, he pulled back. What he needed from her a virgin could never accept, he told himself. But the attraction wouldn't die, the needs wouldn't extinguish. Then she left for a brief time, returning to her home. When she came back, he went to her. Went to her because he couldn't resist her laughter, her smart mouth or touch. And he began to hope. Began to believe that perhaps one day she would understand…

And then the stalker struck again. They found Heather bound, her slender legs spread, the soft mound of her cunt sliced by a madman's scalpel. Sam knew that, no matter how much he loved her, and he did love her, no matter his need for her. The past was rising, swift and sure, and it could very well destroy him as it hadn't during those bleak, dark days of captivity. So he fought…

Why an electronic book?

We live in the Information Age—an exciting time in the history of human civilization, in which technology rules supreme and continues to progress in leaps and bounds every minute of every day. For a multitude of reasons, more and more avid literary fans are opting to purchase e-books instead of paper books. The question from those not yet initiated into the world of electronic reading is simply: *Why?*

1. *Price.* An electronic title at Ellora's Cave Publishing and Cerridwen Press runs anywhere from 40% to 75% less than the cover price of the exact same title in paperback format. Why? Basic mathematics and cost. It is less expensive to publish an e-book (no paper and printing, no warehousing and shipping) than it is to publish a paperback, so the savings are passed along to the consumer.

2. *Space.* Running out of room in your house for your books? That is one worry you will never have with electronic books. For a low one-time cost, you can purchase a handheld device specifically designed for e-reading. Many e-readers have large, convenient screens for viewing. Better yet, hundreds of titles can be stored within your new library—on a single microchip. There are a variety of e-readers from different manufacturers. You can also read e-books on your PC or laptop computer. (Please note that Ellora's Cave does not endorse any specific brands. You can check our websites at www.ellorascave.com or www.cerridwenpress.com for information we make available to new consumers.)

3. *Mobility.* Because your new e-library consists of only a microchip within a small, easily transportable e-reader, your entire cache of books can be taken with you wherever you go.

4. *Personal Viewing Preferences.* Are the words you are currently reading too small? Too large? Too… ANNOYING? Paperback books cannot be modified according to personal preferences, but e-books can.

5. *Instant Gratification.* Is it the middle of the night and all the bookstores near you are closed? Are you tired of waiting days, sometimes weeks, for bookstores to ship the novels you bought? Ellora's Cave Publishing sells instantaneous downloads twenty-four hours a day, seven days a week, every day of the year. Our webstore is never closed. Our e-book delivery system is 100% automated, meaning your order is filled as soon as you pay for it.

Those are a few of the top reasons why electronic books are replacing paperbacks for many avid readers.

As always, Ellora's Cave and Cerridwen Press welcome your questions and comments. We invite you to email us at Comments@ellorascave.com or write to us directly at Ellora's Cave Publishing Inc., 1056 Home Avenue, Akron, OH 44310-3502.

erridwen, the Celtic Goddess of wisdom, was the muse who brought inspiration to storytellers and those in the creative arts. Cerridwen Press encompasses the best and most innovative stories in all genres of today's fiction. Visit our site and discover the newest titles by talented authors who still get inspired - much like the ancient storytellers did, once upon a time.

Cerridwen Press
www.cerridwenpress.com

Discover for yourself why readers can't get enough
of the multiple award-winning publisher

Ellora's Cave.

Whether you prefer e-books or paperbacks,

be sure to visit EC on the web at
www.ellorascave.com

for an erotic reading experience that will leave you
breathless.